ALL FIXED UP

Tor Books by Linda Grimes

In a Fix

Quick Fix

The Big Fix

All Fixed Up

ALL FIXED UP

Linda Grimes

A TOM DOHERTY ASSOCIATES BOOK

NEW YORK

This is a work of fiction. All of the characters, organizations, and events portrayed in this novel are either products of the author's imagination or are used fictitiously.

ALL FIXED UP

Copyright © 2016 by Linda Grimes

A Tor Book
Published by Tom Doherty Associates, LLC
175 Fifth Avenue
New York, NY 10010

www.tor-forge.com

Tor® is a registered trademark of Tom Doherty Associates, LLC.

The Library of Congress Cataloging-in-Publication Data is available upon request.

ISBN 978-0-7653-7639-8 (hardcover)
ISBN 978-1-4668-5127-6 (e-book)

Our books may be purchased in bulk for promotional, educational, or business use. Please contact your local bookseller or the Macmillan Corporate and Premium Sales Department at 1-800-221-7945, extension 5442, or by e-mail at MacmillanSpecial Markets@macmillan.com.

First Edition: May 2016

Printed in the United States of America

0 9 8 7 6 5 4 3 2 1

This book is dedicated to my brilliant, creative, and generally adorable children, Annalisa and Sean. All that morning sickness really paid off.

ALL FIXED UP

Chapter 1

Weightlessness, I decided, was overrated. My stomach concurred.

I took deep and steady breaths, willing the breakfast I now regretted eating to stay where I'd put it. Really, I should have known better. But in my defense, I wasn't supposed to be here. I thought I'd be sitting at a news conference, dropping a bombshell on a NASA-friendly press corps, doing my patriotic part to keep the nation's interest in our space program amped up enough to ensure future funding.

Of course, the press conference was still ahead of me. Only now it would be a tad more challenging to keep a smile on my face—and, you know, breakfast in my stomach—while the cameras were rolling.

The plane providing our zero-G experience by alternately climbing, then diving, at a steep pitch—a fricking airborne roller coaster was what it was, and I didn't even like the earthbound versions—neared the bottom of its arc. Gravity was restored with a vengeance, pressing down with a force that made me feel like

I weighed three hundred pounds, pinning me just long enough for anticipation to build to another crescendo in my solar plexus. I lay quietly on the floor of the cabin, holding myself still, as per the instructor's orders. It was supposed to prevent, in most cases, the nausea a flight on the aptly nicknamed "Vomit Comet" was famous for, but I feared I wasn't a "most case."

This on top of the preflight physical I'd been subjected to that morning. With shots. (God only knew what they were inoculating me against. Airborne cooties?) *Not* a good day for an admitted needle-phobe who had only recently started to get over her fear of flying. But I was coping. I counted that as a victory.

I opened my eyes long enough to check out the ASCANs around me. ASCAN is short for Astronaut Candidate, and it's pronounced exactly like you'd expect it to be. Ass can. (Yes, I giggled like a middle-schooler when I first heard it. What can I say? God blessed me with a juvenile sense of humor.) All the ASCANs looked significantly less green than I felt. Huh. *They* probably actually used the antinausea medication issued to them. Me? Yeah, well, when you're dealing with a nickname like "Iron Gut," it's tough to justify the sudden necessity.

"Behind your ear," the photographer assigned to document my return to the space program said in his adorable Australian accent, speaking loudly enough to be heard over the engines.

I turned my head to see that he'd landed right next to me. Alec, his name was, Alec Loughlin. In his mid-forties, he was the rugged, distilled-by-life kind of middle-aged, not the soft, no-reason-to-even-try-anymore kind. Too old for me, but hey, nothing wrong with appreciating what gifts the future might hold. After a second or three of appreciating the finer points of keeping in shape as you age, it occurred to me that if stray lascivious thoughts were entering my headspace, then maybe my airsickness wasn't going to be as bad as I thought. Was random (and, okay, inappropriate) lust a possible cure for motion sickness?

He reached up and stroked a spot that happened to be one of my most sensitive erogenous zones. I felt my eyes widen, and mentally apologized to my boyfriend, Billy Doyle. Not that Billy had a problem with lust inspired by outside sources—which he claimed was merely a sign of a healthy libido, and therefore a good thing—as long as I came to him to act on it. But after a recent lapse in judgment on my part, I was still a little sensitive about it myself.

"Right here," Alec said. "It's an antinausea patch. New, faster-acting stuff. You'll be fine."

I lifted my hand to check, bumping his hand out of the way. Sure enough, there was a smooth patch I hadn't noticed before. "But I didn't—"

He shrugged, floating upward as gravity released its grip on us once more. "I had a spare. Slipped it on you when I was adjusting your collar before our preflight camera check. 'Iron Gut' or not"— this accompanied by a sardonic lift of brow—"I don't like my footage spoiled by random puking. Should be kicking in by now."

Of all the nerve! I rose next to him, trying my best to control my limbs. Pro tip: Air is not water. Swimming motions are useless for moving around in zero-G. Though apparently highly amusing to others who have more experience with the situation. I gave him a dirty look.

"You had no right," I said, indignation propelling me into an unintentional cockeyed somersault.

He shrugged again (an attractive mannerism on him) and reached out to steady me. "How's your stomach?"

I stilled, considering. No longer felt impending barfage. "Fine,"

I admitted. Grudgingly. "Doesn't mean—hey, wait a second . . ." I eyed him suspiciously. "Are you who I think you are?"

Billy. It had to be. He had a habit of showing up on my jobs under the pretext of helping me, but really he just likes to annoy me. It's a holdover from growing up together, raised as cousins, even though we're *not*. Our mothers were sorority sisters, which makes our cousin status strictly honorary, and therefore not in the least perverted. But that doesn't keep Billy from zinging me with a teasing conversational "cuz" at every opportunity. He claims it's habit, but I suspect he just likes getting a rise out of me.

Mr. Too-Old-But-Still-Gorgeous shrugged again, giving me a decidedly odd look. Suspicious, one might say. "Depends on who you think I am, I suppose."

"*You* know. But I thought you were, um, otherwise occupied." Billy was supposedly busy with one of his vast and varied money-making schemes—something terribly clandestine, and probably not legal in the slightest. He'd never hurt an average Joe, but had no such compunction about those he deemed to be the rich ass-holes of the world.

Alec looked at me blankly. "This is my assignment. Where else would I be? Look, we only have a limited time up here. How about you introduce yourself to the camera? Try to look all gung ho NASA, and tell us why you're back with the program. And if you're going to puke, don't get it on my equipment."

Okay, maybe he really was the photographer.

"Your precious equipment is safe. So, will this be shown at the beginning or the end of the press conference? Wouldn't want to spoil the big announcement."

"The beginning. Do it right, and this will *be* the big announcement."

All right, then. I pasted a suitably patriotic expression on my face and gave him a thumbs-up.

"Hello! I'm Philippa Carson, NASA astronaut and lab geek, soon to be the first woman to conceive a baby in space."

The ASCANs tried to mill closer without spoiling the shot. They'd heard the wild rumors, of course, watercooler gossip being what it was, but it appeared confirmation was still a shock. The women looked incredulous, the men speculative. I quickly went on to explain my field of research was conception in off-earth environments, and that thus far all experimentation with animals had been limited to the tiny variety.

"If all goes according to plan, I'll be the first mammal bigger than a rat to conceive in a microgravity environment," I said, squeezing it in right before the floor came up and hit me again.

I lay back, making sure my pose was as far from "porn star" as humanly possible. After an announcement like that, the last thing you need to do is add any visual innuendo. Of course, if the PR guys at NASA hadn't come up with the bright idea that a zero-G ride would make great "optics" for the mission reveal, I wouldn't have to worry about it at all.

Alec kept shooting, aiming the camera down at me from his kneeling position. (Not generally recommended for those trying to retain their stomach contents. Apparently not a concern for the intrepid photographer.) I tried not to look like I was gripping the padded flooring beneath me with my fingernails, and hoped to hell my oh-God-I'm-being-plastered-to-the-floor-again face didn't in any way resemble an O-face.

"Since my husband and I were planning to start our family soon anyway, and I already have the astronaut training, I figured I'd be the perfect candidate. When I presented the plan to my bosses, backed up with comprehensive research to show the risk to me and my future offspring is minimal, they agreed. Can't wait to get up to the ISS!"

"ISS?" Alec asked on behalf of the future audience.

"International Space Station," I clarified. "I can't tell you how much I'm looking forward to my first visit."

Ugh. *Not.* Thank God it would be the real Philippa Carson going and not me.

Because, yeah, I wasn't Philippa Carson. I was a rather impressive copy of her, though. An exact replica, appearance-wise at least. Even the exceedingly thorough NASA doctors couldn't tell us apart. Well, as long as they didn't decide to run a random DNA profile, which was unlikely.

Thanks to my extensive dossier on the woman, I also had her personality down pat. The one face-to-face meeting I'd had with her—long enough to grab her energy and chat about life in general—had been enough to pick up her mannerisms. I have a knack for people-reading. Which is a good thing, considering my job. What good is looking like people if you can't pull off the subtleties of their behavior?

My job? Ciel Halligan, Facilitator, at your service. I fix other people's problems for a living. Got a situation you, and only you, can take care of? Move over. I can handle it for you. *As* you. And probably better than you, seeing as how I'm not bogged down by whatever baggage is keeping you from handling it yourself.

How is it possible? Easy, if you happen to be an aura adaptor. Because of a genetic anomaly—a mutation that originated quite a few generations back—aura adaptors can alter the energy they project to take on the appearance of another person. There's a complicated explanation for how and why it works (my brother James, the scientist—who, ironically, didn't inherit the adaptor gene from our parents—can explain it better than I can), but I find it's easiest to think of our kind as human chameleons and leave it at that. I mean, I don't know every detail of how my cell phone works either, but I don't lose any sleep over it.

Dr. Carson—"Phil" to her friends, which made her "Dr. Phil" to my giggling inner middle-schooler—was a PR dream for NASA. She had PhDs in aerospace engineering, biochemistry, and human reproductive technology—your basic brainy overachiever. And her atmospheric IQ came wrapped in a package worthy of the cover of a fashion magazine: tall, black, and willowy, with super-short auburn hair, high cheekbones, and translucent honey-gold eyes. In other words, gorgeous.

The reflection I saw in the mirror when I was wearing her aura was enough to set my insecurities nibbling at my ego with piranha teeth. Recently I'd been working on filing those teeth down, but it wasn't easy. When you're a height-challenged, next-to-boobless wonder, with freckles (*ugh!*), strutting through life with bravado takes determination. But at least my own strawberry blond hair and pale green eyes aren't too horrible, and, judging by how often I've caught Billy staring at my lips with lust in his eyes, my mouth must be okay.

One thing I *didn't* envy about Dr. Phil at the moment: she was at one of my undisclosed client hideaways, keeping company with a private (and very discreet) doctor and nurse while passing a kidney stone. A luxurious remote island setting probably doesn't help much when you're in pain.

See, kidney stones are a big no-no for astronauts. Once you have one—even if you pass it without complications—you're pretty much a permanent fixture on the No Go list as far as space flight is concerned. "Prone to kidney stones" is not a label the medical professionals at NASA are comfortable with, no matter how stoic an astronaut might be. If the Powers That Be found out their mama-candidate was dealing with the issue, they might decide to scrub the mission. Or worse, as far as Philippa was concerned, call in a willing understudy.

Phil, having worked long and hard on this project, did *not* want to hand it off to someone else at the crucial time. It would be the scientific equivalent of training your whole life for the Olympics, making the team, and then having to drop out at the last minute due to a minor injury. In other words, soul crushing.

Phil's brother, Rudy, happened to work with CIA agent Mark Fielding, aka my big brother's best friend and the primary star of my deepest fantasies before Billy entered the romantic picture. (Okay, okay. So Mark still sneaks into my dreams sometimes. The nighttime ones, not the daydreams. You can't control a sleeping mind, for Pete's sake.)

Phil's brother, whose Agency clearance was high enough to know about Mark's adaptor abilities, had approached him with his sister's dilemma. Mark could have done the job himself, but since he was pretty much always busy with some super-secret matter of national security, he'd asked me to do it. Which was incredible progress in our professional relationship. He used to be so obsessed with protecting me he wouldn't even consider referring a potential client to me. Proving myself capable in his eyes hadn't been easy, and I still wasn't sure I was completely there. I suspected this job might be some sort of a test—one I fully intended to pass with flying colors.

It was poor timing for me that the Vomit Comet flight popped up during my job. If it had been a few days later, answering questions from the press would have been the worst I had to contend with. But I was used to poor timing—it defined my relationship with Mark.

As the plane went into another dive, Alec leaned back, allowing me the space to rise again. Since the camera was still rolling, I tried to do it more gracefully this time. It was getting easier.

Once up and floating, I tucked my currently long legs (man, was I ever going to miss those) close to my chest and rolled forward— on purpose this time—executing one of the flawless somersaults I'd been told Phil had perfected on her inaugural Vomit Comet flight, back when she was an ASCAN herself. Score one for me.

"That seems more in character," Alec said.

I spun my head toward him. *Crap.* I was supposed to know this guy? He hadn't been in Dr. Phil's dossier.

"It takes a few minutes to get your sea legs back," I said, making it rueful. Maybe he'd attribute my lack of recognition to preflight nerves.

He nodded. When he lowered his camera the expression on his face was perfectly professional.

"Say, listen," I said, "sorry if I've been, um, distant. It's a bit overwhelming trying to reacclimate to the program." I gave him what I knew to be Phil's man-melting smile.

He cocked his head, quirking his mouth. "If you say so."

I didn't know enough about him to delve more deeply into any possible connection between the two of them. If I'd somehow offended him by treating him as a brand-new acquaintance instead of a friend, the good doctor would have to smooth things over when she was back.

On the other hand, if it was only Billy giving me some shit . . . well, I'd just have to kill him later.

When the end-of-flight announcement came, we all drifted toward our seats at the back of the plane. After normal gravity was restored, Alec buckled himself in beside me, in preparation for the gentler descent of landing. One good thing—after surviving this, I doubted flying commercial would ever bother me again.

I settled back comfortably, feeling pretty cocky about how well my first reduced gravity flight had gone. A measly national news conference ought to be a piece of cake comparatively.

Alec leaned close to my ear and said, "Where's Dr. Carson?"

So much for cocky. I swallowed hard and turned toward him, hoping like hell to see the light of Billy's laughter in his eyes. If it was there, it was doing a damn good job hiding behind the cold, hard suspicion.

Still, I tried. "If this is one of your jokes, you can stop now."

"I'm not the one 'joking' here," he said, a hard edge to his voice. "I mean it. Who are you? Or should I say, what are you?"

Uh-oh.

Chapter 2

The Johnson Space Center was a hive of buzzing reporters by the time we arrived from Ellington Field, where the Vomit Comet had mercifully touched down without incident. I'd been whisked away from the plane—and, thankfully, Alec Loughlin—by Steve Richards, the distinguished older PR representative who was my on-the-ground handler for the day. Alec had been driven back to the Center by his assistant, in their work van, so he could edit the footage he'd taken into an acceptable digital video to be shown at the press conference. It's amazing what you can do in a short time with a powerful laptop and the right software.

The screening for the reporters, which began with random, fun scenes of the ASCANs and me performing our floating gymnastics and ended with my rather startling announcement, had been like throwing a lit firecracker into the middle of the press corps. The questions continued, rapid-fire. I'd already responded to umpteen inquiries about the why, when, where, and for-God's-sake-*how* of the mission (and one statement expressing disappointment that the big announcement didn't concern irrefutable proof of aliens among us). The newshounds persisted like they hadn't been fed for a week and I was prime rib on a platter.

An incongruous image of slavering hybrid bee-dog with an Uzi in one hand and microphone in the other sprang into my head. I ignored it, and continued projecting the calm, cool, and collected persona of my client.

"Dr. Carson . . . Dr. Carson! Won't you be taking a huge risk with your future unborn child?"

I smiled and shook my head at the thirty-something, heavily pregnant reporter. I sympathized with her concern, but I'd already answered the question at least fifteen different ways. Did she think I was going to tell her something different this time?

"We are certain the risk is minimal. I will either conceive or I won't. If I do, there is nothing in our data to show a statistically significant likelihood of harm to the developing blastocyst, or later to the embryo. Again, I refer you to the press packet you were handed as you arrived. You'll find the essential parameters of the experiment laid out for you there," I said, hoping I sounded sufficiently like a brainy scientist trying her best not to talk down to the public. Of course, if anyone asked me what a blastocyst was, I was screwed. Biology hadn't exactly been my favorite subject in school.

"Dr. Carson . . . over here!" came a male voice, young and demanding. I ignored it.

"Dr. Carson—hey, Dr. Phil!" a woman's voice called out from the other side of the room.

Ha. Guess I wasn't the only one to note the name similarity to the celebrity talk show host. I scanned the crowd of curious faces, and nodded at the newshound with the sense of humor—a woman who looked like she'd been working the beat since the Apollo 11 moon landing.

"Are you *sure* you won't be sneaking your husband along on the mission with you?" she asked, a prurient gleam in her ancient eyes.

I refrained from rolling my own, not wanting to put a blemish on Dr. Phil's PR skills. What was it with the repeat questions? Only thing I could figure was, it must take at least ten times before the answer sticks.

"Only the essential parts of him, I'm afraid," I said, keeping it light. I was tempted to elaborate with "you know, his wigglies" or "his swimmers" this time, but I was going to assume the grown-ups present knew which parts were essential to conception.

Another reporter—the demanding young man—called out, "But your husband is a cosmonaut, right? He's qualified to go along, isn't he?"

I swallowed a sigh and revived Phil's smile. "*Retired* cosmonaut . . ."

It was true. Dr. Phil and her husband, Mikhail Yurgevich, had met and fallen in love when both were speaking at a European Space Agency symposium in Paris. Yurgevich owned a private U.S.-based company, where he concentrated on research and development of twenty-first-century cargo transport. Spaceward Ho was starting to give Virgin Galactic a run for its money. Most people thought the company's name—the "Ho" part, anyway—was poking fun at the competition, though the founder claimed it was merely a play on the old "Westward Ho" pioneer spirit. Personally, I suspected it was a bit of both.

Mikhail being Russian had probably tipped the scales in favor of Phil as the human guinea pig. The Russians might not be at the point of testing human conception in zero-G themselves, but they sure didn't mind having a fifty-percent PR stake in any future little half-Russian possibly arising from the U.S.'s research. Mikhail wasn't a Russian citizen anymore, but they still laid claim to his heritage.

"Will Spaceward Ho transport you to the space station? Maybe he could go along for the ride. Er, so to speak." The demanding young man couldn't have infused more innuendo if he'd waggled his eyebrows. Hmm. Maybe *he* was Billy.

I looked at him sternly, resisting the urge to slap him down—verbally, of course—for his impertinence. "As far as I know, the transport arrangements haven't yet been finalized. And, as I already explained, the International Space Station is quite small. *This* experiment will be centered around the viability of human *conception*, not sex. One step at a time. Some day, in the future, once we're certain conception itself is a feasible prospect, then the various methods of achieving it might be explored further."

Then, thinking to lighten the moment, I added, "Hopefully when there's more room available and, you know, some privacy. Maybe some Norah Jones"—Norah was listed under Music Favorites in Phil's dossier—"and a little champagne."

During the ensuing laughter, the PR spokesperson for NASA took my place at the microphone and told a disappointed crowd, "That's all for now, folks. We'll keep you updated."

I rode a wave of shockingly personal questions out of the room, thankful I'd be handing the reins back to the real Dr. Phil soon. Let *her* figure out a polite answer to whether her husband was upset about being replaced by a turkey baster. Me, I just smiled, waved, and pretended to be deaf.

Once we were out of the press's earshot, I ditched my handler on the pretext of needing to use the restroom, and found a quiet stall to make a phone call. Billy answered on the third ring.

"Where are you?" I said, using my own voice so he'd recognize me.

"Gee, I was hoping for 'What are you wearing?' Assuming you miss me as much as I miss you, and this is phone sex, which I'm afraid is our only option until my job is over." There was laughter in his voice, which almost always calmed me down, but not this time.

"Billy, you didn't happen to ride along with me on my job today, did you?" *Please say yes, please say yes, please . . .*

"Sorry, sweetheart. Much as I love me some zero-G, I'm in the middle of something that can't wait. Well, not if I want to collect a sum hefty enough to maintain my lifestyle for the next year or so."

"So you're honestly not here in Houston?" I said, trying my best to keep the panic out of my voice.

His voice got serious. "Ciel, what's wrong? Tell me. Now."

I sighed. "It's the photographer. He knows I'm not the client. He *knows* it, Billy! What am I supposed to do?"

"First of all, breathe. Slowly. Don't hyperventilate. You're probably feeling paranoid from the seesawing altitudes. Blood rushing in and out of your head can't be good for rational thought."

"He told me flat out. Asked me what I was. Not who. *What.*"

There was a pause. "Strange. What'd you tell him?"

"I ditched the subject entirely by pretending to feel airsick. Kept my face buried in a barf bag, dry-heaving for the entire descent"— there hadn't been much pretending involved, the possibility of discovery having made me queasy in spite of the behind-the-ear patch, something Billy didn't need to know—"and we were taken back to the Space Center for the presser as soon as we landed. Alec—the photographer—was there, in the back, taking pictures of me the whole time. I'm afraid he's going to come looking for me any second. What if he knows something for real?"

"Well, taking pictures is his job, isn't it? Of course he wants as many pictures as possible of your client—she's the rock star of the day." There was a short pause, presumably him evaluating. "Maybe he meant 'what kind of woman are you to do this.' He could be, I don't know, a 'natural conception' fanatic or something."

"No. The way he looked at me . . . it was creepy. He knew I wasn't Dr. Carson, I'd swear to it."

"Could your client have spilled the beans herself? If this guy knows her, maybe she told him."

"No, she wouldn't have. Her mission is too important to her. I'm certain she wouldn't risk it."

"Okay, if you say so. I think you're probably overreacting, but it's obvious you're spooked. Speaking of which, have you talked to the boss spook yet? Maybe Mark knows something about the guy."

I bit my—well, Phil's—lip. I didn't want to involve Mark if I didn't absolutely have to. How would it look if I couldn't make it through the first assignment he'd given me without his help?

"No," I said. "I'm sure he's got his own job to worry about. Probably something of national importance. I don't want to bother him."

"He's not on a job right now—he took a few days off."

"*What?* I mean . . . good. Really good. He could use a break." Geez, he *didn't* trust me. He probably left his schedule open in case I screwed up and he had to fix it.

Billy's amusement was palpable. "Afraid you're gonna flunk?"

Yes. "Of course not. Shut up."

His laughter filled my ears. "It's not a test, cuz. Mark wouldn't have asked you to do the job in the first place if he wasn't sure you could handle it. You won't blow it if you call him with some questions."

Maybe. Maybe not. I didn't want to risk it. "Look, I already have *you* on the phone, and I don't have much time. Are you going to help me think of something or not?" I said, laying on the exasperation.

"Will you still sleep with me if I don't?"

"No. In fact, if you even approach me in a sexual manner, I will immediately project your mother's aura. Think your libido could handle *that*?"

"Harsh, sweetheart."

"I have your father's aura, too."

"Okay, okay. Look, all you have to do is get away from the guy and lie low until you hand off to your client, right? Where are you now?"

"In a bathroom. I figure I can hang out here five more minutes, tops, before someone comes looking for me."

"Are you wearing the same NASA-issued jumpsuit as the ASCANs?"

"Yeah."

"Any of them about the same size as your client?"

"Yeah . . . all right, I get it. I can probably get past the photographer, if I use the one with hair long enough to cover my name patch, and I'm careful to keep my ID badge flipped. But it's risky. What if I run into the ASCAN I'm impersonating?"

"What can I say? Risky"—I could almost see him giving one of his insouciant shrugs—"is how my mind operates. Anyway, you'll only be wearing the aura long enough to get to Phil's car. If you see the ASCAN, walk the other way. Call me back when you're clear. And next time use a breathy voice and moan a little. It makes phone sex way more fun."

The aura I was projecting was a few inches shorter and ten or so pounds heavier than Dr. Phil, but that didn't matter in a flight suit. Long brown hair, pale complexion. The shoes had pinched at first, nothing a minor adjustment of my feet hadn't fixed. I hoped I didn't run into anyone I'd have to introduce myself to, because hell if I could remember her name. The important thing was, I'd automatically snatched some of her energy when I'd shaken her hand before the flight. You never know when an extra aura will be useful.

The hall outside the restroom was deserted except for my elderly handler, Steve. Darn. I'd thought he'd leave Phil alone once the reporters had been shown the door. Not that it mattered, since I wasn't Phil at the moment.

I nodded pleasantly, hoping to whiz by him without having to talk. No such luck.

"Excuse me, Major, but did you happen to notice if Dr. Carson was okay? I hate to bother her if she's, um, indisposed, but there's some paperwork we should take care of before she leaves today."

"Gosh, I think she's already gone—she told me she had an appointment she had to get to. Maybe you can catch her if you call her cell phone?" I said.

Of course, the call would be routed to the voice mail of Dr. Phil's cell phone, which I was carrying. I'd deal with it later.

"Sure. Thanks, I'll give it a try," he said, pulling his phone out of his pocket as he hurried toward the door leading to the parking lot. Phil's phone vibrated in my pocket. I ignored it and hurried around the corner . . . and ran straight into Alec Loughlin.

Shit.

"Um, sorry," I said, not meeting his eye, and tried to keep moving. He wasn't looking for the ASCAN I was projecting.

He stepped sideways at the same time I did, and we found ourselves doing the awkward people-in-a-rush-trying-to-pass-each-other dance. I shrugged, and laughed in the sheepish way the situation called for, waiting for him to get out of my way.

He didn't.

"Excuse me," I said. "I have someplace I need to be."

His eyes sharpened as he grabbed me by the wrist. "I don't think so, 'Phil.' You're coming with me."

Chapter 3

Loughlin pulled me toward the nearest exit. Jesus. Kidnapping an astronaut? Did he really think he was going to get away with that? What kind of freak was he?

I rotated my wrist until the thumb side of my forearm was aligned with the spot where his finger and thumb joined—the weak point in anyone's grip—and yanked downward with all my might, freeing myself. Since the aura I was wearing was tall enough, and I was close enough, and—most importantly—there was no one else around, I followed up with a quick strike to his throat, leaving him sputtering for air while I ran.

The whole thing hadn't taken more than a second or two. It had been a pure reflex on my part, courtesy of my new sister-in-law, Laura, and the rigorous self-defense training she'd been giving me. Laura was one of Mark's fellow spooks, and had insisted if I wanted to learn to defend myself I'd better do it right. Loughlin was lucky I hadn't been at a good angle to bust his balls with a swift kick—another move I'd recently perfected. As it was, any-one who came across him in the next several seconds would as-sume he was choking, and maybe even Heimlich him, buying me more time.

I hit the parking lot at record speed. Hopped into Phil's dark green 1973 Triumph TR6. (Literally. The top was down.) Calmed myself, and headed out as quickly as I could without attracting undue attention for reckless driving. As soon as it was feasible, I took a small detour behind a strip mall, making sure no one was following me.

Crap. He'd called me "Phil." He knew I wasn't the ASCAN I'd been projecting. Jesus. Had I let Phil's aura leak through somehow? I twisted the rearview mirror and took a good look at myself. Long brown hair, check. Pale white-girl complexion, check. No leaking anywhere.

Maybe he'd seen the name patch? But even if he had, it would be more logical to assume we'd gotten our jumpsuits mixed up. Unless he knew about adaptors . . .

There was nothing I could do about that now, so I switched back to Dr. Phil's aura. It wouldn't do to show up at her house in the gated suburban community as a strange ASCAN.

Before I took off again, I dug out Phil's cell phone and gave Steve Richards a quick call. I told him I'd get to the paperwork the next day, so he wouldn't get worried and send out a search team.

Then I paused, took a deep breath, let it out slowly, and dialed Mark. I hated having to explain a cock-up on my first job for him, but there didn't seem to be a choice after what had happened.

He answered on the first ring. I wasn't sure if that was good or not. Did I happen to catch him at a slow time or had he been on standby, waiting to hear if he needed to come winging to the rescue of incompetent little me?

"Nice work at the press conference," he said first thing. Of course he'd been watching. "You handled yourself in the piranha pool like an old pro."

My cheeks heated at his praise. It was embarrassing how much his approval meant to me. "Thanks. Um, yeah, that part went really well, I thought."

His brief pause carried a frisson of tension. "What happened?" Most people wouldn't have noticed a change in his voice, which he kept carefully neutral, but I knew him well enough to recognize the signs of him going into full alert mode.

"Everything is fine," I said, and swallowed. "Now." And then I explained, as efficiently as I could, what Loughlin had done. Sure, I *may* have downplayed the danger a tiny bit by insinuating Loughlin was a bumbling idiot, and *perhaps* up-played my own badassery in getting away from him, but only so as not to unduly worry Mark.

"Where are you now?" His voice was tight. "I can have somebody with you in five minutes, tops." Which meant he had planted reinforcements nearby. Damn it, he *didn't* trust me.

"Behind a strip mall. But don't worry, I wasn't followed. No need to send in the cavalry."

"Get back to the house. Now. The package"—by which he meant Dr. Phil—"will be delivered on schedule."

"Wait—don't hang up. What do you think is going on?"

"Your paycheck will be in your bank account by the time you're home. If you need anything else, call." By which he meant we weren't going to discuss what happened with Loughlin.

I sighed. Someday, I swore to myself, Mark was going to trust me with work-related stuff as much as he did Billy. But at least he didn't seem to think I'd done anything to precipitate Loughlin's weirdness. That was something, anyway.

Next, I called Billy and explained what had happened with Loughlin. I reassured him I'd already talked to Mark, and told him I was on my way back to Dr. Phil's place. Once *he* was satisfied I didn't need immediate protection he sounded genuinely impressed with my escape from Loughlin, which made me so happy I breathed heavily and moaned for him. My giggling may have detracted from any erotic effect, but, hey, it's the thought that counts, right? He hung up after a promise to squeeze some real moans out of me when he got his hands on me again.

The real Dr. Phil looked to be the picture of health when I finally saw her two days later. Apparently the crisis had passed (so to speak) uneventfully. Her private doctor had given her the go-ahead to resume her refresher astronaut training. She'd been genuinely disappointed to miss the ride on the Vomit Comet.

I was back to being myself again, feeling short, freckly, and generally awkward next to her gorgeous, graceful self.

"So, about this photographer . . ." I said as we were finishing the snack of popcorn and white wine we'd been sharing during our informal debriefing. I felt free to indulge in a second glass, because I wouldn't be driving anywhere. The agent who'd delivered her was waiting around the corner to drive me to the airport.

". . . what can you tell me about Alec Loughlin?" Mark wanted the kidnapping attempt kept under wraps for now, as was his usual practice with anything adaptor related—which was possible, since no one had seen it—but I figured a tiny fishing expedition couldn't hurt. It showed initiative on my part, right?

"Alec? Like I told Mark, apparently he's working for NASA again," she said smoothly, and glanced out the window at her husband.

Mikhail (Misha to his friends), a dark-haired Russian hunk of wiry muscle, was in the backyard, a two-acre lot surrounded by a tall, beautifully structured stone security fence and even taller trees. Privacy was not an issue for the couple. He was playing with his latest "toy," as Phil called it.

Misha had explained to me earlier that it was the latest in drone technology, a large, lightweight quadcopter capable of some amazingly intricate maneuvers. It was his "basement project," the thing he'd been working on for fun at home. Once it was perfected, he had high hopes of using it for payload deliveries to remote areas of the planet that might otherwise take days or weeks for relief supplies to reach if hit by disaster. He felt if Spaceward Ho was going to remain economically viable into the future, he had to set his sights on the ground as well as the stars. Diversification—and a big fat government contract for his special drones—would go a long way toward guaranteeing the financial stability of his fledgling company.

Then he'd grinned and admitted that was his official pitch to his investors, anyway. Really he was developing it because it was so damn much fun to play with.

When Phil turned back to me there was a between-us-girls twinkle in her eyes. She shrugged. "Alec and I dated for a while before I met Misha. I might not have told that part to Mark. It was over so long ago, I didn't think it mattered."

"Might have been a good thing to mention in the forms you

filled out for *me*," I admonished, but gently. One does not alien-
ate clients if one wishes to encourage repeat business.

She looked abashed. "It didn't occur to me—I honestly never
expected to see Alec again. I didn't know NASA had jobbed him
in for the video until after I filled out your questionnaire. As far
as I knew, he moved back to Australia. I was under the impression he only leaves the country to go on shoots for National Geo-
graphic in remote areas of the globe. For him, it was always the
more adrenaline, the better."

Easy to believe, looking at her. She'd give any man an adrenaline rush.

I waved a hand breezily, going for the nonchalant response. No
reason to worry her now. I'd leave it to Mark, aka Captain Need-
to-Know, to decide how much to tell her. I could be discreet, too.
"Don't worry about it. Um . . . by the way, is the security guard
at the community gate armed?"

Swift, Ciel. Real nonchalant.

A line appeared between her eyebrows. "I don't think so. Why?
Are you worried Alec is stalking me all of a sudden? Trust me, the
guy is not pining for me. It was only ever fun and games for him."
She glanced again at her husband, a slow and gentle smile soften-
ing her expression into a thing of ethereal beauty. "Alec never
wanted the same things I want. Misha is the real thing."

The next morning I was back in D.C., after a red-eye on which
I'd slept like a baby, thank you very much, with no noticeable
drooling. Flying was getting easier for me, especially when my
client picked up the tab for a first-class ticket.

I was waiting for Laura at the gym where we always met for

my ass-kicking lessons, having come straight from the airport. No point in stopping by my condo—my gym clothes were here, and it wasn't as if Billy would be waiting in my bed with open arms and a knowing smile on his annoyingly gorgeous face. I sighed. Damn. I missed him. Sure, it had only been a week since I'd seen him (naked), but it was seven days too long as far as my body was concerned.

I sighed again, unsure if having a boyfriend was even good for me. It might be like coffee—something that perks you up and makes you feel *sooo* good, but then you get addicted, and the next thing you know you're in pain when it isn't available.

Plus, it made you sigh in public, which was totally humiliating. I clamped my mouth shut and clobbered the heavy bag with a roundhouse kick. Swore when I stubbed my pinky toe.

I grabbed my injured appendage and hopped up and down on the other foot, skillfully managing to keep from falling on my ass. Barely.

"You need to master your high knee kicks before you hurl yourself into roundhouses."

Mark? *Shit!* What was he doing here?

I whirled around, still holding my foot, looking, I imagined, as awkward as a flamingo on ice, and probably as pink. I didn't bother to adapt away my blush—he would have noticed. He noticed everything. All I could do was hope he'd think my flushed face was due to the exertion of the workout I hadn't technically started yet.

Thoughts started tumbling in my head. How long had he been watching? Damn, he looked good. Tall, blond, and chiseled. Hard, like he'd been carved out of wood that had since petrified.

Except his eyes. His gray eyes could be hard, but they were anything but petrified. They changed constantly, ranging from dove soft to gun-barrel scary, depending on his mood and the situation. Right now they were somewhere in the middle. Neutral, like he was hiding behind them. They'd been like that a lot since a stupid mix-up on my part had culminated in me giving him the world's most awkward can't-we-just-be-friends speech.

I lowered my foot, pretending it didn't hurt anymore. "Um, yeah. Laura said the same thing. So, where is my sadistic sister-in-law, anyway? She was supposed to be here to mete out more of the punishment she refers to so adorably as 'lessons.'"

Mark raised the corners of his mouth in what, for him, was a pretty good smile. He could do better—I'd seen him grin big and wide on occasion—but it was rare. *And devastating when it happens*, I thought, remembering times my insides had melted right out of me at the sight of it, starting when Thomas had first brought him home from college (they'd been roommates at Harvard) for Thanksgiving when I was thirteen.

Good thing he wasn't bestowing one of those on me right now, because combined with the way he filled out his gym clothes, I'd be a puddle on the floor in no time. A remorseful puddle, berating myself for mental unfaithfulness to my boyfriend. Who wanted to be a remorseful puddle?

"Laura had a last-minute appointment your brother wouldn't let her cancel, so she asked me to fill in for her. Told me to keep it real, not to go easy on you because you're a girl."

My chest clutched at the thought of getting hot and sweaty rolling around on the floor with Mark. I swallowed hard. "See, what'd I tell you? Sadistic."

Mark laughed, a deep rumble I could practically feel vibrating through me from five feet away. "Don't worry, I won't break you. Thomas would kill me if I did."

Thomas was the brother in question, a lawyer, married to Laura. He'd always been overprotective to the extreme, though he was somewhat better since marrying Laura. One of the many things I loved about her.

But the ass-kicking wasn't the kind of sadistic I'd meant. Laura was aware of my conflicted feelings about Mark. She also knew how he felt about me. Talk about star-crossed. Or maybe timing screwed. If Mark had told me his feelings for me had moved beyond a tolerant affection for his best friend's kid sister *before* Billy had entered the picture romantically, things might have been different now.

Yeah, right, I told myself. *Then you'd be with Mark and conflicted about Billy.* Same boat, different oars. Frankly, it made my head hurt to think about it. I loved Billy, he loved me, we were good together. The simplest solution for all involved was for me to get past my lingering infatuation with Mark.

What if it's more than infatuation? my inner buttinski said.

Shut up! I screamed at her. Inwardly, so Mark wouldn't call the men in white coats. *Even if it's more, it's not like I don't still have to choose one. Which I've already done. End of story.*

Yeah? the buttinski said. *Ever hear of sequels?*

God, she was such an unhelpful bitch sometimes.

I shook out my arms and legs, holding myself loose and ready, the way Laura had taught me. "Don't hold back on my brother's account. I won't tell on you."

The thing was, Laura wasn't as sure as I was (and I *was*) that I'd chosen the right guy. She adored Billy—nobody could help adoring Billy; he sucked in adoration like a vacuum cleaner—but Mark was her friend and partner, as well as her husband's best friend. She had a vested interest in seeing him happy. She also had the devious mind of a spook. It wouldn't be beyond her to devise ways of throwing me together with Mark, figuring the cards would play out the way they were meant to.

Mark's eyes flicked over me, taking in my stance, sizing me up in an instant. Calculating, no doubt, how to take me down without inflicting too much damage on me, and maybe teach me a few things at the same time.

Use the tools you have, Laura had told me a hundred times during our lessons. *If you're not stronger than your opponent—and women rarely are, when their opponent is a man—you have to outsmart him. Leverage is your best option.*

I darted a glance to Mark's right leg, telegraphing my intent to strike there first. I let my eyes linger a fraction of a second too long, knowing he'd catch it and be ready for me.

Then I skirted around his left side. Kicked the back of his knee, buckling it. Jumped back a few steps. One advantage of being small: I was fast.

But not quite fast enough. He righted himself before he hit the floor, reaching for me as he twisted, and dove in my direction. Quick as I was, he had me by my ankles before I could dance away from him.

If I'd been intent on hurting him, I would have grabbed him by both ears and bashed his head into the floor, using his own momentum against him. We'd moved off the mat, so I could inflict some damage if I chose. Of course, if *he'd* been intent on winning at any cost, he could have already pulled my legs out from under me and broken my neck before I had a chance to do any head bashing.

I looked down and saw the heart-melting smile. "Nice try, Howdy"—his nickname for me, short for Howdy Doody, which

my grandfather dubbed me as a child, for freck-tacular reasons—
"but you should've kept running. *Always* run if you can."

I squared my shoulders, trying to ignore the heat of the big
hands still gripping me. "Running wasn't an option. Your legs are
longer than mine. You would have caught me."

"Not if you'd kicked the side of my knee instead of the back,
and used more force. You had the opportunity—nice feint, by the
way—and it would have incapacitated me long enough for you to
get away."

"Jesus, Mark, are you crazy? I wasn't about to really hurt you!"
I said.

He yanked my legs out from under me, and caught me before
my head hit the floor, lowering me gently. Amusement crinkled
his eyes as he kneeled to one side of me, his hands on my biceps.
"You're definitely getting better, but I don't think you're quite at
the point where you have to worry about that yet. I won't let you
hurt me. So stop holding back." The last part was accompanied
by a squeeze. Not painful, but letting me know his strength.

"Fine," I said, and lifted my head, fast, with as much force as I
could. I was aiming for his nose, but he drew back at the last
second, so I only grazed his chin with my forehead. His grip loosened for a fraction of a second. I pulled my knees up to my chest.
Rolled toward him, connected my feet to his midsection, and
gave a mighty push.

I got my legs under me while he sucked in a breath. Sprinted
across the gym, not stopping until I'd put a big weight machine
between us. He wasn't far behind, but couldn't reach me as long
as I kept to the other side of the equipment.

I grinned at him, skipping from side to side as he tried to figure out a way around the machine to get me. "I can do this all day, spook."

He finally stopped, smiled the heart-and-panty melter, and said, "Good job, Howdy. Now let's get back to the mats so I can show you some moves to use when you don't have anything to hide behind."

I steeled myself to withstand whatever effects further physical contact with him might have on my hormones. Crap. Why did he have to look so good? And when the hell would Billy be back from his stupid job?

An hour and a half later we sat at a festively bedecked coffee bar around the corner from the gym, sipping pumpkin spice lattes and watching Christmas shoppers hurtle past as we dissected my performance. Well, Mark dissected. I tried to absorb and assimilate. But between sore muscles and prolonged exposure to his pheromones, I'd about reached my saturation point.

We'd showered at the gym—separately, of course—so we weren't offending anyone within sniffing distance. Took some doing to wash the sweat off after a rigorous workout, especially when the shower was of necessity a cold one.

I had no idea if Mark had the same problem. When he set his mind to instructing, he *instructed*. Pure focus. No provocative looks, no sneaky caresses, no innuendo. Just the cold, hard, how-to-hurt-the-other-person facts, ma'am. He was way better at compartmentalizing life than I was.

A harried woman with six bags from three different stores came in and approached the counter, struggling to hold on to her toddler's hand. *Thank God for Internet shopping,* I thought as Mark alternately complimented my performance and ripped apart my form. Yeah, I should have been listening closely to his valuable pointers—after all, they might one day save my life—but I was trying to get my focus off his biceps. Forcing myself to think about shopping should do the trick. Hitting the shops and malls is painful for me any time of year, but in the run-up to the holidays it's excruciating. Apparently I lack whatever basic hunter-gatherer gene makes shopping fun for some people.

Better to think about how much I hate shopping than those big, manly hands circled so gently around the coffee mug. They'd be warmer than usual now, maybe even hot . . . Ack! Think of something else, you idiot!

Two preteen girls walked by, giggling as they compared their recent purchases. Which reminded me, I had a promise to keep. Molly, Billy's adorable recently turned eleven-year-old sister, had requested some special girl time. *Yeah, good. Think about that.*

"Got something more important on your mind, Howdy?" Mark said, a hefty dollop of pay-attention-to-the-teacher edging his voice. He'd been all business at the gym, making me work defensive and offensive moves over and over again until my form and reflexes satisfied him.

"Hu—what? Um, no. I remembered something I have to do with Molly. Sorry. What were you saying again? Something about using more thumb pressure in my eye-gouging?" I sipped my coffee extra genteelly, pinky extended, making sure I left a giant whipped-cream mustache on my upper lip. Then, in case he wasn't sure I was doing it on purpose, I crossed my eyes at him.

His eyes softened at once, and he may have even chuckled. "All right, Howdy. Enough violence for today. I'll tell Laura what we covered so she can continue from where we left off."

Damn. Might have been a bad move to break his teacherly concentration. The soft eyes and the almost-laugh were de-solidifying my insides at an alarming pace. And here I'd been about to congratulate myself on not making an embarrassing fool of myself during the rest of our workout. Granted, it's tough to feel warm, lustful fuzzies toward someone barking at you like a drill sergeant, so the credit should probably go to him. Still, I was going to count it. Only now, when I could really use the restraint, I felt myself about to tip over the edge again.

I grabbed a napkin, wiping my mouth as I stood, almost knocking my chair over in my hurry. "I better get going. Thanks for the coffee and for, um"—*rolling around on the floor with me?*—"the lesson. I'll keep practicing."

Mark stood, his expression telling me all I needed to know about whether he understood my dilemma. He took my hand (his *was* hot), leaned down, and kissed the top of my head. "Anytime, Ciel. I'm still here."

Heart pounding with a combination of lust and guilt, I got the hell out of there.

Chapter 4

My phone vibrated in my pocket right after I boarded the Metro train. Normally I would have walked home—the gym was only a mile from my condo—but frankly, I was pooped. Plus, there was my carry-on to deal with. The wheels didn't need the wear and tear.

I hooked my elbow around the pole in the middle of the car, holding on to the extended handle of my bag while I dug my phone out of my pocket. Laura, probably with some lame excuse for not-so-metaphorically shoving me into Mark's arms.

As always, her voice was flavored with the honeyed tones of the South. "Sorry I ditched you, sugar. Your brother insisted on dragging me to the doctor."

"Doctor? Laura, what happened? Are you sick? Did you have an accident? Are you okay?" I said, my voice escalating with every question.

Oh, God. I was channeling my mother.

Her soft and sultry laughter reassured me it couldn't be anything too serious, so I took my worry down a notch.

"I'm fine. Your brother looks a little pasty, though. Shock, I think."

And there it went, right back up through the roof. "*What?* Is he the one who's sick? Or hurt? Should I come over? What can I do?" The idea of my big brother not being completely healthy, strong, and in charge of everything in his world was frightening. "Why are you laughing?" Geez, maybe she really was a sadistic bitch.

"Honey, calm down. Tom is fine. Or he will be, once he gets used to the idea of being a daddy."

My phone slipped out of my hand. I did half a twirl around the bar and picked it up before the guy next to me stepped on it. "Holy shit! You're pregnant?" I said when I was upright again.

"Apparently so. According to the best ob-gyn in the city, anyway. I assume she knows her stuff. When the home test showed a positive this morning, your brother went all caveman on me and insisted we go see the doctor right away. I wanted to wait until after our lesson, but you know your brother."

Did I ever. I loved him dearly, but Laura was welcome to his Neanderthal tactics. She was much better at dealing with his bossiness than I was.

"Forget about it," I said. "This is so cool! Congratulations! Oh, my God—have you told Mom yet? She is going to *freak*."

"Not yet. You're the first. We're still at the doctor's office."

Aw, that made me feel good. Special. Having a sister was the best.

"I think your brother has recovered enough to speak now—here he is."

"Hey, sis." Thomas's voice was shakier than I'd ever heard it. But happy.

"I can't believe I'm going to be an aunt!" I screamed, earning myself major *looks*—some indulgent, some annoyed—from my fellow passengers. I lowered my voice a few decibels. "This is the best news ever."

"It is, isn't it? I still can't quite believe it—we weren't even going to start trying until next year. We've been so careful—"

"TMI, Thomas!" Laura's voice in the background. I thought maybe I heard a *thwack,* too. She probably hit him.

"Sorry, dear." Thomas's muffled reply was to her. He never called me "dear." "We're thrilled. I can't believe I'm going to be a dad."

I giggled. "Wait till Mom finds out she's going to be a grandma. Things are about to get real, big bro. So, are you going call her next? Whatever you do, don't tell her you told me first, or none of us will ever hear the end of it."

"We're heading up"—"up" being Manhattan, where my parents lived in an Upper West Side brownstone—"as soon as I hand off the baton at the office and we get a few things packed. We figured we better tell Mom and Dad in person, so I can catch Mom when she passes out. Besides, if we're not there for her to hug, she'll be on the first flight down. Want me to text you after we tell her, so you can get your 'surprise' on?"

"No need. I'm sure I'll be able to hear her scream from here," I said.

I was still buzzing with the good news when I walked through my front door and saw the roses. All thoughts of my brother's impending daddy-hood flew out of my head. A dozen blooms, in as many colors, in a crystal vase on the hall stand, and more leading up the stairs, one on each step.

A smile stretched my face almost to the breaking point. I

abandoned my carry-on and ran up the stairs, grabbing flowers along the way. "Billy?" I hollered. "Are you here?"

I pushed open the door to my bedroom. He was there all right, gloriously naked from the waist up, barefoot, and stretched out casually on his side across my king-size bed. He was propped up on one elbow, the most gorgeous, deep red rose clamped between his teeth. He waggled the dark eyebrows above his inky blue eyes, and fluttered his lush, black lashes.

I burst out laughing. "You look like the cover of a bad romance novel."

He spit out the rose. "Yeah? Come here so I can rip your bodice. Now, wench! I've been waiting. If you'd been any longer, I might have been forced to start without you."

I tossed the rest of the roses onto the bed beside him (the thorns having been thoughtfully removed by the florist—I'm not an idiot) and dove in after them, my heart near to bursting with laughter and love.

"If you'd told me you were coming, I would have made it a point to get here sooner," I said.

"What, and spoil the surprise?"

He flopped back and pulled me on top of him. Kissed me until I moaned and begged him to hurry. When he let me up for air, I'd somehow lost my jacket, shirt, and bra.

"Damn, I've missed you," he said.

"Prove it," I said with a challenging grin, and tugged at the top button of his jeans.

With a wicked gleam in his eyes, he flipped me onto my back and slowly divested me of my ankle boots and pants. He left my lacy underwear—he was fond of removing that with his teeth.

After he took off his jeans and boxer briefs, he crawled back into bed beside me and planted a kiss on each of my breasts, lingering with his tongue until I was whimpering. If lingering were an art form—and I was pretty sure it was, the way Billy did it—he would be a virtuoso. He certainly made my body sing.

He paused, replacing his teasing tongue with both hands, cupping me, squeezing lightly. "You're beautiful, Ciel. You know that, don't you?"

"I know you think so," I said. "And I'm happy you do."

He nodded. "As long as you realize it. And while I appreciate what you're trying to do for me"—he traced his fingers lightly over my chest—"you know it's not necessary, right? You don't have to enhance anything for me. You're the sexiest woman I know exactly the way you are."

I looked down at myself. Were my boobs bigger? They *were.* What the hell?

Shit. What was I doing? I shrank them back down to normal, mortified my subconscious would do such a thing.

Billy smiled reassuringly. "If you get off on changing things up, you know I'm ready and willing. I'll even enlarge anything you want bigger on me." He winked. "But I don't ever want you to feel insecure with me, okay? Playing games can be fun, but I love *you.* As you."

I didn't think he was intentionally reminding me of my recent mix-up, but I felt guilty all the same.

"I love *you,*" I said, fiercely, clutching him to me. "I don't want you to change *anything* for me." It was true, too, every word of it. Losing him before, if only briefly, had about killed me. The thought of it happening again was too painful to contemplate.

He held me tightly. After a moment, he said, "Nothing? You sure?"

The teasing in his voice, coupled with a new pressure on my belly, made me pull away and look down. *Ack!* Billy, already generously endowed, had doubled his size. I scooted away from him.

"You put it right back the way it was, mister," I said as sternly as I could while swallowing my laughter. "There is no way I'm letting that monster near me. God, I wouldn't be able to sit for a week."

He complied at once. "Come here, you," he said in a voice just this side of a growl, pulling me under him and sliding into me in one smooth motion. His eyes, serious now, held mine as he began to move, slowly at first, then picking up speed until I moaned with my impending release. "*You* are what matters to me, Ciel. Not how you look. *You.*"

I toppled over the edge, staring into those eyes that never failed to mesmerize me, marveling once again at his ability to have me giggling one second and gasping with passion the next. He came seconds later, burying his face in my neck, gripping me tightly until at last we fell apart, holding hands and breathing hard, staring at the ceiling together.

A minute or so later—long enough for our heart rates to slow back down—he turned his head to me, a naughty glint in his eyes. "Of course, the package you're wrapped in is an awfully nice bonus."

I snuggled up to him. How did he always know exactly what I needed to hear? "Oh, you are *good.*"

"Huh. I guess it must be like they say . . ."

The grin in his voice made me smile. "And what exactly do they say?"

"Good things come in small packages."

I cracked up. Yeah, he was the one. The only one, I assured myself. This time I got no argument from my inner buttinski.

•

———

Much later, completely satisfied, and naked except for the blanket (me) and sheet (Billy) wrapped around us like togas, we sat at my dining room table, munching on freshly delivered pizza. I picked the anchovies off mine and gave them to Billy, who happily piled them on his.

"I thought you liked anchovies," he said with a suspicious twinkle in his eye. "Honest."

"Eh. They're okay. But not on Hawaiian pizza. They clash with the pineapple, and the ham is already salty enough. Which you knew when you ordered, because I explained it the last time we ordered pizza."

"Huh. Guess I forgot."

Yeah, right. Billy had the most obnoxiously good memory of anyone I knew.

"Bullshit," I said. "You figured I'd give you my share of the anchovies." I bit into a slice and made a face. I must have missed one of the little suckers. "Bleah. Too salty."

Billy leaned over and kissed me. "Mmm. Salty is good. I like you salty." His tongue played delicately over my lips.

I pulled away with a groan. "Stop! I'm hungry. For *food* now."

"I can't help it. Seeing you wrapped up in a blanket makes me think of the boat in Sweden. That was when I knew for sure I had to have you."

I'd been wearing a blanket then, too, after an unintended dip in the Baltic Sea drenched my clothes (and almost drowned me, but I preferred not to dwell on that part). That little adventure had been the first time I'd started seeing Billy in a romantic light. And the beginning of all my confusion. Before then, I'd been safely and solidly wrapped in the cocoon of my unrequited passion for Mark. Was Billy intentionally reminding me my attraction to Mark was no longer unrequited? Was he fishing? Or was I being too sensitive?

"And now you do have me," I said simply, willing him to believe me, because, God, I never wanted to hurt him.

After a pause, he smiled, seemingly reassured. He picked a piece of pineapple off his slice and put it on mine. "There. I'm atoning."

For what? The fish or the fishing?

I chose to go with the least complicated path. Thank you, Occam's razor, for shaving my conscience. "I gave you *all* my anchovies."

"Yeah, but I love pineapple, so my sacrifice is greater. It balances out karmically," he said.

"You're such a saint. Honestly, I don't know why you haven't been canonized yet."

"Merely a celestial oversight, I'm sure. But enough about me, fascinating though the topic is. Catch me up on you. How'd your lesson with Laura go? I assume that's where you were between the airport and bed with me."

"Laura! Oh, my God, I haven't told you the news! She's pregnant. Can you believe it? I'm going to be an aunt!"

Billy's eyes got big. "Way to bury the lede, cuz."

"Hey, it's your own fault. I was *going* to call you as soon as I got home, but then I saw the roses, and you were there in my bed, all shirtless and sexy, and I hadn't seen you in *a whole week,* and then you started kissing me, and then . . ." I shrugged. "I forgot."

"Excellent excuse." He grinned, and leaned over to kiss me again before turning his attention back to his pizza. "Hell, they aren't wasting any time, are they? Unless maybe that was the reason for the blitzkrieg wedding your mom pulled out of thin air?"

"No, they only found out today. Laura called me from the doctor's office. Apparently, they hadn't planned to start trying until next year. Thomas was still in shock."

"I can imagine. God, impending fatherhood would send me running for—" He shuddered almost imperceptibly, a strange cross between speculation and fear blooming in his eyes. "You don't think . . . I mean, there isn't any way . . ."

My latest sip of beer exited through my nose on the updraft of a cough. "*What?* No! No way. Jesus, Billy, don't say stuff like that."

He mopped my face with a napkin, pounding me—softly— on my back when my coughing fit continued. "Sorry," he said. "Forget it, okay? We're careful. So, Laura still gave you a lesson? Bet Tommy-boy wasn't keen on that."

"No, she sent Mark as a substitute," I said, under control again, keeping it breezy. No biggie, right?

A small muscle contracted in Billy's jaw. "Mark? Guess he thought it would be a good opportunity to go over your NASA job? Two birds with one stone."

I shrugged, and forced myself not to look away from Billy's eyes, holding back a blush. "Not so much. You know how he is with the need-to-know bullshit. Whatever's going on with the photographer, apparently I don't need to know."

Billy nodded, looking at me thoughtfully. "The spook give you a good workout?" he asked, not an inkling of innuendo in his voice or eyes. So why could I still feel it?

"He went all drill sergeant on me," I said, squelching my stupid guilt. "And here I'd been thinking Laura was tough." I shoved some pizza in my mouth and concentrated on chewing.

Billy put his slice down, and took mine from me. He dropped it beside his.

"Hey, I'm not finished!" I mumbled, chewing faster.

He took me by the hand and led me back upstairs. "Neither am I," he said, a determined gleam in his eye.

I woke to a jarring clash of cymbals followed by my mother's voice saying, "Answer your phone!"

Gah. Ringtone hell. Odds were ten to one Billy helped Mom install it on my phone when I wasn't looking. Great in the sack or not, I might have to kill him.

The cymbals crashed again. "Answer your phone!"

Was it my imagination, or did the recording sound more insistent that time?

Thomas and Laura must have told her the news. I pried my eyelids open and looked at the clock beside my bed. They'd made incredibly good time. Maybe if I didn't answer she'd give up and call Auntie Mo to lord it over her instead.

Auntie Mo was Billy's mom. Well, stepmom. (Not that it makes a bit of difference, except to cement the whole cousin issue with Billy as Absolutely Not Perverted.)

Crash! "Answer your phone!"

I sighed. Nothing could douse the sleepy afterglow like a conversation with my mother. Billy had left me practically radioactive when he'd had to skedaddle back to his job; the glow was finally calming down enough for me to relax into the land of Nod. Frankly, after the two workouts I'd had—professional with Mark, recreational with Billy, both physically exhausting—I really needed some shut-eye.

I stared at the phone, debating whether I could get away with ignoring it.

Crash! "Answer your phone!"

I yawned until my jaw cracked. Oh, hell. She'd keep trying every five minutes until she got through. Mom was nothing if not persistent. I reached for the phone.

"Hey, Mom. Wow, *great* news, huh?" I said, thinking, in my groggy state, a preempt would be a good idea. Maybe if Mom found out I already knew, she'd hang up fast and call someone who didn't. "Welp, gotta run—"

Yes, I know I told Thomas not to let on they'd told me first. Trust me, all of us Halligan siblings are accustomed to the view from under the bus. It's a survival mechanism that kicks in when dealing with our mother. Thomas would no doubt claim I'd wheedled the news out of Laura. Since Laura is a saint in Mom's eyes, she wouldn't get in trouble over it. So really it wasn't as much of a betrayal as it might appear.

"Ciel Colleen Halligan, how could you say such a thing? It's *terrible* news. And how did you hear about it? I just found out myself."

"Um, Thomas told me," I said, scrubbing my face with one hand, trying to chase away the residual sleepiness. Regardless of Laura's immunity from Mom's wrath, she hadn't been in the family long enough for me to throw *her* under the bus. Besides, sisterly solidarity. "I've never heard him so happy," I added. "Wait a second—why aren't you happy? You're supposed to be thrilled."

"You think I'm some sort of monster?"

"Of course not," I said. "I would never think—"

"And how did Thomas find out?"

"Well, how do you think? Laura told him."

"Laura? Why on Earth would she—oh, my God! The CIA is involved?"

Okay, what the hell was going on? "Mom, let me talk to Laura for a second, okay?"

"Why would Laura be here? She's working, and so is Thomas."

Uh-oh. "Mom, what did you call to tell me?"

A heavy sigh came through the line. Mom composing herself. "It's Aunt Helen. She's dead."

Crap. A picture of Aunt Helen popped into my head and gave my heart a squeeze. Elderly, frail, and unable to sustain a decent aura for longer than fifteen minutes at a time anymore. We all loved her dearly.

I took a breath and leavened my voice with a hefty dose of sympathy. "I'm so sorry. It's not entirely unexpected, though, is it? Given her age and all," I said.

"She was murdered."

"*What?*"

"Somebody used a stun gun on her in Central Park, then stabbed her while she was still twitching."

Thanks for the visual, Mom. "What kind of fucking sicko does that?"

It was a measure of how upset I was that I let "fucking" slip out while talking to my mother. It was a measure of how upset *she* was that she let it pass without a comment about God punishing me right away.

"How could the police know such a gruesome detail anyway?" I added rapidly, in case she was only pausing to frame an adequate threat of heavenly retribution.

"There was a witness. He was too far away to get a good look at the guy's face, but he definitely saw the stun gun, and then the stabbing. Which I wouldn't know, except Junie Sorensen volunteers at the library where the wife of the police officer who was first on the scene works. Oh, God, Ciel, what is the world coming to when a harmless little old lady can't even take a walk—in the middle of the day!—in Central Park?"

I knew she didn't expect an answer. "How's Dad taking it?" Aunt Helen had been like a second mother to him when he was a kid.

Mom switched gears from impending hysteria to deep sadness with a heavy sigh. "You know your father. He's being strong for me." There was a small pause—a sniffle and a deep breath. "Enough tragedy. What's this 'great news' you were talking about?"

I might have known a simple thing like the murder of a relative wouldn't keep Mom from pursuing a trail.

"Uh . . . nothing." *Crap, Ciel, think of something!* "Look, now isn't the time—"

"Ciel Colleen, now is exactly the right time to tell me some 'great news.' Spit it out this instant!"

"Laura's pregnant." The words were sucked out of my mouth by the force of my mother's will before I could bite my tongue.

I *know.* It was awful enough I'd been willing to admit I'd known something before she did, but then not to wait for Thomas and Laura to tell her? Bad me.

I heard a *thunk*—that would be the phone dropping—followed by a happy squeal.

"Mom!" I yelled. "Mom, pick up the phone right—"

"Oh, this is such wonderful news!" Mom's voice was loud and clear again, glazed with joy. "If it's a girl, they'll have to name her Helen. Well, middle name at least. And Mo will throw a shower, of course, and we'll have a fabulous christening party—"

"Mom! Stop a second, okay? Listen, you can*not* tell Thomas and Laura I spilled the beans. They're on their way up to tell you in person."

Mistake. Mom shifted gears faster than a NASCAR driver on race day.

"Why did they tell you before me? Shouldn't grandparents be the first—"

"They wanted to see your face when—"

"Would it have killed them to wait to tell you? Who else have they told? James? Brian? *Mo?* Am I the *last* one to find out?"

"No! Nobody else knows." *If you don't count Billy*, I thought, crossing my fingers and glancing ceiling-ward for stray lightning bolts. "And the only reason I know is because Laura had to cancel her lesson with me to go to the doctor. She wanted to explain why she ditched me, is all."

"Well . . . I suppose I understand. Still . . . never mind, it doesn't matter." Thank God for Laura's saintly immunity. "Listen, honey, I have to go. I need to call Mo!"

"Mom, you *can't* tell Mo yet!"

"But she'll want to start planning the shower." Mom was already a million miles away, somewhere deep in Baby Land. In fact, I heard the telltale sound of her fingers tapping away on her computer. She was probably already scouring the Babies"R"Us website.

"*No*," I said. Loudly, to break through her haze. "You have to wait until Thomas and Laura tell you. And you have to act surprised when they do. Promise me!"

"Promise what, sweetie? Listen, I'll call you later. So much to do!"

Chapter 5

Aunt Helen's funeral was a suitably somber affair, unless you counted the flashes of joy in Mom's and Auntie Mo's eyes every time they glanced at Laura. They were starting to make me queasy. Seemed like I was feeling queasy a lot lately. Which made me wonder . . . no. I was *not* going to go there, and damn Billy for planting the seed of the idea in my head, anyway.

The seed-planter himself (okay, even as a random thought, that *so* didn't sound right) squeezed my hand reassuringly.

I glanced at Laura, whose auburn hair had grown into a sleek bob, presently shining in the morning sun. She'd met Aunt Helen only once, at the wedding, so her forest green eyes were focused on my brother Thomas with concern for him more than sadness for herself. His dismay lessened perceptibly when he looked at her. The skirt of her dark burgundy suit showed not a hint of a baby bump yet, but her hand still gravitated toward it unconsciously, like she was already protective of it.

I jerked my eyes away from her, fighting the roil in my belly. There was no way . . . was there? I mean, I used birth control. Religiously. Then again, going by Thomas's slip on the phone, so had Laura. If someone as meticulously careful as I knew CIA spooks to be could get caught . . .

Crap. Where were horrible cramps when you really needed them? I did a quick calculation in my head, trying to remember how long it had been since my last period. Had I even had one since Thomas and Laura's wedding? Things had gotten pretty messed up with the client I'd had then, and afterward the rift in my relationship with Billy had upset me so much I hadn't exactly been paying attention to my internal calendar. If I hadn't had a visit from good ol' Mother Nature since—

Holy shit! No, it couldn't be.

I looked at Mark with something akin to terror flowing through me. It had been a stupid, stupid misunderstanding on my part. I hadn't even known at the time he was the one who—holy hell, God *couldn't* be so cruel. Could He?

Billy once again squeezed my hand lightly. "It'll be over soon, cuz."

Would it? I thought weakly, and then gave myself a shake. This was ridiculous.

I nodded up at Billy and tried to smile. Forced my mind to focus on Aunt Helen. Which didn't make me feel one whit better. Funerals sucked, no matter how long and good a life the deceased had had, but then to be taken out in such a senselessly violent way . . . damn. It wasn't right.

Mom and Mo had (naturally) arranged everything. They'd tried to respect Uncle Foster's wishes for a small graveside service with only the closest friends and family members in attendance, difficult as it was for them to plan anything low-key, but there were still a lot of people in there, most of them adaptors.

At least the setting was beautiful, I thought, trying my best to find something positive to focus on. Aunt Helen and Uncle Foster had bought a double plot at the Woodlawn Cemetery in the Bronx back in 1974, when Duke Ellington was buried there. They were big jazz fans. The weather was crisp and clear—cold enough to be seasonal, but not to give you frostbite.

The only disconcerting thing about the morning was the presence of several undercover security guards posted around the perimeter, trying to blend in with the mourners. Mark had insisted on it. He was working with the police on the murder case (if by "working with" you mean "had taken it over entirely") because it involved an adaptor. He hadn't told the local law enforcement officers that, of course. He'd merely flashed his government credentials, said something about "national security" and "need to know" (big surprise), and set them to doing the mundane groundwork, without allowing them to follow any trails that might lead to discovering the existence of adaptors. (Yeah, I'll bet the local LEOs *love* when the feds come to visit.)

I put it all down to Mark's tendency to be extra cautious where the anonymity of the adaptor community was concerned. (Thomas had once hinted that Mark's extreme caution had something to do with his family—whom none of us knew—but refused to discuss it more than that.) Still, somebody purposely singling out Aunt Helen? It was a ridiculous notion. She was the most inoffensive person you could imagine. There was no possible reason anyone would kill her, other than pure random malice.

When the minister—a friendly older woman who looked like

she'd be right at home baking cookies in Santa's kitchen—finished listing all the wonderful things about Aunt Helen (it was a long list), Uncle Foster picked up the saxophone from a stand between two huge wreaths of anthuriums. The waxy red flowers, with their obscene protrusions, had been Aunt Helen's favorite—she said they always looked happy to see her.

If there'd been tears before, the floodgates opened on everyone when Uncle Foster handed his prized possession to my brother Brian, the musician in our family, who started playing "In a Sentimental Mood," Aunt Helen's favorite. Uncle Foster closed his eyes, holding on to my father and mother for support, an achingly sad smile on his face as he swayed, ever so slightly, to the melody. I buried my face in Billy's shoulder (yeah, that suit jacket was going to need a trip to the dry cleaners) and momentarily lost myself in memories of the sweet old lady who'd snuck me candy and told me scandalous stories about her days entertaining the soldiers as a USO volunteer.

My snuffling was interrupted by an extra hand on my shoulder. Mark.

"To your left, Howdy," he said, barely moving his lips. "Recognize anyone?"

I glanced. A man appeared to be photographing us from twenty or thirty yards away, documenting our grief for whatever reason. "Maybe he works for Woodlawn?" I looked again, more closely, after blinking away excess tears. This time the camera was away from the man's face. "Wait a second—that's Alec Loughlin. What's he doing here?"

"Good question," Mark said quietly.

What the hell? I thought. Mark stepped away before I could voice it. He must have signaled his men somehow, because they closed ranks—quietly, casually—around our small group. Mark walked toward Loughlin, also not rushing. Unfortunately there was no way he could sneak up on the man. Instead, he gave a friendly wave. When the man bolted, so did Billy, joining Mark in the chase.

Mark and Billy were fast, but the man had a vehicle idling close by, and was in it, tearing out, before they could reach him. Traveling much faster than the fifteen-mile-per-hour speed limit, too, the asshole.

"Are you sure it was Alec Loughlin?" Mark said. "I've only seen pictures of the man, but you've met him in person."

We were in my parents' study, along with Billy, taking a brief break from the gaiety in the dining room, where all the in-town Halligans and Doyles were gathered to toast Thomas and Laura's good news. Perhaps it wasn't in the best of taste to hold such a celebration on the evening of Aunt Helen's funeral, but Mom had pointed out Aunt Helen would have been the first to insist on it. She'd always made such a fuss about each and every new Halligan baby, and would have been thrilled at the news of the newest generation.

Uncle Foster was settled back at the exclusive senior living community next to Central Park where he and Aunt Helen had lived for the last ten years. As a new widower, he would be well looked after by a few dozen widows who also resided there, God help him.

I thought hard about Mark's question, struggling to see the man's face in my mind. "I *was* sure. At the cemetery. When I saw him," I said. "There was something about his stance, about the way he held his camera—it reminded me of the news conference. But, no, I suppose he was too far away for me to be a hundred percent certain. Say, ninety-eight percent?"

Mark had shown Billy and me pictures of the real Alec Loughlin on his cell phone. It was definitely the same guy who'd been on the Vomit Comet with me. Or his twin, I supposed, but Mark probably would have mentioned if he'd had one.

Billy's usually playful eyes were serious. "It makes sense Loughlin was hired by NASA to document Dr. Carson's announcement. He knows her—there's a connection. But how could he know Ciel wasn't the real Dr. Carson? Sure, he might wonder why she was ignoring their previous romantic relationship"—I'd already explained how she had neglected to include that little tidbit in her questionnaire—"but that shouldn't be enough to make him think it wasn't *her*. And, if it was Loughlin at the cemetery, why was he taking pictures of everyone?"

"More good questions." Mark's mouth settled into a hard line. He didn't like unanswered questions, especially where adaptors were concerned. "Do you think Dr. Carson told him?"

I shook my head. "And risk her mission? Highly doubtful. It's too important to her."

Molly, Billy's youngest sister, a shorter, long-haired female replica of him, stuck her head in the door. "Hey, you guys, Auntie Ro"—my mom, the inimitable Aurora Halligan, was "Auntie Ro" to Billy and his sisters—"says to come back for the toast. Guess what! Dad said I can have a sip of champagne!"

She skipped off, happily anticipating her first parentally approved taste of alcohol. Of course, if she was anything like her brother and sisters (Sinead and Siobhan, currently home from college on winter break), she'd already illicitly sampled the fruit of the vine. Doyles were precocious.

"Be right there," Mark called after her, then turned back to Billy and me. "What are the chances of getting your families to take Christmas vacation to someplace remote this year?"

"Ha. Mo and Ro, the Christmas queens, leave the city at the height of the holiday season? Slim to none," Billy said.

"No kidding," I said. "But why would you want them to?"

"Call it an abundance of caution." Mark looked like he was about to say more, but was interrupted by my mother's voice telling us to get a move on. Instead, he herded us out of the study. "Come on. Let's go make the newest Halligan's existence official before the wrath of Granny comes down on our heads."

Dad was already pouring when we rejoined the festivities. The amount he put in Molly's glass was minuscule.

"Not even one good swallow," she complained.

"Hey, at least you get real champagne," Laura said, eyeing her own glass of sparkling cider suspiciously. She looked over at James, appealing to the scientist in our family for support. "Are you sure alcohol is bad for the baby?"

James, the brother who looks the most like me, with his strawberry blond hair and pale green eyes (no freckles though, the lucky bastard), shrugged. "Current medical opinion on the consumption of small amounts of alcohol while pregnant varies, but the official recommendation is still not to risk it."

Thomas looked at his wife's disgruntled face and hugged her to him with one arm (his other was busy lifting his full-to-the-brim glass). "Don't worry, honey. Since you'll be eating for two, I'll be happy to drink for two."

"Thanks a lot," Laura grumbled indulgently as everyone else laughed. It's possible my laughter was a tad forced.

My father finished topping off the rest of our glasses and raised his. "To the next generation!" he said, looking about as happy as I'd ever seen him.

I didn't let myself look up at Billy or Mark, standing on either side of me. Fighting down the tiny seed of panic taking root inside me, I wanted nothing more than to guzzle my whole glass in one good swig. Instead, out of some superstitious dread, I barely let the liquid touch my lips.

Chapter 6

I stood in line at Macy's Santaland, wearing the clothes and aura of Molly's good friend Olivia Hawkins, a cherub-faced child with a halo of golden-brown curls and eyes the color of old pennies. Even from as far back in line as Molly and I were, I could see Santa's eyes matched his rosy cheeks. I had a sneaking suspicion the contents of his cocoa thermos went beyond the usual kiddie drink. Not that I blamed him. Hell, I was tempted to see if I could get him to share.

I'd about convinced myself the insidious "what if" thoughts I'd been having were purely a psychosomatic response to Laura's pregnancy, so joining the jolly old elf in a quaff of something strong enough to deaden the pain of being trapped in this store with dozens upon dozens of joyously—and some not so joyously—screaming children and their harried parents sounded pretty good. But of course, it was only a pipe dream, considering the age of the aura I was projecting.

Plus, part of me was convinced if I avoided alcohol, then

I wouldn't be pregnant. Superstitious? Probably. But that was the way my mind worked. The same way I didn't want to take a pregnancy test, because as long as I didn't *know*, then I wasn't pregnant. (Yeah, I know. Stupid. But when you thought about it, it was like the Schrödinger's cat dilemma—which made it totally scientific—only with my belly. Until I took a test, I both was and wasn't pregnant. As long as I covered my ass on the "was" possibility by not drinking, I could safely remain "wasn't" in my head. Not that I wouldn't take the damn test eventually, if necessary. I was superstitious, not stupid-stitious.)

"Are you sure this is a good idea, Molls?" I said. "I mean, I hate for your friend to miss out on the fun."

Molly, tall for her age—all the Doyle kids were tall, like their dad—wore her dark brown, wavy hair in one long braid. Her bright blue eyes (almost identical to Billy's, again courtesy of Uncle Liam) sparkled.

"Oh, it was Olivia's idea. Her mom has a picture of her sitting on Santa's lap every year for the last twelve years. She started in utero"—Molly had a great vocabulary for her age—"and made Olivia promise to keep doing it until she's twelve. It's a family tradition, and Olivia hates it with a *passion*. So I told her I'd do it for her as a Christmas present. I was so *sure* I'd be adapting by now, after what happened before."

Molly had recently gone through a phase of being able to adapt—after a fashion—at a younger than usual age. The vast majority of aura adaptors don't acquire the ability until they hit puberty. We'd all assumed Molly was as precocious at adapting as she was at everything else, but it turned out her early onset had been a short-lived fluke. She'd been waiting on pins and needles for it to reappear ever since.

"If it's a family tradition, shouldn't she be doing it with, you know, her family?" I said, nudging my youngest honorary cuz in the ribs. I would have been concerned about Molly telling her friend about us and what we could do if I hadn't known Olivia's grandmother was an adaptor. None of her offspring had inherited the trait, but our existence would be no surprise to the family.

Molly giggled. "You'd think, huh? But Olivia threw a major fit, and told her mom she'd only do it this year if she could do it with me, no parents involved. She told her mom you'd take us. Which is kind of true, isn't it? If you don't get too technical about it."

You had to admire their proficiency at scheming, if not their honesty. "I hope Olivia stays out of sight until we're through here. If she's seen two places at once . . ."

Molly, raised in a family of adaptors, was well drilled in the dangers of discovery. "She's hiding out in the tree house her dad built her. We stocked it up ahead of time with sodas and popcorn, and she has her iPad with her to watch videos. With headphones, so nobody will hear her."

"Good thinking. But what if her brother finds her?" There was very little possibility Olivia's mom would make the climb, but her kid brother was half monkey. As far as I knew, he had not been let in on the adaptor secret yet, being somewhat ill-equipped for keeping his mouth shut about anything.

"He's not allowed in the tree house since their mom caught him up there last summer spying on Chrissy next door with binoculars. Chrissy was sunbathing." Molly lowered her voice to whisper, lacing it with giggles. "Topless."

Ha! Chrissy was a newly minted teenager who'd recently started filling out a bikini. "You really think being forbidden will keep him from trying for another peek? Isn't Chrissy's bedroom window right across from the tree house? As I recall, he's a persistent little bugger."

"Nah, we're good. If he gets caught again, his parents will take away all his electronic privileges for a month. He won't risk losing access to his video games. Not even for boobies."

One of Santa's elves—a short, middle-aged lady with bright red lips stretched wide, bleached hair, and way too much jingle in her bells—handed us each a candy cane. We were getting close to the front of the line, thank God.

"So, how big should I smile?" I asked Molly out of the side of my mouth.

Molly weighed the matter. "You know how you look when Auntie Ro makes you go shopping and you don't want to hurt her feelings? Like that."

"Gotcha. Martyred it is," I said with a wink. The look came naturally to me, perfected during the many times during my adolescence Mom had decided my wardrobe needed updating. Shouldn't be a problem transferring it to Olivia's face.

As soon as the kid in front of us was off Santa's lap, Molly shoved me toward the chair. "I'll wait for you in the shoe department," she said, fleeing.

"But it's almost your turn," I hollered after her.

"Me? No way. Santa is for babies!" And then she was gone.

Great. I took a deep breath, plastered on my martyred half-smile, and climbed onto the red velvet pants. Santa looked at me, glassy-eyed, and let loose with a fragrant "Ho! Ho! Ho!" Whew. As I suspected. Whiskey fumes.

"So, little girl, what do you want Santa to bring you for Christmas?"

"Nothing. Really, I already have everything I want. Let's get the picture, okay?"

He joggled his leg, bouncing me up and down until my teeth rattled. "Come now, there must be something you have a hankering for. A great big *package*, maybe? Heh-heh-heh."

What the hell?

I looked up at the jolly face. Was there a leer hidden behind those gold-frame spectacles? There *was*. Why, the old perv! But I was determined to go through with it. A job is a job, paid or not. Besides, if I didn't get the picture here, we'd have to hunt down another Santa, and I'd already wasted too much of my day in line.

"The picture, fat guy," I said through gritted teeth. "Now. Or you'll lose your package before you can give it away."

His eyes sparkled like a naughty boy. "Somebody might be getting a lump of coal in her stocking this year," he said. But at least he signaled the photographer. The camera flashed at the same time I yanked—hard—on his very real beard. That should provide an interesting addition to the family Christmas album.

Before I slipped off his lap I said, "Just so you know, I'll be reporting your disgusting comments to security. I expect you'll be unemployed by the end of your shift."

Santa leaned forward, rubbing his jaw, and whispered, "Jesus, cuz, can't you take a joke?"

Billy met us in front of girls' shoes, back in his own clothes and projecting his own mischievous self. The real fake Santa was back on duty after his unexpected—and, according to Billy, very welcome—break, which he'd spent knocking back a few tall ones at the Cellar Bar. Guess he really was a self-medicator. But apparently not a pedophile, so I didn't feel obligated to get him fired. He'd been under the impression Santaland had been temporarily closed due to a behind-the-scenes problem with a robotic reindeer. Fortunately, he wasn't the sort to question his luck.

I'd ducked into a stall in a ladies' room and switched back to myself, now carrying Olivia's clothes in a shopping bag. My own jeans and sweater weren't much bigger than hers, but I refused to parade around the store as myself wearing a Justin Bieber sweatshirt.

"You are such an ass," I said to Billy first thing. I'd like to say I kept my voice low enough that Molly couldn't hear, but her giggle told me otherwise.

Besides, it wasn't as though she'd never heard me call her brother that—and worse—before, practically from her birth onward. Growing up with Billy had, at times, been a frustrating proposition. His teasing at family gatherings had more often than not culminated with him standing in a handy corner and me with a bar of soap in my mouth.

"What? Can't I have a little holiday fun with my favorite girls?" He tugged Molly's braid.

"If I'd known it was you, I would have stayed," Molly said. "You should have told me you were coming."

"That goes double for me," I said, giving him the evil eye. "You said you had something important planned for today."

"And so I do. Ladies, if you'll follow me . . ."

He led off with long strides, not looking back. After a quick glance at each other, Molly and I followed, walking double time to keep up with him. Molly held on to multiple copies of a picture of Olivia with Santa, a happily malevolent smile on her face. The look on Santa's face—mouth wide open, eyes squished shut in a major wince—might leave a little to be desired, but, hey, those were the breaks. At least Olivia's hand was hidden. I'd taken care to pull his beard from the underside, so Molly's buddy wouldn't be blamed for spoiling the picture. I was sure Olivia herself would love it. Her mother? Possibly not so much.

Molly could barely contain herself as we stood in front of the g-force simulator at the Intrepid Sea, Air & Space Museum. Me? I was starting to wish the taxi ride hadn't been so short.

We'd swung by Olivia's house first. Molly had snuck around back to the tree house with the clothes I'd worn, so Olivia could change, and then we made a big show of dropping her off after our supposed shopping-slash-Santa expedition. Olivia's mother thanked me profusely for ensuring the tradition lived on, despite the pained look on Santa's face in the photo. Olivia and Molly had giggled conspiratorially at each other, garnering nothing more than an indulgent look from Mrs. Hawkins. Job completed without a hitch.

Until now.

I gave Billy a dirty look. "This? *This* is the surprise? Like I haven't had enough g-forces lately?" I whispered.

"I promised Molly I'd take her this year. There isn't much of this year left, so . . ." He shrugged. "Anyway, it's all part of your ongoing desensitization process. Two birds, one stone. At the rate you're coming along, you'll be begging to fly everywhere before long—don't look at me like that. Come on, cuz. If you can handle the Vomit Comet, this will be a piece of cake."

"Yeah, well, I got paid a crap-ton of money for the Vomit Comet, thank you very much."

He pulled out his wallet and started peeling off bills.

I rolled my eyes. "Put your money away, idiot."

"Hey, if you don't want it, I'll take it," Molly said, reaching.

I had to grin. Molly was exactly like her big brother, opportunistic to her Doyle core. Not a mean bone in her body, but definitely willing and able to turn situations to her financial advantage.

Billy snatched his hand away. Molly batted her eyelashes at him. "I'll be able to afford a better Christmas present for you."

Billy twisted his mouth, making a big show of weighing the matter, and finally handed her a twenty. "No more Christmas ties," he said, his voice laced with threat.

Molly stuffed the bill into her pocket, a wicked gleam in her eye. I was pretty sure I knew exactly what she'd be getting for Billy. And he'd wear it, too, grumbling the whole time.

I cleared my throat. "Oh, look. There are only two seats on it. Guess I'll wait out here and watch your charming Doyle faces on that handy-dandy screen," I said, pointing at the monitor next to the ride. The current occupants seemed to be enjoying themselves, if in a rather terrified way.

"No!" Molly said, grabbing my hand. "I want to ride it with you, Ciel. Today is supposed to be girl time. Billy won't mind riding with a stranger. Pleeeease . . ."

She employed the Doyle eyes, full force. I could feel myself weakening.

"You heard the kid, cuz. She wants you." Billy tried to disguise the I'm-getting-my-way gleam in his eye, but I could still detect it.

"But your motion sickness . . ." I said, as delicately as I could. Molly couldn't even go on a merry-go-round without plastic bags. I shuddered to think what being tossed around inside a small capsule on the end of a giant robotic arm would do to her delicate constitution.

"I'm getting better! I didn't even feel a bit sick in the taxi on the way here. Besides, Billy says you have to keep stretching your limits if you want to get over something."

Yeah, I was familiar with Billy's line of thinking on stretching your limits. I even agreed with it, in theory. But I wasn't fond of being barfed on, and neither was Billy. Which, I was sure, was why he'd arranged to keep his promise to Molly while staying safely out of the splash zone.

"Fine," I said with a final glare at her brother, and allowed myself to be loaded into the machine. "But I'm warning you—if you hurl on me, I will hurl back on you." It was only as the words came out of my mouth that it occurred to me if I *was* pregnant (*please, please, please no*), this might not be the best activity to participate in.

I was about to signal the ride controller to let me out when Molly said, "Deal! This is going to be *awesome*!"

Then it was too late. The last view I had of Billy's face as the door closed over us was dominated by his dimples. Naturally. It was to be expected—his evil plan had worked. The disturbing thing was what I glimpsed several yards behind him: Alec Loughlin.

"Crap," I said, evoking Molly giggles. The slim possibility of pregnancy fled my mind in an instant.

"Don't worry, Ciel. Even if the ride makes us feel sick, we probably won't barf until after we get off."

Comforting as that thought was, it didn't help with my dilemma. How could I warn Billy without frightening Molly? Had that even been Loughlin? The glimpse had been so brief, and I was extra sensitive about him since the funeral. Maybe I was seeing things.

Then I remembered the monitors. Surely Billy was watching us. I searched the cabin. There. There was the camera. I gestured madly at it, trying to get across "look behind you" with hand motions.

"Ciel! It's starting—quick, take the controls! You don't want us to crash, do you?"

"Um, yeah. I mean, no." I grabbed the stick beside me and tried to hold it steady with one hand while mouthing "Behind you!" at the camera. Only there was a big swoop, and it felt like the seat was falling out from under me, so if Billy *was* reading my lips, he might possibly have deciphered it as "Oh, shit!" followed by "Fuuuuck!" My mouth tends to have a mind of its own in certain situations.

Molly was whooping wildly next to me, having the time of her life. Which didn't necessarily mean she wasn't going to get sick, only that the "I'm having fun" part of her brain was temporarily overriding the "I'm turning green and am gonna puke" part. But I had more important things to worry about.

Crap. Now I was glued to my seat, experiencing the g-forces for which the ride was named. Huh. Not as bad as the Vomit Comet— Billy was right about that—but still not my preferred way to spend six minutes of my life.

During a brief period of relative calm, when I was almost certain we were right-side up, I once again attempted to tell Billy to turn around, this time using a spinning hand gesture. Bad move. The cockpit—whether coincidentally or by human intervention— seemed to take it as a signal to ramp up the rocking and rolling.

Forget warning Billy. If Loughlin didn't kill him, I would.

———

Molly and I exited the ladies' room on legs a lot steadier than when we'd stumbled in after the ride. Neither one of us had actually tossed our cookies, thanks to the judicious application of cold water to our necks and wrists, but it was close.

I hadn't noticed Billy—or Loughlin either—between the ride and the restroom. Then again, finding either of them hadn't exactly been paramount in my mind right then. Or Molly's. But now our stomachs were settled, and I had a thing or two I wanted to say to my significant other.

Which would be a lot easier to do if he hadn't disappeared.

"Man, I can't wait to tell Sinead and Siobhan we did it without puking," Molly said, her natural ebullience returning along with the color in her face. Kids. They bounce back fast. "Now maybe they'll take me on the Cyclone next time we go to Coney Island!"

Better them than me. "Let me know if you need me to back up your story. Say, do you see your brother anywhere?"

She craned her neck, searching every direction. "No. Huh. Wonder where he went. Hey, I know—he's probably in the other simulator." She ran back, ducking between tourists. I stuck to her heels, an uneasy feeling building inside me, one that had nothing to do with motion sickness and everything to do with sudden, overwhelming worry.

Both g-force simulators were in full swing; neither monitor showed Billy in a cockpit. Had he picked up on my warning about Loughlin? Was he following him right now?

I dug my phone out of pocket and called him, leading Molly by the hand toward the nearest exit, and heard the nearby strains of Randy Newman's "Short People"—Billy's special ringtone for me. He'd teased me with that annoying song for years when we were growing up, and claimed he was sentimentally attached to it. He had to be close. I twirled in place, dragging Molly around in circles with me. Still no sign of Billy.

"There!" Molly said, pointing down. On the floor, near the Plexiglas barrier to the simulators, was Billy's phone, faceup, with a picture of my smiling, lightly freckled face on the screen, playing the opening notes of the Newman song over and over.

A cold fear slithered down my spine. Where was Billy?

Chapter 7

My phone buzzed in my hand, quickly followed by the James Bond theme song. Billy (of course) had programmed it into my phone as a ringtone for Mark, whom I could only hope was calling to tell me he'd had to pull Billy away suddenly, and was now looking to retrieve his dropped cell phone for him.

"Tell Billy I found it," I said. "You know, if I were inclined to take a page from Mom's handbook, I'd mention losing his phone was God's punishment for setting me up on that god-awful ride."

"Howdy, what are you talking about? I'm calling because I couldn't get through to Billy, and I knew he had planned to spend time with you and Molly today. Are you telling me he's not with you?"

Cue the return of the cold fear. "He was. But when Molly and I got off the ride, he was gone. We found his phone on the floor—oh, Jesus, Mark. Loughlin was here! At least I think he was. I caught a glimpse of someone who looked like him from the window of the ride."

"Ciel, stay where you are. Don't turn off your phone."

"What's going on? Damn it, Mark, tell me! Is Billy okay?"

There was a pause. I could almost hear Mark's thoughts as he tried to decide what to tell me.

"Look, if ever anyone *needed* to know something, I do now. *Tell me.*"

I could hear the sound of a car door closing in the background. Wherever Mark was, he was already moving. "There's been another killing. Mason Pickering. He was stabbed as he was leaving his apartment."

Shit. Mason was a friend of Auntie Mo's, the man she'd been dating when she met Uncle Liam, in fact. They'd remained cordial after that, though not close. He was an adaptor.

"Was he stunned first?" I asked, mouth dry. Very quietly, so Molly wouldn't hear.

"We don't know yet. Howdy, I'm on my way."

"Okay. We're at the—"

"The *Intrepid*. I'm tracking you now. Keep Molly where there are plenty of people around. I'll be there as soon as I can."

Molly and I waited for Mark at the food court, sipping on sodas, pretending we weren't worried about Billy. I sure wasn't going to tell her about Mason—that would only add to her worries.

I coped by focusing my thoughts on Mason instead of Billy as I listened to Molly babble about what she was getting everyone for Christmas. I was trying to think of the last time I'd seen him myself when it hit me. He'd been at the funeral. Everyone in the nearby adaptor community had been. Aunt Helen had been universally loved among all those who knew her.

Crap. Was that why Loughlin had been at the funeral? To get close to adaptors so he could kill them?

As soon as Mark got there, Molly ran to him and hugged him tight. Honestly? I wanted to do the same thing, but I was trying to exercise my grown-up muscles.

He nodded at me over Molly's head, hugging her back before gently disengaging her from his waist. He dropped a kiss on top of my head and gave my arm a reassuring squeeze. "You have it?"

I handed him the phone. He checked the call log. Maybe he'd be able to make more sense of it than I could—I didn't recognize three-quarters of the numbers I'd seen there. Which didn't mean anything, really. Billy had a complex encryption system on his phone for dealing with his less savory clients.

"Anything?" I asked.

"Nothing unusual," he said. "Why don't you show me where you found it."

Molly took the lead, speed-walking all the way back to the simulators.

Billy was there, talking to one of the simulator operators, pointing at the floor. His dimples were out full-force, as if he could charm the young lady into making his phone reappear.

"Billy!" Molly ran the last thirty feet to him and jumped up into his arms, practically choking him in her glee at finding him. Again, I wished I could do the same thing. Especially the choking part.

"Where'd you go?" Molly said. "We looked *everywhere*. And then we found your phone—"

"You have my phone? Thank goodness for you, monkey girl. I thought I'd lost it for sure," Billy said, tugging her braid as he put her down, deftly not answering her question.

Mark handed him the phone. I gave him a more sedate hug than his sister had. Well, if you don't count slugging his shoulder. (What? He'd scared the crap out of me. I needed to release a little tension.)

"Do we need to find somewhere quieter to talk?" Mark said.

"Might be a good idea," Billy said, with a significant glance at Molly. "But first we better get the munchkin home."

"But—"

"No buts, Molls," I said. "I promised your mom I'd get you back in time to do your homework before dinner."

"Homework sucks. Anyway, I already did it. It was stupid easy."

"Good," Billy said. "Then you'll have time to research Christmas gift ideas for your brother online. Think gadgets. Or toiletries. I'm almost out of bubble bath"—he gave me a knowing look—"and I could use a new loofah, so you might start there."

"Okay. What's your favorite bubble bath, Ciel?" she asked, without missing a beat. My cheeks heated, much to Billy's amusement. Honestly, the kid was way too savvy for her own good.

Billy, Mark, and I sat in a booth at the back corner of my favorite dive of a deli, Billy and me on one side, Mark across from us. My immediate fear for Billy having been alleviated, I was starving. Sure, I was upset about Mason, but that didn't make my stomach any less empty. Same with the guys, so we'd ordered huge Reubens all around, a pile of greasy onion rings and another of fries, and giant kosher dills. Beer for the guys, lemonade for me. Billy had looked at me oddly when I'd ordered it instead of my usual brew, but hadn't commented on it.

Mark had told Billy, along with Auntie Mo and Uncle Liam,

about Mason when we'd dropped Molly off, once the munchkin had run off to the study to begin her Internet research on Christmas presents for Billy. They were all shocked, of course. Mark said there was no way to know if there was a connection to Aunt Helen's murder at this point, but that it wouldn't hurt for everyone to be extra cautious.

"So," Mark said after we'd all taken the edge off our appetites. "What happened with you? I've told you everything we know so far about Mason Pickering. Your turn."

Billy wiped his mouth and took a long swallow from his pint glass. "Well, after I succeeded in my mission to get Ciel into the simulator with Molly, I was preparing to take what I assumed would be a highly entertaining video of their faces on the monitor."

"You rat!" I said, and elbowed him in the ribs. He was ready for it, so it didn't faze him. I really had to learn some better moves.

"It was for your own good. I knew worrying about Molly would distract you from your own fears. Anyway, after watching some"—he glanced down at me, laughter dancing a jig in his eyes—"*interesting*, shall we say, sign language from our tiny friend here, I realized she wanted me to see something—"

"I thought I saw Loughlin as the simulator door was closing," I explained. "And you try signing while you're being spun around like a freaking gyroscope," I added to Billy. "We'll see who's laughing at whom then."

He nudged me with his shoulder apologetically. "You were adorable, as always. Anyway, when I finally figured out I wasn't watching some weird new form of performance art, I turned around and there he was, the photographer from the funeral. He bolted like a jackrabbit on crack when he saw I'd spotted him. I took off after him. Someone jostled my arm, and I dropped my phone. Couldn't take the time to pick it up, or I'd have lost him for sure."

Mark chewed quietly, not saying anything, knowing Billy would give him all the pertinent information without prompting.

"He caught a cab on Twelfth. I flagged another one down. Thought for a minute I'd be able to keep him in sight, but for some reason my cabbie was averse to breaking a few measly laws, no matter how much money I waved under his nose."

Billy turned to me. "I would have called you, cuz, but . . ."

"Yeah, no phone. I'm glad you're all right." And I was. I wasn't even mad about the simulator. He was right—I needed to get over my fears about crap like that, if only to keep up with Molly.

Billy kissed the tip of my nose. "Don't worry about me. I'm a slippery son of a bitch. Ask Mark if you don't believe me."

The corner of Mark's mouth lifted ruefully. "He is. Billy can take care of himself. Listen, you look beat. You staying at your folks' place?"

I automatically adjusted my aura to remove any traces of tiredness. "No, Thomas and Laura are using my room there while they're in town. Mom wants them right under her nose as much as possible. I'm at Billy's. Well, officially—as far as Mom and Dad know—I'm at James's, but really I'm at Billy's."

The guys exchanged a look, and Billy said, "Maybe you should stay with your parents tonight, cuz. I have an early meeting with one of my clients in D.C. tomorrow, so I'm leaving in a little while. And James and Devon are out with Devon's family."

"So?" I said.

"So maybe it would be good for you to stay with family, that's all," Billy said.

I threw down my napkin. "Oh, come on. Are you serious? You

think I can't handle being alone? You *know* I can take care of myself, Mark. Hell, I almost kicked *your* ass. Jet-lagged."

To his credit, Mark kept his amusement confined to his eyes. "You did fine, Howdy. But kicking ass doesn't help much against a stun gun and a knife."

"What are you saying? You think *Loughlin* killed Aunt Helen? And Mason? But that doesn't make any sense. Heck, we don't even know if Mason's murder is connected to Aunt Helen's."

"It makes as much sense as anything else right now, cuz. And Loughlin *is* here in New York. We know that from the funeral."

I sucked more too-sweet lemonade through my bendy straw, thinking. "Right. Okay. I can help you find him, Mark. With Billy gone, you'll need me."

Mark shook his head. "I gave the police his picture. They're looking for him as a 'person of interest,' and will let me know when they have him. *I'm* going to get some much-needed sleep." He punctuated his statement with a huge yawn, covered by the back of his hand.

Billy hit me with the Doyle eyes, full power. "Look, will you please stay with your parents tonight? As a favor to me?"

I divided a glare between the two them. "Okay. But I'll have to sleep on the couch in the basement. And I'm not happy about it."

Mom and Dad already knew about Mason's murder, of course. Auntie Mo had probably called Mom within seconds of our dropping off Molly. They were upset, of course. Ditto Thomas and Laura, but they agreed it was pointless to assume there was a connection to Aunt Helen until Mark found out more. Still, they all seemed happy I was staying under the same roof with them.

I pleaded exhaustion as soon as Billy and Mark left, and decamped to the lowest reaches of the house, suddenly longing for the oblivion of sleep with a passion I normally reserve for hot fudge sundaes.

Contrary to what I had implied to Billy and Mark at the diner, the couch in Mom and Dad's basement is exceedingly comfortable. I used to fall asleep on it all the time when I was a teenager, watching fascinating shows on cable stations my parents didn't know I knew they had. I could have slept in one of the bunk beds in James and Bri's old bedroom, but Mom would've had to clear out a bunch of as-yet unwrapped presents. Thomas's old room was now Mom's office, so that wasn't an option either.

Besides, the basement was the warmest, most welcoming place I knew, especially during the holidays. Nobody could decorate like Mom. (Well, except maybe Auntie Mo. There was a friendly rivalry between them.) The day after Thanksgiving, Mom always mobilized all her kids, along with Dad, and we transformed the house from top to bottom, turning it into a place it was easy to imagine St. Nick living with Mrs. Claus and a passel of cheerful elves. There was no getting out of the forced labor either. If any of us tried to opt out on the grounds of, say, having to work at our paying jobs, she merely said fine, we'd have to clear the turkey off the table and work all night on Thanksgiving to get it done. Yeah, right. Like any of us could even move then.

The real reason I didn't want to stay there was Laura. Don't get me wrong—I loved her as much as ever. But the whole pregnancy thing was needling its way into me. As long as I stayed away from her, I could mostly keep myself from thinking about—

Yeah. *That.*

Sleep, the elusive bitch, decided to play hard to get. Of course.

I pulled the pillow over my head and balled myself up under the plush comforter, for the first time in my life willing myself to feel something starting up in my nether regions. A cramp. A backache. A twinge. Anything indicating an impending visit from my good friend Flo, as Mom so euphemistically called it. (I'd include cravings for excessive amounts of salty snacks and chocolate, but I pretty much always had those.) I mean, I'd never been regular, so lack of a timely period wasn't unusual. Then again, I'd never had any reason to worry about the reason behind its absence before either.

After tossing and turning most of the night, my head whirling through twisted dreams of a hugely pregnant me sitting in an interrogation room, with either Billy or Mark—I couldn't tell which; probably some combination of the two of them—behind the blinding light shining in my eyes, I gave up on rest. Apparently my superstitious avoidance of alcohol and pregnancy tests was not enough to let my subconscious relax. Never in my life had I been so relieved to wake up at the butt-crack of dawn.

Screw this shit, I thought, my hand firmly pressed against my belly, seeking reassurance from its flatness. *I'm outta here.*

I'd have to take a damn test, of course. If I could figure out a private place to do it, because I sure as hell wasn't going to bring one back here.

But first I was going to hit my brother James's gym and subdue my stupid mind with extreme physical activity. I knew it was open, because when James worked out, he liked to get it over with early. Said it cleared his head and made tackling scientific conundrums easier. (I suspected keeping in shape for his gorgeous boyfriend might have had something to do with it, too.) I wasn't sure how well strenuous exercise worked with emotional conundrums, but it couldn't hurt. At least it would keep me from having to make happy baby talk around the breakfast table.

Yeah, right. Like I could be so lucky. I smelled food in progress as soon as I got up the stairs.

Mom and Dad were in full-on breakfast mode, with Mom (festively dressed in a cashmere sweater with a big Rudolph face, complete with battery-powered blinking nose—nobody could marry expensive and tacky quite like Mom) whipping up eggs for omelets, and Dad (topped with a Santa hat I knew he only wore for Mom's sake) manning the griddle for his famous buttermilk pancakes.

There was bacon sizzling in a big cast iron skillet, and—I sniffed the air, sorting and organizing the various delectable aromas in my head—Mother of God, was that Moravian sugar cake heating in the oven? Mom always ordered it from Dewey's down in North Carolina this time of year, but she usually made us wait until Christmas morning to eat it. Too bad none of it smelled appetizing in the least. (Well, possibly the sugar cake.)

So much for sneaking out.

Thomas and Laura sat at the kitchen table, Thomas sipping strong black coffee, Laura with what looked to be some sort of weak herbal tea. Yikes. You had to give up coffee, too?

Laura was the first to see me, and greeted me much too cheerfully for the early hour. "Hey there, sugar. Sorry we bumped you out of your bed last night."

Thomas looked up from the headlines he was reading on his latest tablet. "Hi, sis. Laura may be sorry, but I'm not. Your bed is comfortable."

Dad abandoned the griddle briefly to give me a hug. "Good morning, sweetie pie. Hope you slept well."

"I did, thanks," I lied.

Mom crossed to give me a kiss over the bowl she held between us, still stirring the eggs. "You're up early."

"Not as early as all of you. What's up?" I said, wrapping it around a yawn.

"I need to get started on some casseroles for poor Mason's family. His mother—you remember Miss Alice, the nice lady who used to make her own pickles?—I spoke to her a little while ago. She's always been an early riser, and I knew she wouldn't be sleeping anyway, so I took a chance and called. She said Mason's will stated explicitly that there was to be no funeral service. I don't understand it, but if that's what he wanted . . ." Mom paused for a breath and stopped stirring long enough to dab at her eyes with a dish towel. "And your brother has an appointment with one of his clients who's up here for the holidays. Laura and I"—the tears turned to a happy glow as she looked at the mother-to-be—"are taking the opportunity to go shopping for maternity clothes. It's never too early to start stocking up. You're welcome to join us, of course."

I tried unsuccessfully to suppress a shudder, and hoped Mom would take it as nothing more than my loathing of shopping in general. "Um, no thanks."

"All right, sweetie. What kind of omelet do you want? Plain, cheese, or Western?"

Gah. If I stayed to eat, they'd notice if I didn't drink my usual half a pot of coffee. But if I did drink it, and it turned out I was— *don't go there. Leave. Leave now.*

"No omelet for me. I have to get going. I'm meeting James at the gym for an early workout." It wasn't a complete untruth. He went most mornings, and just because he didn't know I was coming didn't mean I wouldn't meet him there.

Supremely skeptical looks were lobbed at me from everyone except my sister-in-law. She didn't know me well enough yet to realize how out of character my excuse was.

"Hey, it's Laura's fault. I have to keep in shape for her lessons," I said.

She smiled encouragingly at me (not one bit green around the gills, in spite of her confirmed pregnancy—how was that fair?) and said, "You're doing great, Ciel. All your hard work is really paying off."

"You have time to eat," Mom said. "I'll make your omelet first."

"Sorry, but I'm already late. I'll take some coffee in a travel mug." They'd be all over me with questions if I didn't have coffee. Mom would probably drag me to the doctor, thinking I had the plague or something.

"That's not enough to start your day."

I sniffed the air again. "Maybe I can eat a piece of sugar cake on the way." That had better be okay. If it turned out I had to give up sweets on top of booze and coffee, I might as well shoot myself and be done with it. It would be easier.

"Well, all right," Mom said. Reluctantly. "It's done. I'll cut you a piece while you pour your coffee. But you better promise me you'll eat a healthy breakfast after your workout." She bustled as she spoke. Her culinary creations might not always turn out, but she was a champion kitchen bustler.

"I'll make James take me out for breakfast before he goes to work." Again, not necessarily a lie. If I happened to run into James at the gym, I *would* wheedle him into taking me to breakfast. He'd expect it. And he, at least, was absentminded enough not to notice if I didn't drink coffee.

I snapped the lid on and pretended to take a sip. *Gah.* One tiny taste and I had to fight my impulse to drain it dry.

What the hell are you doing, Ciel? This is stupid. You can't possibly be . . .

I lifted the mug again, determined to take a real sip. Because, now that I considered it in the light of day, there was no way I was pregnant.

Yeah, but what if? the troublemaking little fearmonger in my head said. *And think of all the coffee you've had in the past few months. The Big Guy Upstairs can't hold you responsible for what you drank before you knew, but . . .*

I tore the mug away from my mouth. Coughed to cover the jerky motion. Big mistake to cough around Mom. Her hand was on my forehead before I could inhale.

"Are you coming down with something? Should you go back to bed? You do look kind of peaky—have you been getting enough rest? Maybe I should call the doctor."

"No! Mom, I'm fine. I, um, swallowed wrong. Relax, okay?"

"Open your mouth. I want to look at your tonsils." She stood eye to eye with me (she's short, like me), pinched my chin, and tugged my mouth open.

I dutifully stuck my tongue out at her. I'd learned from long experience it was faster to let her examine me and get it over with. Besides, it was the only time I could get away with sticking my tongue out at her without her calling down the wrath of God on me. Not seeing anything to alarm her in my mouth, she double-checked for fever on both sides of my neck. Finally, she seemed satisfied.

"Okay, then. Remember, sweetie, breathe first, then swallow.

It never works well when you try to do it at the same time"—she raised one eyebrow at me—"no matter how big a hurry you're in."

"Yeah, yeah. Got it." I *was* in a hurry, so I didn't take time to give her an exaggerated eye roll. "See you guys later," I called over my shoulder.

"You be careful! Do you need money for a taxi?" Mom hollered after me.

I waited until the door was safely closed behind me to roll my eyes.

As it happened, I had plenty of money for a taxi. Sure, only because Billy had pulled me aside and slipped a roll of twenties into my pocket before he'd left the evening before, but whatever. When I'd told him I didn't need it, he'd asked me how much cash I had on me. Checking, I'd been forced to admit I was down to seventy-three cents and a fuzzy Life Saver.

"But I *have* plenty," I'd told him. "Really. As soon as I get to an ATM."

"Ciel, I don't want you going anyplace without ready cab money in your pocket. You never know when you might need to get somewhere—or *away* from somewhere—fast."

"Cabs take plastic nowadays, you know. And I almost never forget my credit card anymore," I'd pointed out.

"Very good, sweetheart. I'm proud of you"—I'd stepped on his toes; he'd only grinned, because he was wearing heavy hiking boots—"but it's easier to bribe them with cash. You know, in case you want to go somewhere they don't want to take you."

Before I could argue further, he'd kissed me goodnight, and

then I hadn't felt like arguing anymore. His kisses tended to have that effect on me, which might have annoyed me more if I couldn't tell they had the same effect on him.

Within a block, I was awfully glad for the extra cash in my pocket, because I *had* forgotten my wallet (sue me, I had a lot on my mind), and I was starting to get the creepy feeling someone might be following me.

An SUV I didn't recognize, parked across the street from my parents' house, had started up right as I reached the sidewalk, and had made a U-turn, so it was heading the same direction I was. Could be a coincidence—maybe somebody happened to be leaving at the same moment I was—but it was traveling pretty slowly.

I picked up my pace. When I glanced over my shoulder, I saw the driver was looking at his phone. Probably checking directions, or maybe texting. If Mom saw him, she'd give him holy hell for not keeping his eyes on the road and both hands on the wheel.

I was even more reassured when the glow of a streetlight caught his face and I saw it wasn't Loughlin. Hadn't even realized I'd been holding my breath until then. Still, I hurried to the cross street—a major road where you could always find a taxi this time of morning. It didn't take long for one to stop for me. The driver wasn't thrilled with the address I gave him—he would have preferred a longer fare—but jollied up fast enough when I assured him I was a good tipper.

Once we were moving, I peeked out the back window. The SUV was two cars behind us. It was a common model, but I recognized the driver's haircut, so it had to be him.

Calm down, Ciel. Stop being so twitchy. Lots of cars go this way. Just because someone is behind you doesn't mean he's following you.

Unless, of course, he stayed behind you all the way to the

relatively obscure gym you were going to, and held up traffic in his lane while he watched you leave your taxi and walk into the building, staring at you the whole time he was talking to someone on his cell phone. Then, I hazarded a guess, he was probably following you.

Chapter 8

Okay, I thought later, while I was beating the shit out of a heavy bag. The guy definitely hadn't been Loughlin. Might be connected somehow, might not. For all I knew, he was some pervert who got his jollies following women, seeing if he could get them to react. Kind of like catcalling, only without words.

Creepy? For sure. Dangerous? Hard to say. I'd mention it to Billy or Mark later, and see what they thought. There was no point in bothering them this early, not when I was now safely in a gym surrounded by well-muscled witnesses.

I hit the bag with a rapid-fire barrage of punches. My form no doubt sucked—it was my first time wearing boxing gloves—but it was a great release all the same. The nice old man with the battered face at the desk up front had been unpacking some new youth gloves when I'd arrived. I admired their bright green color, and jokingly said something about how they must make you feel as powerful as the Hulk when you wore them. He'd laughed, and told me I should try them and see.

He didn't know it yet, but he'd made a sale. I did feel rather Hulk-like when I lit into the bag. Like I said, *great* release. Plus, as I'd suspected, a hell of lot more fun than wondering if I was pregnant. Time to figure that out later.

I felt a warm hand on my bicep and reacted without thinking, twisting my torso and aiming up by instinct, connecting with the face before I could stop myself. He fell backward, landing on his butt, cradling his jaw with one hand.

I'd never seen Mark look quite so surprised.

I sank down beside him, reaching for his face with both hands. He flinched away from the gloves, understandably leery.

"Crap." I untied my right glove using my teeth, wedged it under my arm, and yanked my hand out. "I didn't know it was you. I am so sorry!" I pulled the glove off my other hand.

He pushed himself up to a steadier position. "My fault, Howdy. I shouldn't have tried to adjust your form without telling you first. Good reflexes, by the way."

I blushed at his praise, as usual. "Thanks. What are you doing here, anyway? James never told me you came to his gym."

"I don't. One of my guys told me you were here."

"How did he—wait, did you have somebody watching Mom and Dad's house? Was that who was following me?"

"Yeah. Obviously, he didn't do a great job of it if you spotted him. My fault. I told him to watch out for anything odd around the house, but not to be stealthy about it. When you left so early, he decided he better see where you were going. Once he reported to me, he went back to watching the house."

"But why?"

"Billy insisted. Said he wouldn't leave you there unless I put men on the house."

That made me feel all warm inside, and kind of pissed off at the same time. "You think it might have been nice to tell me? You know, so I don't get the freaking shit scared out of me when a strange man follows me around?"

Mark smiled. It was sort of lopsided, because the left side of his face was getting puffy. "I told your dad while you were saying good-bye to Billy. I guess you didn't hear." There was a rueful look in Mark's eyes, which made me remember every second of Billy's good-bye kiss. Yeah, it was safe to say I hadn't heard anything. "The guy made you a little jumpy, I take it?"

No wonder Mom and Dad hadn't made more of a fuss when I left the house on my own. I huffed a wry laugh. "Tiny bit."

"Think it might have been a good idea to call Billy or me if you were worried?" he said, sounding a tad perturbed.

"I was here by then. Presumably safe. Didn't want to disturb your beauty sleep."

He looked around the training room. All the gym rats had paused their various workout activities to stare at us, probably trying to decide which of us required assistance. Mark waved them off, indicating he was fine.

"So, why are you here, Howdy? Isn't this a little out of your usual New York routine?"

I sat back, wrapping my arms loosely around my knees. "Had to get out of the house. You know how crazy Mom gets around the holidays. This year she's positively manic. I needed some breathing space."

His eyes sharpened, delving beneath the words, as usual. "You're happy about the baby, aren't you? I know Thomas is thrilled, and so is Laura."

My breath caught when he said the word "baby." Stupid, I know.

"Sure I am," I said breezily. "I'm as thrilled as they are. Hey, I'm gonna be an aunt"—please, God, *only* an aunt—"to what will no doubt be the most gifted child ever born. According to Thomas, anyway. What's not to be thrilled about?"

Mark cocked his head, still absently rubbing his jaw, looking like he wanted to ask more but wasn't sure he should. Ultimately, he stood and reached down to give me a hand up. "So, are you meeting James here?"

I grinned, happy to get off the baby topic. "Damn, I sure hope so. Otherwise I lied to Mom, and you know that never works out well—never mind, here comes reprieve."

James joined us, looking fit and trim in his stylish workout clothes. His boyfriend, Devon the Gorgeous, must have bought them for him, because James normally didn't care what he wore, as long as it was functional, comfortable, and reasonably appropriate to the occasion. He steadfastly claimed not all gay men were fashionistas.

"Fancy meeting the two of you here. Thinking of switching teams, Mark?" he said, teasing.

Mark laughed, a pleasant rumble no one heard often enough. "Afraid not. I'm trying to keep tabs on your sister."

I looked around, for the first time noticing the predominance of supremely—one might go as far as to say scrupulously—fit men. "Geez, my gaydar sucks," I muttered.

James caught it, and whispered, "Don't worry, sis. I don't think you need it." And was that a wink? My normally staid brother was loosening up. Go, Devon!

"So," James continued, "Mom called to make sure I didn't 'forget' about our date. She seems to be under the impression I am the proverbial absentminded professor."

"Well, if the proverbial shoe fits . . ." I said.

He lifted an eyebrow very similar to the one our mother had lifted at me earlier. "Be that as it may, I'm fairly certain we did *not*, in fact, have a date to meet here this morning."

"You didn't tell Mom, did you?"

"I did not."

I hugged him, throwing my arms around his neck, and kissing his cheek for good measure. "Did I ever tell you you're my favorite brother?"

"Of course I am. Thomas is a domineering ass and Brian, God help us all, is an indie band member whose only redeeming quality is that he doesn't play bass. Why wouldn't I be your favorite?" Humor glinted in the green eyes that were mirrors of my own, his affection for our mutual brothers obvious.

Mark acknowledged the teasing with a smile. "Listen, if you're going to be here with Ciel, maybe I better get going. Think you could see her back to your parents' place when you're done?"

"Does this have anything to do with what Mom told me about Mason Pickering? You think it's connected to Aunt Helen somehow?" James asked. I felt a pang at the mention of Aunt Helen, and Mason, too, though I'd barely known him. "Is Ciel in danger?"

"To answer all your questions, yes, don't know, and not necessarily. But like I keep trying to tell your sister, caution doesn't hurt."

"I don't need a babysitter," I said, sounding more grumpy than I intended. I needed some time to myself to take the stupid pregnancy test so I could stop worrying about *that*.

"Don't get pissed, Howdy. It's only until we find out who's behind the murders," Mark said.

"It's a stupid waste of your resources. Geez Louise, I just decked *you*! I think that proves I'm perfectly capable of getting myself where I want to go when I leave here without a man's help." Which wasn't going to be back to my parents' house, though I didn't feel the need to mention that.

Both of James's eyebrows had shot up at my declaration about Mark.

"Not on purpose," I explained. "He startled me—I didn't know it was him." *A common problem for me*, I thought wryly.

"Listen, if Billy thinks you're wandering off someplace on your own—no matter how capable you are of taking care of yourself—he'll be useless to me."

Okay, that got my attention. Billy was doing something for Mark? "Did he really go to D.C. to meet with a client? He's not going after Loughlin on his own, is he? Is he okay?"

"He's fine. Yes, he went to meet with a client—we didn't lie to you, if that's what you're worried about. But I did ask him to scope out NASA's headquarters while he was there, to see if he could dig up anything useful on Loughlin." He paused, looking at me intently. "Howdy, I need Billy's head in the game, so we can finish this up fast. It won't be, if he's worried about you."

"Damn it," I said, lowering my voice even more. The emotion still came through loud and clear. "I should have gone with him. I'm the one who has Loughlin's aura. Did you ever even consider that *that* might be handy?"

"Cool your jets, slugger." Mark stroked his jaw. "Billy was already down there when I thought to send him to NASA. It's a long shot. And he couldn't use Loughlin's aura anyway—what if he'd run into him? I promise to keep you in mind if we need the aura. But it won't be happening today." Mark finished with one of his devastatingly appealing smiles. Seriously. Half the men in the gym were drooling over him.

James looked around, and announced to the room in general, "Forget it, guys. He's straight."

There was a chorus of groans, but it didn't take them long to get back to the serious business of maintaining their temples.

Mark hadn't taken his eyes off me, and I have to admit, it was hard to resist the pull of his smile. Besides, I knew if I didn't agree, he'd stay with me himself, and I didn't want to keep him from his work. "All right. James, may I hang out with you today?"

"Happy to have the company, sis. I promised I'd go shopping with Devon after we're through here, and he'd love to spend time with you. He's always saying how he wants to get to know my family better."

Gah. Shopping? Was this retribution for lying to my mother? I glanced heavenward. *Go for the thunderbolt next time, Big Guy. It would be more merciful.*

"Last stop, I promise!" Devon the Gorgeous pulled me into the baby store by my elbow. He used to say he was bisexual because it would have been too cruel to deprive either gender of his company. (I think he was teasing.) These days he had eyes only for James.

I dug in my heels. "Guys, I'm all shopped out"—absolutely true—"and I'd only slow you down. Why don't I wait for you out here? Oh, look, there's a bench."

"Nonsense. It won't take a minute. We absolutely must find something fun for your new niece or nephew," Devon said.

I shifted the four shopping bags I carried to my other arm. "No, really. You go ahead. I'll find something for the"—I swallowed hard—"baby later."

James gave me a small shove, juggling his own bags. "Come on, sis. If I can do this, you can, too."

Crap. And I'd been doing so well up until then. Hadn't thought about any uncomfortable what-ifs since I'd chased down the waitress at breakfast and changed my coffee order to decaf, asking her not to mention it when she brought it to the table. James might not notice what I drank, but Devon tended to be a lot more observant about people than my brother.

The splitting headache I was getting from caffeine withdrawal wasn't helping my nerves any.

Since breakfast we'd hit what felt like every store at the Long Island outlet mall Devon had insisted had the best bargains. I'd joined in on the shopping with determined merriment. As long as I had to do this, I might as well get my own Christmas shopping out of the way, or at least part of it. The tie I'd found for Billy (with lumps of coal on it, each one printed with the word "naughty" in different fonts) almost made the trip worthwhile. Between the tie and the kitschy assortment of Christmas bathroom decorations I'd found for Mom, the wad of twenties Billy had pressed on me ran out pretty fast, but I could replace them as soon as I laid hands on my wallet again. Which, granted, wouldn't be until I stopped avoiding Laura.

God, Ciel, grow up already.

I took a deep breath and marched myself into the store, secretly starting to hope Loughlin would show up. Dealing with a possible killer would be less painful than fake-smiling at infant paraphernalia.

Devon was oohing and aahing over miniature clothing, soft toys, and crib accessories that made *me* want to scream and run the other way. Even James had a besotted expression on his face he normally reserved for the contents of petri dishes.

"If only we knew the gender of the baby," Devon lamented, fondling a tiny leather jacket with "Heck's Angels" printed on the back. "Then we'd know whether to get the lettering in pink or blue."

"Well," I suggested, antsier than ever to leave, "if we *waited* until . . ." I trailed off when a petite woman who looked about my age rounded the corner of our aisle, pushing a double stroller with twin boys, one with spiky blond wisps of hair, the other sporting a head full of brown curls.

I gasped, assailed by a horrible new thought. Then, to my everlasting mortification, right there in the middle of a happy crowd of holiday shoppers, I burst into tears.

Chapter 9

Back at James's apartment, seated on his comfortable overstuffed sofa between him and Devon, I reiterated for the umpteenth time that I was fine, maybe a little overtired was all, and possibly affected by the combination of Thomas and Laura's baby news and the murders of Aunt Helen and Mason. That kind of emotional pendulum was enough to overwhelm anyone, right?

Only they weren't buying it. James, even if he didn't quite believe me, would probably have left it alone. He respected people's privacy to a ridiculous extent (something I loved about him, even if I didn't share the trait myself).

Devon, however, was another matter. I could tell by the dangerous combination of concern and curiosity in his lovely violet eyes that he wasn't going to let it go. He was tucking one of Auntie Mo's ugly afghans (a relic from her yarn phase—we all had them) around me in a mother hen-ish way so far from his usual sex-on-a-stick persona I almost couldn't recognize him.

"It is a lot to take in all at once, I know," he said gently. "James, why don't you make your sister a drink? It's cold out there—maybe a hot toddy?"

I sat bolt upright. "No! I don't want a drink."

Surprise and alarm flared on James's face. Oblivious he might be, but even he knew I rarely refused a drink at happy hour.

"It's okay, sis. You can stay here tonight. I'll call Mom and let her know. I'll tell her we're wrapping presents or something."

"Thanks," I said. "That would be great. Only do you maybe have some"—gak!—"herbal tea?"

James screwed up his brows, examining me with new interest, like I was one of his lab specimens. "Sure. Devon, could you see what we have? And start the kettle?"

Devon seemed reluctant to leave the room, but, after a pointed look from James, went to make my tea. James, once we were alone, took my hand awkwardly. Dealing with strong emotions wasn't within his usual purview. We sat there for several minutes, being quiet. I'd chalk it up to sensitivity on James's part, but I suspected it was more him trying to come up with a rational way of dealing with an obviously upset female.

Eventually he spoke, his voice calm. Soothing. Careful. "Ciel, what's really wrong? We're all upset about Aunt Helen and Mason—naturally so—but this is something more, isn't it?"

It was the steady, concerned look on his face that did it. This was my reserved brother who always held himself in check, not only with me, but with the whole family. None of us doubted his love, but we all understood he wasn't at his most comfortable displaying it overtly. He was more at home with the cut-and-dried, provable or disprovable aspects of scientific study. Facts were clean. Emotions were messy.

I tried to think of a good excuse. Even surreptitiously crossed the fingers of the hand he wasn't holding, in case I had to out-right lie. But when my mouth started moving, something even more horrifying than crying like a baby in front of all those strang-ers at the mall happened: I told him the truth.

"I'm afraid I might be pregnant and I don't know who the father is, and what if it's twins, and they're *both* the father! Is that even possible? Because if it is, and I am, and they are—oh, God, I am so screwed!"

I *know*. The words spilled out of me, surfing a tsunami of guilt and fear.

There was a crash. James and I jerked our heads around to see Devon, mouth open, tea tray at his feet, broken china scattered, and steaming liquid spreading in puddles. The delicate aroma of grassy citrus hit me, and I burst into tears for the second time that day.

"It was a completely understandable mistake. No one could pos-sibly blame you," Devon said, patting my hand.

The three of us were at the small kitchen table, James having decided the mess on the floor could wait until after the mess who was his sister was cleaned up. Knowing how difficult that must be for someone of his orderly nature made me feel even worse. But he'd insisted.

Devon had quickly brewed more tea. This time he'd served it in sturdy mugs. Guess he had a pragmatic side.

I'd completed, with great difficulty, my halting explanation of how I'd inadvertently mistaken Mark for Billy, under the tipsy assumption that Billy, well aware of my decade-long crush on Mark, had decided to help me get Mark out of my system by satisfying any lingering curiosity causing me to cling to an old fantasy. (Trust me. It had made perfect sense at the time.)

"I mean, who *wouldn't* assume that?" Devon continued. "Right, James?" he prodded.

My brother still looked stunned, but was manfully trying to hide it from me. He nodded, probably wishing he'd never come to the gym that morning, longing no doubt for the test tubes and microscopes of his lab.

"Of course. Yes, perfectly normal assumption, I'm sure. Er, does Billy know?" he added delicately.

"That I might be pregnant? God, no. How can I tell him? He doesn't even want kids!"

Devon handed me a tissue, which I automatically raised to my cheeks. Shit. This was all so *stupid*.

"I think what your brother was asking is if Billy knows about the, um, confusion with Mark."

I blew my nose. "Oh. Yeah. Yes, of course he does. I wouldn't keep a thing like that from him."

James, still looking uncomfortable, said, "And Mark? Does he . . . ?"

"Yes. He knows, too." I looked from James to Devon and back again. Sighed. "To answer the question you're both being too polite to ask, yes, they were both mad at me. But they got over it. Even—kind of—understood how it could happen."

Devon smiled, a touch of his more familiar sauciness sparking in his eyes. "Well, as long as we're being all open about things, why would Mark take you to bed if he knew you and Billy were together? Admittedly, I don't know him well, but it doesn't sound like him. He's always struck me as stick-up-your-ass honorable, if you'll pardon the expression."

"Devon! Please," James said. "Of all the things to ask."

"What? It's relevant. And you want to know, too, you know you do."

"It's okay," I said. "Apparently, Mark's feelings toward me have . . . evolved. He may have been under the impression I was reconsidering my relationship with Billy, and when I, um, kind of"—I couldn't bring myself to say "threw myself at him"—"when I made my intentions for the evening known, he . . . *gah*, this is all so embarrassing. Damn it all to fucking hell!"

I threw my tissue down next to my mug. James handed me a fresh one. I took a deep breath and pushed forward.

"Look, I thought Billy and I were playing a game. You know, like those role-playing things you read about? Dress up like a pirate, put on a French maid's outfit, that sort of thing, only more realistic."

Devon stared at me, plainly fascinated. James, having grown up with adaptors, didn't look the least surprised. Or shocked. So I plunged forward. There was hardly any point in stopping now.

"Billy had offered before to . . . I mean, he knew I hadn't, well, sampled the dating pool as much as he had, and he never wanted me to feel like I'd deprived myself of, um, the normal amount of, er, experience . . . shit. I was a virgin before him, okay?" As if they hadn't figured it out by now. "Billy offered—more than once—to provide me with any 'variety' I might someday want." Okay, my face was officially on fire.

"Oh!" Devon said. "I remember now—I was there for your deflowering!"

"*What?*" James's eyes bulged ominously.

My face, if anything, flamed even more.

Devon twisted his gorgeous lips at James. "Oh, stop. Not 'there'

there. This was back when we were broken up. I'd dropped by, hoping to see you, and found your biometric lock still accepted my palm print. I thought it was an invitation of sorts. Imagine my surprise when I found it wasn't you in your bedroom."

I groaned. "Devon, you're not helping."

James looked like he was about to pop. "You . . . Billy . . . in my bed?"

"I washed the sheets after!" I said.

"Really, James, it was so sweet. Everything you'd want your sister's first time to be. Not that I saw it *all*, of course"—the look on Devon's face told me he'd seen enough—"but Billy was very tender with Ciel. I can see why she loves him."

James was taking deep breaths. I thought I saw him counting under his breath. "All right. Fine. It's my own fault for letting you and Billy and everyone else treat my home as your own. Let's get on with the problem at hand, shall we?"

I took a gulp of tea that tasted like lawn clippings soaked in lemon juice, and tried to compose myself. "You should know I'm careful about birth control. There's really no way I should even be pregnant. I use a patch, and they're supposed to be *very* reliable. So I'm probably being stupid, right? Paranoid? Please say yes! Things are only now getting back to normal with Billy and Mark. If it turns out I'm . . . God, I don't know what to do!"

James patted my arm, and settled into clinical scientist mode. "When was your last period?"

"Before the wedding. I think. No, I'm sure I haven't had one since then."

"How long before?"

"I don't know. Before my Hollywood job, so maybe a few weeks?"

"In other words, you haven't had a period for at least two months?"

"No," I said, my voice sounding reedy. I cleared my throat. "No, I haven't. But I've never been regular. It's been better since I started using the patch—that's why I started using it in the first place, the doctor said it should help even me out. Not because I needed it for . . . I mean, before Billy . . ."

Ugh. Why was holding on to your virginity for as long as I had humiliating? It was what worked for me at the time. I should own it and be proud. I lifted my chin and looked James in the eye. He gave me a brief smile and a nod. I'm pretty sure brothers don't like to think of their sisters as having sex at all, so kudos to him for handling this as well as he was.

"Any other symptoms? Nausea, frequent urination, tender breasts?" James might have been a doctor himself, the way he sounded.

I nodded bleakly, looking down at my chest. Not huge, but my bra was definitely snugger than usual.

"Okay, then." He reached for his keys.

"Where are you going?" I said, fighting back a touch of panic. Now that I'd unburdened myself, I kind of wanted him to keep holding my hand, and tell me everything was going to be all right.

Pathetic as it was to admit, I was conditioned from childhood to expect my big brothers could and would fix everything for me. It's tough not to revert to baby-sister syndrome in a crisis. Which was probably why I'd spilled the beans the way I had. In a way, it was Pavlovian.

"To buy a pregnancy test. There's no point in panicking until we know for sure what we're dealing with."

"But—wait!" I had a sudden urge to run away. Hell, even

hopping a plane to somewhere, anywhere, didn't sound half bad. As long as I didn't know for sure I was pregnant, it might not be true. Which, of course, ran totally counter to my previous plan to get myself a test and take it as soon as I was alone. What can I say? There's no accounting for panic.

James's face softened. "Listen, sis, there's a good possibility this is all some sort of stress reaction to Laura's announcement. You're an adaptor. If, somewhere deep down inside, you're worried you might be pregnant, then you could be mimicking her subconsciously."

I relaxed. Somewhat. "You really think so?"

He hesitated. Then said, with what I hoped wasn't forced confidence, "Yes. I do. But we have to be sure, don't we?"

I wanted Devon to go to the store with James—some time to pull myself together would have been welcome—but James insisted he stay with me.

"One man buying a pregnancy test wouldn't necessarily look strange—it would be assumed it was for his wife or girlfriend. Two men together might raise eyebrows," he'd said.

After he left, Devon and I picked up shards of china and mopped, chatting about TV shows and movies until the floor dried.

"Do you think Herbert is hungry?" I said during a conversational lull. Anything to avoid more awkward questions.

Herbert was James's chameleon. He'd started out as part of an experiment, but had quickly become a pet. His habitat took up one corner of the cozy living room, and gave the whole space a real indoor-outdoor vibe.

Devon shrugged. "It's hard for me to tell. I'm better at reading dogs and cats."

When he saw me approach his cage, Herbert stepped slowly and deliberately along one branch of the live tree that was his usual perch. Chameleons don't have a lot of facial expression, but I thought he was glad to see me. Probably expected I was going to offer him a juicy mealworm from James's stash, like I usually do whenever I come over, but this time I didn't have the stomach for it. The thought of touching one of those squirming critters made me want to gag. If Herbert was hungry, he'd have to make do with one of the crickets already hopping around his cage.

"Listen, Ciel," Devon said after a few minutes. "I know we got off to kind of a bumpy start, what with the way we first met and all, but I want you to know you can count on me. On my friend-ship, I mean."

I studied his face. Saw the sincerity. "Thanks, Dev. That means a lot to me."

"Look on the bright side. If you and Billy had let me into bed, you might have had another possible baby daddy in the mix. Think about it—you *could* be worrying about triplets right now."

"What the—" I almost slugged him for implying I would have slept with him, but then I saw the naughty sparkle in his eyes, and started laughing so hard I had to sit down. "Damn, I was so mad at you then. Not only because of your rude proposition either. I thought you'd broken my brother's heart."

Devon, laughing himself, sat on the floor next to me. We both leaned back against Herbert's cage. (Herbert twitched his tail and crawled back up his tree, apparently bored with us now that he knew mealworms were not on the menu.)

"I had, I'm afraid," he said, reining in his laughter and sounding serious all of a sudden. "But I never will again."

I gave him a sideways look. "Are you really bisexual, or do you only pretend to be because you enjoy being an equal opportunity object of lust?" I said. Hey, why should my private life be the only one being discussed intimately?

He laughed, but answered me seriously. "I really, truly am bi. But it doesn't mean I love your brother any less. Listen, Ciel, none of us can help who we're attracted to—we're all wired how we're wired. But the *love* we choose to commit to . . . that we can help. And I choose James."

I nodded, part of me envying how simple he made it sound.

I heard the front door open, and hopped up. "There he is. Hey, James," I hollered, "did you get it already? Did anybody look at you funny? I want stories!" Because if I didn't start seeing a glimmer of humor in this situation, I was going to lose my mind.

But it wasn't James. "Hey, cuz. Mark told me you might be here. Oh, hey, Dev. How's tricks?"

Chapter 10

"Billy!" I said, and stared at him like a fool. "You're back."

He pulled me into his arms. "Very good, cuz. Got it in one. So, where's James? More importantly, what's he cooking for dinner?" He paused, holding me away from him. "Are you all right? Nothing else happened, did it?"

Crap. Billy could *not* be here when James got back.

"No. Nothing," I said quickly.

"Does this mean you've found Ciel's photographer?" Devon said, skillfully distracting Billy from me with a beer he'd procured from the fridge. James had explained the situation with Loughlin to him over breakfast. "Let's celebrate, shall we?"

"Not quite yet, but Mark has more agents on it now, so I'm comfortable taking a short break. Cheers!" He clinked his bottle with Devon's. "Where's yours, Ciel?"

"Oh, I've already had plenty. Couldn't drink another thing," I said. Total truth. If he assumed I meant beer instead of tea, it wasn't my fault. "And James isn't cooking tonight. Maybe you and I could go out to eat. I'm sure James and Devon are tired of babysitting me." I tugged Billy's arm toward the door. "Bye, Dev. Thanks for today. It was fun!"

"Hold on a sec. Where's James? I have something for him," Billy said.

"He's, uh . . ." My brain stalled out. Normally I'm proficient at avoiding outright lies, but nothing was coming to me.

"He's running a few errands," Devon said, smoothly catching the ball I was fumbling. "I'm afraid I dragged him—and Ciel, too, of course—all over hell and creation looking for Christmas presents. Of course, my dear absentminded professor totally forgot a few things on *his* list, so he had to run back out." He pulled his phone out of his back pocket. "Here, I'll text him that you're here waiting, shall I?" He gave me a significant look.

Errands. Of course. Simple, true, and non-revealing. My head must truly be scrambled if I couldn't come up with that. And texting James? Brilliant. I tried my best to convey my gratitude to Devon using only my eyes. He seemed to catch my drift, judging by the understanding curve of his gorgeous lips. I was going to have to find him a really great Christmas present, even if it meant more shopping.

"Um, yeah," I said. "And you know James. Who knows when he'll read Devon's text? If he even remembered to take his phone with him. Wouldn't surprise me if he stops by the lab while he's out. No telling how long he'll be. Maybe you better leave it for him. I'm sure Devon will see he gets it."

"I need to get something from him, too." Billy plopped down on the sofa, kicked his shoes off, and put his feet up on the coffee table. He patted the spot next to him. "We can wait a bit."

I ignored his invitation to sit. "But I'm starving. Let's go eat and swing by after, okay?"

"Kind of rude, isn't it? Maybe James and Devon would like to join us for dinner."

"No thanks," Devon said without missing a beat. "I'm dieting for a beachwear job, and James is dieting with me to be supportive. But thanks for the offer."

God. So smooth. I was going to have to make James propose to him so we could keep him in the family.

Billy looked from Devon to me. He picked up a shoe and started putting it back on. "Fine. Devon, I better go feed Ciel before she collapses from starvation. Tell James his sister has no patience whatsoever. Never mind, I'm sure he already knows—Ciel, I am perfectly capable of tying my own shoes. Have been since kindergarten."

Oops. "I know. I'm hungry, is all. Hurry, okay?"

"Since when does James not have a full refrigerator?"

"It's all diet stuff. Hideous, awful, *yucky* diet stuff." I glanced at Devon, apologizing with my eyes. "Nobody with functioning taste buds could possibly choke it down."

Devon nodded, dutifully keeping the grin off his face. "Ciel's right. Good thing my taste buds lost all function when I became a model. It's the only way to survive in this business."

I yanked Billy up by one arm and dragged him toward the door. "See you later, Dev. Thanks again for today. We'll do it again soon. Tell James we'll be back after we eat."

"Jesus, cuz, slow down. Devon, stay inside when you're not with James, all right? Just for tonight."

"Why? Is the crazy stabber out to get all of us or something?" Devon asked, only mild concern in his voice.

Billy didn't deny it. "We'll talk more when we get back."

Now Devon was concerned. "Wait a second—is James all right out there by himself?"

"Should be, yeah. He's armed."

"He's *what*?" I said, and stopped tugging on Billy.

"Mark assured me you would be guarded. You don't think he would have let you go shopping with James and Devon if one of them wasn't armed, do you?"

"With what, a test tube?"

"Guess again." He lifted his thumb and extended his index finger.

"James doesn't own a gun."

Billy's dimples made a gotcha appearance. "And exactly how would you know, cuz?"

Damn it. I wasn't about to admit to my inherent nosiness. I cleared my throat. "I'm sure he would have told me."

"Right," Billy said, and gave my hair a tug. "Don't worry, your snooping—pardon me—*sleuthing* skills are in good working order. Mark slipped him a pocket pistol this morning, which I'm going to need back. I've got something else for him."

"Well, I wasn't worried *before* . . ." I said. "Can he even shoot?"

"Quite well, actually," Billy said. "He was fascinated for a while with the science of weaponry, notably projectiles. We spent a lot of time together at the range while you were doing mundane things, like actually attending college classes."

"Hmph. Mark could have given the gun to me. I'm good."

"Which is why you'll be getting it as soon as I retrieve it from James. It's more your size anyway. Besides, I figure it's only a matter of time before you slip the guards, being so inconveniently claustrophobic about such things," he said with a wink.

He was right. I had a thing about being able to go when I wanted to.

The door opened again. "Got them! Four different kinds, to be—"

Crap. He didn't get the text! No fucking way did I want to explain what James had.

"James!" I hollered. "Look who's here! It's Billy. He wants your gun, but don't worry, he has a new one for you."

Please, please, please don't let Billy see those test kits . . .

"Ah, Billy," James said, casually dropping the thankfully generic bag on the small cabinet next to Herbert's habitat. He reached into his coat pocket. "Got it right here."

"Oh, how adorable!" I said, taking it before Billy could, hoping to draw his attention away from the bag. "What kind is it again? I know I've used one like it on the range before, but I never can remember what they're called."

Yeah, not exactly true. I knew exactly what it was, but shifting Billy's focus was for once more important than proving myself smarter than him.

Billy looked at me oddly. "Smith & Wesson featherweight thirty-eight special. Highly concealable, no cocking. Point, and pull the trigger." His eyes drifted back to the cabinet.

"Oh! Right. Now I remember. What did you bring for James?" I said brightly, feigning an interest I didn't really feel. For me, guns were a sometimes necessary tool, one I sincerely hoped I'd never have to use myself. But in my line of work, every skill set was an asset, so I'd trained on the range until I was proficient. (Okay, it hadn't hurt that Mark was the one who'd trained me. Back then, I would have done anything to spend time with him.)

James and Devon gathered closer (conveniently blocking the

view of the cabinet) as Billy pulled a slightly larger handgun out of his leather jacket. "Kahr P380. Not quite five inches long, and only three-quarters of an inch wide. Should fit your hand well. Oh, and here's a concealed carry permit for each of you."

James pulled out his wallet and placed his permit in an open slot. I stuffed mine in my back pocket. Neither of us questioned how Billy came by the permits. They would without a doubt hold up under the closest scrutiny; Billy was good at that sort of thing.

"Needless to say, emergency use only. But if you have to use it, then *use* it. No screwing around with any shoot-to-disable nonsense. Because you know what a disabled attacker can still do? *Kill you.*"

James nodded thoughtfully. "What about Devon?"

"I wasn't sure what he could handle. You want me to get you something, Dev?" Billy said.

Devon shuddered. "A gun? God, no. I wouldn't know what to do with one."

"Pepper spray? Taser? Brass knuckles?" Billy winked at him.

"*Billy* club?" Devon winked back. "Or how about a switchblade? I've always thought those were sexy, the way they . . . pop up."

I gave James a sidelong glance to see what he thought of our boyfriends' banter. He was studiously trying to suppress a smirk. *Guys.*

"As long as you make sure it only pops up in an *appropriate* situation"—Billy pulled me to him with a grin—"I can get you one, but you're on your own if you get caught with it. No permits for those—they're flat-out illegal here."

"Never mind. I don't think I'd cope well with jail," Devon said. "Besides, I already have pepper spray, so I'm good."

"Welp . . . James, Dev, it's been all kinds of fun. Thanks for today." I shoved Billy toward the door. "Come on, I'm starving."

"Don't you want to stay and feed Herbert his new bugs?" James said, glancing at the bag.

Nice, bro. Subtle. I telegraphed my gratitude with my eyes. "Next time," I said. "I'll be over soon."

The trouble with claiming to be ravenous is that you have to eat, even if you're so tied up in knots you couldn't squeeze a single strand of spaghetti through your esophagus if you lubricated it with a gallon of olive oil.

Billy waved an aromatic piece of garlic bread under my nose. I did my best not to turn green. "Go ahead, cuz. Dig in. You know you want to."

We were at my favorite Italian restaurant. It was situated, conveniently enough, close to James's place, near NYU. Billy knew how much I loved their meatballs, so boyfriend points to him for bringing me here. Still . . . ugh. Not what I wanted right now. Especially since there were no fewer than five women at various stages of pregnancy seated throughout the homey dining room. Made me want to crawl under the red-checkered tablecloth and quietly drain a carafe of Chianti.

I gulped some ice water. "I'm saving it for the pasta. Mmm-mmm, nothing tastes better than Jo-Jo's"—Jo-Jo was the cook; imagine a female Robert De Niro, only not as pretty—"garlic bread with her spaghetti." Why the heck hadn't I ordered something easy to swallow, like soup?

"It's not like you can't have more with your meatballs—there's plenty." Billy bit into a piece, closing his eyes briefly in bliss at the flavor.

"I, uh, read somewhere that delaying gratification can enhance a pleasurable experience," I said, assuming a virtuous expression I hoped didn't look as phony as it felt.

He leaned close and said, softly, wickedly, "I'm going to make you regret those words when we're in my tub later."

A tingle traveled the length of my spine, ending in a great big exclamation point at my . . . never mind. Billy had a huge bathtub, and was extremely adept at maneuvering in it.

I snatched the bread from his hand. It did smell good. Maybe I could push it past my gullet if I chewed it really well first. I bit into it carefully. Started grinding my jaws. Kept at it while Billy took another slice and finished it.

"Better keep up, cuz. Eat fast or eat less."

I gave up. "Look, Billy, I wasn't exactly honest back at James's." And I wasn't about to be entirely honest—in spirit, anyway—now either, so I crossed my fingers in the folds of the napkin on my lap. "I'm not really starving. Or even hungry. I needed an excuse to get out of there."

A look of sympathetic understanding came over his face. I had to fight an overwhelming urge to confess all my fears to him. If we'd still only been best friends, and I'd found myself in this situation with some other guy, I would have run to Billy in an instant. He'd always been my go-to fix-it guy, the superhero of finding the best way out of any tight spot. But this tight spot might prove too constrictive for him, given his views on having children. And if I had to admit the possibility of Mark being in the picture . . . no. We'd weathered that storm once, and I did not relish the thought of heading back into the cyclone again, especially if it proved not to be necessary.

"Shopping with the guys a bit much for you?" Billy said.

"It was a nightmare. Devon was so afraid we'd miss a bargain—we must have hit every freaking store at the outlet mall. Honestly, we didn't leave until I was in *tears*." Absolutely true, as far as it went, though I *may* have made it sound like I was exaggerating the crying thing for effect. Little did he know . . . and I hoped he never would.

Billy signaled the waiter and asked him to box up our dinner. "We can eat it later," he said once the waiter was out of earshot, "after I've relaxed you enough to enjoy your meatballs."

Which sounded wonderful, on the face of it, but I wasn't sure I'd be able to enjoy letting Billy "relax" me any more than I could enjoy the meatballs now. Not before I knew.

Damn it. What I needed was a private moment to pee on a fucking stick.

Billy hugged me to his chest in the cab, rubbing my arms against the chill. Either the heater was broken, or the cabbie was part polar bear.

I wanted to relax and enjoy snuggling with my boyfriend, but instead found myself desperately trying to come up with a good reason for refusing the drink he was sure to offer me as soon as we got to his place. It was a simple matter to adapt my boobs down to normal (honestly, they weren't *that* much bigger than usual—probably wouldn't even be noticeable if I weren't so meagerly endowed to begin with), but me refusing to share a drink with him? It could easily make him suspect something wasn't right, and might lead him right down the rabbit hole to where I was trying to bury my Big Fear.

And there was absolutely no good reason to worry Billy at this point. Why put him through the angst when it might not turn out to be an issue? It would be cruel, in fact, to do so.

The thing was, Billy's possible reaction terrified me more than anything. If he drew back, if he pulled away from me, it would break something inside me. Even if it turned out I wasn't (*please, oh please, oh please*) pregnant, could a reaction like that ever be fixed?

I didn't want to find out.

Coward, a piercing voice from my inner mob of insecurities rang out.

Yeah, so what? Screw you, I silently shouted back at it.

So I had to have a justifiable excuse for refusing a drink. I could always strongly imply it was part of my new training regimen. Would he buy it? Probably, I decided. Back in middle school I'd once given up chocolate for a whole month when someone told me it caused pimples, so abstinence on my part wasn't unheard of. Since adaptors don't typically acquire their ability until puberty, back then I couldn't be sure I'd be able to adapt the prospective zits away, so I'd decided it was best to be proactive against the dreaded acne monster.

Billy had teased me mercilessly at the time, telling me zits wouldn't show through my freckles anyway. I stuck to my guns . . . right up until the first indication I'd inherited the adaptor capability. Once I knew I'd be able to hide any complexion woes the easy way, I ate a whole pan of triple dark chocolate chip brownies in one sitting, and threw up for the rest of the afternoon. (It was totally worth it.)

So, yeah, he'd maybe swallow the training implication, if I fed it to him the right way.

My phone buzzed, breaking me out of my frantic planning with a start. Must be Mom, wondering when I'd be back home.

I dug it out of my pocket before it could start ringing, switching excuse gears to quickly formulate a reason to give Mom for not staying overnight again. I wouldn't go so far as to *say* I'd rather have sex with my boyfriend than string popcorn and sing Christmas carols with the parents-to-be, though if I handled it right it was exactly what she'd think. Which might not be classy, precisely, but was better than the truth. Plus, if I sounded strained, she'd chalk it up to me not wanting to admit I was sleeping with Billy instead of not wanting to be around Tom and Laura. You had to be subtle with Mom.

Only the call wasn't from Mom. I felt a perverse twinge that she obviously didn't care about *me* as much now that she had her precious grandchild on the way, but it was immediately overshadowed by a great big thud when I saw it was Mark. I sat up so fast my elbow almost knocked the breath out of Billy.

"Um, hi, Mark," I said, and mouthed a "sorry" to Billy. "What's up?"

"Hey, Howdy. James said you went to dinner with Billy. Everything okay? No more sightings?"

"Nope. Haven't seen a sign of Loughlin, or anyone else suspicious, since I last saw you."

Of course, I hadn't exactly been paying close attention either, what with my mind being otherwise occupied noticing every freaking pregnant woman in the city. There went two . . . no, three . . . more on the sidewalk next to our taxi. Didn't women have anything better to do than repopulate the planet?

I looked at Billy, relaying the question to him via raised eyebrows. (Mark's question about the sightings, not my inner rhetorical one about pregnant women.) He shook his head. "Billy hasn't seen anything weird either."

"Well, I wouldn't say that, exactly," Billy said. "This is New York. We're surrounded by weird. But nothing suspicious."

"Did you hear that, Mark? No, nothing important, only Billy being amusing. Do you want to talk to him yourself?"

"Yeah, but first I need to ask you a favor," Mark said.

"Shoot," I said. Anything to get my mind off of babies.

"Would you be up for filling in for Dr. Carson again for a few days? I can guarantee you no more reduced gravity flights."

"Not another kidney stone, I hope," I said, my brain shifting into high gear, rearranging plans. If I went back to Houston for a while, I wouldn't have to make any excuses to anyone. I could do my job. Maybe grab a pregnancy test with no one watching, and put this whole stupid thing behind me.

"No, she's fine physically. It's her husband who's the problem."

"He doesn't want her to go on the mission? Did he change his mind about the baby?" I said. If he wasn't behind her on this, I didn't see how it could possibly work out for her.

"No, he's on board with the experiment. What he's got a problem with is Alec Loughlin. Rudy—Phil's brother, the one who approached me about the job to begin with—told Misha about him trying to grab you at NASA, and now Misha doesn't want Phil anywhere near the place until we've questioned the guy."

"I'm in," I said at once. "When do you need me?"

"Yesterday," he said.

Even better. "I'll be there."

"One other thing. Better put the phone where Billy can hear this, too."

I leaned close to Billy and held the phone between our ears. "Go ahead."

"There's been another murder. An adaptor."

Billy and I looked at each other. The concern in his eyes mirrored what I felt. "Who?" I asked hoarsely, afraid to hear the answer.

"Jenny Harrison."

Oh, God. Jenny was a friend of Mom's and Auntie Mo's. She was several years younger, and they had kind of adopted her because she had no immediate family of her own. Unless you counted . . . "Her cats," I said inanely. "Who's taking care of her cats?"

"I don't know, Howdy. A neighbor, maybe?"

Billy's questions were more relevant. "Knife? Taser?" He spoke quietly, shielding his mouth with one hand so the cabbie wouldn't hear.

Somehow, I didn't want to know the answer. "She wasn't really friendly with her neighbors," I mumbled.

"Throat slit. Taser marks were plain. The coroner found them on Pickering, too, hidden beneath his hair."

I shut my eyes, but I couldn't get rid of the image. "She mostly kept to herself. Mom and Auntie Mo were trying to get her to go out more . . ." I told myself to stop babbling, but myself didn't seem to want to listen. In fact, Mom had suggested fixing her up with Mark. I'd shot down the idea at the time. Now I couldn't help wondering if I'd let Mom play matchmaker, and it had worked out, if Mark would have kept Jenny safe and she wouldn't be dead. (Yeah, I knew it was stupid even as I was thinking it, but the guilt fairies couldn't seem to resist the opportunity to lob more guilt balls at me.)

Billy swore softly, presumably about the Taser marks, and hugged me closer to him. "What do you need me to do, Mark?"

"Make sure Ciel gets to the company plane I have waiting for her at the airport. And then I guess you better check on the cats."

Chapter 11

"Here you go, Dr. Carson. I'll leave you to get reacquainted with everyone's favorite facility. Remember, practice makes perfect!" said the man with a clipboard, cheap pen, and fabulous facial hair. Seriously. Elvis sideburns and a handlebar mustache. I'd say it worked for him, only . . . it didn't. On the other hand, it probably kept most people from noticing he had ears the size of a Ferengi's.

It was my second day in Houston place-holding for Dr. Phil while she and Misha waited out the manhunt at my tropical island hideaway. Billy hadn't been thrilled—at first—to take me to the airport instead of his bed, but he understood how jobs worked. He was called away unexpectedly often enough himself; he could hardly complain when I was. Besides, he was going to be busy enough helping Mark. And they both seemed happy enough to get me out of the city where all three murders had occurred.

Mom and Auntie Mo had divvied up Jenny's cats between the two households for the meantime. Molly had wanted to take them all, but Auntie Mo had put her foot down at three, leaving Mom to herd the other four. After the funeral, which was put on hold pending the murder investigation, they would work on finding them all good homes. (Ha! Good luck to Auntie Mo on ever getting their three away from Molly.)

I chuckled at my scheduler (he seem to expect it) and said, "Thanks. I know the drill."

Except I really didn't. Dr. Phil may be space-potty trained, but I definitely wasn't. So when I closed the door behind him—and dead-bolted it—I started examining the equipment, and fast, because I had to pee. Urgently. (There was a regular toilet available, but if someone heard me flush it, they'd think Dr. Phil wasn't doing her duty. Er, so to speak. I had her reputation to maintain.) What was it James had said about "frequent urination"? That it was a symptom of—

No! Ciel Halligan, do not go there. You are wearing Dr. Phil's aura, and if you have to pee, it's because of her, not you. Think about your personal problems on your own time.

From the research I'd done before I'd taken the job to begin with, I knew there was a functional training toilet, and a "positional" one. I peeked at the one on the right. Inside the four-inch hole in the seat there was a video camera. It was hooked to a monitor in front of the toilet, so you could make sure the pertinent part of your anatomy was centered over the relatively small target before you released your figurative bombs. The idea was to get the feel of the right position before you practiced on the functional throne.

This kind of repetitive toilet training was essential, because once you're in space, using the real thing, accidents can get not only messy (imagine human waste floating around), but dangerous. You do not want to accidentally inhale or (*ew*) ingest any stray poop or pee floating around because you didn't hit your target.

I took a deep breath. Dropped Dr. Phil's drawers and took a seat. It was amazingly awkward to situate myself properly, but not nearly as embarrassing as turning on the monitor to the view of Dr. Phil's nether region. There are parts of this job I am never going to get used to. Snapping my eyes shut after the briefest peek possible, I memorized the feel of my position so I could duplicate it on the working trainer.

Satisfied I could do it, I shuffled over to the more intimidating functional replica. Buttons and switches and hoses . . . *gah.* Luckily, someone had taped easy, step-by-step instructions on the wall behind the space john. (*Or would that be a "John Glenn"?* I thought irreverently.)

First thing, you flipped the footholds down. Check. (There were straps to help hold your feet steady, and thigh restraints to keep you from floating away. Honestly, it looked like some futuristic version of a medieval birthing chair. Ugh.)

To urinate, one had to attach the proper funnel to the correct hose and turn on the fan. No gravity in space meant you had to use suction to control the flow of human waste to the containers where it was held for later recycling (liquid) or disposal (solid).

Trouble was, there were four different funnel types. How in the hell was I supposed to know which one to use? I supposed I could go back to the positional trainer and take a closer look at, um, things to get an idea of which one might be the best fit, but that seemed needlessly invasive of Dr. Phil's privacy, not to mention time-consuming. Like I said, I had to *go.* So I eenie-meenie-miney-moed it, and hoped for the best.

Phwoop!

Wow. Talk about a singular sensation. Even though my bladder felt like it was about to burst, I had a hard time getting started. (Go attach a funnel to your vacuum cleaner, press it close to your pertinent anatomy, and see if *you* can relax.) But eventually my need won out, and relief was had. Until I had to remove the funnel from its, um, docking station.

I tugged. It stuck.

Then I remembered—vaguely—that the funnels for the female astronauts were vented around the rims to avoid this kind of situation, because of the necessity of placing them directly against the body. The guys only had to aim into theirs from a few inches away (honestly, guys have it *so* much easier in the peeing department), so no vents were necessary for them—only a nice, strong suction to keep their fluids flowing where they needed to flow.

I'd obviously grabbed a guy funnel. (Damn it, I'd had to *pee*, all right? Urgently having to pee is not conducive to forethought.)

I tugged again. *Ouch.*

There was a loud knocking on the door, followed by an eager "Dr. Carson? Everything all right in there? If you need assistance . . ."

Yikes. "No! I'm fine."

"Very well. I don't mean to rush you, but it looks like PR has scheduled you for another interview. This one is with a reporter from a local elementary school, and he's getting a little antsy. You know kids."

"I'll be right there . . ." I said, doing my best to keep the desperation out of Dr. Phil's voice. One more good yank and—

Gah! I bit my lip against a filthy word.

My interviewer was a big-eyed little boy with a blond buzz cut and more freckles than my primary aura, poor kid. He wrote painstakingly in his composition book with a blunt-pointed pencil, his tongue switching from one corner of his mouth to the other with each new letter he put down. He was in the second grade. But as excruciating as waiting for him to finish writing was, that wasn't my real problem.

My real problem was the videographer recording the interview for NASA's PR department.

A shiver had gone through me when I'd first seen him. He resembled Alec Loughlin in build and coloring, and was equally good-looking, if you go for that rugged, I've-lived-an-outdoor-life type. My handler introduced him as "John Smith." Such a nice, ordinary name. My relief might have stayed with me past the introduction if, while shaking my hand, he hadn't stroked my palm with one finger and whispered, in a faint Russian accent, "Alec sends his regards." That turned my initial shiver into a full-blown chill down my spine.

I tried to stay focused on the kid—Eddie, his name was—but my mind was flying. What was this guy doing here? Was there going to be another kidnapping attempt? Or maybe worse? Did he think I was Dr. Phil, or had Alec told him I was someone— some*thing*—else? How much did he know? How should I be acting around him?

Thus far I'd kept it to a pleasant but distant "pleased to meet you." I didn't think Miss Manners had any set rules for greeting possible kidnappers-slash-murderers, so I was working blind.

I glanced at the camera, adopting a façade of magnanimous-adult-being-patient-with-the-kid. From the amused smirk on Smith's face, he wasn't buying it.

I turned to Eddie's teacher (Mr. Brooks, according to his name tag), an earnest older black man who obviously took his job as educator of tomorrow's scientists seriously. He'd made it a point to tell me the original journalist for today had been a girl who had called in sick to school, and the first alternate had also been a girl, but she too had been sick. I had applauded his efforts to encourage girls in the fields of science and technology, and assured him I was perfectly happy to talk to boys as well.

Now all I could think about was how to get both of them the heck out of here as soon as humanly possible. If this asshole was sent by Loughlin to get me, I didn't want any collateral damage.

"So," I said to the teacher, "don't you think it might be a bit, well, redundant for Eddie to write down all my answers? I mean, since the interview is being recorded."

Mr. Brooks smiled. "It never hurts to have a backup. What if the video is corrupted? Technology is far from infallible, you know."

I suppressed an eye roll, Dr. Phil not being the eye-rolling type. "Yes, I do see your point. Perhaps if *I* wrote down my answers . . ." I suggested delicately.

"Oh, no," Mr. Brooks said. "We like to foster independence in our students. Besides, this is good practice for Eddie. Dictation is rapidly becoming a lost skill for our youngsters."

I nodded, keeping the patient smile on Dr. Phil's face, and decided to limit my future replies to three words or less. Three *short* words.

I darted another look at the Russian. His smirk seemed slier somehow. He knew he had me squirming, and was enjoying it.

Eddie looked up, eyebrows squinched together. "How do you spell 'international' again?"

I was about to answer, but was stopped by a raised palm from the teacher. "Sound it out, Eddie."

Eddie finally reached the end of his sentence—I-N-T-E-R-N-A-S-H-U-N-U-L . . . S-P-A-S . . . S-T-A-S-H-U-N; not a bad, if exceedingly time-consuming, effort—jabbing the period at the end of it like he was spiking a football after a touchdown.

"Next question?" I said, consciously not drumming my fingertips on the table between us. "Um, not to rush, but I do have another appointment soon." A very personal appointment with my cell phone, to tell Mark that Loughlin definitely wasn't working alone.

Hmm. Maybe I didn't have to wait. I could shoot off a quick text while little Eddie was laboriously laying lead down on the page. But as soon as I reached for my pocket, the videographer (whom, I somehow suspected, was *not* named John Smith) started talking, his Russian accent not as subtle as before.

"Patience, Dr. Carson. Put yourself in the boy's place. That would be much better than putting him in your place, wouldn't it?"

I forced myself to keep my focus on my interviewer, terribly afraid I couldn't hide my shock at what he seemed to be threatening. Would he really harm a child?

Eddie put his pencil down and flexed his hand, grimacing.

I feel you, kid.

"Go ahead, Eddie," Mr. Brooks said with an encouraging smile, looking like he had all the time in the world. Not that I could blame him for stretching things out. This was probably way more fun than dealing with a whole classroom full of seven-year-olds.

Eddie looked at the next question on his list, a mischievous grin appearing on his face. "How do you use the bathroom in space?" He snickered.

Great. How could I explain *that* in three words?

"Keep it serious, Edward," Mr. Brooks said sternly.

"Hey, you told me a good journalist asks the questions other people want to know. Well, that's what Sam wants to know." He shrugged.

Under less tense circumstances I probably would have had trouble maintaining Dr. Phil's decorum. As it was, I only smiled, keeping her professional attitude intact. "We have a special toilet. It sucks the"—would he understand "urine" and "feces"?—"pee and poop into special containers, kind of like a vacuum cleaner."

Mr. Brooks frowned slightly at my word selection, but I didn't care. "Pee" and "poop" were easier to spell, and I didn't want to wait for Eddie to write "Y-E-R-I-N" and "F-E-E-S-E-E-S." The sooner the two of them were out of Smith's reach, the happier I'd be.

"My dad said you have to use a hose."

"For"—I glanced at Mr. Brooks, and decided to be more careful with my words—"um, number one, yes—a hose with a funnel on the end of it. For number two it's more like a regular toilet," I said, keeping my voice as matter-of-fact as I could.

Eddie looked thoughtful. "I'll bet the hose thing is a lot easier for the guys than the girls, huh?"

Kid, you have no idea. But you may have just given me one . . .

"Hey, I know," I said. "Would you like to see a space toilet close up?"

"Heck, yeah!" Eddie said, eyes alight with curiosity. Even Mr. Brooks looked intrigued.

The Russian, however, didn't seem to care for the idea.

"Come on, Mr. Smith," I said brightly. "You can document it for us. I'm certain whoever watches this interview will be as fascinated with space plumbing as Eddie here is."

His eyes narrowed on me. "Sure," he said, patting Eddie on the head, allowing his hand to slide down to the back of the boy's skinny neck. He gripped it lightly, in a way I was sure Mr. Brooks and my handler found friendly, but I found nauseatingly threatening. "And then maybe you can come with me to take some random footage around the grounds outside. For additional viewer interest."

I nodded, my mouth too dry to speak.

He let go of Eddie. "Lead the way, kid. I'll be *right* behind you."

Message received.

I set Dr. Phil's normally brisk pace to match Eddie's shorter stride, knowing it was what she would do. It also gave me slightly longer to fine-tune my plan, which so far consisted of "find a way to get Eddie and Mr. Brooks away from Smith." Admittedly, it could use some fleshing out.

Smith shouldn't be armed. Security was tighter than ever for the building—Mark had seen to that after the incident with Loughlin—but I had no idea what kind of hand-to-hand skills he had. He might be as well trained as Mark, for all I knew, and Mark could probably take down anyone who wasn't holding a bazooka on him. So I had to be extra careful. Isolating him somehow would be my best option.

When we got to the restroom door, Eddie was ready to barge right in, but I held him back with a hand on his shoulder. "Wait a second. I have a better idea," I said, the details of a plan materializing in my head as I spoke. "Let's let Mr. Smith go in first, so he can capture the look on your face when you get your first up-close and personal view of the space potty."

Smith gave me a suspicious look. "Good idea," he said with a tight smile. "Why don't you come in with me and show me how you want the shot set up?" He hooked a long-fingered hand above my elbow and pulled me after him.

Okay, so that hadn't been part of my plan. "Um . . . sure. Happy to. Let me just tell Eddie and Mr. Brooks what to do when I call them in."

Turning my back on Smith, who waited just inside the open door, his grip still firm on my arm, I focused on my Ferengi-Elvis look-alike handler and mouthed the words "Call security" as distinctly as I could, praying he could read lips. He looked confused.

Smith's grip tightened.

"Um, so when I holler 'go,' Eddie, you just open the door and walk right in. And, you know, pretend you're impressed or something," I said, the whole while staring at Elvis and rolling my eyes wildly in an effort to make him realize something was very, very wrong.

Eddie shifted from foot to foot, impatient to play his role. "Gotcha! Just like when I open a present from Aunt Doris. Only I bet this is going to be way cooler than the stuff she gets me!"

Elvis cocked his head at me. "Are you quite all right, Dr. Carson?"

"Yes. I, um, got something in my eye." I tried mouthing the words again, exaggerating the movement of my lips even more.

Mr. Brooks said, "Here, let me take a look."

"Uh . . . okay. It's the left one."

When he was close enough, I whispered frantically, barely moving my lips, "As soon as the door closes, get Eddie the hell out of here. *Fast.*"

Surely the man hadn't survived this long in the teaching field without being quick on the uptake. He cleared his throat, still looking at my eye, and gave one quick nod. "There. I think I got it."

God, I hoped so.

Elvis tucked his clipboard under his arm. "Wait just a moment, please. I didn't catch what you were trying to tell me, Dr. Carson." He tugged on one of his earlobes. "I'm afraid this new hearing aid might be malfunctioning. It seems to be fading in and out."

Oh, for fuck's sake. "I *said* call security!" I shouted, and spun around, breaking Smith's grip on my arm. I shoved him into the room and stumbled in after him, kicking the door shut behind me.

He dropped his camera and came at me with a roar. If he got me pinned, I'd never get away from him. Not alive, anyway.

I lowered my head and charged him like a bull, aiming to hit him in the solar plexus and knock the wind out of him. It might have worked, too, if he hadn't had abs of titanium. A grunt was all I got out of him, followed by a dirty laugh.

He grabbed me by the hair and shoved my face down a few inches, into his crotch. "You want to go down on me, little imposter? That can be arranged. But later. First we are getting out of here."

Fortunately, Dr. Phil's stylishly short coif kept Smith from achieving a strong grip. I twisted my head and pulled away, hard, leaving him with a palm covered in auburn hairs and me with a burning scalp. Before he could grab my head again, I jerked my knee up, aiming for his balls. I figured they must be a big target, considering how he strode into the Space Center intending to snatch me right out from under everyone's noses.

Unfortunately, whatever protect-your-junk-at-all-costs instinct men come equipped with kicked in before I could make a solid connection. I must have winged him, though, because he was pissed off. Big time.

He dragged me—by my ears this time—to the training toilet and attempted to push my head, face-first, into the bowl. Good God, was he trying to drown me? Didn't he know space toilets use suction, not water?

When he saw my head wasn't going to fit—because, of course, the hole was too small—he pulled me back by one ear, and lifted the seat, obviously thinking to attempt it again with a larger opening. Instinctively, I braced my hands against the base of the toilet, trying to push myself away. My fingers brushed up against a knob.

Aha! The suction switch. I twisted it to the highest setting. While he was still occupied with the seat, I grabbed the urine-disposal tube and, with as much force as possible, jammed it right between his legs.

Smith doubled over, his own head landing in the place he'd been trying to put mine. He let go of me by reflex, and tried to push himself up from the toilet, but apparently he'd wheezed the strength right out of his arms. I held firm, pushing the hose as hard as I could against the most tender part of his anatomy. With my other hand, I reached up and slammed the toilet seat down on his head. Repeatedly.

He sure as hell wasn't laughing now.

"How do *you* like it, you motherfucking douche bag?" I know. My language deteriorates when I'm under stress. It's a quirk.

I gave the hose another upward shove, twisting. I must have connected a little more solidly to the anatomy beneath his pants, because this time it stuck. Ha! "Sucks, doesn't it, asshole?" I said, and dropped the toilet seat on his head one final time.

———

John Smith was still clutching his man-bits when three security guards burst into the room. He'd slid to the floor in front of the space potty, and was balled up in a fetal position, pale and sweaty and glassy eyed. I'd removed the hose. Let him explain his busted balls any way he chose.

I played dumb with security, claiming I had no earthly idea who the man could be or what he wanted. Mark could decide what to tell NASA. As far as they were concerned, I was Dr. Carson, and I wasn't about to tell them otherwise. When they wanted to escort me to see a flight doc, I pleaded the need for a few moments in the ladies' room first, and called Mark, quickly relating the bare bones of what had happened. It's possible the groin-punishing interlude in the bathroom got condensed to "I incapacitated him," which somehow struck me as more professional.

"Are you injured?" he asked tensely.

"Nope. Right as rain," I said, keeping Dr. Phil's voice bright and steady.

"Hang tight. I'm sending someone to pick up Smith. And you." His voice had become more controlled, but I detected an underlying grimness.

"Take Smith, and good riddance, but I'm on a job here and plan to finish it."

"Howdy"—the phones were encrypted, so he wasn't giving anything away to any would-be eavesdroppers—"if there was one guy, there could be more. It's not safe."

"Look, if it makes you feel better, have someone follow me"—I knew he would anyway, so I figured I might as well make it sound like a concession on my part—"but I'm driving myself home in that sweet ride, same as always. Oh, and tell whoever follows me not to freak out when I stop for a burger. I'm starving."

Chapter 12

I dropped my double cheeseburger and fries on the kitchen counter, along with another bag, and went to the fridge for a bottle of designer water. Nobody had recognized Dr. Phil at the busy burger joint, but I hadn't wanted to stay long enough to press it. Greasy burgers weren't really her thing, and I didn't like to appear in public out of character. But desperate times call for desperate measures—I *needed* a cheeseburger to fortify me.

After my visit to the flight doc I'd been freed for the day. Naturally, I'd projected Dr. Phil in peak physical condition, not a bruise or blemish on her. It was likely another story beneath her aura, but nothing that need ever show to anyone but me. Luckily, Dr. Phil's mission wasn't set to launch until January, so she wasn't scheduled for the mandatory weeklong pre-mission quarantine until after the new year. Thank God I wouldn't be filling in for her then.

Mr. Brooks and Eddie were given a police escort back to their school, something that thrilled Eddie to no end. From the shine in his elderly eyes, I suspected Mr. Brooks was enjoying the excitement, too. The next edition of the school newspaper was sure to be a doozy.

Mark had spoken with the big boss of NASA security and convinced him Dr. Carson would be adequately watched over, so nobody in that department gave me any shit when I went to leave.

The drive back to Dr. Phil's house in her cool TR6 was exactly what I needed after my bathroom brawl with Smith—fresh air and open sky. I kept the top down in spite of the cooler-than-average December weather. (This works pretty well if you put the heater on high. Warm legs offset the chilly ears and nose.)

Misha was with Phil, so I had the house to myself. He went out of town a lot for his job with Spaceward Ho, so the neighbors wouldn't think it was strange he wasn't here. His coworkers thought he was taking leave to spend more time with his wife before her mission. Which was true enough.

Tonight was the night I was going to do it. I was going to pee on the stick.

The first night, I'd come straight here after work, sure the job would keep my mind occupied and I'd be able to stop thinking about my own dilemma for a while. Yeah, not so much. I'd stayed up most of the night, unable to stop generating scenarios of me with one baby, with two babies, with Billy, with Mark . . .

I'd even stood in front of Dr. Phil's full-length bathroom mirror and projected myself with a big belly. It was a scary sight.

I didn't intend to spend another night wondering. Hell, I'd just faced down a big Russian intent on harming me, and thoroughly kicked his ass. That took guts, right? Surely I could be brave enough to face the truth in my personal life. So before I'd hit the burger joint, I'd visited a pharmacy far from Dr. Phil's neighborhood and purchased a test kit, which was in the other bag, next to my dinner. I was determined to use it.

Right after I ate my pickle-laden burger while refusing to think what my sudden craving for extra dill pickles might mean. (I mean, come on. My subconscious couldn't be that clichéd, could it?)

"Mmm. Smells good. I don't suppose you have enough for two?"

Crap.

I spun around to see Billy lounging against the frame of the door leading to the living room. Clad in dark slacks and a midnight-blue fitted dress shirt (with no tie, loosened collar, and cuffs rolled up to display his ridiculously sexy forearms), he looked even more delicious than my burger smelled. "What the hell are *you* doing here?"

"Gee, I love you, too," he said, dimpling enough to show me he hadn't taken offense. He was used to me blurting out the first thing to cross my mind when I was surprised.

I crossed to him, my heart beating faster, either out of love, or out of terror that I might wind up blurting something I definitely didn't want him to know at this point. Not before *I* knew, and could figure out the right way to handle it. Either way, immediate physical contact was called for, so I wrapped my arms around his waist and pulled him tightly to me, reveling in the comfort of his familiar arms until another thought occurred to me.

"Wait a second," I said, pulling back slightly. "Did Mark send you here to babysit me? Damn it, I knew he gave in too easily after . . ." I trailed off when I saw confusion being replaced by suspicion in Billy's eyes.

"Tell me. Now."

I took a deep breath and told him the whole thing. I could see he was upset at the idea of another person acting with Loughlin, but I did manage to coax some humor into his eyes when I related how I'd accomplished the space-potty takedown.

"Jesus, cuz. Remind me never to piss you off," he said, his dimples finally making a welcome reappearance. "Anyway, to answer your question, Mark didn't ask me to come—that was purely my libido's idea—but he does know I'm here."

Which probably explained why Mark hadn't argued more strongly for yanking me off the job right away. "Did you fly in yourself?" Billy had a Mooney 252 he was fond of using to hop around the country.

"Yeah. Doesn't take much longer than commercial, and it's way more fun. I got here this morning. Mark gave me Mikhail's aura—"

"Phil calls him 'Misha,' " I said.

"*Misha's* aura to use as needed—with permission from the man himself, of course. I told him I'd check out some places in Houston Loughlin might have been seen. When I was done, I thought I'd come here to wait for you. Didn't want to bother you at work."

I grinned. "Yeah? Since when?" Showing up to bug me on a job was one of Billy's favorite pastimes.

"Hey, I can try new things."

I raised a skeptical brow.

"Okay. I decided not to bother you on your job for the spook, seeing as how it's so important for you to impress him and all."

"Technically I'm on the job right now," I pointed out.

"Baby steps. At least we're not in public this time. You don't expect me to reform all at once, do you? Now, drop the aura so I can kiss you properly."

"Wait—did you find any sign of Loughlin?"

"Yes, but nothing recent enough to be relevant. Now drop it."

I waggled my eyebrows. "You sure? Most men seem to find Phil exceedingly attractive."

"No doubt she is. But I've become addicted to a certain petite blonde with freckles. And the last time I tried to take her to bed I was rudely interrupted by her work. Therefore, I feel perfectly justified in interrupting her work now."

I laughed, a soft and sultry sound in Phil's aura. "You've convinced me. Let me make sure all the blinds are shut—"

"Already did. Come on, hurry."

I stopped projecting Phil's aura, instantly losing half a foot in height. Billy lifted me right out of her shoes and laid his mouth across mine, teasing my lips open with his clever tongue. My major worries—whether or not I was pregnant, who was killing adaptors in New York, how Loughlin could apparently see through my auras, and, newest of the bunch, who Loughlin was working with—all disappeared into a fog of passion. Hell, even the cheeseburger was taking a backseat, which said a lot about how good Billy was at kissing.

He pulled his head away long enough to say, "Living room okay?"

I took a deep breath and released it raggedly. "Yeah, good. The rug in front of the fireplace is soft."

He carried me there, and laid me gently on the plush earth tones of the deep pile. There was a fire already going in the gas fireplace, and what looked like an expensive bottle of wine on the slate coffee table, open and breathing next to two delicately stemmed wineglasses.

I pushed myself up on my elbows. "You raided my client's wine rack?"

"Well, it seemed like the sort of thing a good husband would have waiting for his wife after a hard day of astronaut training. Shall I pour you a glass?" He reached for the bottle.

I grabbed his hand and pulled it back to me. "No, thanks. Right now all I want is you." I'd figure out how to avoid drinking it later.

He lay down next me and nibbled my neck. "More than your cheeseburger?" he murmured.

A soft moan escaped me. "Well, it was close, but you squeaked out ahead. Barely."

"Speaking of *barely*"—he divested me of Dr. Phil's clothing, not a difficult task considering how easily they slid off now that my size had been diminished—"and *squeaking* . . ." His hands zeroed in on all my most ticklish places until I was, in fact, squeaking with laughter.

"Stop!" I said. "I can't breathe!"

He ceased immediately. One of the things I loved about Billy—as big a tease as he was, he never turned tickling into torture. His hands became gentle, applying enough pressure to leave me breathless for another reason entirely. While I could still form words, I whispered, "You have too many clothes on."

He remedied the problem with a quick, but remarkably hot, striptease.

"You know, you could make good money doing that for a living," I said, only half jokingly.

His grin told me he appreciated the compliment but didn't take it seriously. "You're the only audience I want. Think you can afford me?"

I pulled him down on top of me. "I'm fresh out of ones. Can I run a tab?"

"I don't know." He kissed my neck, unerringly hitting *the* spot.

"I'm thinking barter arrangement might be more mutually beneficial."

I moaned as he slid into me. "*Mmm.* Definitely. Barter works for me."

As did procrastination.

The cheeseburger was a cold—and some might say aesthetically disgusting—mess by the time we got to it. Fortunately, I wasn't picky about my burgers, and neither was Billy. I sawed it in half with a serrated knife I'd located when I was doing my extensive recon of Dr. Phil's home.

It wasn't that I was nosy . . . okay, I *am* nosy, but the fact is, it's essential to be familiar with your setting when you're impersonating someone. Something as simple as not knowing where an everyday object was kept could trip you up if, say, a neighbor stopped by to chat. I was sure Billy had also gone through the house from attic to slab while he was waiting for me. He was nothing if not vigilant.

"You sure you don't want this nuked?" I asked, handing him his half.

"Do you really think it would help?"

I shrugged. "Why don't you try? If it works for you, I'll nuke mine, too."

He tugged my hair. "Fine. I'll be your guinea pig."

While he had his back to me, futzing with the fancy microwave, I dumped most of my wine down the sink. When he turned around, I had the glass to my lips, like I'd taken a big sip.

He picked up the bottle to offer me more.

"No thanks," I said. "This is plenty."

"But it's the good stuff. What's the point in working if you don't take advantage of the perks?"

"You go ahead. I'm saving my taste buds for my meager dinner." Lame, but the microwave beeped before he could call me on it.

He retrieved his half-burger and waved it under my nose. It might look like something retrieved from a Dumpster, but it smelled divine. Before I could snatch a bite, he downed half of it, as usual not spilling a bit.

"Well, what's the verdict?" I said.

"Mmm. Nuke it. Definitely nuke it."

I loaded my half into the microwave, fiddled with the reheat function, and turned to find Billy staring into the sink. A flash of panic killed my burgeoning appetite. He turned on the water, extended the sprayer from the faucet, and rinsed away the wine residue.

"You know, cuz, I can understand your not drinking," he said after carefully replacing the nozzle. "It's okay not to be in the mood to imbibe. Heck, even I don't drink *every* day. But what I don't get is why you're taking such pains to hide it from me. Back at your brother's with the beer—yes, I noticed, and at the restaurant, too, when you wanted to leave before they brought the wine. And at the diner with Mark. Lemonade with a Reuben? You want to tell me what's going on?"

My mouth went dry. "Not really, no."

"How 'bout you do it anyway? In our newfound spirit of communication. Or have we suspended that?"

After our last misunderstanding, we'd vowed to be more open with each other, and it had been working great. Did I want to risk whatever ground we'd regained just to spare him what might prove to be a fruitless worry? Especially when, if I was honest with my-self, I was mainly trying to spare myself the discomfort of telling him. (Being honest with yourself *sucks*.)

I took a breath. Released it slowly. (It didn't help.) "Look, it might not be anything. I'm probably being stupid, and I *hate* being stupid, around you especially . . . damn it!" I picked up the drugstore bag and tossed it at him. "There. You want to know so bad, that's it."

I braced myself for his reaction. Told myself I could handle it, whatever it was.

He reached into the bag and pulled out the test kit. Studied it for a good thirty seconds, as if unable to comprehend what it was. I held my breath, hugging myself, my hands gripping the sides of Dr. Phil's shirt, which was more like a short dress on me. I hadn't bothered with her pants. Billy was back in Misha's clothes.

Eventually he smiled. His dimples grew until I could see he was struggling not to laugh. "This is it? You're worried you're pregnant?"

I snatched the kit away from him. "I told you it was stupid. Don't laugh! You're the one who put the idea in my head, you with your comment about my boobs being bigger. And I thought . . . I mean, it happened to Laura . . . and then she stopped drink-ing because apparently it's *bad* to drink when you're . . ."

He wrapped his arms around me. Leaned his chin on my head and held me tight. "Cuz, it's okay. You're freaking out about Tom and Laura, and being an aunt, and hell, even your client is getting ready to inseminate herself. You have babies on the brain, is all."

"But . . ." I took a deep breath. ". . . my period's late."

"How late?"

I shrugged. "Hard to say. I'm not very regular."

"Well, there you go. And lots of things can make your period late. Stress, for one. Think you might have been under some lately?" he said, sounding so perfectly reasonable I felt like kicking myself for not coming to him when I first started worrying.

"Maybe." I hugged him tighter.

I *had* been under a huge amount of stress recently. My Hollywood job had been a real doozy, and then there was the wedding and all its related hoopla, and the misunderstanding with Mark (something I really didn't want to think about right now), all topped off with the murders in New York. No wonder my body was staging a protest.

I finally looked up at Billy. His beautiful eyes were full of empathy and, yes, humor. Oddly, I found the humor the most reassuring thing of all. He wouldn't think it was funny if he thought there was the remotest possibility I was actually pregnant.

"You think I'm being crazy?" I asked hopefully.

He tugged my hair, and stroked my cheek with his thumb. "Little bit."

"But what if . . . I mean, I know we're careful, but no birth control is a hundred percent foolproof."

"Birth control patches are extremely reliable. I'd be willing to bet the vast majority of statistical 'patch failure' is actually user failure. And I happen to know you're very careful with yours. I've never seen your naked ass without it"—he winked at me—"unless you count the time I walked into your room without knocking back when we were in middle school."

"I still think you did that on purpose," I said, laughing. I certainly hadn't found it amusing then.

"And punished me adequately at the time, as I recall." I had thrown my hairbrush at his head with deadly accuracy, resulting in a black eye he'd had to spend a week adapting away with his fledgling skills. "So you can stop pinching me now. The point is, I'm sure this is a false alarm. But if it will ease your overanxious mind to pee on the stick, let's do it." He ended with an encouraging smile, and led me to the downstairs powder room. I was feeling better about the whole thing already.

We stared at the stick together, holding hands.

"That's a p-plus sign," I said.

Billy swallowed, so hard I could hear it. "Yes. It is."

The brittle quality of his words drew me out of my own shock. Because I *was* shocked. It didn't matter how worried I'd been, how afraid it might be true, I hadn't really believed it. I'd somehow expected this would turn out to be another warning from The Big Guy Upstairs. That I'd be saying, *Ha ha, good one, God. You sure got my attention. Whew! I'll be a much better person from now on.*

Only . . . plus sign.

And worse than the plus sign: Billy's face.

He'd joked throughout the test, reading the instructions in funny accents, even insisting on holding the stick for me while I peed on it, because girls were such lousy pee-aimers. As he'd probably intended, his teasing humor had gone a long way toward relaxing me.

There was no humor in his eyes now. No hint of a dimple on his stiff cheeks. Only a stark paleness that extended to his lips and made his eyebrows stand out like two slashes of black paint on clean canvas. He looked so unlike his usual animated self that I found myself checking to make sure he wasn't projecting a different aura.

"Billy?" I said, making his name into a question I couldn't find the words to frame.

"I can't do this," he said.

The panic inside me was bubbling up for real now. It felt like acid in my throat. "We'll talk. We'll figure it out. The test—maybe it's wrong—I'll take another one—"

He finally looked at my face. "Queasy. Bigger boobs. Positive test. It's real, Ciel." When I didn't respond (I didn't know what to say—I'd barely had time to process it myself), he leaned down and kissed me, fiercely. "I have to go."

"But—"

He turned and strode out, grabbing keys from the kitchen counter on the way to the garage. I had no doubt he'd don Misha's aura before he pulled out—no matter how upset he was, he wouldn't risk blowing his—or my—cover. That much was pure instinct for him.

"You're *leaving*?" I called after him.

"You're safe. Mark has men on the house," he said, without breaking his stride. It almost sounded like he was reassuring himself more than me.

My legs finally started to work, and I trailed after him. "Will you be back?" I hated the pleading that had crept into my voice, but I couldn't seem to control it.

He hesitated. "I don't know."

Anger welled up in me, crowding out the helpless feeling threatening to drown me. How could he do this?

He's a leaver, the insidious voice in my head whispered, the one that had tried to warn me about Billy from the start. The one I'd refused to listen to, because I'd convinced myself it didn't know what it was talking about. *He's left every girlfriend he ever had—and there've been plenty. It was always a matter of time, wasn't it? And you knew he didn't want kids. He's never made a secret of it. Of course he's leaving. What'd you expect?*

"It might not even be yours, you know! It could be *Mark's*," I shouted, surprising myself with the sudden intensity of my need to hurt him, knowing instinctively what would wound him more than anything. "I haven't had a period since that night."

He stopped. Turned back to me slowly. I fully expected to see a corresponding anger on his face, and was prepared to deal with whatever he lashed out at me with—I'd give it back as good as I got. What I saw instead floored me: relief.

"That might be best," he said quietly. And then he was gone.

Chapter 13

Four sticks were lined up on the bathroom vanity, like soldiers in a firing squad, each aiming straight for my gut. One set of parallel lines, two plus signs, and, presumably for those who needed the news to be literally spelled out, the word "pregnant" appearing digitally. They all meant the same thing. And all claimed ninety-nine percent accuracy. What were the odds I'd fall into the one percent for every single one of them?

The first thing I'd done after Billy left was go to four different pharmacies to buy more tests. Because it was always *possible* the first one had been wrong, no matter what Billy said, and it would look stupid to buy four of them at the same pharmacy, right? And if I only got one more, and it was negative, well then I'd have to go out *again* to break the tie. Four more would make five in all, and there could be no tie. (Trust me, it had made all kinds of sense at the time.) Besides, driving all over town from one pharmacy to the next beat the heck out of crawling into Dr. Phil's king-size bed, hiding under the covers, and bawling my eyes out. I had apologized to the agents following me, making up some shit about a specific brand of feminine hygiene product I needed, so they would give me some space. Men tended to be squeamish about tampons.

The second thing I'd done was stop for gas, because yeah, driving all over town.

I dug my own phone out of my luggage, where I kept it stowed so as not to accidentally use it when I was being my client. *Not*, I told myself, to check for messages from Billy. (There weren't any.) There were seven voice mails from Mom (mostly requests to call when my job was done, because she had *plans* to make and needed my input) and one from James. I had a pretty good idea what he wanted to talk about, and I wasn't up to it yet.

There was also one from Mark, asking me to call when I got the chance. Probably an update about Loughlin. My chest clutched at the idea of talking to him, but I couldn't *not* return his call when I was technically working for him. Just because my personal life was falling apart around me didn't mean I couldn't concentrate on my job. That's what being professional was all about, right?

He picked up after the first ring. "Good news, Howdy." *Well, that would be a refreshing change of pace*, I thought wryly. "Your client has decided she's placated her husband long enough, and is insisting on getting back to work."

"But is that safe? What about Loughlin? What if the Russian wasn't the only one working with him?"

"Her brother finished his other assignment, and has been given leave to stick close to her. Rudy's a good agent, and Misha knows it. And we'll leave a complete security detail, too. Dr. Carson will be well looked after."

"Great," I said. "So, when's the handoff?"

"Later tonight, after the neighborhood is asleep. My guys will bring Phil and Misha straight to the house from the airfield, and take you back. Billy, too, if he's there with you. His Mooney should be at the same field."

"Billy's not here. He was, but he had to leave." There. I sounded natural. My voice hadn't even cracked.

"Did he say where he was going?"

"No. He left in kind of a hurry. It might have been one of his side jobs." Hey, it *might* have been. Sure, it would have to be the mother of all coincidences for him to suddenly remember something he had to do on one of his side jobs at the precise moment he'd learned I was pregnant, but it was poss—okay, so it wasn't possible. If God wanted to strike me down for the lie, He was welcome to have at it. It wasn't like my day could get much worse anyway.

There was a pause, maybe half a beat too long. Mark's spook antennae going up, no doubt, but he didn't pursue it. "All right. My guys can take you to D.C., or back to New York, if you'd rather. Laura tells me your mother is anxious to get everyone settled close to the nest for the holidays."

Ack. No way could I see Mom yet. Even thinking about it made my belly flip. Hell, she'd probably sniff out another grandbaby like a bloodhound, and I could *not* deal with that now. "D.C. would be perfect. I need to get some stuff done there before I dive into the crazy."

Mark chuckled. He'd spent many a Christmas holiday with the Halligan clan, and knew exactly what kind of insanity I was talking about. "All right, Howdy. But don't let your guard down."

"Don't worry, I won't," I said. *Not for a minute*, I thought, one hand automatically moving to my belly.

Chapter 14

The roses on the hall stand weren't dead, but they were seriously drooping. Probably something symbolic there, but I didn't want to examine it too closely.

I left my bag in the hall and took the roses to the kitchen, trying on the way to decide if they could be saved or if I should go ahead and toss them. In the end, I left them on the counter and went upstairs, unable to tend to them without crying—which I refused to do—but equally unable to throw them out. When in doubt, put it off.

Seeing my bed didn't help my mood any. Stray rose petals, dried and crushed, littered the sheets. (*The way broken dreams littered my soul* . . . I, um, *might* have thought if, you know, it hadn't been so nauseatingly trite.) I yanked the sheets off the bed and stuffed them into the hamper, petals and all. I'd shake them off before I washed them. In the meantime, I didn't need the reminder of how giddily happy I'd been to see Billy here in my bed.

Getting fresh sheets out of the linen closet and making the bed seemed like too much trouble, so I went across the hall to the guest room. But then I remembered the night not long ago I'd spent there with Billy, and couldn't bring myself to crawl into that bed either.

Get a fucking grip, Ciel. What are you going to do, go to a hotel? Hmm. Not a bad idea . . .

The more I thought about it, the less crazy it seemed. I might actually be able to sleep in a hotel, someplace impersonal, someplace I'd never been with Billy. My bank account was, for once, healthy enough. Mark had made sure I received a hefty bonus for tacking those extra days on to the NASA job, so I might as well make use of the windfall.

I called a taxi, repacked my bag with a clean change of clothes, and got the hell out of Dodge.

The pounding on my hotel room door was my first clue upon waking that something was amiss. I looked at the bedside clock. Jesus, I'd been asleep for, what, twelve hours?

Thomas's voice was even louder than his incessant pounding. "Ciel! Sis, are you all right? Open the door!" Honest to God, with a voice like his, he could fill in for Metatron.

"One second!" I hollered. He'd obviously escaped Mom's grip up in New York. I wondered if Laura had been lucky enough to get away with him.

My mouth gaped into a yawn. Why was I naked? Oh, yeah. Forgot to pack pj's. I grabbed a terrycloth hotel robe, belting it tightly as I tried to clear my head. What the hell was Thomas doing here? I hadn't told anyone where I was going.

The pounding kept up a steady rhythm until I finally opened

the door. Thomas pushed his way in and pulled me into a bear hug. When he let go, I saw Laura was behind him, looking much less perturbed. Guess she'd managed to elude Mom, too. I waved at her, and smiled at both of them. Laura waved and smiled back, giving me an apologetic shrug.

"What's up, guys?" I said, trying to sound a lot more chipper than I felt.

"Damn it, Ciel, you can't just disappear. You *have* to tell some-body where you are," Thomas said.

"My cell phone is charged. You could have called."

Thomas made what I think of fondly as his "apoplectic eyes." Laura patted his arm (or else she was trying to keep him from throttling me with it, one or the other) and said, "Well, sugar, that only works if you *answer* your phone."

I peeked behind me at the nightstand. Saw the light on my phone indicating a missed call. Checked the log. Okay, fourteen missed calls (none of them Billy, not that I was searching for his name), seven of which were from either Thomas or Laura.

"Sorry. I guess I was really tired. Um, do I want to listen to any of your voice mails?"

Laura glanced at Thomas and suppressed a smile. "Well, the first few are perfectly polite. Then I'm afraid they get"—she glanced at her husband, holding back a smile—"repetitive."

Thomas quelled her with a look. "Sis, why are you staying in a hotel when we live in town? When Mark called looking for you after your condo was broken into, I was terrified you'd been taken. And if you think I ever want to explain to Mom and Dad—"

"Wait . . . *what*? Broken into? When?" I said. Shit. What was going on? I needed coffee. Which, I belatedly remembered, I wasn't going to get.

"Last night." He looked at me closely, no doubt noting my shock with his super-lawyer observational skills. "After you left, I presume."

"How did Mark know?" I said, defaulting to the trivial because it was easier than dealing with the fact that my condo had fuck-ing *been broken into.* "Did he have someone watching me?"

"After what he told me happened in Houston? Of course he did. The problem was, the guy he had watching you took ill— violently—and there was a space of time before his replacement was there. It must have happened then. And, yes, that makes the whole thing even more suspicious—Mark thinks his guy might've been poisoned somehow."

"Jesus," I said. "Is he going to be all right?"

"He won't be running any races for a while, but he'll recover."

Thank God. "So, if the guy didn't tell him, how did Mark find out?"

"The security system routes directly to the Agency. And before you get all huffy about being monitored, it's been that way since Mark was my roommate there. I'm the one who asked him to keep it when you moved in."

"It's the same at our house," Laura added quickly, in case I thought I was being singled out.

"But how did you find me here? I haven't been microchipped, have I?" I said, only half joking.

"Tempting," Thomas said under his breath.

Laura shrugged. "I tracked your last credit card transaction— here, at this hotel, strangely enough. Oh, and your phone. GPS is a wonderful thing. Don't be mad, hon. I had to do it to calm your brother down."

I glared at Thomas. It had no effect. "Fine. You found me. Now you can take me to my condo so I can see if anything is missing."

Thomas and Laura looked at each other, doing that annoying nonverbal communication thing couples do.

"What?" I said.

Thomas sighed. He's not normally a big sigher. "Not a good idea right now, sis."

"Why not? Look, I get it. You're trying to shield me from the trauma. But my place has been broken into before—I know what to expect."

"Ciel, hon, they torched it after they broke in," Laura said gently. "There's not a lot left to go through."

I froze. Stared at her for a second, then looked to Thomas for confirmation. He nodded, a grim look on his face. "You can see why we were concerned when we couldn't reach you."

I nodded numbly. There had to be questions I should be asking, but I couldn't think of them. "I don't have any pets," was all I could think to say. "That's good, right? It's the only thing that really matters. I mean, I've thought about getting a dog, or maybe a cat would be better—I love animals—but it wouldn't really be fair, would it? Since I'm gone"—damn, why couldn't I stop babbling? The clinical part of my brain knew it was the shock, but I still couldn't shut up—"so much for work and all. Of course, I could always get a turtle. They probably don't care much if you're not there all the time. But they're not good cuddlers, and I think if I had a pet I'd really like one I could cuddle . . ."

Laura put an arm around my shoulder and gently herded me toward the bathroom. "Come on, sugar, let's get you dressed. Tom, why don't you wait in the lobby? We'll be down in a bit."

"Yeah. Right. I'll give Mark a call and let him know Ciel is okay. Sis, do you want me to call Billy?"

"No!" I said, stopping. *God, not Billy.* I couldn't deal with him right now. I pulled myself up straight, shrugging off Laura's arm. "He's, um, busy with something . . . one of his . . . he can't be reached. I'll take care of it later. Laura, go on down with Tom. I'll throw some clothes on and meet you in the lobby. And then I'm going straight to my condo."

"Can't. Mark wants you kept out of sight for now," Thomas said.

"What the hell? Why?"

"I'm sure he has a good reason, sugar," Laura said. "And I'm sure he'll tell us what it is when we see him later," she added when I was about to protest again. I recognized the spook stubbornness in her eyes and dropped it. For the moment.

It didn't look too bad from the outside, only some broken windows and water-streaked soot stains. And, of course, the crime scene tape. Because arson. I was still trying to wrap my head around the fact that somebody had intentionally set my home on fire.

The fire had apparently been contained by strong firewalls, so my neighbors' homes had suffered only minor damage, thank God. At least I didn't have to add guilt to the host of emotions I was feeling.

I had convinced Thomas and Laura I'd never be able to relax until I'd seen it for myself. I was wearing the aura of one of my old high school teachers—Mrs. Denton, a young first-year teacher I'd had when I was a senior, who now lived overseas—so technically "I" was out of sight.

Thomas returned to where Laura and I were standing on the sidewalk in front of the building. At one time it had been a huge single-family home—a mansion, really—but some enterprising owner along the way had converted it into four two-story units, the front right of which was owned by Thomas and rented by me. (He was planning to buy up the other units as they became available—Thomas collects real estate the way I collect Spiderman comic books.)

"I spoke with someone from the firehouse. There's fire damage both up- and downstairs, and all up the stairwell, but the floor joists seem to be sound. There's a lot of smoke and water damage throughout. Once we get clearance from a structural engineer, I'll have the place gutted and redone. Sis, you can stay with us in the meantime."

And watch you two brimming over with joy as Laura's belly grows? Yeah, no thanks.

"Are the stairs still there?" I asked.

"I assume so. Why?"

"Good. I'll be back in a minute." I took off, slipping under the crime scene tape and through the door that was no longer capable of closing all the way.

"Ciel, wait—we can't go in!" Thomas came after me, but not until after he admonished Laura to stay where she was, so I got a pretty good head start.

It was the smell more than anything. Smoke, acrid and biting, mixed with the chemical fumes from burnt paint and synthetic carpet, overlaid with a dank, *wet* smell that made me want to gag. That, or the fact that if I hadn't been running away from my memories of Billy I would be dead right now, as charred as all my belongings. Somebody wanted me dead, and I didn't even know why. The very randomness of the act made me feel more vulnerable.

Holding one hand over my nose and mouth, I hurried up the stairs and into my room.

"Hey!" Thomas hollered from the front hall.

"Up here!" I ignored the scorched, sodden mess that was my bed and went straight for my burnt-up dresser. Yanked open the top drawer—the front of it splintered in my hands—and started riffling through wet underwear and bras.

Thomas came to a halt at the door to my room. "Sis, don't be ridiculous. We'll go shopping, get you some new clothes. You can't save those."

My hand finally hit wet velvet. I squeezed the small jewel box tightly, sending up a wordless prayer before I opened it. I held back a sob of relief when I saw it there, unharmed.

The pin, made of white gold and diamonds and shaped like an open parachute, had been a gift from Billy after my first terrifying ride on his airplane. It was his way of telling me he'd always be there, providing security for me as I faced my fears and tried new things. Shutting the case and enclosing it in both hands, I held it to my waist, as if it could magically shelter the new life growing there.

I felt Thomas's hands on my shoulders. "Stupid risk, sis, sentiment or not. He could have always gotten you another one."

Somehow I didn't think so. "Come on. Let's get out of here," I said.

"This is the surveillance footage from the gas station three blocks from Ciel's condo," Mark said.

We were at my office, on the third floor of the building that housed my brother's law firm (he owned it, of course), staring intently at my laptop screen. Thomas and Laura were with us. Thomas had tried to assure me his security system would have alerted him if anything were amiss, but I'd insisted on going there to see for myself it was okay. It wasn't until I was seated behind my antique wooden desk that I stopped shaking on the inside. I drew comfort from its solidness, its age, its aura of permanence. Not everything had been ripped away from me. Something of mine was left, a small cave I could crawl into, where I could lick my wounds.

While we'd waited for Mark, I'd asked Thomas to put my pin in his office safe, fairly sure there was no place more secure in the whole city. If he and Laura thought it odd for me to put it away, they didn't say anything. Maybe they figured wanting to protect it was an aftereffect of the shock of seeing the rest of my possessions ruined by fire, smoke, and water. Hell, maybe it was. All I knew was, I couldn't wear it anymore, and I couldn't let it go.

We all leaned closer to my laptop. I squinted at the grainy, black-and-white image. The camera was focused on the area in front of the cashier, but in the background you could see two of the pumps.

"There," Mark said when a man approached one of the pumps on foot. He filled a gas can, using a credit card at the pump to pay.

"Is that . . . ?" I said.

The man turned his head enough to catch his profile.

"Keep watching," Mark said. The man glanced toward the camera, affording us a brief view of his whole face.

"Loughlin torched my condo?" I said. "But why?"

"Don't know, Howdy. We can't find any connection between him and you, other than your client. We've already put extra people on Dr. Carson, of course, but when we add Mason and Jenny together with Aunt Helen, it's starting to seem more like it might be some sort of vendetta against adaptors. I don't know if he has something particular against you, or if you're just next on his list." He looked me right in the eye. "I want somebody on you at all times. I don't want you out in public without armed protection."

I thought about protesting—it was almost a reflex at this point to argue my ability to take care of myself—but frankly, after seeing my condo, I was feeling a tad vulnerable. And, you know, not stupid. Plus, as much as I wanted to hyperventilate whenever I thought about it, there was the little bun in my oven to consider. So I nodded my agreement.

"What about Thomas and Laura?" I said.

"I've put people on everyone in your extended family, as well as everyone who attended the service. As for Tom and Laura . . ." He looked at Laura with a small smile.

Laura cleared her throat. "I'm actually pretty good at taking care of myself. I was trained by the best, you know." She grinned at Mark, and glanced at Thomas.

"But you're . . ." I said. "I mean, didn't the doctor tell you not to, um, kick people's asses?"

Laura laughed. "She said I was in great shape, and that unless I experienced any unusual difficulties, it was fine to continue my usual physical regimen for the time being."

Huh. Good to know. I was going to assume I'd get much the same advice when I got around to seeing a doctor. Which I supposed I'd have to do soon, but frankly right now catching a killer was a little more pressing.

Laura patted Thomas's arm. "And I promise I'll watch out for this guy."

Kudos to my big brother for not wincing at the idea of his pregnant wife guarding him. Clenched his teeth a little, but didn't full-on wince. "Mark, remember when you said you could get me a gun and a permit and I told you not to be ridiculous? I changed my mind," he said.

Mark nodded. "Done. Howdy, you still have yours, or was it lost in the fire?"

"I left it with Billy when I went to Houston." I didn't even trip over Billy's name. I couldn't stop my heart from beating faster, but my high collar probably covered the pulse in my neck.

"I'll get you one for D.C."

"No need," I said. "I'm going back to New York tonight." Because if I remained in D.C., Thomas would expect me to stay with him and Laura, and I couldn't. I would adjust to being around their happy family unit eventually, but I wasn't there yet.

"What have you found out from John Smith?" I said. "I'm assuming that isn't his real name."

"You can't assume anything in this business, Howdy," Mark said, his tone seasoned with a touch of teacher, which he then softened with a smile. "Though in this case you're right. Ivan Petrovich is a second generation Russian American whose family never quite assimilated. If they're as tied to the Russian mafia—Bratva—as we suspect, there isn't much hope we can scare him into talking. Nothing we can do to him would be worse than what Bratva would do if he gives away anything."

"Great. So he's useless."

Mark shrugged. "Maybe, maybe not. If I can manage a moment alone with him—unofficially—he might be more forthcoming. In the meantime, I'm heading back to New York myself. You can come with me on the company plane. That way I won't have to put another man on you until we're there. Maybe Billy, if he's finished with his business. Do you know if he will be?"

"I, uh, don't know for sure. His business sounded pretty open-ended." Ha. Totally true. I only hoped I didn't look as uncomfortable saying it as I felt.

Mark cocked his head, a question in his eyes. I ignored it.

"You're with me, then," he said at last. "We'll leave as soon as you're packed."

I quirked my mouth. "Ready when you are. Everything I have is in my carry-on in Thomas's trunk." An awful thought occurred to me. "*Shit!*"

Three sets of alarmed eyes drilled into me.

"What?" Mark said. "Tell me."

I sank back into my cushy leather desk chair and let the misery engulf me. "I have to go *shopping.*"

Chapter 15

"Do you want to stop by Billy's and pick up your gun before I take you to your parents' place?" Mark said, after we left the airport in a hot yellow Porsche 911, top up in deference to the subfreezing temperature. (Mark changed cars all the time. I thought he must have some sort of secret goal to get through every make and model in existence. Well, except a Yugo. I couldn't picture him in a Yugo.)

The plane ride hadn't been as awkward as I'd feared. There were several other agents with us—reinforcements to supplement the ones already guarding all the people who'd attended Aunt Helen's funeral—so Mark couldn't ask me any probing personal questions. Bonus: I'd had plenty of time to concoct natural-sounding answers to things he might be tempted to ask once we were alone, so I was ready for this one.

"I had a voice message from James." Which I'd finally gotten around to listening to. He'd asked how I was doing (in a rather pointed way) and said to call him as soon as my job allowed. "Billy left the gun with him when he went to Houston. I can pick it up tomorrow. You can drop me at Brian's."

Mark nodded. "Don't you think your parents will want you with them?"

"You know how Mom will get when she hears about my condo. I'm too tired for frantic mothering tonight. I'll have more energy to face her tomorrow," I said.

"And Brian's couch is more comfortable than James's futon?"

I laughed. "Not really, but James and Devon have already put in their time babysitting me. It's Bri's turn. Unless he has a new girl I'm not aware of?" Brian was forever drifting in and out of relationships, apparently addicted to the bloom of fresh romance. He wasn't promiscuous for promiscuity's sake—as near as I could tell, he honestly thought he was in love every time.

"No, he's on his own for now. I've asked him to swear off the groupies until after we find Loughlin. He'll probably be happy for your company. But maybe you'd better call and give him a chance to get rid of anything incriminating."

I grinned. Like a lot of musicians, Brian did tend to indulge in recreational "creativity enhancement" (aka smoking weed) on occasion, but he wasn't a pothead by any stretch. "I gave him a heads-up while you were pulling the car around. Anyway, he keeps it pretty well hidden ever since Mom stopped by unexpectedly with a pot of calamari noodle soup when he was sick. She thought it was dried oregano and added it to the soup before she left."

Mark chuckled. "I'm surprised it bothered him."

"It probably wouldn't have if he could tolerate Mom's calamari soup. As it was, he claims it was a waste of—and I'm quoting here—some 'really good shit.'"

Another chuckle from Mark as he expertly negotiated through

traffic—honestly, it was almost a relaxing ride—and then, out of left field, he said, "You gonna tell me what's up with Billy?"

My stomach clenched. "What do you mean?"

"He's not answering my calls. I haven't been able to track him by other means either. Which means he's purposely avoiding me. I'm curious as to why, since I can't think of anything I've done to offend him"—he gave me a meaningful look—"lately."

Crap. So not ready to deal with this. And I couldn't pretend everything was fine, not with Mark and his super-spy senses. I'd have to be straight with him.

"It has nothing to do with you." Okay, maybe not totally straight. But only slightly bent, so almost as good. "It's me. And I'd really, *really* appreciate it if you'd give me some time to work things out with him before you dig into it any further. Please."

He glanced at me (he never took his eyes off the road for long when he was driving). I could tell he was dying to ask more. "All right. As long as he's not in any kind of trouble. I hope you guys work it out soon, though, because I could sure use his help with Loughlin."

An awful thought struck me, one my mind had been too tangled with other thoughts to contemplate. "You don't think Loughlin, or someone he's working with, might have . . . I mean, Loughlin knows Billy's face from the funeral, and after Billy chased him at the museum . . ." I couldn't finish. My mouth was too dry.

Mark reached over the stick shift and covered one of my hands (which were currently gripping my knees tightly enough to leave bruises) with his own. His felt so warm I knew mine must be freezing. "Billy can take care of himself. There is no scenario I can imagine where Alec Loughlin could get the jump on him."

I nodded stiffly, needing to believe it. *Damn.* What I needed was to *do* something. "Yeah. You're right. Look, I'm available, even if Billy isn't. Let me help. I think I proved I'm capable in Houston."

"You did great in Houston, Howdy. I'm proud of you. But your skill set isn't—yet—up to Billy's. Not nearly."

I couldn't exactly deny that. "I might not be in his league, but I'm better than nothing," I said.

"Don't take this the wrong way, but at this point you're not. If I'm worried about you in the field, that's a distraction for me. And distractions are dangerous."

I might have argued more, but it occurred to me—once again— that, as much as I'd welcome a distraction of my own, it wasn't only about me anymore.

Brian was ready for me, having ordered two large pizzas, one pepperoni, one Hawaiian. Not an anchovy in sight. Perversely, that brought a lump to my throat. Which made me feel like such an idiot I hit a pillow when Brian wasn't looking. Remarkably cathartic, hitting things. Boxing might be worth continuing.

Mark had walked me into the Williamsburg apartment, leaving his car under the watchful eye of a member of the security team assigned to Brian. He hadn't stayed, only told me to tell Billy to call him if I heard from him.

"Hey, sis," Brian called from his tiny kitchen, "what do you want to drink? I have PBR, a couple of craft IPAs, and some fancy imported crap Thomas left here last time he visited."

"Water for me, thanks," I said, ripping the tops off the pizza boxes so we could use them as plates. "Bring some napkins, too, okay?"

He joined me on his lumpy sofa (honestly, he could afford better, but it wouldn't jibe with his image of himself as a poor indie musician), bringing a PBR, a generic bottled water, and a handful of paper towels. "Hey, just like old times, huh?"

I used to crash on Brian's couch after going to his shows, mainly to save him the trouble of seeing me all the way back to Mom and Dad's. Not that *I* expected him to, but Mom and Dad would have killed him if he'd put me in a taxi on my own in the middle of the night back then.

"Yeah," I said, smiling at his open and friendly face. "Fun. Thanks again for letting me stay over."

"No problem. Hell, I sure wouldn't want to tell Mom my place had been lit up." He looked at me thoughtfully, his pupils only slightly dilated. "You okay? Really? It can't be easy losing all your stuff."

I sighed. "It sucks. Still, it *is* only stuff, right? Nothing that can't be replaced."

"Good attitude, sis. Hey, you wanna stream a movie or something? I don't have a gig tonight."

"Or a date?" I teased. There were very few non-show nights Brian didn't spend with a girl.

He grinned. "Nah. Kirby dumped my ass. Said I wasn't 'evolved' enough for her."

I'd never even met Kirby. Just as well. It was hard enough to keep their names straight without having to worry about attaching faces to them. "Don't you usually have one or two waiting in the wings?"

"Mark asked me to give it a break. And a few nights off won't kill me. Frankly, I could use the rest."

If he were any other guy, I'd think he was kidding around, or maybe bragging. But not Brian—he was way too ingenuous.

I gave him a friendly shove. "Poor exhausted baby. Okay, what do you want to watch?"

He grinned. "I'm cool with chick flicks, if you want. See? I can be evolved."

Gah. Anything romantic would make me weepy for sure. "Yuck. No chick shit," I said.

"Well . . . I *was* going to watch a Three Stooges marathon . . ."

Slapstick wasn't really my thing, but if that's what he'd been planning, I wasn't going to spoil his evening. Besides, random wacky violence actually sounded pretty good. "Perfect," I said.

A few hours later I was convinced I'd been totally wrong in my earlier assessments of the Stooges. They were obviously comedic geniuses. I couldn't remember the last time I'd laughed so hard.

"This is brilliant!" I said, for probably the fifth time. "Curly's the sweetest, of course. Moe's grumpy, but he's *smart.* In his own way. And Larry is underrated—he's a lot deeper than he first appears."

"What about Curly Joe?" Brian asked seriously, like my opinion on the matter was the most important thing in the world.

"Let's pretend he never happened," I said, and giggled. "Maybe we can start an online petition. Get him removed from all things Stoogie."

"Dude! Fantastic idea. Let me get my laptop. We can start with a web page, and then see if we can get it linked to Reddit. We'll need the exposure."

I sat up straight. "Yes! Whoa. Bri. You know what we should

do? Call Sinead and Siobhan—they could design us an awesome website!" Lurking beneath Billy's sisters' excessive Doyle gorgeousness were the hearts and brains of dedicated Internet geeks.

"Great idea, sis!" He reached for his phone.

"Wait. Let's get something to eat first. I'm starving." And, boy, was I. Must be because I hadn't been eating much for the past few days, what with one worry and another. Funny, but it all seemed kind of fuzzy and far away now.

Brian looked at me kind of funny. "You ate three-quarters of a pizza."

"I know. I had some cookies, too, while you were in the bathroom. They tasted *sooo* good—did one of your girlfriends make them? If so, you should totally keep her."

Now he looked really strange. "Um, sis . . . which cookies did you eat?"

"The chocolate chip ones. Oh, no! Should I not have done that? Were you saving them for something special? Tell me they weren't your Christmas gift for Mom!"

He grinned. "Nope, definitely not a gift for Mom."

"What, then?"

"Ciel, those were my, um, *special* cookies."

I giggled. "Special? So, like, did you give them names? Did I eat little Sammy or Harry? Stephanie or Gloria?"

"You don't understand. They're the cookies I eat before I write a new song. The ones that *free my muse.*"

"Oh," I said. "OH! Oh, my God! Bri, are you telling me I ate *pot* cookies? That I'm *high*?"

He shrugged. "You are if you ate those cookies. Don't worry—it'll wear off by morning. And you'll probably sleep really well tonight."

Shit! I ran to the bathroom. Hung my head over the toilet and stuck two fingers down my throat. I had to get it out of me. I mean, my God, if alcohol was bad for the baby, I didn't even want to contemplate what pot would do to it.

Brian pulled my hand away from my face. "Stop. It won't do any good at this point. It's already in your system. Relax, sis. Honestly, it's no worse than the martinis and Manhattans you like— better, probably. It's organic."

"You don't understand!"

He nodded. "I think I might. Is this your first time? Man, I knew Mom and Dad were more protective of you than the rest of us—being a girl and the youngest, and all—but you went to college. How can anyone get through college without—"

"What? Of *course* it isn't my first time." Technically, it was my second. I hadn't cared for it much at the one party in college where I'd tried it, and I hadn't ever been inclined to indulge again. But I'd been smoking it that time. And honestly? I hadn't inhaled. (Yeah, I know. Me and Bill Clinton.) "This feels . . . different."

"You ever had an edible before?"

"Well . . . no. But it doesn't matter. I *can't* be high right now." I was pacing the apartment, shifting direction like a pinball every time I came up against a wall or large piece of furniture.

"Calm down. Like I said, it's no worse than a few drinks."

"But I'm not drinking anymore!"

"Whoa. Dude. That's extreme. Why not?"

I stopped pacing. Tried to gather my thoughts. "I, uh, I've been working out with Laura. Trying to get in shape, you know, learn to defend myself. I need to take care of my body."

There. At least I hadn't spilled the beans to another brother.

That showed presence of mind, right? Maybe I was only a teensy bit high.

Brian cocked his head, considering my revelation. "Cool. I get it. Your body's a temple. Well, you can start over tomorrow."

I swayed, overcome with a wave of dizziness.

Brian caught me, held me steady. "How many cookies did you eat?"

"I don't know . . . two, I think. Maybe three. They were really good." I gulped in air. "Oh, God, did I overdose? Don't tell Mom and Dad how I died! Make something up. Tell them . . . tell them I developed a sudden allergy to pineapple. Say it was anaphylactic shock from the Hawaiian pizza!"

Brian smiled, guiding me back over to the couch. He sat next to me and took both my hands in his. "Sis, listen to me. Sis! Are you listening?"

I slowed my breathing and stared at his face. "You have pretty eyes. They're like Mom's, only boy-ier . . . -ish . . . I mean, *man-ier*. Um, manlier."

His smile got bigger. "Thank you. Now listen. First of all, you didn't OD. It's practically impossible to eat—or smoke—enough pot to kill you. So you're safe. Understand? *Safe.*"

I nodded.

"Second, I'm right here with you, and I'm not going anyplace. You are not alone. Remember that if you start to feel paranoid."

I nodded again, comforted in spite of my swirling thoughts. "You're a good brother. You're my favorite, did I ever tell you that?"

"Why wouldn't I be? Thomas and James are workaholics. I'm the fun one." He winked.

"Bri? I don't think I'm having fun."

"I promise you will get through this. We'll watch more TV—

it'll keep you focused. Your choice. More Stooges? Oh, hey look—it's *A Christmas Story.*"

He'd stopped flipping through the channels at the Santa scene, which normally cracked me up, even if it was a little mean. Only this time all I could think of was sitting on Billy's lap at the mall, and how now he'd never tease me like that again. I laid my head on my brother's shoulder and closed my eyes, wishing I could shut out my thoughts as easily as I could the picture on the screen.

Chapter 16

I bummed a ride to my parents' house with one of the security guys (young, dark, hunky-homely, and, I was sure, very well armed). When I apologized for putting him out, he told me he was the one assigned to follow me anyway, and giving me a ride actually made his job easier.

As Brian had promised, I'd made it through my incredible-edible trip. A sneak check of the Internet on my phone while Brian was absorbed in Ralphie shooting his eye out with the Red Ryder BB gun had assured me I probably hadn't irreparably damaged the bun in my oven. Somewhere in the middle of the *Home Alone* marathon that followed *A Christmas Story*, I was finally able to sleep.

Brian woke me at noon, handed me a jug of orange juice (which, following his instructions, I guzzled, feeling better almost at once), and told me Mom had called, and wanted to know when I was coming over. I wasn't sure who told her I was in town. I suspected Thomas. He must not have told Mom about my condo, though, or she would have been pounding on Brian's door instead of calling him.

Now I'd have to tell my parents myself, without freaking Mom out. I took a deep breath and reached out to knock on the door, adding "new key" to the shopping list I had going in my head. Before I could lay knuckle to wood, the door swung open and I was pulled inside, into my mother's arms. Dad's arms followed, encircling us both, pulling us into the house and shutting the door behind us without letting go. Apparently they *did* know about my condo.

I held on tight, inhaling security along with the familiar scents of Mom's light floral cologne and Dad's spicy aftershave, flashing back to all the times I used to insert myself into one of their hugs when I was a kid.

"Ciel sandwich," I said, same as I always had. They squeezed tighter, same as they always had. Aurora and Patrick Halligan, the best parents on Earth. Or, as Billy used to tease when he saw this maneuver, the bread to my bologna.

I finally pulled myself away when a congregation of cats started slaloming between our legs. Mom shooed them away. "Sweetie, are you okay?" she said.

Dad waited expectantly for my answer. Seeing the love overshadowed by concern on both their faces squashed me harder than the group hug. "Guess you heard, huh?"

"Thomas told us everything this morning," Dad said. "He said you were absolutely fine, and since you got in so late you decided to stay with Brian, because you knew he'd still be up. He suggested we not wake you up too early, as he was sure you could use the sleep."

Mark must have let Thomas know my whereabouts. Trust Thomas to know the right thing to say to soothe the parents.

"You know you can always come here no matter how late, sweetie. We *want* you to disturb us," Mom said, picking up and petting the calico cat who'd returned and was rubbing itself against her legs. "We like to be disturbed, don't we, darling?" I wasn't sure whether she was talking to the cat or Dad.

"Haven't found new homes for Jenny's cats, I take it?" I said.

"Not yet, but I have feelers out. Nobody seems to want to adopt this close to Christmas." There was a crash in the living room. Mom looked heavenward and sighed. "There goes the tree again."

Dad perked up. "I'll take care of it. I just need to get a ceiling hook and some clear fishing line."

Mom took my hand and dragged me behind her. "Never mind that now, Patrick. I have lunch waiting in the kitchen. Ciel, honey, you still look peaky, and no wonder. Thank God you weren't at your condo when the fire started. I don't know what we would have done if . . ." She stopped and gathered me into another hug. "Never mind. You're fine and you're here. Let's eat."

"Give me a sec," I said, and ducked into the powder room. I dug out my phone and texted Thomas: *Thanks for breaking it to Mom and Dad for me. Know what? You're my favorite brother.*

He texted back within a minute: *Naturally. James always has his head in a test tube and Brian is forever plugged into an amp. (You're welcome.)*

My luck must have been turning, because the casserole Mom took out of the oven was her divine macaroni and cheese, my favorite. I dug into my heaping bowl of steamy, cheesy goodness (browned bread crumbs on top—yum!) with the gusto it deserved. The flavor carried pure love to my soul via my taste buds.

"Thanks, Mom. You're the best," I said, unabashedly talking

with my mouth full, knowing she was too happy at seeing me in one piece to call me on it.

"Oh, pish. I had it in the freezer," she said, removing the obese Siamese from the table. I'd been petting it with one hand while shoveling in my lunch with the other. "All I did was warm it up."

"Whenever you made it, it's still delicious—the best thing I've eaten in days," I said. "May I have some more, please?"

"Of course, sweetie. As much as you want." She beamed as she dished out more for Dad, too, who appreciated it every bit as much as I did.

I finished the second serving even faster than the first. Miraculously, I felt stuffed, but in a good way, not at all queasy, which I attributed to the legendary antinausea properties of pot. I wouldn't be adding it to my medicine cabinet, but hey, I might as well enjoy the effects while they lasted.

"Come on, sweetie," Mom said when I had scraped the last bit of melted cheese off the bottom of my bowl. "I have your room all ready for you. You can rest. Read, relax—whatever you like. We'll have hot cocoa by the fire later."

I groaned. "That sounds so good, Mom, but I can't. I have to go buy some clothes. Most of mine are unsalvageable."

Mom's eyes lit up. She was probably thrilled to have an excuse to take me shopping. "Come with me. Patrick, could you give the herd some tuna? I don't want them in the bedrooms."

Dad grabbed a can from the pantry and headed for the electric can opener, all four cats shadowing his every step, yowling at him to hurry it up already.

Mom led me upstairs, which was kind of weird. It wasn't like I didn't know where my room was. When she opened the door and let me in ahead of her, I realized why she'd come along. Laid out over my queen-size bed (which had replaced my twin canopy bed when Mom and Dad upgraded theirs to a king) were stacks of new clothes, their tags still attached. There were jeans and tees, sweaters (including a spectacularly tacky one emblazoned with what looked like the dogs-playing-poker picture, only with reindeer), blouses, skirts, dresses, underwear, bras . . . everything I could possibly need. Shoes, even. And some really kick-ass boots.

"But how . . . when . . . ?" I didn't know what to say.

"I did a little shopping this morning after Thomas called. It should all fit—I tried on everything except the underwear using your aura from the neck down."

Aurora Halligan, Power Shopper Extraordinaire. I threw my arms around her. "I don't have to go shopping! This is the best Christmas present ever!"

She patted my back. "Now, if you don't like something, leave the tag on it and I can return it tomorrow."

"Don't be silly—I love it all," I said. And I did. Right now I loved anything that meant I didn't have to try on clothes at stores crowded with impatient holiday shoppers. Even the tacky sweater.

"Ro! Ciel!" Dad's voice called from downstairs. "Mo and Liam are here."

Ack. I didn't know if I was ready to face Billy's parents. They'd probably ask about him, and what could I tell them? Sorry, but your son hightailed it when he found out I was pregnant, possibly by another man? A conversation I definitely did not want to have.

"You go ahead, Mom. I'll be right down after I change. Thanks again, for everything." I gave her another hug, and gently pushed her out the door.

I stripped quickly and pulled the tags off underwear, a bra, a white long-sleeved shirt, and jeans. The bra and jeans were a tiny bit snug. I made an adjustment down to my normal size, trying not to think about it, and topped it off with the tacky sweater (the card-playing reindeer stood out nicely against the bright green background), because I knew it would make Mom happy, and added the kick-ass boots. Those, I genuinely loved.

I didn't bother to concoct any fibs about Billy, because anything I said would depend on whether or not his parents had heard from him. I didn't want to trip myself up with contradictory lies.

They were all in the living room when I came down. Auntie Mo grabbed me into a hug, pressing my face against a sweater that rivaled mine for sheer kitsch. Hers had a Santa in overalls, standing in a garden, with "Hoe! Hoe! Hoe!" in a word bubble over his head. (Yes, he was holding the garden implement in question.) With her dark red hair and green eyes, she was looking more than ever like the young Maureen O'Hara she'd been named for.

"Ciel, honey, how are you? When I heard, I was so upset. Jesus God, it's bad enough having a crazy killer on the loose, but for someone to go after you, in your home . . . never mind that now. You're safe."

She handed me off to Uncle Liam, who enveloped me in strong arms that felt so much like his son's I almost couldn't let go. He didn't rush me. "There, pumpkin. It's all fine now. You're home." When I could tear myself away, he smiled at me with eyes as blue as Billy's and said, "If you get tired of the craziness over here, you know you always have a place with us. We're no less crazy, of course, but maybe for a change of pace."

"Here now, I've brought you something," Auntie Mo said. She handed me a large wrapped box. "It's your Christmas present from us, but we thought you could maybe use it now."

Grateful they hadn't said anything about Billy yet, I tore into my gift. I was thrilled to see a gorgeous, dark brown leather jacket that matched my new boots exactly, which I was quick to point out when I tried it on. It fit perfectly, even over my sweater.

"I was with Mo when she found it," Mom explained. "When I saw those boots this morning, I knew I had to get them."

"You look wonderful, sweetie pie," Dad said.

Uncle Liam nodded in agreement. "You'll knock my son flat when he sees you in that."

I tried hard to keep the smile from melting off my face, but I wasn't sure how successful I was. Not very, judging by the piercing look Auntie Mo was giving me.

"Speaking of Billy, we thought we might find him here with you," Auntie Mo said.

I cleared my throat. "Um, no. He"—I stuck my hands in the pockets of my snazzy new jacket and crossed my fingers—"got caught up on a lead. But don't worry, he's fine"—*I hope*—"and will be calling you soon, I'm sure."

Mom stepped up to defend Billy. "I know he'd be right here with you if he could. But helping Mark find whoever's responsible for all this is so important. That lunatic has to be caught before he can harm anyone else."

"Of course," Mo said, and smiled at me. "Sinead and Siobhan are making their armed keepers take them shopping tomorrow. I know they'd love for you to come along."

I stifled my impulse to say "No way in hell," which might be construed as rude. Instead, I said, "Do you think we should? With the murderer still out there, I mean?"

"Don't worry, you'll have lots of security, and you can always adapt," Mo said.

They didn't know Loughlin had somehow seen through my astronaut aura in Houston. Could he recognize adaptors, whether or not they were wearing another aura? Was that how he'd targeted Aunt Helen, Mason, and Jenny? I hesitated to mention the possibility without clearance from Mark, especially since we weren't absolutely certain Loughlin was responsible for the New York murders. Though, frankly, I thought it would be a damn big coincidence to swallow if it turned out he wasn't connected to them. But for now, I'd have to come up with another excuse.

"Uh . . ." I said (I know—so articulate), and cast a panicked look at my parents.

"It'll do you good to get out, sweetie," Mom said, benignly throwing me under the shopping bus. And to think, she'd come *that* close to making it to the top of my Saints on Earth list.

Tomorrow might be ruined . . . wait, was that harsh? Maybe "marred" would be a better word. Or "blemished." Tomorrow might be *blemished* by a dive into the retail maelstrom, but I still had the rest of today to take stock of my current state of affairs— ugh. Wrong word again. Not that my mix-up with Mark qualified as an "affair," but still. The current state of my *life*—and figure out what to do next.

As much as I loved my mom and dad, hanging around the house with them was not conducive to clear thinking. If I stayed, it wouldn't be long before I was afloat on a sea of hot chocolate and Christmas carols, jabbing my fingers with needles while stringing yards of popcorn for Mom's newest tree. (She'd finally found one skinny enough to fit in the main-floor powder room, and was sure "old fashioned and homey" was the proper theme for it.

Me, I thought empty cobs would be more appropriate to the setting.)

I needed to be outside, where my head was open to the sky and my thoughts weren't ricocheting off walls. A long walk was definitely on the agenda. Outside, with no shoppers, so Central Park.

Mom wasn't thrilled with my plan, but she, having raised me, was perfectly aware of my claustrophobic tendencies. "Make sure your bodyguard sticks close," she said, and handed me a bag of Christmas cookies to give to him. "And here, use this aura—I already ran it by Mark and he approved it." She called up a young Japanese woman about my size, so my clothes would fit, and pronounced me "absolutely adorable" when I reproduced the energy.

After what happened in Houston, I wasn't certain a different aura would make a difference if Loughlin came after me, but I sure as heck wasn't going to worry Mom by mentioning it. And if Mark had approved it, I supposed it couldn't hurt.

Mom filled the few minutes necessary to transfer a secondhand aura with happy chatter about the impending addition to the family. Every time she said "grandbaby" I winced inside, but kept any external reaction from showing on my new Asian façade.

"Okay, Mom, got it. Better get going—my keeper is waiting."

Mr. Homely But Hunky wasn't surprised to see me in a new aura. He, along with the others on the various security details, had been read in to our special situation by Mark, who considered all our watchers to be part of the need-to-know gang. I directed him to James's place first, so I could pick up my gun. It was all well and good having a bodyguard, but I'd still feel better with my own weapon.

Devon answered the door. (I could have let myself in using a partial aura of James's palm, but I didn't want to be rude.) There was no one in the corridor, so I switched back to my own aura as he opened the door.

"Ciel! Come in, come in. James, your sister's here!" Avid curiosity lit Devon's eyes, making them appear a darker violet than usual. I knew I wouldn't be getting away without answering questions.

"Hey, homeless person," James said, pulling me into a brief hug.

I quirked my mouth. "Hey yourself. Fortunately, thanks to Mom, I'm a homeless person with a snazzy wardrobe." I pirouetted, opening my jacket to show the sweater.

"Oh, my God, I *love* it!" Devon said, laying his gay on heavily. He mainly did that to get a rise out of James, who was doing his manful best to ignore him.

"You do? Are you blind?" I said.

Devon lifted his lips in a droll smile. "The jacket. Not the sweater. Though it's kitschy-cute, I suppose, in its own special way."

James looked at him with an evil glint I rarely saw in my staid brother's eyes. "I can't wait to see what Mom got you for Christmas."

A look of horror flitted over Devon's pretty face, but he recovered quickly. "I'm absolutely sure I'll adore whatever Ro picks out for me."

"Uh-huh. But will you wear it?" I said.

"Only when your parents invite us for dinner . . . and then only if we're eating in," he said. "Now come, Ciel. Sit, sit. We have so much to talk about."

"I can't stay. I only came for the gun."

James retrieved it, along with its pocket holster, from the coffee table. He hesitated before handing it over. "Sis, have you . . . ?" He cleared his throat, a small blush blooming on his cheeks.

"I'm not worried about my period anymore," I said before he could ask me about a pregnancy test, forcing a big, relieved smile. Convoluted, maybe, but true. I *wasn't* worried about my period anymore, because I was no longer expecting it to happen. But I didn't want them worrying about a pregnant me. Time enough to deal with that later.

Their smiles were much more genuine than mine.

Devon clapped his hands. "Let's celebrate! We have ice cream . . . and chocolate . . . and potato chips . . . and bourbon!"

In other words, everything a woman on her period could want. I couldn't help but laugh. "Tempting, but I have to go. Next time, okay?"

Back in the car with Mr. HBH (who'd told me his name was Carl), I thought maybe it hadn't been fair to run out on James and Devon, considering how sweet they'd been to me when the emotional time bomb inside me had exploded. But if I'd stayed any longer, I would have wound up telling them the truth about Billy, and I couldn't. Not yet.

Part of me was holding out hope he'd contact me, that he'd apologize for flaking out on me, and tell me everything would work out.

That he still loved me . . .

Pathetic, Ciel.

A more realistic hope would be that we could discuss the situation rationally, and present our breakup to our families in a way that wouldn't cause anyone to get out a shotgun. Bonus points if we could manage to leave Mark out of it entirely, because, yeah, awkward.

"Where to?" Carl said.

I thought about it. In my current mood, I didn't think a mere walk was going to cut it. I felt the need for speed. (Normally, I'd rather yank my eyelashes out individually with tweezers than quote a Tom Cruise movie, but if a quote fits, it fits.) Running for any length of time wasn't an option, not with the kick-ass boots, no matter how comfortable.

"Do you know how to ice skate?" I said.

His forehead wrinkled as his eyebrows rose. I could see him struggle with the question. "I grew up down south. I've never tried," he finally admitted. "But I'm great at Rollerblading."

Huh. This could be entertaining, I thought. I really shouldn't . . . oh, hell. I needed the distraction. "Close enough," I said.

Chapter 17

The milky sun was low in the sky by the time we got to the Wollman Rink in Central Park. It was crowded—it always was this time of year—but at least there was no wait, thanks to the weather. Freezing drizzle isn't nearly as picturesque as snow, but the hardiest tourists were there in spite of it, determined to check another must-do off their Christmas-in-Manhattan lists.

"So, you sure you want to do this, Carl?" I asked as we laced up rental skates that smelled strongly of antifungal spray. I tried not to think of how many feet had worn them before. "You can always watch from the side, you know."

He shrugged, and swiped a gloved hand over the reddened tip of his nose. "How different can it be from Rollerblading?"

"The balance is similar, so you should adjust fairly quickly," I said. Honesty compelled me to add, "Or you would, if those weren't rentals, which are by definition lousy. But at least it looks like they've been sharpened recently—that will help. Good luck." I grinned.

He stayed upright on wobbly ankles for a good thirty seconds before falling on his ass, whereupon he looked so shocked I had a hard time not laughing. When I circled him and asked if he needed help, his surprise was quickly replaced by a look of profound determination. He waved me off. Spooks. They all think they can do anything.

Then again, it only took three more falls before he was gliding along like he'd been raised on skates, so maybe his confidence wasn't misplaced. Once I was sure he was steady, I took off, increasing my speed as much as I could without triggering a reprimand from the staff. The frigid air stung my cheeks and made me puff out clouds of visible breath, which entertained me as much as an adult as it had when I was a kid. I used to like to pretend I was a dragon, breathing fire as I flew over tiny villages below.

Carl stuck close to me for several circuits. I was hitting the groove—the sweet spot where the combination of physical exertion and sensory input didn't leave room for intrusive thoughts—when a budding wannabe hockey player darted between us and practiced his hip check on my skating partner. The boy, from what I could tell as he whizzed past, looked to be twelve or thirteen, prime age for ice-rink assholery. Carl went down hard. I turned my feet sideways, skidded to a quick stop, and circled back around to help him. Again, he waved me off. Sheesh. Spooks.

I left him to get himself up, and went after the kid instead, intending to give the little shit a piece of my mind about rink manners. Judging by how swiftly and gracefully he was maneuvering around the other skaters, it hadn't been an accident.

I caught him three-quarters of the way around, hooking elbows with him and slowing him down to a crawl. "Hey, brat, what you did wasn't funny. It was rude, and downright dangerous. How about we skate over to my friend so you can apologize."

He gave me a coolly appraising once-over. "You give me five bucks and I'll say 'sorry' as nice as can be."

"What? Why the he—um, heck, would I do that?"

The delinquent shrugged. "Same reason the guy gave me ten to trip him to begin with?"

Shit. I whipped my head around. "What guy? Where?"

"Dunno, lady. Give me twenty bucks and maybe I can find him for you."

I let the juvie go and skated toward where Carl had fallen. He wasn't there. I spun slowly in space, scanning the crowd on the ice. Three guesses how many guys there were with dark jackets and black knit hats exactly like Carl's.

But only one was being half-led, half-carried out of the rink by two staffers on the far side of the rink. Why was Carl's head listing to one side when he'd been fine a minute ago, right after he'd fallen? Head injuries were funny things—you could seem okay one minute, and be dead the next.

Shit. I took off after them, cutting straight across the ice, trying my best to avoid the other skaters. I sent one middle-aged woman spinning, hollering a hasty "Sorry!" It was answered with a snarled "Up yours!" (Civility is not every New Yorker's strong suit.) I was about ten yards from the exit when I was hooked through my elbow in much the same manner as I'd latched onto the juvie.

My trajectory was altered. A large man eased me back into the clockwise circle of skaters. I tried to yank myself free, but gave up when I felt something hard poking me low in the ribs. I kept skating. My first thought, stupidly enough, was, *If this asshole puts a hole my new jacket I'm going to kill him.*

My second thought: he was holding me too close for me to get to the gun in my pocket. *Damn it!*

I looked up. The bottom half of his face was covered with a black felted-wool scarf, and his eyes were partially obscured by the thick black frames of his glasses. Even with his face obscured, I could tell I didn't know him. I'd never before seen eyes so flat black you couldn't even discern a pupil. Against the pasty backdrop of his complexion, they were creepy as all get-out.

The sinking sensation in my stomach made me fairly certain it hadn't been staffers leading Carl off the ice after all. "Who the hell are you, and what have you done to my friend?" I said, anger keeping my fear temporarily at bay.

The first sound I heard out of him was an ugly laugh. "You can scratch him off your list of worries," he said, with a voice so low-pitched it wouldn't surprise me if elephants at the zoo could detect it.

I stifled my immediate urge to ask him if he'd ever sung "Ol' Man River" from *Show Boat*, because, yeah, it was an absurd question under the circumstances. One of my brain's crazy defense mechanisms to keep me from being overwhelmed with worry about Carl. If he was hurt, or worse, because of me—

Stop. Stay focused or you'll be in the same boat. Fat lot of good you'll do Carl then.

"What do you want from me?"

"I want you to come with me quietly," he said.

Yeah, right. My position might be precarious—assuming it *was* a weapon poking my ribs—but I was at least smart enough to know it was better to remain in public, with a lot of witnesses, than to let him get me alone somewhere.

"Not gonna happen, asshole." I tried again to pull away, but he was gripping my upper arm too tightly. His other hand shoved the weapon harder into me.

"Hey, watch the coat, you shit-eating dickwad."

Yeah, I know. The stress-language thing. I was probably going to have to learn to control my mouth after—

Argh! Ciel, not now!

If anything, he jabbed harder. I definitely felt a point now.

"Look, I don't know who you think I am, but you're obviously mistaken," I said, toning my voice back down to "reasonable." It was worth a try.

"I know who you're *not*," he said with another blast of ugly laughter. "You're *not* an astronaut."

Crap. He'd connected me to Dr. Phil?

"How do you *know* that?" I asked in frustration, not expecting him to answer.

But he did. He jerked his head toward the skimpy crowd of people on the sidelines. "*He* told me."

I glanced to the side. Alec Loughlin stood with the other spectators, watching us. My vertebrae lined up like a stack of ice cubes. Jesus. He really *could* tell an adaptor when he saw one. But *how*?

I might be able to get away if I made a big enough ruckus, but who was to say this guy wouldn't cut off my screams with a stab to my kidney? I happened to be even fonder of my kidney than I was of my coat. And even if I managed to get away from the asshole who'd apparently been sent to grab me for Loughlin, how was I going to avoid someone who could see through my auras?

The exit was approaching too fast. I could *not* let this bass-voiced moron get me to it. If he was going to hurt me—or kill me—he could damn well do it in front of everyone.

I stuck my foot out to the side, tripping him.

The good news was, he let go of me. The bad news: I spun out and hit the ice, landing on my back. Didn't skid far before he came down on top of me, his weapon—a fat-handled ice pick, I now saw all too clearly—still gripped in one hand.

If I could keep him down until a rink monitor got there, maybe I'd stand a chance. Unfortunately, Creepy Eyes recovered from his fall almost at once. Unless I could pull myself out from under him as he tried to stand, I was as trapped as ever.

Hell, he might decide to kill me right on the spot. He was good enough on the ice to stab me and get the hell out before anyone official knew what had happened. If he chose a spot covered by my clothes—basically, everything except my face—it would take a while before someone realized I wasn't just stunned from the fall. I knew from watching way too much television crime drama that lethal wounds from an ice pick didn't tend to bleed much. (I vowed inwardly to stop watching those shows—some shit you didn't need in your head.)

In the two seconds it took for that to go through my mind, he'd brought the pick close to my chest—right about heart level—and bared his teeth in a cheap imitation of a smile his scarf, unfortunately, no longer covered. Evidently the same scenario had occurred to him. He got his feet under him, ready to flee as soon as the deed was done.

It would take significant force to jab an ice pick through the leather of my jacket, no matter how sharp it was. Before he got his weight behind him enough to press down on it, I pulled my knees toward my chest, as I had with Mark during our lesson. I pushed with all my might, thinking to repeat the same maneuver and make a similar, if slipperier, getaway. But he was too heavy. I couldn't get any purchase on the ice with my back. His way-too-long arms still held the ice pick firmly against my chest, his black eyes glinting with his intention.

"So long, bitch," he said, and bore down on me with all his weight.

The leather wasn't going to hold much longer. I had seconds at best. One thing crystallized for me in that moment: I would do anything to stay alive. Anything.

I gave one last mighty heave with my legs, pushing up his torso instead of back against him. My blades slid on the drizzle-slick Gore-Tex of his coat. I tilted both toes inward, kicking up with as much momentum as I could. I felt a burst of something—relief or satisfaction, maybe both—when one blade caught his cheek and nose and the other sliced a ragged gash on the side of his neck.

The blood spurted over my legs, onto my face, a fountain of red heat blinding me, clogging my nose with a sickly metallic smell. The clinical part of my brain told me I'd severed his carotid artery. I clamped my mouth shut. Too late. I could taste it anyway.

I completed the backward roll I'd inadvertently started. Wound up on my knees, gasping for air, staring at the creepy man bleeding out all over the ice in front of me. As the black-red pool grew, steaming against the ice, it was all I could do not to scream out my primal rush of victory.

I killed a man.

The words tapped at my head like inside-out water torture.

Aside from a few monosyllabic responses to essential questions (like whether or not I was hurt), I didn't say a word to the police until Mark got to the station. The medics had examined me at the scene and released me to the cops with the caveat to keep me warm and watch for signs of shock. One of them had done some sort of rapid-result AIDS test on the man and told me it was negative.

He said the risk to me was low, but I could have myself tested in a few months if I was concerned. I'd nodded my understanding, frankly numb to any new worry.

I'd called Mark as soon as I'd been given access to a phone. Not only was he the only one I could think of who could possibly help me in a situation like this, he was also the only one who might understand what I'd done.

Once upon a time, I would have called Billy before anyone, trusting him to get me out of any mess I'd landed in. But obviously it wasn't true anymore. So . . . Mark.

My God, I killed a man. I really killed a man.

The burner phone I'd been carrying was confiscated, along with my gun. I hadn't been carrying my own phone—or any identification—because it wouldn't match the Japanese aura I was wearing. The gun, coupled with my lack of ID and my unwillingness to talk for fear of digging myself deeper into the hole I was in, was why the police were holding me. All I'd said to Mark on the station phone was, "Howdy. I need your help." Then I'd handed the phone to the officer and let him explain where I was, trusting my hint was enough for him to figure out who I was regardless of my different voice.

I killed a man . . . I killed a man . . . I killed . . .

Mark came into the small, dimly lit room where I'd been placed for questioning after showering and changing into a set of tan scrubs they must have kept handy for occasions like this one. They were too big, but at least it wasn't an orange jumpsuit, and infinitely preferable to my bloodstained clothing, which had been bagged as evidence. Strangely, it was the thought of never wearing the ugly sweater again that almost unleashed a flood of tears. But I'd held them back.

I killed a man . . . killed . . . killed . . .

"Who are you?" Mark asked as soon as we were alone. I wasn't sure how he'd swung it, unless he'd shown them his super-secret spy credentials, or maybe told them he was my lawyer.

I assumed he was referring to my aura. "I don't know," I said. Mom hadn't given me a name to go with it, never dreaming it would prove necessary, I supposed.

"Howdy," he said, adding only a hint of a question to it.

I nodded once.

"Show me," he said, ever cautious.

I flashed my own eyes at him briefly, throwing in a few freckles for good measure.

His face hardened, lips set in a grim line. "Hang tight. I'm getting you out of here right now."

"Wait," I said as he turned. "Is Carl okay?" I hadn't asked the police, because I was unsure how much Mark wanted them to know.

He hesitated. "We'll talk later."

I swallowed a reflexive breath, nodding because I was unable to find words.

I killed a man . . . maybe two . . .

Mark's SUV (basic black, about as nondescript as you could get) had tinted windows, so I pulled up the hood of the coat I'd been provided with (a lost-and-found special smelling strongly of cheap perfume and pot, but at least it was warm) and dropped the Japanese aura. I hoped like hell I could shed some of the guilt I was feeling along with it, but no such luck.

Mark nodded his after-the-fact permission and pulled out of the parking space.

I killed a man . . .

The words bounced around my cranium like pachinko balls. I wanted to hit my head against the window until they stopped, but that would no doubt worry Mark more than he already was. Besides, I suspected it wouldn't work.

Like an automaton, I reported everything I remembered from the rink. Mark took in all in, processing it without comment, allowing me to let the facts slip out while holding my emotion in check.

"Carl. Tell me," I finally said.

"He's alive."

"But?"

"He's in critical condition. Stunned and stabbed, left for dead in a wooded area of the park. It . . . doesn't look good."

"Jesus. It's my fault. If I hadn't—"

"No," Mark said, taking his eyes off the road for a second to bore into mine. "This is *not* your fault. He's a trained agent. Sometimes shit happens. It's part of the job, and he knows it."

"But if I hadn't insisted on ice skating, even after he told me he'd never done it before—"

"Yeah, and the same thing could have happened if you were out for a walk. You were being watched more closely than any of us realized. If anything, this is my fault. I should have kept you with me when you offered."

"You couldn't know!" I said.

He hazarded another look at me, raising an eyebrow.

"Point taken. Not my fault either," I conceded. "But, damn it, Loughlin *knew* it was me. How the hell can he do that?" I said.

"I don't know. But we *will* catch him, and I will find out. One way or another. At least now we know for sure he's connected to the New York murders." The stony set of Mark's face didn't bode well for Loughlin's future. "I've requisitioned more agents. Even brought in the FBI—he's at the top of their Most Wanted list as of now."

"I thought you said the FBI were a bunch of idiots."

He quirked his mouth into an almost-smile. "Even idiots have their uses. They're good at finding people."

I recognized the neighborhood we were headed toward and sat up straight. "No! Mark, I can't go home now. I *can't*." There was no way I could face my family yet. If I had to explain what had happened, I'd lose it for sure, and I wasn't at all certain I'd ever find it again. "*Please*," I said, panic creeping into my voice, trying though I was to keep it out.

"I've put more people on the house. Nobody can get at you there, I promise. I need you someplace safe."

"Please," I said again. "Anywhere else. I can't . . . I can't see them right now. I can't tell them what I did. Not yet."

"Ciel, it's not your fault—"

"*Please.*"

He nodded. "Billy's place okay? Is he back in town? I can put more men there, too."

I stiffened, willing myself to keep my face from crumbling, but I couldn't keep my eyes from pooling. "Not a good idea."

Another sharp look from Mark. He made an illegal U-turn at the next intersection and sped toward a section of town I hadn't seen since a visit I'd made with Thomas back when I was in high school.

Chapter 18

Mark's off-the-grid apartment was in a sketchy part of town, a tiny jewel hidden behind a façade that would embarrass a slumlord. Once we were up the six flights of scuffed wooden stairs and through a door with hospital-green paint peeling off it, it was a high-tech wonderland of minimalist luxury.

But yikes, those *stairs*. I fought to keep the wheeze out of my breathing. No wonder Mark was in such great shape.

"Would it have killed you to find a building with an elevator?" I said.

"Builds character," he said with a teasing smile.

I'd called my dad from the car and told him I was with Mark. That was all I'd squeezed out before I'd handed Mark's phone back to him. He told Dad that I was helping him on a lead, and wouldn't be in any danger. Didn't mention anything about what happened, for which I was grateful. I knew my parents were of the opinion there was no better protection in the world than Mark, so they wouldn't worry.

I started to smile back at him, but it froze on my face, guilt stabbing me again. I was starting to think the ice pick would have been less painful.

"I killed him, Mark. I killed a man."

He took the coat I was clutching (I'd removed it after the second flight of stairs), tossed it onto a chair along with his, and pulled me into an embrace, cradling my head against his chest with one large hand. "I know, Howdy. I know. It sucks. It sickens you, it terrifies you, destroys a part of you, and I'm sorry you had to do it. But listen to me. You had no choice."

"Maybe if I'd—"

"Stop. Don't 'if' it, Ciel. It was what it was. He had an ice pick"—the police must have told Mark that—"and he was going to kill you. You stopped him. That is *all* that matters."

I nodded into one of his pecs, and tried to believe him. "How do the police know he was trying to kill me? I didn't tell them— I was afraid to say anything before you got there."

"The ice pick was still in the guy's hand, and he had a rap sheet longer than his arm. Wasn't tough to put it together."

"Don't they wonder who the Japanese girl is? Won't they want to question me more?" I shuddered at the thought.

"As far as they're concerned, she's a foreign national under the protection of Uncle Sam. They know better than to ask anything more."

He led me to the sofa—small, modern, upholstered in soft gray Ultrasuede. I sat, relieved I wouldn't have to face the police again anyway, while he went to the bar area of the peninsula that separated the living area from the kitchen. He poured hefty slugs of some fancy bourbon into short glasses, and brought one to me.

"I'm not as good at making Manhattans as your dad is, but this will take the chill off your stomach," he said, sipping his.

I hesitated, my mind slamming up against a wall I didn't want to face right now. I gripped the glass until I was afraid it might shatter.

Screw it. *Sorry, kid, I need this,* I thought, and knocked it back. But a great big ol' lump of guilt blocked my throat before I could swallow.

Shit, Ciel, haven't you done enough damage for one day?

I ran to the kitchen sink and spat it out, but not before swishing it around in my mouth a few times. What a waste of good whiskey. But at least it had helped rid my mouth of the taste of blood I hadn't thus far been able to squelch.

I felt Mark's hand on my back. "That bad?"

I coughed, and pretended he was talking about the bourbon. "No. It tasted great. Really. It's . . . um, maybe some tea would be better."

"Sorry. I'm not much of a tea drinker. But I have coffee."

"Decaf?" I asked.

He looked at me like I was crazy.

"You know, in case I have trouble sleeping . . ."

"Ciel, if you have trouble sleeping, I'll stay up with you. If you want to talk—about anything—we'll talk. If you want to be quiet, we'll be quiet. Whatever you need, I'm here."

God, the dove-gray eyes, soft and tender. In my current emotional state, if I wasn't careful, they were going to undo me.

I looked down at my ugly scrubs, noticing a few suspect stains. "Do you have an old shirt or something I can borrow? I feel like a reject from *Grey's Anatomy*," I said, forcing a light tone.

"Sure thing." He disappeared behind the door of a compact

closet and returned with a dark green thermal and a pair of wool socks. "I'd give you some pants, but I'm afraid they'd fall right off you."

Normally the inherent innuendo in a statement like that would have me stifling giggles. It appeared my juvenile sense of humor was another casualty of the day's events.

"Thanks. This will be fine," I said.

I changed in a small bathroom so artfully laid out it seemed downright spacious. But first I took another shower, because even after scrubbing myself nearly raw at the police station, I didn't feel clean. Maybe Mark's soap would work better. At least it was a comforting smell, light and fresh, not at all overpowering like the industrial deodorant stuff they'd had at the station.

The thermal came almost to my knees, and I had to roll up the sleeves multiple times, but the color worked for me. The socks added a warm and goofy touch that might have amused me under different circumstances. I peeked in the medicine cabinet, found a new toothbrush, and proceeded to make use of it for at least double my normal brushing time. When I joined Mark in the main room I felt slightly more human.

"What do you think?" I said, striking a silly pose. "New fashion trend?"

Mark pretended to study me critically. "The socks make the outfit."

I held a foot up, toes extended. The heel of the brown sock was above my ankle, the top almost to my knee. Alluring they were not, but they were warm. I opened my mouth, willing a witty sock comment to come to my lips. Came up empty. I dropped my leg, sucked in some air, and started to shake.

"I can't do this. God damn it, it's not fair, not when I'm—"

I swallowed the words in time. "I want a do-over! I don't know how to be a killer," I said, giving up my futile attempt at normalcy.

Mark led me back to the sofa. He sat next to me, holding my hands steady in both of his, looking straight into my eyes. "You don't know how to be a killer because you're *not* a killer. You defended yourself, and someone died—a huge distinction."

"Even if . . . if . . ." I didn't want to say it, didn't even want to think it.

He squeezed my hands lightly, rubbing his thumbs across my knuckles. "If what, Howdy? Tell me. Let me help."

"When I saw the blood pouring out of him . . . when I saw the life fade out of his eyes . . . I was glad. No, I was *ecstatic*. I took a *life*, and got the same kind of rush as when I hit a home run, or win at bowling. What kind of sicko am I?"

"Ciel, that's a human reaction. You were flooded with adrenaline, fighting for your life, and you *did* win. You won a life-or-death contest. Of course your instinct is to feel satisfaction. It's normal."

"But the blood . . . I think, if I'd been able to stand . . . I think I would have kicked his dead body. Stomped him to ribbons with my skates. God knows I *wanted* to."

"Adrenaline," he repeated. "Nature's motivator when it comes to survival. Look, Ciel, your body was in fight-or-flight mode. You couldn't flee, so you fought. And I am damn glad you did."

He was starting to get through to me. It made sense. "Was it . . . was it like that for you . . . the first time?" I asked hesitantly. I knew he'd had to kill people—in his line of work it was inevitable—but he never talked about it.

He nodded. "Yeah. Only there was nothing to stop me. I was caught off guard, a stupid rookie mistake, and didn't have a weapon. He did, a knife, and he liked playing with it. He toyed with me, slicing me randomly while we fought, all the while telling me which parts of me he was going to cut off before he killed me. Scared the living shit out of me. When I managed—by pure luck—to knock the knife out of his hand, I jumped on him and started pounding. Kept pounding long after I knew he was dead. He didn't have much of a face left when I was done."

I squeezed his hands back. Somehow it was easier to understand the reaction in someone else. "How did you deal with it? After, I mean."

"Harvey"—Harvey was Mark's mentor at the Agency—"made me see a company psychologist. I resisted. Thought I could handle it myself. But Harvey insisted, and I'm glad he did. Doc's a smart woman. Might be a good idea for you to see her, too. I can arrange it if you like."

The idea of talking to anyone else about what I'd done—no, I couldn't see it. "Maybe later."

Mark didn't press it. "No rush. For now, you can talk to me as much as you want." He quirked a half-smile. "I'm not a doctor, but I can listen. And I do know what you're going through, if that helps."

I relaxed. "It does. More than you know."

He nodded. "Think you might be able to eat something? I can fry a mean egg. I don't usually burn toast either."

I wasn't hungry, but it would be something else to focus on. "An egg and some toast would be great," I said. "I'd offer to help, but . . ." I shrugged. Mark was well aware of my deficiencies in the kitchen.

He ruffled my hair, and for a second I almost felt normal. "Watch and learn, Howdy. Watch and learn."

The trouble started when I closed my eyes.

I'd made it through dinner, managing to eat most of my toast and half an egg before my stomach put up a roadblock. We'd stuck to non-stressful topics, like how freaking cold it was, what kind of car Mark was considering trying out next, and old-school video games, after which I thought I was tired enough to sleep.

But every time I closed my eyes the world turned red. The color flowed over me, harsh and ugly, oozing into my field of vision, making my heart race as the adrenaline punched me in the gut again and again.

So I kept my eyes open, staring at the light coming from the bathroom door Mark had left open a crack, in case I needed to get up in the middle of the night. I was snuggled into the best sofa bed ever—apparently if you pay enough you don't wind up with a bar digging into your back—but it couldn't keep the red away.

Mark was in the chair where he'd thrown our coats earlier, the coats having been banished to the floor. The chair reclined, and he'd claimed it was perfectly comfortable. I'd told him it made more sense for me to take the chair, since I'm a good foot shorter, but he'd insisted.

"Want me to make you some warm milk?" Mark's words gave me a start, low though he'd kept his voice.

"How did you know I was awake?" I'd been trying my best to stay silent, figuring one of us should get some sleep.

"You're too quiet. Sleeping people are full of tiny noises. Even if they don't snore, their breathing has a different quality than when they're awake."

I sighed. "Anyone ever tell you you're way too observant?"

"It's a curse," he said. I could hear the smile in his voice.

He went to the kitchen area, turned on the light over the stove, keeping it at the dimmest setting, and got out a mug and a quart of milk. I joined him, still wearing his wool socks and thermal.

"You're going to have some, too, aren't you? I hate to drink alone," I said, again trying for a touch of humor. It sounded flat to my ear.

He got out another mug. "Sure. Can I add a little something to sweeten it up for you?"

"Do you have any cocoa powder?"

"No, but I have some honey."

"I guess it will have to do. At least now I know what to get you for Christmas," I teased. If I kept working at it, maybe it would start to sound natural again.

While the milk heated in the microwave he leaned back, his hands resting on the counter on either side of his hips. He was still wearing clothes, but at least he'd taken off his shoes and sweater. Guess the T-shirt kept him warm enough indoors. Heck, it was starting to make me feel warm, and I wasn't even the one wearing it. I came close to asking him why he didn't get comfortable and change into his pajamas, but figured it wouldn't be wise. For all I knew, he didn't even sleep in pajamas, and I certainly didn't need to add that image to the muddled mess already tumbling in my head.

Though it was certainly more pleasant to contemplate than the other ones . . .

The kitchen felt smaller all of a sudden.

Of course it does, idiot. He's a big guy. Naturally the room looks smaller by comparison, I thought, staring at his biceps. He gripped the edge of the counter, the muscles in both arms flexing to life.

The microwave beeped, pulling me out of my mini-trance, and my eyes shot up to his face. I could tell he'd caught me staring, and prayed the dim light would hide my blush.

"Howdy . . ."

I coughed, and turned to study the apples in the bowl on the counter. "Yeah?"

"Never mind," he said after a short pause. He got the mugs, gave each a squirt of honey and a stir, and placed one carefully in my waiting hands, his fingers brushing my knuckles in passing.

All right, *that* felt way better than it should. I lifted the mug to my lips with trembling hands, sucking in the honeyed liquid like it was the antidote to what ailed me.

"Delicious," I said. "Almost as good as hot chocolate. Yup, I think this is going to do the trick." I gulped down the rest, afraid to move the mug for fear of what Mark might read on my face.

God, I really must be some brand of warped. Pregnant, deserted by my boyfriend, fresh off killing a man, and now here I was wanting nothing more than to jump Mark on the kitchen floor.

He set his mug on the counter after a token sip, took my empty one from me, and put it next to his. Then he held my hand with both of his, keeping some space between us. "*That's* normal, too. After." His eyes were understanding, reminding me of the way he'd looked at me when I was nothing more than a kid crushing on him.

"It is?" I said, not bothering to pretend I didn't know what he was talking about.

He nodded. "It doesn't mean there's anything wrong with you. It'll wear off soon."

I looked at the hands cupping mine. So big. Strong and vital and *alive*. Without conscious intent, I uncurled his fingers and placed his palms over my breasts. "What if I don't want it to wear off?"

His fingers gripped me lightly, then tried to pull away. I held them close. "Can't you help me not think for a little while?" I said softly.

He kept his hands still, not yanking them away, but in no way caressing me either. "Ciel, this isn't a good idea. Not now."

Funny, it felt like the best idea in the world to me, the only idea worth having at the moment. The one thing that might override everything else I was trying so desperately to keep out of my head. I stroked the backs of his hands, circling his knuckles with my fingertips. "One night. If I can get through tonight I think I'll be okay."

"What about Billy?" he asked gently.

"Billy ran out on me," I said, my voice harsher than I intended. "I can't think about him right now."

He moved his hands up to my shoulders. "Ciel, what happened?"

"Damn it, Mark! I don't want to talk. I want to *fuck*. And so do you." I looked pointedly at his crotch. He'd have trouble denying *that*.

His jaw tightened along with his hands. He took a deep breath and visibly relaxed himself. "Yeah, I do. But it's not happening if we don't talk. Why did Billy leave? Was it because of me?"

I sighed. He'd have to know sometime. This day was already in the toilet. Might as well flush it.

"He didn't seem to care for the idea of becoming a father," I said, going for ironic understatement but probably stumbling into rancor.

Mark stared at me blankly for a second, then looked even more shocked than when I'd punched him at the gym. "You're pregnant?"

"Afraid so. Looks like Thomas's heir is going to have a cousin to grow up with," I said, and immediately regretted it because it couldn't help but remind me that Billy and I had grown up together as cousins, albeit honorary ones.

"How long have you known?"

"Since my last day in Houston. Billy was there. He was as supportive as could be, even helping me with the test I was scared spitless to take. He was the perfect boyfriend . . . right up until he saw the little blue plus sign. Then he suddenly had somewhere else he needed to be, and I haven't heard from him since."

Mark's forehead wrinkled, like he was having trouble wrapping his head around what I was telling him. "Are you sure that was the reason? Billy has a . . . complicated . . . work life. Did he get a text or anything before he left? Maybe something came up he couldn't tell you about."

I thought back to the lovely reveal in Dr. Phil's bathroom. "No, I'm pretty sure it's the pregnancy thing. I knew he didn't want kids—he's never pretended to be father material, and frankly that was fine with me. It wasn't like I got pregnant on purpose. I lost my temper when he started to go—justifiably, I think—and yelled at him that it might not even be his baby, that it might be . . . yours." If Mark had looked stunned before, it was nothing compared to now. "Instead of getting angry, he told me 'that might be best.' And then he was gone."

"Jesus, Howdy, I—is it true? Or were you just trying to hurt him?"

I took a deep breath. "It's true. I haven't had a period since that night. I didn't think anything of it before Laura . . . I mean, I've never been very regular. God, Mark, I don't even know which of you is—"

He dropped to his knees and hugged me around my waist, pressing his lips against my belly. "It doesn't matter. It will never matter to me, Ciel."

Once again, I was blindsided by the reaction to my news. I placed a hand on his head, shaking in earnest now, and said, "Can we go to bed now?"

Chapter 19

Mark stood. I took him by the hand and led him back to the sofa bed, lying down once we were there and pulling him on top of me. He still seemed hesitant.

"I know you're Billy's friend," I said. "I know there might be more to his reaction than I realize. Maybe he'll come back. Maybe"—I swallowed hard, about to be brutally honest, both with Mark and myself—"maybe I even want him to. You can't stop loving someone on a dime." How often had I made the same explanation to Billy about my leftover feelings for Mark? "I don't know any of that. But I do know I need you to hold me right now more than I need my next breath."

He kissed me then, wrapping strong arms around me, giving me what I wanted. Selfishly, I took it. I held on to him the way a drowning person clings to a buoy in a stormy sea, using him to keep all the terrifying thoughts in my head at bay. One more thing for me to feel guilty about tomorrow, but at the moment I didn't care. Tomorrow could go fuck itself. Tonight was my haven, and

I was damn well going to crawl into it and lock out the rest of the world.

He was tender with me, too tender for my present state of mind, undressing me and himself with agonizing slowness. I wanted him fast and hard, to match the pounding of my pulse. I wanted him to drive every ugly thought, every hideous image, out of my head by his sheer strength.

"*Please*," I said, demanding more than begging. I dug my fingers into his shoulders as hard as I could. I tried to shake him, but he was like stone in my hands, immovable.

"Shhh . . ." he said, the sound a whisper of breath in my ear. He ignored my efforts to spur him on, choosing instead to gentle me with unhurried hands and soft lips. "Be still. Let your muscles relax. I promise it will be better."

I lay back in frustration, doing as I was told, not sure I deserved to enjoy it more, but what choice did I have? He wasn't giving in.

His hands and mouth continued their leisurely exploration of my body. It was almost more of a massage, and eventually I did relax, receding into a boneless state of blissful nothingness. Then he switched gears and started ramping up the tension in my body again, minus the rage at life that had been threatening to overwhelm me.

When he finally entered me it was in one silken motion, filling not only my body but also the place that had been excised from my soul at the skating rink. He moved inside me with infinite patience, not rushing, lifting me so gradually that when my peak came it took me by surprise, both with its intensity and its duration. Not the violent release I'd wanted, but the deep and gentle one I'd needed.

As it ebbed, he joined me with his own, holding himself still as he pulsed into me, kissing me so softly, so reverently I couldn't stop my tears from flowing. He withdrew and rolled onto his back, tucking me next to him.

I snuggled close, burrowing my face into his chest. "Thank you," I said, sniffling. "Thank you, thank you . . ." And then I drifted off to sleep.

The first thing I realized upon waking: I hadn't had a single nightmare. Mind-blowing sex, the cure for all ills. Beat the heck out of seeing a shrink. No offense to psychiatrists, but I didn't think I'd enjoy having my psyche dissected. I figured my subconscious deserved its privacy.

The second thing I realized: Mark was gone. Before I could panic, I saw the note he'd left on the pillow beside mine, telling me he'd gone downstairs for a quick meeting, assuring me he wouldn't take his eyes off the building and would be back soon.

The wave of relief that spread through me was embarrassing. *Come on, Ciel, grow a pair. You can't expect him to hold your hand forever.*

And I didn't. I could take care of myself. I'd proved it, hadn't I? Someone had tried to kill me, and here I was, still alive. I was going to focus on that, and ignore the fact that I'd pretty much crumpled on the inside afterward. Because so what?

So. The. Fuck. What.

I dug through the covers for the thermal, and pulled it over my head. The important thing was, I could function in a crisis. Who cared about the immediate aftermath? I was fine now. *That* was what mattered.

Still, I jumped like a scared mouse when the door opened.

I knew it had to be Mark, and jumped anyway, pure reflex. Crap. Jangled nerves sucked.

"Sorry, Howdy," he said in a perfectly normal voice, like my idiot reaction was somehow his fault. He put some bags on the kitchen counter. The smaller appeared to be from a nearby storefront diner.

"Nothing to be sorry for," I said. "Guess I'm a little . . . never mind. Whatcha got there?"

He pulled two large, lidded paper cups out of a bag and handed one to me. "I can't guarantee the quality, but it's decaf."

It smelled heavenly. "Thanks. At this point, if it's black and made from a bean I'm willing to give it a go."

Next out of the bag was the biggest, gooiest cinnamon roll I'd ever seen. My mouth watered, and without thinking I blurted, "Oh, my God, I love you!"

I froze. *Crap, Ciel, what the hell?* "Um, I mean . . ." I ventured a look at his face.

He was smiling. "Gee, if I'd known it was that easy I would have plied you with pastries weeks ago," he said.

"Mark . . ." I said, then stopped, biting the inside of my cheek.

"Howdy, eat. We can have the 'about last night' talk later."

I'm totally cool with procrastination, especially when it involves cinnamon and sugar. I dug in and put off thinking about the day ahead of me for the few precious moments I could.

While I was eating, Mark pulled some clothes out of the other bag. Some very familiar-looking clothes. I dropped the roll, rinsed my hands, and went for a closer inspection. It was the reindeer-playing-poker sweater, along with everything else I'd been wearing the day before.

"But how . . . ?" I said, running my hands over everything.

"I mean, they were soaked with . . . they were *ruined*. These look brand new!"

Mark smiled. "They are. I had someone go to the station yesterday and inspect your clothes. She tracked down the stores where your mother shops—don't worry, your mom doesn't know—and bought duplicates of everything."

My eyes started leaking again. "I won't have to explain what happened. I won't have to tell my parents I—" I dropped the sweater I'd been clutching and hurled myself at Mark. "Thank you."

"No problem. I thought it might make it easier for you go home."

I pulled away from the hug. "But I can't—"

"Ciel, I have to get back out on the street. I *have* to find Loughlin and I can't—I *won't*—leave you here alone."

"You don't have to—I can go with you. I can help! I can handle myself, you know I—"

"No."

"But you know I'm capable. And you said . . ." I was about to remind him he'd regretted not keeping me with him before, but somehow that seemed like a low blow, so I stopped myself.

"Howdy, after how you've handled yourself this past week, I damn well believe you're capable of anything. But *I'm* not. I can't worry about you out there on the street with me, not when you're pregnant."

Damn it. I knew I had a responsibility to the tiny alien growing inside me, but it was going to take some adjusting. I sighed my reluctant agreement.

Relief softened his eyes. "You can stay with your parents, or James. Even Brian. Or I can have you flown back to D.C. to stay with Thomas and Laura. Your choice."

"I don't think I can be around Thomas and Laura right now," I said quietly. Mark was a smart guy. He'd figure out why.

He nodded. "I suggest your parents. You can't avoid them for long this time of year, and your mom will keep you too busy to worry about . . . things."

I took a deep breath. "Yeah, okay. You're right. I suppose it's too much to expect Mom and Dad don't know about what happened at the skating rink. Did it make the news?"

"It did. But a police spokesperson, at our suggestion"—yeah, right, "suggestion"—"told the press a mentally disturbed homeless man was harassing a woman at the rink, which led to a horrific accident. No names were released in order to respect the privacy of all involved."

"Did they mention the woman was Japanese? Because Mom was the one who gave me the aura."

Mark smiled a tiny bit. "I believe that fact was omitted."

"Maybe Mom won't connect it to me then. I never told her I was going skating."

"That's the idea."

"Do you think the press will leave it alone?" I said.

He shrugged. "This is New York. It won't be long before something crazier comes along to distract them."

True enough. "Let's hope it doesn't involve another adaptor."

"I'm going to see that it doesn't," he said. "Do me a favor and put your clothes on so we can get going."

"Sure. Only, um, about last night . . ." I began hesitantly.

"Ciel, last night was for you, no strings. You were hurting, and I hope I helped." He paused, then seemed to come to a decision. "There's only one thing I'm going to ask from you. If you and Billy wind up back together"—my heart clutched at the thought—"and it turns out the baby is mine, I need to be a part of its life. We don't have to tell people I'm the father—my aim isn't to make life complicated for anyone—but I *have* to be there, in some capacity, for my child."

Seemed only fair. I nodded. "And if Billy and I don't get back together?"

A strange—for him—look settled on his face. I couldn't quite read it. "You could always marry me."

I stared, stunned. "But it's more than likely not even your baby."

"I told you last night that doesn't matter. I meant it."

I twisted my mouth into a wry smile. "Oh, right. Mark to my rescue yet again. You really need to do something about that savior complex, you know."

He shook his head, slowly. "It's not that, Ciel. Not even a little bit. I'll settle for being your friend if I have to, but I *want* it all. With you. I thought you knew that."

Chapter 20

Mark dropped me at my parents', leaving me in what one of my favorite high school science teachers would have referred to as a state of disequilibrium. Funny how your dearest adolescent dream can come true and leave you more bewildered than you've ever been in your life.

Why did Mark have to be so goddamn perfect? It made me feel small by comparison, and not size-wise either. The relief I felt at the giant safety net he was offering me, no strings attached, was not something I found attractive about myself. But it was the truth.

An even bigger truth? I couldn't stop thinking about Billy. Where was he? Was he okay? Would he come back once the shock wore off, or was he out of my life for good? Was he even safe? Or had, God forbid, Loughlin somehow gotten to him?

Ugh. Being honest with yourself is *so* overrated.

Mom had Dad deep in the present-wrapping cave when I got there. After a hello and good-bye to Mark, who'd walked me in,

Mom reminded me of my planned shopping excursion with Billy's sisters. Sinead and Siobhan had called earlier to ask what time I'd be there. Mom had told them no later than one o'clock.

When I'd mentioned that perhaps holiday shopping so soon after Jenny's murder was not in the best of taste, Mom said she'd already been to the nearest Catholic church and lit a candle for her, and there was nothing more any of us could do until the body was released to the funeral home.

"But, Mom, you're not Catholic," I pointed out.

She shrugged. "No, but Jenny was. I thought it would be a nice gesture. I said a rosary, too. I'm not sure I got all the words right, and I had to use your great-great-aunt Maria-Louisa's rosary beads—she was Catholic, married to my great-uncle Harold; she tried to get him to convert, but he never would, such a stubborn man—but I'm sure Jenny wouldn't have minded."

"Is that even allowed?" I said.

"It is. I checked with the priest. He said non-Catholics were welcome to use sacramentals as long as they did it in a respectful manner. Which I did. So I think it's okay to go Christmas shopping. After all, God would want us to celebrate His son's birthday, right? And so would Jenny. Now, why don't you go shower and change while I make you some lunch."

I almost told her I didn't need to change, but as far as she knew, I'd been wearing the same clothes since the day before, so I went with it.

It was all so ridiculously normal. The incident at the ice rink was starting to seem like a freakishly terrible nightmare—horrible, and yet distant from reality. I wasn't sure if that made me feel better or worse about the whole thing.

Up in my room, I looked in my dresser mirror, jabbed my reflection, and said, "You took a life." I felt the pain I needed to feel, because I couldn't bear to think of myself as someone who could kill a person and shrug it off the next day. Then I did shower again. I told myself it was because Mom might be listening, not anything Lady Macbethian.

Lunch was . . . interesting. Mom had seen a recipe for grilled Brie sandwiches on French bread, with apricot jam. Only she didn't have exactly the right ingredients, so she figured grilled blue cheese on raisin bread with grape jelly would probably be as good. (She was wrong.) Even the cats were hiding.

During lunch she attached a truly hideous Rudolph pin—with a battery-powered nose—to the soft white lambswool sweater I had purposely chosen for its lack of kitsch. Why did I even try? But I did manage to hide half my sandwich in my purse while she was hunting for a fresh battery, so yay, Rudolph. Also, it could have been worse. At least she hadn't added tinsel to my jeans. And my treasured new boots (which had, of course, been safely in a locker at the rink, and so had emerged unscathed) were still classy.

Sadly, as I headed out into the shopping abyss, I couldn't even bitch and moan about it inwardly anymore without feeling petty. Yet another casualty of the asshole at the rink.

My new bodyguard was older, bigger, and altogether tougher-looking than Carl, whose condition, according to Mark, was improving. It could still go either way, but the odds were starting to tilt toward survival, thank God.

Mark had introduced the new guy to me only as "Davis." He'd been parked in front of the house when we'd arrived, not making any attempt to conceal himself or his reason for being there. It wasn't like it was any secret we were being guarded.

"So, is Davis your first or last name?" I said by way of making conversation after he'd safely escorted me from the front door to the big SUV, and slid into the driver's seat.

"Last," he said, his cheeks reddening, which was oddly sweet on a face that looked like it belonged on a prize fighter.

I kept looking at him until he expelled a grumpy sigh. "Al."

"Al?"

He nodded.

"Alexander? Alfred? Alan? Alcott?" (Yeah, I know. Nosy. But it was better than dwelling on all the other shit.)

His mouth tightened. "Alastair," he said, sounding so pained I felt compelled to bite the inside of my lower lip to keep from laughing.

"Ma thought it would class up the family," he explained.

"It's nice," I said.

Al looked disgusted. "I told everybody in school I was named for my uncle, Al Capone."

I laughed. I'd have to bear that in mind when it came time to consider what to name—*crap. For God's sake, Ciel, think about something else.*

A woman tapped on the driver's side window. Al didn't seem alarmed, so I guessed he knew her. He unlocked the back door and she climbed in.

"Sorry I'm late—I got called off another job. So, I hear we're going shopping," she said, and stuck her hand over my seat to shake my hand. "Hi. I'm Candy. I'll be tagging along with you today."

To say Candy was Amazon-esque would be an understatement. She was tall and athletic-looking, with close-cropped brown hair and large (for a woman) hands. But she had a serious sprinkling of freckles on her pale cheeks and nose, so I felt an immediate kinship with her.

"Ciel," I said, though I was sure she already knew who I was. I was her assignment, after all.

She smiled broadly, exhibiting a small gap between her front teeth. It worked for her. "Six-three, and I have no interest in playing for the WNBA." She shrugged, laughing. "Everybody wonders."

I grinned back at her. "Damn. And here I was hoping you could help me refine my jump shot before I try out for the Mystics." The Mystics were the D.C. women's basketball team. I didn't follow them, but Thomas did. I suspect he has a thing for tall, kick-ass women. Which would explain, of course, how he wound up with Laura.

Candy laughed again and said, "Might be easier to toss you at the net and let you dunk it." Yeah, I liked her. When she was finished laughing, she sniffed the air around her. "Christ, Al, what's that smell? Did you spill milk on the carpet?"

Oops. Blue cheese and raisin bread. Guess it hit you harder if you hadn't just eaten it. I should 'fess up, but it would be embarrassing to explain my childish hide-the-food behavior. I was supposed to be an adult. I'd find someplace to dump it later.

"Huh, I don't smell anything," I said. Which wasn't a lie, because I really couldn't smell it anymore. Strong odors cause nasal fatigue, and after that lunch my nose was exhausted. "So, what did you guys do to piss off Mark and get roped into this gig?"

"Are you kidding?" Candy said. "Mark loves us, doesn't he, Al? We're his favorite flunkies."

Al gave her a wry look via the rearview mirror, only taking his eyes off the road for a millisecond. He was obviously from the Mark Fielding school of driving. "Speak for yourself. He hates me ever since I got in a lucky punch in the ring with him. He couldn't wait to give me a shopping gig."

"Aw, lighten up, Al. A little retail therapy never hurt anyone," Candy said.

Personally, I shared Al's pain, but we pulled up in front of the Doyle homestead before I could express my solidarity. Auntie Mo and Uncle Liam didn't live far from my parents—same neighborhood, in fact.

Uncle Liam caught me at the door before I rang the bell. "Ciel, hon, could I have a word?" He drew me quietly into his study before Sinead and Siobhan spotted me. Candy and Al waited with the car.

"Sure," I said. "What's up?"

"It's about Billy," he said, his voice more serious than I was used to from him.

I stilled, a chill taking me from top to bottom, falling over me like some god-awful ice bucket challenge. "What about him?" I said. *Please, please, please don't let him be hurt.*

Uncle Liam hesitated. Cleared his throat. "I better give you the background first. I don't know what Billy has told you about his mother . . ."

"Is Auntie Mo all right? She's not sick, is she? Or hurt?" I couldn't imagine a germ strong enough to take on Auntie Mo and win, but an accident, or Loughlin . . .

"No, not Mo. Billy's birth mother."

"Oh." We all knew Uncle Liam had married Auntie Mo when Billy was a baby, of course, but nobody ever spoke about his bio mom, least of all Billy. "Has something happened to her? Is Billy all right?"

"I was hoping you'd be able to tell me. I haven't talked to him since . . . well, since before he visited his mother a few days ago."

"She's alive? I always assumed she'd died soon after Billy was born. Where is she?"

He took a deep breath. Came to some sort of a decision. "You should know. Billy's birth mother was institutionalized shortly after his birth. She's been there ever since—it's a very nice place, and she receives the best of care. But she's . . . easily upset. Billy's known about her since he was quite young. Mo and I were as honest with him as we could be."

I nodded, trying to assimilate this new information. Why had Billy never told me?

"When he got older, and started asking more questions—he must have been about ten—we explained as gently as we could that the woman who'd given birth to him was in a special hospital for people who couldn't cope with the world. He got it into his head it was his fault—that he'd somehow made his mother lose her mind."

God, poor Billy. Back then, all he'd ever been to me was a best-friend-slash-tormenter. I'd had no clue at all—he was always the dimpled charmer, happy no matter what kind of trouble he'd managed to get into.

"I'm so sorry, Uncle Liam. I never realized. It must have been so hard for you," I said.

His eyes—the beautiful Doyle eyes, Billy's eyes a few decades older—saddened briefly. "Only until I met Mo. Then life became . . . what life should be." His smile, warm and genuine, was overshadowed by worry. "I have an alert set with the home where Chastity lives. That's her name—Chastity Oglethorp. They call whenever anything out of the ordinary happens."

"I take it Billy's visit wasn't ordinary?" I said.

"You could say that. It was the first time he'd seen her since the day he was born."

My mouth went dry. "Never before? Not once?" I said.

It wasn't hard to figure out what had precipitated the visit. The idea of having his own child had obviously spurred him into finally seeking out the woman who'd abandoned him at birth in the backseat of the '57 Chevy that was now his pride and joy.

"Never. You have to understand how complicated the situation was. Chastity was raised in an extremely strict religious offshoot sect. Think Westboro Baptist on steroids. We met by accident when she was trying to run away. She was hitchhiking. I was driving along in my fine set of wheels"—that would be the Chevy Billy had now—"when I saw her, looking so pretty and scared and in need of rescue. We fell in love and things got . . . well. When she became pregnant, I wanted to marry her. It was then she finally told me she was already married. She'd been running away from her new sixty-year-old husband when I'd found her."

Yikes. That was messed up.

"We decided a marriage certificate didn't matter. We were as good as married anyway. She was always . . . fragile . . . but it didn't matter to me. I was the big rescuer, the one who would take care of her, protect her from the world. Everything was good until the day I came home from work and found two men—big men; either of them would have been more than a match for me—trying to drag her into their car. I found out later they were from her former . . . I can't dignify it with the word 'church' . . . her former *cult*. I lost it. I knew I'd never be able to fight them off as myself, so I adapted to the biggest, burliest aura I had, right there in front of them. In front of her."

Uncle Liam paused for a second, letting the ramifications set in. Adapting in front of non-adaptors is not done, not unless they are a part of the community and already know about us. It wasn't exactly a law, but it was the closest thing our community had to one.

"Did it work?" I asked hesitantly.

"Only too well," he said. "The men let Chastity go and ran off, shouting that I was the devil. Chastity's water broke, and her contractions started coming fast, one on top of another. There was no time to lose, so I put her into the backseat of the Chevy and headed for the hospital. We lived pretty far out in the country, and I knew an ambulance would never get there in time.

"She started screaming the baby was coming before we were halfway there. I pulled over, totally out of my depth. I had no idea what I was doing. Through the grace of God, I caught Billy, and had enough presence of mind to tie off his umbilical cord with one of Chastity's shoelaces. I put him on her belly and got back behind the wheel. The car wouldn't start. I panicked and flooded the engine. Kept trying and trying, until I totally drained the battery, all the while listening to Chastity whimpering in the backseat, mumbling prayers, begging for forgiveness.

"She was so out of it. God, I was terrified, until I remembered we'd passed a gas station four or five miles back. I told Chastity to hold on, I was getting help. And then I ran, faster than I ever had, until I thought my lungs would burst from it. Running as much from the fear I'd seen in her eyes—the fear I knew was of *me*—as I was for help.

"When we got back to the car—the station owner and I—

Chastity was gone. Billy was on the backseat, wrapped in a bloody slip. I thought the men had come back for her, had taken her. But we found her a mile down the road, babbling incoherently about laying with the devil and giving birth to an abomination. She blamed herself, thought it was her punishment for thwarting God's will by running away from her husband. I'm afraid she never recovered.

"She was disowned by her 'people.' Her husband denied the marriage. I was all she had, and she reacted to me like I was the devil incarnate trying to drag her into hell. She refused to even look at Billy. So I found a place. She lives there peacefully, for the most part, spending her days reciting Bible passages to anyone who will listen.

"I did try to see her a few times, but it always made her so much worse. Eventually I stopped. My days were full of work and taking care of Billy. I moved to the city to get a better job—the place Chastity stays is nice, but it isn't cheap—and to be closer to my parents, who helped me with Billy. I met Mo through a mutual adaptor friend. She was a godsend—but you already know that part." He broke off with a weary smile.

I wiped the tears from my cheeks, aching for him, and for Billy. "How did Billy's visit go? Did they say?"

"Not well, I'm afraid. You know how much Billy looks like me even now? Well, he's the spitting image of how I looked back then. Chastity thought it was me coming for her again, and reacted badly. Billy took off, and I haven't been able to reach him."

"God, Uncle Liam, I don't know what to say. I am so sorry."

"By the way, I haven't told Mo about Billy's visit to the home. She worries so much . . ."

I nodded. "I won't say anything to her about it."

"I didn't want to worry you either, but if there's a chance you might see him or talk to him, I thought you should be prepared. And . . . well, I'm hoping you'll have better luck tracking him down than I have. I'd rest easier if I knew he was okay."

You and me both.

"I'll do whatever I can, Uncle Liam, I promise. I'll—"

The door to the study burst open and Hurricane Molly blew in. "Ciel! Tell Mom—ew, what's that smell?"

I shot a look at my purse, which I'd left on Uncle Liam's desk at the beginning of his tale. Guess he was too much a gentleman to mention the odd aroma that had hitched a ride with me.

"Never mind," Molly said before I could explain. "Ciel, tell Mom I can go with you guys. It's not fair to leave me here. It's *discrimination!*"

Uncle Liam scooped her up and twirled her around, coming perilously close to knocking over one of Auntie Mo's prized Tiffany lamps. "But who'll watch Christmas movies and drink hot chocolate with me if you desert me, too?"

Molly looked torn. "With marshmallows?"

"Of course."

"And cookies before dinner?"

"We'll sneak them out of the cookie jar when you mother isn't looking."

"Can we watch the *Grinch* twice?"

Uncle Liam screwed up his face, considering. "You drive a hard bargain, Molly-my-love. But yes. We can."

"Yay!" Molly wriggled out of his arms and ran to me. "Why don't you stay with us, Ciel? You hate shopping."

I tapped my chin, considering. "Well, I suppose I *could* . . . if a certain eleven-year-old wouldn't mind not having a present from me to open on Christmas morning."

"Never mind. Go! Go!"

Sinead stuck her head in the door. "Yeah, Ciel, move it. It's time to 'go, go!'"

Siobhan's head appeared next, looking enough like her sister to be a twin, though they were almost a year apart. They were both gorgeous, with chestnut hair and their dad's deep blue eyes.

Siobhan gestured toward the front door with a hooked thumb. "Let's blow this joint."

Uncle Liam nodded at me. "Go on. We'll talk more later."

"About what?" Molly said, eyes alight with curiosity.

"Sorry, can't say. Santa swore us to secrecy," Uncle Liam said.

"Yeah, right. Oooh, I bet I know! It's about Ciel and Billy and, you know . . ." She puckered up her lips and made kissing noises.

Siobhan gave me a giggling poke in the ribs. "You asking for Dad's blessing to propose to our brother?"

I made myself laugh, but it sounded kind of anemic.

"Can we watch? Hey, we can video it for you! I bet we could make it go viral," Sinead said.

"Don't be crazy. I am *not* proposing to your brother. Man, you guys are the worst. Wasn't Tom and Laura's wedding enough trouble for you?"

Or maybe that was only me.

Molly started hopping up and down. "I call dibs on maid of honor!"

"Well, if you get to be maid of honor, then I'll have to insist they name their firstborn after me," Siobhan said. I could feel my face freeze. I tried to laugh, but you know. Frozen face.

"Ha! What if it's a *boy*?" Molly said.

"It will build his character."

"*Stop it,*" a voice rang out, and the rest of me froze to match my face.

Chapter 21

"I'm sure Ciel doesn't appreciate your planning her life for her," Billy said good-naturedly, his questioning eyes meeting mine briefly before he was surrounded by Doyles large and small.

Somewhere in the happy jumble of voices I heard him tell his father everything was fine. Uncle Liam didn't look convinced, but apparently seeing his son whole and sound was enough for the moment. Auntie Mo magically appeared, elbowing her daughters out of the way so she could get at Billy for her own vigorous embrace.

"Billy, you know better than go off without telling us, especially this time of year," she said, her voice a mixture of exasperation and maternal forgiveness.

Billy was typically pretty good at letting his family know when he'd be gone. He didn't always tell them *where* he was going—his jobs, both the ones he set up on his own and the ones he did for Mark, didn't allow for complete disclosure—but he told them *that* he was going, so they wouldn't worry any more than could be helped.

"Sorry, Mommo. I got caught up in something unexpected." Again, he looked at me with searching eyes. Searching for what? A clue? How the hell did he expect me to react?

How did he *want* me to react?

"Look at us, keeping the lovebirds apart! Sorry, Ciel—you know how we are." Auntie Mo took me by the arm and pulled me into the fray, shoving me up against Billy's chest.

I swore to myself if I felt him stiffen, if he seemed at all hesitant, I'd walk out then and there, and leave him to explain things the best he could. But he didn't. He hugged me tight, lifting me, putting his mouth next to my ear. He spoke so softly amid the happy chatter that I couldn't quite make out what he said.

But it sounded an awful lot like "forgive me."

I clung to him against my better judgment. My mind was wary, calling up the recent hurt, replaying in high-definition his reaction to the plus sign. I was still pissed as hell at how he'd left me to cope with the biggest shock of my life alone, no matter what his reason. But I couldn't get rid of the image of him, *infant* him, being abandoned by his mother within minutes of his birth, and my arms wouldn't let go. Part of him was broken, and, fixer that I was, I couldn't turn my back on him. I buried my face in his neck, hiding it as well as I could from everyone else in the room, unsure what my expression might reveal.

"Um, Ciel, I hate to break up your reunion, but our heavily armed carriage awaits. To Fifth Avenue or bust!" Sinead said.

"Billy, you can come with us if you like," Siobhan said. "Sure, it's *supposed* to be a girl date, but we can stand you if we must. And I'm sure our bodyguards won't mind having an extra along."

Billy set me down and searched my face again.

"Um, guys, if it's okay with you, I think I need to spend some time with your brother," I said.

"Hey, no fair!" Siobhan said.

"Yeah, we had dibs on you for today!" Sinead said.

"That's enough, you two," Uncle Liam said. Quietly. When Uncle Liam said something, his kids listened. "Billy hasn't seen Ciel since her apartment burned"—Billy pulled me more tightly to him, and yeah, I couldn't help thinking that was another time he hadn't been there for me—"and I'm sure they have a lot to discuss. You girls go ahead. And be careful—you do whatever your bodyguards tell you."

"There's that smell again," Candy said. She was up front with Al; I was in the back with Billy, who looked at my purse, a grin twitching on his lips. I ignored it, as I did Candy's comment.

Al and Candy had insisted on driving us to Billy's place, and Billy hadn't argued, since they would have had to follow us anyway. Besides, his car was nowhere to be seen. When I'd asked him where it was, he'd mumbled something about it being in the shop.

Sinead and Siobhan's security detail would be the ones who had the pleasure of maneuvering them safely through the holiday throngs. If Candy was disappointed to miss the shopping expedition, she didn't let on.

The ride to Billy's was mostly silent, even the garrulous Candy realizing, and respecting, that Billy and I weren't being especially communicative. I sat a little apart from him, pulled back from my initial inclination to forgive and fix by an upwelling of confusion. My compassion for his situation was muddied by the persistent, fiery ball of anger in the pit of my stomach. I was stuck on the tipping point between needing to hug him until my arms creaked and wanting to slap him silly.

Which, come to think of it, pretty much summed up my relationship with Billy going all the way back to toddlerhood.

Candy and Al escorted us up the stairs and checked the condo before going back down to keep watch on the building while Billy and I were there. They would call up a warning if they saw anything suspicious.

As soon as I walked through the door I knew it was a mistake. There wasn't a place I could rest my eyes that Billy and I hadn't been intimate. Couch, loft, the rug on the floor, bathtub, kitchen counter. (Um, yeah. But it was only once, and we'd sanitized it afterward. Trust me, once is enough when it comes to cold, hard granite. "Adventurous" can be fun, but "comfortable" doesn't give your butt cheeks frostbite.)

Billy seemed to know what I was thinking, and shrugged apologetically as he took my coat and purse. He hung them, along with his coat, on a rack made of old steel pipes welded together. "I didn't know where else to bring you."

"It's fine," I said, and walked to the big window beyond the seating area. His condo was a large open space, modern in design, with lots of masculine black leather, softened by a few colorful (all right, ugly) afghans from Auntie Mo's knitting phase. She must have made a ton of them, because every time one of us "lost" or "accidentally" ruined one she always had another ready. I fully expected to unwrap one on Christmas morning, to replace the one I lost in the fire. Truth be told, I'd be disappointed if I didn't.

The window didn't have much of a view—only similar buildings across the way and the street down below—but it did let in a lot of light. I could see the SUV, and wondered what Al and Candy were talking about. Whatever it was, it had to be less tension-filled there than it was here.

"Ciel . . . I'm sorry. I was stupid. I thought of a hundred different ways to explain it to you, to excuse it, but that's the simple truth."

"Why are you telling me this? You still don't want a kid, do you?" I said, not looking at him.

He sucked in a breath. "No. I don't."

I flinched, automatically hugging my middle. The scale just tipped. Anger for the win. "Then why are we even here?" I said harshly, keeping my back turned.

Billy came to me. Leaned over, hugging me from behind. Like he was sheltering me. But from what? Himself? I tried to pull away and, failing that, to elbow him in the gut. He held on.

"I'm not going to lie to you, Ciel. I *don't* want a kid. The idea of it scares me shitless, and you know I don't scare easily. I think you have a right to know why."

I stilled, needing to hear what he had to say.

He took a deep breath. "The woman who gave birth to me is in an institution. For a very good reason." He swallowed hard. It obviously wasn't easy for him to talk about.

I twisted around in his arms, compassion, for the moment, pulling ahead. "I know. Your father told me about it right before you got there."

Anger sparked in his eyes, at Uncle Liam I supposed, for telling me what Billy had obviously wanted kept a secret over all these years.

"He was worried about you, about what you might do. He never would have said anything otherwise."

Billy nodded, resignation replacing anger. "The thing is, as much as I don't want a kid, I do want you. I want you so much more than I don't want a kid. So I'm here, admitting I was an ass in Houston." He looked deep into my eyes, his face stripped of his usual brash, take-on-the-world confidence. "Ciel, I regret that more than you can possibly imagine."

My shields went up, and I pushed away. He let me go. "You once told me you don't do regret, that it was a waste of time. That mistakes were nothing more than life-enriching experiences."

"I still believe that's mostly true. But not with this. This is the first time in my life I honestly know what regret means. Deep-down, soul-searing regret. I should not have left you there, alone with this." He spoke the last sentence slowly and deliberately, his eyes emphasizing the sincerity of every word.

"Damn straight, you shouldn't have," I blurted, poking his chest with my finger. *Because if you hadn't, I never would have slept with Mark*, I thought, *and I wouldn't be feeling so damned guilty right now!*

And not guilty on Billy's account either. Guilty at what I'd done to Mark. How I'd used him as some sort of giant Band-Aid for my psyche, without considering how it would make him feel afterward.

That was part of my problem, I realized. Sure, Billy had made a mistake. But would I really be having such a hard time forgiving him if I wasn't trying to avoid my own damn conscience?

Billy laid his hands on my shoulders. My anger deflating, I let him. "Ciel, I'd sell my soul if I could take back the hurt I caused you"—one corner of his mouth lifted wryly—"not that seared souls are worth much, and anyway, that's stupid. I can't. All I can do is tell you if you still want to keep the baby, even knowing about my birth mother, I'll be right there with you, doing my best to be a father."

I stared up at him, stunned. Until that moment it hadn't once occurred to me that I didn't necessarily have to have the baby. If pressed, I would have considered myself pro-choice, but somehow I'd never thought to apply it to myself.

"You want me to—" I couldn't say it. My God, if my mother ever found out . . .

"What I don't want is for you to be saddled with a kid from my gene pool." Bitterness clouded his eyes. And something else. Fear.

The silence stretched out as I tried to consider the possibility. In a way, it made sense. And, God, if it would erase the terror I saw in his eyes . . .

I was a fixer, and it was certainly one way I could fix a complicated situation. But in the process I would break something inside *me*. And I'd never be able to put it behind me, because every time I looked at my new niece or nephew I'd be reminded.

I shook my head slowly. "I don't think that can be on the table, not for me. I'm no more ready to be a mother than you are to be a father, but the way I was raised . . . I don't think I could."

He nodded. Accepted it. "Okay then. Let's do this thing."

I sagged into him, laying my head against his chest, grateful he wasn't going to push it. "Why didn't you tell me about your birth mother before? In Houston, if not sooner?"

"Before, it never seemed to matter. Frankly, I didn't want to think about it, much less talk about it. And in Houston . . . it all kind of reared up and swallowed me. I knew I finally had to see her for myself. To see exactly what kind of crazy I'm carrying around inside me."

I looked up at his troubled face. "Billy, she's mentally ill, not some sort of monster," I said as gently as I could.

Pain twisted his handsome features. "No, that would be Dad. And me."

"According to a woman who doesn't have a firm grasp on reality. It sounds to me like she's a product of her early environment. It's sad, but your father is doing the best he can for her."

"But what if it's genetic? What if *I* lose my mind down the road? What if I pass it on? Jesus, Ciel, aren't you even a little bit afraid of what we might bring into the world?"

"No. I'm not," I said firmly. "I have never met anyone more grounded than you, and I've known you all my life. I think I would have noticed anything off by now." I reached up to stroke his cheek. "Your dad said she reacted, um, poorly to seeing you."

"If by 'poorly' you mean screaming that I was the devil and collapsing into a catatonic heap on the floor, yeah, that happened. Not very good for my ego, let me tell you. I left, quickly. Probably a little too quickly."

Something about the way he said the last part worried me. "What happened?" I said.

He looked uncomfortable. "I was agitated. Took a curve faster than I should have. Banged up the Chevy a bit, that's all."

"How banged up?"

He shrugged. "More than scratched paint, but it fared better than the tree."

"You hit a *tree*?" Billy was one of the best drivers I knew. Other than Mark, I didn't know anyone better.

"Only a small one," he said.

"Jesus Christ on a piece of toast. Are you okay?"

"Look at me, cuz. I'm fine."

Ha. I knew better than to take that at face value. "Show me," I said, narrowing my eyes so he'd know I meant business.

He dropped the adjustments he'd been making to his aura, revealing a bruised and abraded cheek. Across his forehead was a long gash, perilously close to one eye. It had been stitched neatly, but still stood out starkly on his face.

"Windshield?" I said, compressing my lips.

He nodded.

"Is that all of it?" I said, proud of how well I was controlling my reaction.

He lifted his sweater. Above his drool-worthy abs was a spectacular eggplant-colored bruise. I ran my fingers over it lightly, swallowing hard. No wonder he hadn't been able to come back any sooner.

"Steering wheel?"

Again, he nodded.

"Did you break any ribs?"

He dropped his sweater back into place. "No. I told you, I'm fine. My car and I will both be back to our excessively handsome selves in no time." The words were pure Billy, but the delivery lacked his usual panache.

I made myself look at the long cut on his face again. "Will it scar?" I asked. He had enough scars from his birth mom; he didn't need a reminder of her every time he looked in a mirror as himself.

"Probably. But it will fade in time, according to the doc. And meanwhile"—the visible remnants of the accident disappeared—"it's not like I'll be frightening the general public. Or my family." He stressed the last part, looking at me significantly.

I sighed. "I won't tell on you. You know a scar doesn't matter to me, right?"

He nodded.

Okay, enough is enough. Time to lighten this shit up. "I mean, you've always been prettier than me anyway. Frankly, I was getting tired of all the how-did-she-ever-score-him looks I was getting from other women."

He grinned. "Want me to rip out my stitches so it will leave a grizzlier scar?"

"Aw. You'd do that for me?" I said.

"Say the word. And then get me some Vicodin and lidocaine, because damn, this is going to sting." He reached up to his forehead.

"Stop that, you idiot," I said, and hugged him gingerly.

He pulled me to him harder, as if he felt like he deserved the pain, and his voice turned serious again. "Ciel, I mean it. I am so, so sorry. All I can say is, in my warped frame of mind—then, in that moment—I honestly thought you'd be better off without me. My biggest fear now is that I was right, that you would be. But I'm not strong enough to stay away from you."

Tears sprang to my eyes at the thought of Billy being afraid of anything, and clogged my voice when I spoke. "Stop it. I need you, damn it. Warts and all." I managed a small laugh. "Not that I won't use it against you for the rest of our lives. Just so you know."

His laugh was suspiciously watery, too. "Deal. And worth it, as long as our lives are together."

We stood there a few minutes longer, digesting our emotions, realigning our relationship's equilibrium. When we finally pulled ourselves apart, Billy said, "Okay, enough about me and my shit. What about you? Are *you* all right?"

"Oh, hell yeah," I said brightly. "Heck, I wasn't even in the condo when it was torched. My landlord"—I winked—"is taking care of everything. And on the upside, I got a whole new wardrobe out of it from Mom and Dad. I didn't even have to go shopping for it. Hey, counting today, that makes twice I've gotten out of shopping this week. It almost makes up for having to do the whole damn mall with James and Devon."

Billy listened patiently to my rah-rah-I'm-fine speech. "I'm glad, but that's not what I meant. I knew Thomas would handle your condo. How are you after the skating rink?"

The blood took a nosedive out of my head at the reminder, leaving me wobbly. "How do you know about that?"

He gripped my elbows and held me up. "Mark told me."

"Mark's been trying to reach you for days. Why'd you answer him now?"

"The message he left this morning said Loughlin had almost succeeded in killing you. I'd ignored all his previous messages because I knew you were safe—"

"And stupidly thought I was better off without you?" I said.

"And, yes, *misguidedly* thought you were better off without me—"

"Stupidly," I insisted.

He quirked his mouth. "Have it your way. Stupidly. But that message got my attention. So I called him."

I imagined the conversation, and my stomach constricted. "Did he tell you I killed a man?" I said, my voice flat.

"Yeah. He said you had to—the guy had an ice pick to your chest. Jesus, cuz, is that true?"

I nodded. "I sliced his carotid with the blade of my skate. There was a lot of bl—" I swallowed the word, almost gagging on it. I tried again. "Blood. It g-got in my eyes"—I'd begun trembling badly; Billy wrapped me in his arms—"and my nose and my m-mouth." And there went the sobs. Goddamn stupid pregnancy hormones. Seemed like every stray thought was an emotional bear trap, ready to snap and set me off.

Billy picked me up and carried me to the couch, and sat, keeping me on his lap. "It's all right, sweetheart. Shh. It's okay. You did great. You hear me? That asshole was going to kill you and you didn't let him. You're fucking *awesome*."

"No, I'm not. I was scared and I panicked, and got lucky. I pretty much imploded afterward."

"You wouldn't be human if you didn't. God, I wish I'd been there for you. You don't know how sorry I am I wasn't with you when it happened. That I wasn't the one to slaughter that worthless piece of shit."

"Huh. You and the owners of the rink," I said with a weak laugh, getting hold of myself. "I'm sure you would have been able to accomplish the deed without getting the place shut down as a hazardous waste site."

"No doubt. Snapping a neck isn't usually bloody."

I pushed myself up from his chest so I could see his face. "Have you snapped someone's neck?" I asked.

He tilted his head, considering me. "You really want to know?"

"Yeah, I do," I said, fascinated in spite of my churning stomach.

"I have."

"When? Where? Why did you have to do it? Was it a man or a woman?" Call me morbidly curious, but I had to know.

"Which time?"

" '*Which time*'? You've done it more than once?"

He shrugged.

"Tell! All of them," I said, tears turned off like a faucet, my misery brightening at the prospect of company, as misery is prone to do.

"Well, okay, but you have to promise me you won't turn this into some sort of gruesome competition . . ."

I slapped his chest. But lightly, on account of his injury. "Tell me already."

"I mean, you do have a competitive streak. I don't want you to feel like you have to go out and break some malefactor's neck just because I have."

I gave him the evil eye. "I won't have to go far."

"All right, all right. The first time was on my third job for the spook—see, you're already ahead of me there, so you can relax." The teasing glint in his eyes was wrong on so many levels, but humor—even when it was of necessity dark—was a coping mechanism that tended to work for me, and Billy knew it. "I was filling in for a midlevel diplomat on an overseas trip. I can't tell you which country, or Mark would have to kill *me*. One day, my driver took the scenic route to our destination. Along the way we met up with a man who obviously meant us no good. The diplomat's wife and five-year-old daughter were with me. The wife was shot between the eyes before I could do anything to stop it, and the bastard was about to do the same to the girl. He turned his back on me. I had an opening and I took it."

Billy had lost the humor as he related the story, and by the end was looking grim. I guess dark humor will only take you so far.

"How did you feel afterward?" I asked.

"Immediately? Good. Pretty damn heroic, in fact. Later? Sick to my stomach. Small price to pay for saving a little girl's life."

"Did you throw up?" I asked. Billy had a really strong stomach, so if it had made him vomit, it would be a good indicator of how much it had affected him.

He tugged my hair. "Yes, smarty-pants. I did. By the way, it takes a lot more force than you might imagine to break someone's neck, so don't go getting the idea that you could have stopped your attacker that way and avoided the mess. You did the only thing you could do under the circumstances."

I nodded, knowing he was right. "You said 'first time.' How many more?"

"One. But it was a bit more . . . deliberate. I'm not sure you want to know."

I looked at him, waiting.

He finally nodded. "Okay, but remember—you asked. It was the same diplomat. I'd thought it was odd that the man who'd killed his wife hadn't put me out of commission right away—most attackers will take out the man first, to avoid exactly what happened. I could only figure the attacker had reason to believe the diplomat wouldn't fight back. Mark did some digging, and found out he'd set the whole thing up to get rid of his wife."

"That's horrible," I said.

Billy nodded. "Worse, the daughter was seen as collateral damage. Being a diplomat, the guy couldn't be brought to justice through official channels—it would have amounted to the dreaded 'international incident,' which naturally had to be avoided at all costs, at least according to Mark's higher-ups. But they were willing to turn a blind eye if some sort of tragic 'accident' happened to the guy. Say, a mugging gone awry. I volunteered to be the accident. Mark didn't want to let me—he said it was different from killing in the heat of the moment, and he didn't want me to go there. I did it anyway."

I was quiet for a minute, absorbing what he'd told me. I came to the conclusion he'd done the right thing. "Was it?" I said at last.

"Different? Yeah. I was prepared. Told myself I was protecting

the girl. I still believe that. And, no, I didn't throw up that time."
Billy hesitated. Swallowed. "But Mark was right. The planning,
the preparation . . . it adds a layer of . . . I don't know if I'd call it
guilt exactly—the bastard deserved it. Maybe 'culpability' is the
word I'm looking for."

I took his face in my hands and kissed his forehead—lightly—
offering him the same absolution he'd given me.

"So, shall we start a tally board or what?" he said, quirking his
mouth. "Should there be extra credit for coming close to biting
the big one? Or according to how big an asshole they are? We
could color code it for evilness, black being for the most heinous
villains we dispatch, of course. And maybe partial credit for
roughing someone up? On a sliding scale, depending on how
much blood is drawn. I should at least get a gold star for those
neo-Vikings last summer."

I tried not to laugh—but yeah, dark humor. It helped. This was
the Billy I loved, warped humor and all. He understood me, and
I thought I understood him, too. I saw the pain beneath his
joking, and I couldn't give up on him.

But if things were going to work between us, we had to maintain our hard-won openness. I took a deep breath. "There's something you should know. I told Mark I'm pregnant . . . and that it
might be his. Not likely, but possible."

Billy closed his eyes. His Adam's apple bobbed up and down
once as he worked to compose his face. When he opened his eyes,
I saw acceptance, if not complete understanding. "Well, I'm hardly
in a good position to complain, am I? And what did Captain Honorable do? Propose?" Billy said, attempting humor.

I just looked at him.

Chapter 22

Comprehension hit Billy's face like a hammer. "My God, he did, didn't he?"

He lifted me gently off his lap and set me beside him. Stood, shaking his head in apparent amazement. "On the minuscule chance one of his little tadpoles got to your egg instead of mine." He was at the bar, already pouring a drink. "Gotta hand it to the guy, nobody does 'hero' better than he does. So, when's the big day? Am I invited?"

I would have been mad if it hadn't been so obvious he was in pain. I was, however, plenty exasperated. "Don't be stupid. I'm not marrying Mark."

"Why not? You love him—don't look at me like that. You know you do. Maybe not as much as you love me—I'm not so modest I won't concede that—but he's better husband material. Well, if you don't mind his dangerous career choice. But then again, what's danger to Superman? No doubt bullets bounce off him."

"Oh, like *your* jobs aren't dangerous? Never mind, it doesn't matter. I'm not marrying *anyone*," I ground out. "God, you are such an idiot. How I can still love you beyond reason is incomprehensible!"

I stomped off to the kitchen and got myself a glass of water. He followed. Leaned over me from behind again. "Beyond reason?" he said softly.

"*Yes.* What reasonable woman would put up with you?" I might have sounded grumpy.

I felt his lips touch a sensitive spot behind my ear. "Ciel, at the risk of repeating myself . . . I'm sorry. And I hope you didn't mean it about not marrying anyone, because you know our mothers will have us at the altar five seconds after they find out."

I spun around to face him. "God, Billy, we can't tell them! They'll plan a *wedding*."

"Horrifying," he said, the humor popping back into his eyes.

"You *know* I hate weddings!"

He ran his fingers through my hair, finishing with a tiny tug. "We could always elope."

"We can't—they'd kill us," I said, conveniently forgetting that a moment before I wasn't going to get married at all.

"They'll forget all about it once they hear about the baby."

True. "But what if it *is* Mark's?" I said. "How would you feel then?" It had to be asked.

A slew of emotions flitted over his face. "Honestly? I think more relieved than anything else. If you're worried I wouldn't love it, all I can say is you're wrong. I would love any child of yours. Even"—he smiled ruefully—"mine. But I admit I would be a more relaxed father if I knew the baby wasn't loaded with my genes, like some kind of ticking time bomb."

Something we'd obviously have to work through. Later.

A determined look settled over his face. "Come on. Let's do it right now."

"*What?* Are you crazy? It's not like going out for ice cream, Billy."

"Sure it is. We can get a license at City Hall. Hell, they can probably make it official right there. And then we *will* go for ice cream. Or maybe hot chocolate would be more in keeping with the weather."

"But—"

"You know once our mothers find out you're pregnant they won't rest until we're married. Why not do it on our terms? Think of it as the anti-wedding," he said.

It did make sense, and he was right about our mothers. "I don't know . . ."

He hit me with the Doyle eyes. Big, blue, and beseeching. What choice did I have?

You do have a choice, my inner troublemaker said as an image of Mark appeared in my head. Mark hugging my belly instead of running away from it. Mark offering me whatever I needed without hesitation, no matter what it cost him personally.

Shut up! I thought back—loudly—at the meddlesome bitch. *Billy had a reason for running. He came back—that's the important thing. And those eyes . . .*

I swallowed hard. It was one thing to keep what I'd done with Mark from Billy if I was honestly trying to spare his feelings. And I *was.* But didn't he deserve to know all the facts, no matter how painful, before he committed himself to something as serious as marriage?

"Billy, there's something else I think you better know."

He held a finger to my lips. Closed his eyes briefly and gave a small shake of his head. "The *only* thing I need to know is that you love me. I don't need to hear more."

I pulled his hand away. "I *do* love you, you know I do. But you should know—"

"No. I . . . I don't want to know anything except that you love me. That's all that matters to me, Ciel."

I nodded, blinking back tears, and looked down at my pretty lambswool sweater. Rudolph's nose was still flashing. "Well, I *am* wearing white." I took a deep breath. "What the hell. Let's do it."

"One thing first," he said, the fear in his eyes receding. "Can we please throw out whatever crawled into your purse and died? Because I don't think they'll let us into City Hall with a biohazard."

The Marriage Bureau at the Manhattan Office of the City Clerk was only moderately busy. We filled out some forms, showed our driver's licenses, and boom, we had a license. There was a minor hiccup when we found out we'd have to wait twenty-four hours to do the deed unless we got a judicial waiver. Billy batted his gorgeous eyelashes at a few harried city employees, who promptly contacted a handy judge, and boom, waiver on the way.

Al and Candy had agreed to be our witnesses. Candy was actually excited about it—she thought it was the most romantic thing ever. We didn't mention the reason behind the big rush, and she was couth enough not to ask. Al . . . well, he didn't say much, but I suspected he was beginning to wish the shopping expedition hadn't been cancelled.

Candy had come in with us while Al found secure parking. Not wanting to draw attention to her occupation, she'd left her fire-arm locked in the car, but she told us not to worry, she was "pretty good" with her hands. If she was anywhere near as proficient as Laura—and from the way she carried herself, I suspected she was—I knew there was no reason for concern. If Loughlin, or one of his minions, had the temerity to come into this building after us, at least we could be sure they didn't have a gun. And I had a feeling none of them would stand a chance unarmed against Candy, much less Al or Billy. Possibly even me. (Okay, that was probably a stretch. But I *was* getting better at the hand-to-hand stuff.)

After we got the judicial waiver, we took a number and hung out with half a dozen other couples who'd chosen to join their lives together without the fuss of a big wedding. The waiting area was pleasant enough for a municipal building, furnished with mod-ern sofas upholstered in some sort of industrial-strength green fabric. (Billy said it really set off my eyes.)

When Al joined us he had a bouquet of white roses tied together with red ribbon, which he handed to me. "Every bride oughta have flowers," he said.

"Why, Al, you big ol' softie!" Candy said. "Where'd you find those?"

His cheeks reddened, and he shrugged. "My brother's a florist. He brought 'em over for me."

I held them to my nose. Surprisingly for modern roses, they ac-tually had some fragrance. "This is so sweet. Thank you!" I said, and stood on tiptoe to kiss his cheek. He had to lean down so I could reach.

"Aw, it's nothing. I have a daughter about your age. I hate to think she wouldn't have flowers at her wedding."

My father's face popped into my head, quiet and handsome and strong. Now he'd never get to walk me down the aisle. He'd never complain about it, never say a thing to make me feel guilty (Mom would pick up the slack for him), but I knew it would matter to him.

I turned to Billy, tears starting to fog my vision. "I can't do this. I can't get married without my father! Please say you understand," I said, practically hyperventilating in my effort to get the words out before I dissolved into an embarrassing heap of weeping womanhood.

Gawd. I didn't even have a tissue.

Billy took me by the shoulders and looked me right in my watery eyes. "You know this will mean a wedding, don't you? And our mothers won't do small. It will be a full-on Mo and Ro extravaganza," he said seriously.

"Are you trying to scare me into going through with this?"

He tilted up one corner of his mouth, a mischievous glint in his eyes. "Maybe. Is it working?"

I chuckled through my snuffles, and almost snotted myself. Candy handed me a man-size tissue she'd dug up from somewhere. I could get used to having a bodyguard.

"I'm his only daughter," I said, trusting the explanation to be sufficient.

Billy quirked his mouth, looking like he still wanted to argue his case, but finally leaned over and kissed me. Chastely, on the forehead. "Come on, cuz. Let's blow this joint."

We went back to Billy's place, deciding we'd had enough excitement and would wait until the next day to gather our parents around and break the news. Candy and Al resumed their post across from the door to the building, taking the latest minor upheaval in their professional stride.

The beautiful white roses were in a vase on the slate-and-metal coffee table across from the sofa where we sat holding hands. Billy alternated, as usual, between being super sweet and teasing me mercilessly, mostly about the wedding hell I was about to descend into. It felt good to be back on a normal footing with him.

"You know, a good adaptor fiancé would volunteer to go dress shopping with my mother for me." I slugged him playfully on the bicep closest to me, pretty sure that part of him hadn't been injured in the car accident.

"Yeah. Too bad you're stuck with a *smart* adaptor fiancé," he said with a wink.

"Smart, huh? Idiot savant, maybe."

"I'll savant you." He pulled me closer and proceeded to demonstrate one area where his expertise definitely qualified him for savant status.

"You know," he said during a pause I didn't especially want him to take, "just because we didn't get married doesn't mean we can't have a wedding night."

I pretended to weigh the matter while I ruthlessly trampled down flashes of sleeping with Mark the night before. That guilt was my burden to bear, not Billy's. "But wouldn't it be improper, Mr. Doyle? Isn't there supposed to be a certain protocol to these events?"

"Screw protocol. Haven't you heard? 'Life is short. Eat dessert first.'"

"That is an unfair metaphor to employ with me. You know how I feel about dessert."

"What can I say?" He pointed back at himself with his thumb. "Savant."

My cell phone took that inopportune time to buzz in my pants pocket. Since Billy's hand was already in the area, he dug it out for me.

"It's Mark. Do you want to take it?" He kept his eyes neutral.

I couldn't help feeling the wise thing to do would be to hit "ignore," but I really didn't think I could. "It might be about Loughlin."

Billy nodded, with only the slightest downturn of his lips. I'd already decided to respect his wishes not to know what I'd attempted to tell him about my night with Mark. That was an aberration, a reflection of my trauma more than anything else. When you really thought about it, it was more therapy than sex. And therapy sessions are supposed to remain private, right?

Okay, that was rationalization on my part. But, honestly, not that far from true. I'd needed it at the time, but to tell Billy would be unnecessarily cruel. Confession might be good for *my* soul, but I had a feeling it would shred his.

If I felt guilty about anyone, it was Mark. But I'd been honest with him about Billy even then. He could have refused.

Yeah, right, Ciel. Like he was going to turn down your plea for help. When has Mark ever done that?

Gah. I couldn't think about that now. I swiped the screen and kept my voice light. "Hey there."

"Hey, Howdy. I have some good news."

"You caught the bastard?" I said. "Fantastic!"

"Slow down. No, we don't have Loughlin yet, but we have a few more leads."

"Is it Carl? Is he out of intensive care?"

"No, but it's looking better for him. He's showing signs of waking up."

"What's the good news then? Did Mom and Auntie Mo swear off parties?" I grinned at Billy, who was close enough to hear both sides of the conversation.

Mark chuckled. "Not a chance. But I found out something interesting when I was speaking with Dr. Carson about Loughlin. She mentioned she'd peeked at her medical records to make sure there weren't any hints about her kidney stone. She also said she hoped you weren't feeling any ill effects from the fertility hormones she saw you received before the reduced gravity flight—she never meant for you to get those."

"What are you talking about?"

"Did you happen to get any injections while you were filling in for her?"

"Well, yeah. It was part of her preflight physical. The doctor called them her 'special vitamins.' I assumed it was to keep her healthy for the mission."

"It was for mission prep all right, but only to make sure she's ovulating at the right time. The side effects can be uncomfortable for some women." He paused for a beat. "They can also cause a false positive on a pregnancy test."

"So you mean . . . ?"

"You might not be pregnant after all."

Chapter 23

I turned to Billy. He looked as stunned as I felt.

"Listen," Mark said, "tell me when you're finished shopping and I'll swing by and get you. You can take another test at my place if you don't want to do it at your parents' house. The hormones should be mostly out of your system by now."

"I'm not shopping," I said, dazed, not knowing quite what to feel. "I'm at Billy's. He came back."

There was a pause. A long one, by Mark standards. "Good. That's good. Maybe he can—"

Billy took the phone from me. "I'll take care of it and call you after. And Mark . . . thanks. For everything. You're a better friend than I deserve."

I winced inwardly, knowing it should be me telling Mark that.

"So," I said after Billy slipped my phone back into my pocket.

"So," he said, watching me closely.

I took a deep breath. "Let's see what we're dealing with before anything else."

"Agreed," he said. To his credit, he wasn't doing backflips of joy, or even smiling in a relieved manner. Of course, that might come if he saw a minus sign on the pee-stick.

As for me, I was keeping all thoughts on hold until after the test. Superstitiously, I didn't even want to think—about *anything*—until I knew for sure. I especially didn't want to examine the niggling jab of disappointment I felt. Not that I wanted a baby—I absolutely didn't. Not now, anyway. But I had begun to, I don't know, get used to the idea or something.

Which was stupid, and I refused to entertain that line of thinking, so I redirected my thoughts to the practical. "How are we going to buy a test without raising Candy and Al's eyebrows? They probably already wonder, after our field trip today, but to confirm it . . . I mean, I know they aren't paid to judge, but . . ."

"They can wait in the car while we go into the store."

"Yeah, right. If they wouldn't let us go into a highly secure government building without them, you think they're going to let us traipse into a drugstore alone? Would you, if it were *your* assignment?"

"I can sneak by them. You wait here. I'll go get it."

"Don't you think they might notice you leaving?"

Billy shrugged. "I won't be me."

"Mark has read them in about adaptors. I'm sure they've been told to keep track of *anyone* coming or going, no matter what they look like."

"So I'll go as one of my neighbors. I won't look like a 'suspicious stranger.'"

"And if the neighbor you choose happens to come or go at the same time?"

"Fine. What do you suggest then?"

"Well, it's not ideal, but . . ." I dug my phone back out and dialed.

"Oh, this is so exciting!" Devon said. "I've never been to a pee-stick party before!"

James cut him a look while shaking Billy's hand. He'd already hugged me. "This *isn't* a party," he said.

"Sure it is. We brought pizza and beer. That makes it a party," Devon said, depositing the goodies on the kitchen counter. "Heck, we even brought extra for the security details—with soda, not beer, naturally. Can't go dulling those protective reflexes, now, can we? But we thought it would be cruel to leave our guys pizza-less after making them inhale the delicious aroma for blocks. And your guys shouldn't be the only ones left out, so there you are. Party all around!" He took a bag from James and handed it to me. "Ciel, honey, we brought four test kits. Hope you've been holding it!"

I had, of course, already explained to Billy what had happened when I went shopping with James and Devon. (He wasn't surprised—he'd known something was up then.) Then I'd called James and explained about the fertility hormones, and he'd confirmed what Mark had said about the possibility of a false positive. He was understandably confused, since I'd led him to believe I wasn't pregnant. I had to admit I'd *implied* my period had started, even though it hadn't, but only so as not to worry him. Fortunately, he'd kept the test kits (no doubt thriftily figuring his wayward little sister might one day need them again).

I had also explained to James (via a text message while Billy was informing Al and Candy we were expecting visitors) that Billy did *not* know that James and Devon knew about Mark being a

possible baby-daddy, and I'd appreciate it if he acted like they assumed Billy was the only one. Because the whole damn situation
was difficult enough without Billy knowing they were in on the
who's-your-baby-daddy game. Yeah, yeah. I know. So much for being open. But this was different. Why make Billy feel even more
awkward around James and Devon?

My plan had been for James to discreetly make the delivery,
pretending it was something innocuous, like a piece of mail, or a
DVD of some movie Billy and I wanted to borrow, and then leave.
Apparently, Devon had had other ideas.

"Well, thanks for bringing the pizza, guys," Billy said, hover-
ing at the door. "We'll let you know how it goes."

Had James been alone, he might have taken the hint—he's sensitive to nuance—but when Devon walked over to the couch and
plopped down on it, my brother rather sheepishly joined him.

"Don't worry, we can wait. Go pee, hon. Hurry up now, before
the pizza gets cold," Devon said. He held up both hands, fingers
crossed, nudging my brother with his shoulder until James did the
same thing. "Bring the sticks back out here—we'll pop a cold one
for you the second we see a minus sign."

"But—" I said, darting help-me glances at Billy, who only
shrugged an *I tried* back at me.

Well, crap. I supposed it wasn't really fair to expect them to leave
before the reveal, not when they'd gone to the trouble of arrang-
ing the pizza party cover story for us.

"Fine. Who needs privacy?" I muttered.

Billy followed me into the restroom, like he had before. He
didn't joke around with me this time, though, and I held my own
sticks. He did, however, take each stick as I was done with it,
quickly handing me the next one. (If you think starting and stop-

ping a full bladder four times is easy, think again.) Eventually we had all four laid out on a thick stack of paper towels on the vanity counter (because *ew*), and the waiting began.

Billy took my hand and we stared in silence. After three minutes, all the tests were negative. I squeezed Billy's fingers. After five minutes—the longest any of the instructions said to wait—they all still showed a negative result.

We looked at each other tentatively, like we were both afraid to read what was in the other's eyes. Our smiles started at the same time, mirroring each other's, until both of us were laughing and crying, entwined in our relief.

And it *was* honest-to-God relief I was feeling. If a few of my tears were maybe due to a tiny, stubborn sense of loss, I wasn't going to dwell on it, because when have my emotions ever been simple? It was probably because of the fertility hormones, anyway.

A tentative knock on the door, followed by James's voice, brought us back to reality. "Ciel? Billy? Is everything okay?"

Billy and I pulled apart and wiped our faces with a hand towel. "Yeah, we're great!" I said, and opened the door. Billy held up all four sticks, fanned out like a poker hand.

"Hooray!" Devon said, and grabbed both of us, sandwiching himself between us. (Yeah, probably not the first time he'd been squeezed between a guy and a girl, but I tried not to think about that.) James patted our shoulders, his relief evident if more restrained.

"Where's my beer?" I said. Because, damn, I needed a drink.

A beer and three pieces of pepperoni pizza later (no anchovies), I was feeling pretty mellow. James had succeeded in dragging his boyfriend away, reminding him they both had to work the next morning. Billy and I were alone, sipping our dessert—fully caffeinated Irish coffee with double shots of whiskey. Because I *could*.

"I suppose we should tell the spook," he said, as if reading my mind. "Shall I call him, or would you rather do it?" Again, he had a neutral look. He hadn't done more than hold my hand since James and Devon left, apparently giving me some emotional space.

"I . . ." I cleared my throat. "I think I should do it," I said, keeping my voice businesslike.

The truth was, I wished I could tell Mark in person, and alone, so I could thank him for everything he'd done for me the night before. For being there, for being the cushion that saved me from breaking when I crashed. To apologize for using him the way I had, and explain how I didn't know how I would have made it through without him.

How could I say any of that in front of Billy?

Billy looked at me thoughtfully, head cocked. Nodded. "I'll be in the bathroom. Can't buy beer, you know. You can only rent it," he said.

Yeah, right. Like Billy didn't have the world's strongest bladder. But I was grateful for his tact.

"Good news," I said as soon as Mark answered. There was a pause. I rushed to fill it. "The tests—four of them—were all negative. I'm not pregnant."

"Good. Great. I'm happy for you, Howdy." Another pause. "Listen, I have to run. Tell Billy I'll call him tomorrow. I think I might know a way to lure Loughlin out of the woodwork, but we can't do anything tonight." All business again.

"Mark . . . thank you. For everything. You . . ." I lowered my voice. "You saved me."

Then I said goodnight, hoping like hell he understood what I meant. He was a smart guy. I was pretty sure he must. Still, I cursed the lousy timing of everything in my life, starting with Dr. Phil's kidney stone. If I hadn't been on the job when her NASA doc administered the hormones, none of this would have happened. Barring that, if only I'd found out about the freaking hormones before I'd opened my stupid mouth to Mark, then he need never have known.

"Everything okay?" Billy's voice came from the doorway of the bathroom.

"Yeah. It's safe to come out now."

He came and took me in his arms. "I don't know what you mean. When a man has to pee, he has to pee."

"Uh-huh." I tilted my head up and saw the understanding in his eyes. "You're a good guy, you know that?"

"Good enough to marry even if you aren't pregnant?" he asked.

I sucked in a breath. How did you diplomatically answer a question like that without hurting the feelings of the man you love? Or, you know, without winding up married?

I made a valiant stab at it. "You are most definitely good enough. But could we keep eating dessert for a while longer before we order the whole meal? Now that we aren't under a deadline crunch?" I said, giving him my most seductive smile.

He laughed. (Yeah, maybe not as seductive as I hoped.) "Is it weddings or marriage that terrifies you more?"

"Weddings," I said at once, mostly sure it was true. "And since Al's roses made it inconveniently plain I can't elope, I'm afraid we're going to have to wait until I feel mentally prepared to face the white lace and organ music."

"How do you feel about black silk sheets and playing a 'flute'?"

he said, with exactly the right amount of wicked innuendo to get my heart racing through my giggles.

Laughter and lust, a salty-sweet combo more addictive than kettle corn.

Twenty minutes later I was breathing heavily and swearing at the same time. "What do you mean you don't have any condoms? How can you not have condoms?"

"I'm sorry, but I threw them all out because I *thought* I didn't need them anymore, you being on the patch and all. I didn't want you find them here and jump to the mistaken conclusion I hadn't given up my wayward lifestyle."

I heaved a disappointed sigh. "I took off the patch when I thought I was pregnant."

Which, it occurred to me with a thousand-watt jolt, meant I hadn't been fully protected when I was with Mark.

No. God cannot be that cruel.

"Look, it's probably okay," I said, trying to convince myself as much as him. "I haven't had the patch off for very long."

"Uh-uh. No way. Not after you had a dose of fertility drugs."

Crap. Crappity, crappity, crap-crap-crap. He was right. "Argh!" I said. "This is so not fair."

Fortunately, Billy seemed to think it was my sexual frustration talking, and not my new worry about Mark's swimmers. "I can call James and see if he'll come back over with some. I'm sure he'll understand our dilemma," he teased.

I rolled away from him, pulling a sheet around me. We were in his loft, on his king-size bed, but my clothes were still downstairs. "Oh, yeah. Sure. Or why not ask Al if he has a spare in his wallet? Because that wouldn't be embarrassing either."

"Come back here. We don't need a condom."

"But you said—"

He pulled me to him. Started nibbling my neck. "Ciel, there are lots and lots of other ways we can make this"—he licked one of my nipples, and blew on it softly—"a very satisfying experience"—his hand found its way up my thigh, fingers teasing and delving everywhere, gliding over places that would normally make me flinch, but somehow not with him—"for both of us. And I know all of them." His voice held a world of promise.

I moaned and stopped thinking about condoms, patches, and Mark's swimmers. *Sufficient unto the day . . .*

Chapter 24

I looked out over the small auditorium at fifty or so alert and interested faces. Every one of them appeared honored to be included in this special NASA presentation, ostensibly set up to explain in greater detail the parameters of Dr. Phil's mission on the space station.

Man, I hoped Loughlin would come after me before anyone asked me a question I didn't know the answer to, because dodging death seemed, at the moment, preferable to what I was about to do.

Mark had given me a folder full of facts to study on the flight back to Houston (in an Agency plane, so I didn't have to worry about nosy passengers reading over my shoulder), so, theoretically, I had all the knowledge I needed to get through the next hour. And I was pretty sure all the details *were* in my head. Somewhere. Only I was terribly afraid they might have gotten scrambled a bit in my rush to wedge them into my memory.

Didn't matter, I told myself. It wasn't like the people in the audience were really scientists. Mark had set up the whole thing using the best agents at his disposal, each of them posing as a representative from the science department of a university or college. The thing was, knowing Mark's standards, they had all studied assiduously for their roles, and could no doubt come up with super-intelligent questions to fill the time until Loughlin might strike.

Yeah, I was bait. Mark's big plan was twofold: one, to set up something too tempting for Loughlin to resist, and thus lure him away from preying on the adaptor population in New York, and two, to catch the bastard. The venue he'd rented for the day was specially selected to look invitingly open while in fact being highly containable, with the right personnel.

Billy had objected—big-time—until Mark had assured him I would be surrounded by the best field agents in the country. Billy himself was sitting right next to me onstage, in the guise of Phil's husband. Misha was a strong guy. With Billy's defense skills behind the aura, I felt pretty safe.

The real Phil and Misha were locked down at their house with yet more agents. They knew enough not to answer the door or their landline. Billy and I had their cell phones, so no worry there.

In the front row, about as close to the stage as you could get, was Dr. Phil's brother, Rudy, the one who'd come to Mark about the job in the first place. It wouldn't seem out of place for Rudy to be there—why wouldn't a brother attend an important event for his sister?

Mark was in a back corner, pretending to be a generic NASA employee. He had a good view of every way in or out of the big room. He was himself, though with his loose-fitting suit and black-framed glasses you'd never guess it at first glance.

The "host" of the event—an especially pompous-looking

gentleman of about sixty, who Mark had assured us could kill someone a hundred different ways if the need arose—said something about mankind thus far being in a gestational period, but on the brink of our true birth into the universe. (Good God, was I *never* going to escape the pregnancy allusions?) He went on to say that with the advent of procreation in space, we would be able to explore our galaxy unbound by our short life spans, and the future was full of unlimited potential, yadda yadda. Applause, applause. All very inspiring, but I was too busy scanning the auditorium for Loughlin's face to give it the attention it no doubt deserved.

No sign of him. Mark had warned us this whole thing might be a wash if Loughlin got skittish. If we didn't catch him today, we'd just have to keep our collective guard up longer. Which would be a total pain in the ass for all involved, especially the security details who'd have to miss their own holiday celebrations to watch over us through ours. Of course, Mom would make them cookies. (And if they were truly fortunate, they wouldn't get her Snicker-doodle Surprises, the "surprise" being caviar, because "everyone loves caviar!")

When it came my time to speak I faked my way through the first few softball questions obviously planted with agents by Mark to put me at my ease. Faking became more difficult as time went on. My answer to one question about zygote morphology elicited raised eyebrows and a delicate cough from Billy-Misha, who probably not only knew the real answer (which apparently had nothing to do with goats), but could tell you which page of the file it was on. Fortunately, the audience pretended to think I was joking.

I pointed to a woman raising her hand in the second row. She stood and said, "You explained how you're getting hormone treatments to make sure your ovulation syncs with your time on the ISS. How are you feeling?"

Ha. At last something I knew the answer to firsthand. "You mean aside from the bloating, queasiness, and mood swings? Super!" I said with a big smile, to the amusement of all in attendance. (Hey, they already thought I was a comedian. Why not make the most of it?)

Inspired (or desperate, take your pick), I invited Misha up to the podium with me. He was asked about his "involvement" in the mission. He described it, very scientifically, as "me, a dirty magazine, and paper cup." The audience roared. Good thing the reporters among them weren't any more genuine than the scientists, or the general public might get the idea he wasn't taking his wife's mission seriously.

After the questioner recovered he said, "Thanks for the visual, but I meant your company, Spaceward Ho."

"Oh. I see," Billy said, with Misha's adorable Russian accent. "I will tell you, but frankly it is not so fun." And then he (of course) proceeded to outline Spaceward Ho's innovative improvements in cargo ("human and otherwise") hauling, ending with "I am, of course, the best ride available to my wife."

When the clock hit twenty minutes past our allotted time, we were forced to admit Loughlin was a no-show. None of the agents set up covertly in concentric circles outside, covering all possible routes to and from the auditorium, had reported a sighting. Mission failure. Mark dismissed the indoor agents with a prearranged announcement about hoping they would all keep their respective schools tuned in on launch day. They wouldn't break character until they were safely out of the city.

"Good try," Billy said to Mark. Misha's voice, minus the accent.

Voices come with the aura you're wearing unless you consciously use your own. Accents are a separate talent, one that must be learned, and Billy didn't need it in present company. "Back to the drawing board?"

Mark nodded, only the tension around his mouth showing his displeasure. He knew no mission was a guaranteed success, but he hated it when things didn't work out the way he planned. "We'll meet back at the hotel after you take your auras home."

Because of course Billy and I had to be seen driving back to Phil and Misha's place. We'd drop the auras there, and they'd be free to be seen in public again.

Rudy shook Mark's hand. "Thanks for trying," he said, and then added, to me and Billy, "Hey, can I get a ride with you? My back tire is leaking air, and my spare is flat, too. Guess I'm back on duty watching my sister. And here I thought I was done baby-sitting her when she went off to college."

"Sure," I said. Fortunately, Billy and I had driven over in Misha's gray Nissan GT-R, which Billy had assured me was even cooler than Phil's TR6, though frankly I couldn't see it. Billy had told me I'd understand if I knew more about cars. Whatever. At least it had a backseat. Which I, with Dr. Phil's long legs, wasn't about to volunteer to occupy. "You might be a little cramped, but we'll get you there."

He smiled, showing perfect white teeth in a face rivaling his sister's for good looks. "Not a problem. I've been in tighter spots."

We were barely out the door when Rudy remembered something he needed to tell Mark, who was settling up with the venue's owner. "You go ahead—it'll only take a minute."

It was more than a minute, for which he apologized profusely when he met us by the car. "Mark had some follow-up questions. And then some follow-ups to the follow-ups."

"The King of Spooks is nothing if not thorough," Billy said, opening the door for Rudy, who crawled into the backseat looking like he was trying to hide a wince.

"You okay?" I said. If he thought a wince was going to make me offer up the front seat, he was sadly overestimating my altruism.

"Leg cramp. I keep telling Misha he needs a bigger car, but the Russki won't listen."

Damn it. "Um, would you like the front seat?" I said. I swear, being nice is a curse.

"No, I'm good. I've learned the secret to this backseat is stretching your legs out sideways."

Okay, I tried. I was going to count it as my good deed for the day. Rudy was quiet, but Billy kept us entertained with his running commentary on everything we passed, using an exaggerated version of Misha's accent.

When we got to the turnoff for Dr. Phil's neighborhood, Rudy interrupted Billy's humorous patter. "Keep going."

Something about the tone of his voice made me twist around to look at him. The gun barrel pointed right at my face was the last thing I expected to see. My yelp (hey, I was surprised) drew Billy's attention.

"Don't do anything stupid," Rudy said to him. "You know I can put a giant hole in her before you can twitch. And if you try to wreck the car, she'll be dead before the air bags go off."

Billy gripped the wheel tighter as he passed the turnoff. "Where exactly am I taking us?" he asked. His voice was remarkably calm. And accent-free.

"Keep driving. I'll tell you when you need to turn." Rudy's voice carried a lot more tension, and he was starting to sweat. His spook instructors would be disappointed by his lack of emotional control.

"Turn around, Ciel. Stop looking at me with—" He cut himself off. Obviously he didn't like his sister's eyes watching him. Not being a fool, I acquiesced at once, pointing my face straight ahead, but keeping my eyes on Billy, watching for any signal he might give me.

"Don't forget for a second what's right behind you, *Ciel*"—he seemed intent on reassuring himself I wasn't his sister—"and don't think your seat will stop a bullet. This forty-five will go through it like butter." I got the feeling he was saying it for Billy's sake.

Billy kept his speed steady, his hands at eight and four on the steering wheel. "Ciel won't be making any sudden moves." That, I knew, was for my benefit.

"We're coming up on the highway. Get on it," Rudy said.

Billy nodded. "I'm going to need to shift gears."

"Go ahead."

Billy's moves were slow and deliberate. Nothing that might jar Rudy into firing. I kept completely still for the same reason, hoping like hell Billy had a plan forming behind Misha's outwardly serene eyes, because I had zilch.

Once he was at speed he spoke. "You know Mark will come after you, right? If not right away, then soon, and relentlessly," he said as calmly as if he were discussing an upcoming sporting event.

"I'm not worried about Mark." The implication behind Rudy's words hit me like a punch in the gut. And I'd been punched in the gut for real before. The comparison might be a cliché, but it was accurate. If he'd hurt Mark, or worse . . .

Billy darted a glance at me. I took a deep breath and steadied myself, trying to convey without words that I wasn't going to panic.

"Give me your phones. Now. Slowly."

Okay, now I might panic. Without the GPS in our cell phones, how was help going to find us? But Billy was doing as he was told, so I did, too. Rudy took them both and removed the batteries one-handed, never lowering his gun. "I didn't want to do this, you know," he said. "I had no choice."

"There's always a choice," I said. "Look, why don't you tell us what happened. We can help."

"Stop talking to me with—" He cut himself off. If voices could sweat, his would be dripping.

Maybe I could use it. "Does my sounding like your sister bother you, Rudy? What would she think of your doing this?"

"She might not understand now, but she will later. After . . ."

"After what?" Billy said.

"After she has kids. Jesus Christ. They took my kids, okay? *They took my kids.*"

Billy and I didn't even pretend not to look at each other.

"Who?" I said. "Who took your kids? And why?"

"The Russians. The ones Misha used to work with before he met my sister. They've had them for weeks. I tried everything I knew to get them back, you have to believe me, you *have* to." He was winding tighter by the second.

"Why would they take your kids?" I asked, dumbfounded.

"It doesn't matter now. I'm going to get them back. Take the next exit. Then turn right at the light."

Billy complied. "Listen, man. We really can help. Give us the background. We'll help you any way we can, I swear."

"You're helping me the only way you can right now. I'm sorry, but my kids have to come first."

"How many kids do you have? How old are they?" I said.

"Two. My boy is six. My baby girl"—his voice broke—"is three. They said they'd—hey, slow down! Take the next left. Then keep on driving until I tell you to stop."

"I take it you're trading us for your kids?" Billy said.

"What would they want with us?" I said.

"Phil," Billy said. "They wanted Phil, didn't they? Either to sabotage the mission, or to get to Misha."

"They don't give a crap about the mission. They only want my sister so they can control Misha."

"But you didn't want to give them your sister, did you? Not even for your kids," I said.

He gave me a look so desperate it chilled my bones. "You're wrong. I would give them my sister in a heartbeat to save my kids. I love her, but they're *my kids*. But then, when the kidney stone happened, it was like a gift from God. Suddenly there was a way to let them have my sister without really giving her to them. Mark would have been able to get away from them. And so will you. My sister and her husband wouldn't have stood a chance."

I shook my head. "I still don't understand why you didn't just *ask* Mark for help. You must know he would have done everything he could to get your kids back," I said.

"I couldn't risk it. If he'd refused, he would have known my plan, and I never would have been able to pull it off."

"Where does Alec Loughlin fit in?" Billy said.

"He was the Russians' idea. Phil was supposed to be taken on the day of her zero-G flight. They needed someone who'd worked with NASA before, someone they knew had the right security clearance. A photographer was a good idea. A photographer desperate to pay off a debt to Bratva—the Russian mafia—was better. They could control him. And someone they knew Phil would trust and go with quietly? Perfect."

"Wouldn't it have been easier to take her from her home? Or at least somewhere without so much security?" I said, instinctively trying to keep him talking. If we could get him to approach the problem rationally, to dial back his panic about his kids, maybe we'd all get out of this alive. Because, honestly? Even though Rudy was the one with the gun, I still thought Billy could bring him down. But maybe not without killing him, and I was sick to death of killing.

"Yeah, but then what excuse could Rudy give Mark for needing someone to take her place? Isn't that right?" Billy said, playing along, keeping the conversation going. "What'd you do? Tell the Russians security around her was even tighter when she wasn't at work, due to the nature of her mission? That's what I would have done."

Rudy didn't answer directly, which I took as an admission Billy was right. "It was never supposed to be you, Ciel. It was supposed to be Mark. I knew he'd be able to handle the Russians. He never told me he'd farmed the job out to someone else until it was too late. Hell, I didn't even know there were more of you until Phil told me about Ciel."

Sounded like Mark, all right. Captain Need-to-Know didn't disclose the existence of other adaptors unless there was no way around it. It had probably about killed him to have to tell our security details about us.

"And then something went wrong. Loughlin knew Ciel wasn't Phil. How?" Billy said.

"How the fuck should I know? Maybe they were closer than I thought. Maybe Ciel did something, or said something, that was too far off for Alec to swallow. Hell, maybe he *can* see through auras."

Okay, that was the scariest thing Rudy had said so far. Even Billy gripped the steering wheel tighter. "But you confirmed it for him, didn't you? You told him about all of us."

"I didn't have a choice! He was so pissed off when his mission failed. The Russians were going to come after him. I'd never seen him so angry. He told me he was going to let them kill my kids if I didn't tell him exactly what you were."

"And then what? He decided it was his new mission in life to rid the world of us?" Billy said.

Rudy shook his head, though not in denial. "He just . . . he went full-on crazy. Said the world wasn't safe with your kind in it. You have to believe me—it wasn't supposed to happen this way. Nobody was supposed to get killed."

"Is Mark okay?" I had to ask. I couldn't stand not knowing.

"He will be. After he wakes up, which won't be anytime soon."

I took a deep breath, steadying myself. He was alive. *Focus, Ciel. Do what you can do. Fix the problem in front of you. Save the kids. Worry about the rest later.*

"God," I said. "He's going to come after you so hard."

"Won't matter. By then my kids will be safe and he can do whatever he wants to me."

Billy looked at me, a question in his eyes. I nodded. "All right. What do you need us to do?" he said.

Silence. I peeked between the seats. Rudy still held the gun behind me, but was gripping his chest with his other arm. He looked surprised. And in pain.

"You're hurt. Mark didn't go down easily, did he?" I said.

"I'll be fine. I just need to get my kids. What did you mean, what do I need you to do? You're saying you mean to help me? After what I've done?"

"That's exactly what I'm saying," Billy said.

"Why should I believe you? You're trying to put me off guard. Sorry, not happening. This gun stays on Ciel until I have my kids. And if either one of you tries any of that sneaky adaptor shit, I will blow her away." He was sweating badly now, either from nerves or pain. I was guessing pain.

Billy shrugged. "Maybe you should believe us because we're the ones who can rescue your kids after you pass out. Broken ribs are tricky things. I'm guessing yours might have punctured something sensitive."

I peeked again. If anything, he looked worse. He was starting to suck in air like it was beer and he was a freshman at his first frat party.

"I'm good," he said.

"Rudy," I said gently, "how are we going to find your kids if you do lose consciousness? At least tell us where to go for the handoff."

Something in his face relaxed. Either he believed we were going to help him, or else he knew he had no choice. He lowered the gun. Tears started streaming out of his eyes. "Keep heading toward Dayton. Get off at Shady Lane. Go left. There'll be a truck stopped on the side of the road. White panel. Plumber. They didn't say a name."

"How much time do we have?" Billy said.

"Window closes in half an hour. After that . . . oh, Jesus . . ."

I unfastened my seat belt and, reaching between the front seats, gingerly took the gun now hanging limply in his hand. Tears rolled down his face.

Billy kept driving. "Don't worry, I can get us there in time. And here's what we're going to do when we get there . . ."

Chapter 25

Rudy was looking dazed but better. He'd improved considerably once it sank in we were, in fact, going to help him get his kids back. He was still in considerable pain, but his breathing had slowed, and he no longer looked to be on the verge of passing out. Billy had told him broken ribs hurt like a son of a bitch, but likely hadn't really ruptured anything, and talked him through some slow breathing exercises to help his anxiety, which had apparently caught him up short. He said it had never happened before—the Agency didn't tend to employ field agents with anxiety issues. Then again, no one had ever threatened to kill his children before either.

"I don't know how to thank you guys. After what I did . . . after I was about to throw you to the wolves . . . I can't believe you're doing this for me."

Billy glanced at the rearview mirror. "Don't thank us yet—save it until we have your kids back safe and sound. And I still might kick your ass after your ribs heal."

Rudy produced a small, if strained, smile. "I'll take it, and gladly."

He had his gun back. I personally thought it was mighty trusting of Billy to give a loaded weapon to a desperate man prone to anxiety attacks, but it was essential to our plan, such as it was.

It was a simple idea. Basically, we were going to do exactly what Rudy had intended before we teamed up with him: he was going to hand us over, at gunpoint, in exchange for his son and daughter. We were going to play it from the angle that Phil and Misha were not such a loving aunt and uncle that they would willingly trade themselves for the kids. Seemed to us it was the scenario least likely to set off alarm bells in the Russians. And when the safety of children is at stake, you don't want alarm bells fogging up the situation.

Once Rudy removed the kids from harm, Billy and I would reassess and decide where to take it from there. There was no way to plan for that part until we knew what we were up against.

I, of course, had dozens of questions I wanted to ask him about Loughlin, and I was sure Billy did, too, but the kids were our priority. Questions would have to wait.

The truck ("Joe's Plumbing—you plug 'em, we'll plunge 'em!") was at the appointed place when we got there with ten minutes to spare. I got out first, keeping my Phil demeanor stiff and fearful (oddly, not tough to do). Rudy unfolded himself out of the backseat, never taking the gun off me for a second. Billy got out, keeping his eyes glued to the gun, as Misha would have. Rudy signaled him to come stand beside me; he did, taking my hand when he got there.

We stayed a good distance from the truck, waiting patiently. After a minute, two men got out. One tall, one shorter, both beefy as hell. They were looking at first at cell phones, then at Billy and me, like they were comparing us to pictures of Phil and Misha. I wasn't worried about passing inspection. I *was* worried about the guns in their hands, hanging low to their sides. The men looked almost casual if you didn't notice the tension in their fingers.

"Where are my kids?" Rudy's voice was stronger than I would have thought possible after his breakdown in the car. He must be pulling the dregs of his courage up from somewhere. "If I don't see them in the next five seconds, these two will be dead before you get close to them."

Damn. He sounded way too sincere. And I couldn't help but notice he was careful to keep Billy and me between him and the two of them.

"Relax. Your kids are fine. Cute little buggers." It was the tall one who'd spoken. Funny, I'd been expecting an accent. The Russians must have jobbed it out locally.

"One . . ." Rudy didn't sound like he was bluffing. "I don't think your bosses would like it if you show up empty-handed. Two . . ." Jesus. I shot Billy a look. He squeezed my hand. "Three . . ."

"All right, all right. Hold on." The shorter one walked to the back of the truck and unlocked it.

"Four . . ."

Shit. Couldn't Rudy see the guy was getting his kids?

"Don't get twitchy. Here they are."

Shorty opened the door. A skinny little boy with light tan skin and dark, curly hair jumped out, squinting against the sudden light. His sister, with soft brown curls and the lingering chubbiness of toddlerhood, stood at the opening rubbing her eyes.

"Simon! Phoebe!" Rudy's voice was full of relief and fear.

"Daddy?" Simon tried to make a break for his father, but Shorty grabbed him by the shoulder and held him back. "Aunt Phil, Uncle Misha!"

Phoebe, meantime, had turned around, flopped onto her belly, and was attempting to scoot backward out of the truck. Shorty scooped her up by her waist with his gun arm. I tried not to gasp.

The tall one had been keeping his eyes trained on Rudy. "You can see they're all right. Now how about you tell the dynamic duo of astronauts there to go ahead and walk this way, nice and easy, so we can send these children back home with their daddy."

Billy still held on to my hand, holding me back.

"*Go.*" If Rudy's voice were any tighter it would snap in two.

Billy and I stepped at the same time, taking it slowly. When we were halfway to the truck, Shorty let the kids go, and things started happening fast. Simon and Phoebe ran for their father, screaming "Daddy, Daddy!" the whole way.

The tall guy covered the distance to Billy and shoved a gun against his lower back. I got the same treatment from Shorty. They hustled us both to the truck. While the tall one held the gun on us, Shorty pulled our arms behind us—Billy first—and wrapped our wrists with duct tape. Put a piece across each of our mouths for good measure.

"Up you go." Shorty's hand on my ass spurred me to move faster, if only to get away from him. Billy-Misha's eyes were full of the anger Billy was no doubt feeling himself.

I twisted my head around in time to see Rudy climb into the driver's seat of the Nissan and peel out.

Thank God, I thought, as Shorty wound the tape around my ankles.

———

It didn't take long for the *Thank God* to morph into *What the hell have we done*. Apparently, my generous and helpful nature is severely curtailed by duct tape and darkness.

"You okay?"

Now, how the hell had Billy managed to talk? *"Mmmph!"*

"Roll over and rub your face on the carpet. Hurry up—I need your teeth."

What the fuck? Oh, well. I did as I was told, trying not to think about what sorts of nasty things had been hauled in the truck. But at least Phoebe and Simon hadn't had to sit for God knew how long on a hard metal floor. I tried to be grateful for that as I pushed my cheek along the rough pile until the edge of the tape caught and stuck enough to peel off the tape.

"Ouch! Shit, that stings."

"Try it with stubble and see how you like it. Now, move closer and see if you can get your teeth on the tape around my wrists. You might have to gnaw a bit."

My eyes were getting more accustomed to the gloom. A tiny bit of light must be getting in from somewhere. Billy was on his side, his back to me.

I scooted down and latched on, immediately deciding duct tape would never make my top ten list of favorite flavors. Plasticky, adhesive-y, and smelly. Bleah. I didn't make much progress until I remembered the kid from college who'd filed his canines into sharp points in some sort of freakish homage to vampires. He'd claimed "chicks dig it," no doubt having seen our classmates' reactions to the *Twilight* franchise. I, of course, had grabbed some of his energy to freak my parents out at Halloween. (They'd loved it. It's hard to freak out adaptor parents with anything appearance-related.)

I called up the canines, managed to get a tear started, and ripped it the rest of the way with a good hard yank. It didn't take Billy long to free his ankles and unwind the tape from my wrists.

"Now what?" I said, untaping my ankles. The rumble of the vehicle made it plain we were moving at a good rate, so even if we could get the door open, it wasn't like we could jump out and escape. At least I hoped that wasn't what Billy had in mind.

"Now we start looking for anything useful. You take that side. Feel every place—it's too dark to rely entirely on our eyes. And be careful—you don't want to 'find' the wrong end of something sharp."

We started at the front, working our way down both sides, laying hands everywhere from floor to ceiling. At the back corner I felt something plastic and boxlike, with a hinged lid. When I lifted the lid, there wasn't much doubt what it had been used for. A camping toilet. When you kidnap two young children, you'd better have lavatory facilities close at hand. It looked—and smelled—like the kids had made use of it. Poor things. No telling how long they'd been kept in here. Good thing it wasn't summer, or they would have roasted.

"I found a portable toilet," I said. "Used."

"Oh, good. For a second I thought it might be you, and I was about to be concerned."

"Shut up. What have *you* found, smart-ass?"

"Half a case of water, some sodas, and what appear to be crackers. Where's a good tire iron when you need it?"

"Well, at least we won't go thirsty. Or hungry," I said.

"Or wet our pants." He made his way over to me and put a can of soda in my hand. "Drink up, cuz."

"I'm not thirsty." Besides, I didn't want to fill up my bladder. The idea of using the camping toilet was not appealing.

"I need the can." He'd already popped the top of his and was downing it.

"Why?"

He slurped out the last few drops, flattened the can in the middle, folded it back and forth a few times, and pulled it apart at the crease, after which he compressed the top and inserted it into the bottom, lining up the sharp edges and flattening them together. Then he wound some of the duct tape around the bottom and tested the grip. "Voilà! Sharp edge, relatively sturdy. Alas, not much good for stabbing, but if we get close enough to slice it'll work brilliantly. Come on, drink up so we can make yours."

I felt a little dizzy at the thought. I'd had quite enough of slicing people. "Um . . ."

"Cuz, I want you as armed as possible when those guys open the doors. We only have one shot at surprising them. If we screw it up, it looks like a trip to Russia for us. Don't know about you, but I'd rather spend the holidays at home."

Good point. I popped my top, took a big slug, and almost spewed. "Grape soda? I *hate* grape soda. Ugh. It tastes like watered-down cough syrup."

"Really? Huh. Mine was cola. Sorry, I couldn't see in the dark." It wasn't so dark that I couldn't see his grin.

"I'd wipe the smile off your face if I were you, buster. I'm going to be armed in about thirty seconds."

He laughed and took the can from me, downing the rest of it before making my shiv. "Careful of the edge. It doesn't look like much, but it will open up your skin like a razor blade. I found that out the hard way when I was ten and practicing my manly squashing of beverage containers."

I tested the feel of it in my hand. It was remarkably easy to grip by the bottom of the can, and if you held it right, it wouldn't be obvious. Infinitely better than nothing, especially against two burly armed guys, but . . .

I swallowed, memories of hot blood pouring over me flashing into my mind. "Billy, I don't know if I'll be able to do it."

I felt two strong hands on my shoulders. "Ciel, you will be able to do any fucking thing necessary to get out of this. Because I can't do it alone, not against both of them."

I nodded.

"Now, they'll still have their guns, and it won't take them long to realize we're no longer taped up. So, as soon as the doors open, we're going to . . ."

I listened attentively to his plan. "Simple. Almost Stooge-ian. I like it."

He laughed. "Stooge-ian? Since when do you appreciate the tremendous trio?"

"Since Brian enlightened me as to their genius."

"Sounds like there's a story there somewhere."

"Oh, there is," I said, and proceeded to share, stretching it out, because no telling how much time we had to kill.

A leg-cramping stretch of time later, we sat close to the doors, occupying ourselves by playing Twenty Questions while we waited for the truck to stop. After Billy's fourth turn, I had to laugh. "You can't *always* be an erogenous zone."

"But there are so many good ones," he said.

"You'll run out of them eventually."

He grinned wickedly. (Well, I assumed it was wicked. It was a little dark to say for sure, but it usually was in conversations like this.) "I haven't yet, have I?"

"Fine," I said, and cut to the chase. No point in wasting questions. "Are you a body part?"

"Yes."

"Are you something I would be touching right now if we didn't have to stay alert for our big escape?"

"No. Although I suppose it's possible . . ."

"Yes or no only. Are you something *you* would be touching if we didn't have to stay alert for our big escape?"

"Definitely. Over and over and over again . . ."

"*Yes or no.* Hmm. You've already been a dick—"

"I believe the proper term is 'penis.' "

"That's not what *you* called it. Now, shush. I'm thinking. You've already been a nipple and a 'love bud'—speaking of proper terms."

"Come on. You have to admit it sounds much more appetizing than—"

"Hush! Now, let's see. Are you a vagina?"

"Well, I prefer 'tunnel of love.' But, technically, the answer is no."

How I could giggle so much in this situation was beyond me. But that was Billy for you. "Are you located *inside* a vagina?"

He groaned. "Don't I wish!"

"Is that a no?" I said.

"No, it's a yes."

"Are you difficult to find, and considered by some to be mythical?"

"By amateurs maybe."

"*Aha!* You're a G-spot!" I said triumphantly.

"Congratulations! You got it in six. Your turn. Try not to be boring this time."

"National monuments are not boring. They're educational," I said primly.

"Can you see me yawning? No? Trust me, my mouth is wide—" He cut himself off, tense and listening, all business in a flash. "The truck is slowing. Get ready."

I patted my soda-can shiv, reassuring myself it was within easy reach, and picked up another can, as did Billy. When the truck lumbered to a stop, we were as prepared as we could be.

The lock rattled. We shook our soda cans. As the door started to move, I squeezed the tip of my finger under the ring of the pop-top. I squinted against the glare when the door rolled all the way open, pulling back on the ring with a nervous energy that ripped it right off the can. I aimed left, Billy aimed right. The spray hit each of our targets right in the face.

Their hands flew up, trying to protect their eyes. The guns they held were, for the moment at least, not pointed at us. Billy dropped his can, grabbed his shiv, and rose to his feet in one smooth motion. I followed suit, though possibly not as smoothly. Dr. Phil's body was taller than I was used to driving in combat situations.

Billy jumped, kicking the gun out of Mr. Tall's hand and knocking him to the ground. He had the shiv to the guy's throat before the soda was done fizzing.

I kicked, jumped, and somehow managed to land on Shorty's back when he spun to go after his gun. He didn't stop, not even when I put my shiv to his neck. *Argh.* "If you make me cut you I will laugh as you bleed out! You hear me? *Laugh.*"

Huh. Dr. Phil's voice could sound creepy-scary when you

pushed it, kind of like that possessed girl in *The Exorcist*. Who knew?

Shorty froze. He seemed to take my threat seriously.

Meantime, Billy had retrieved Mr. Tall's gun after apparently deciding Mr. Tall needed a nap. Being otherwise occupied, I hadn't seen what he'd done to put the big man so thoroughly to sleep. Could've been a Vulcan nerve pinch for all I knew. Whatever it was, I was going to get him to teach it to me as soon as we were out of this mess.

"Why don't you get the duct tape, *kotyonok*? But pick up the other gun first," Billy said, reverting to Misha's Russian accent, using the endearment I knew from Phil's file meant "kitten."

"With pleasure, my love." I pointed it at Shorty, enjoying the fear in his eyes more than I probably should. But I knew my schadenfreude wouldn't last long. I just hoped the postadrenaline shakes held off until after the police arrived.

Chapter 26

Mark was sitting up in the hospital bed, champing at the bit to get dressed and get out, waiting to be released by the company doctor who'd been sent to see him. The doctor, a slight elderly man with more hair on his eyebrows than his head, was currently conferring with the ER doc who'd been taking care of Mark until Uncle Sam had taken over. They were waiting for lab results to tell them precisely what Rudy had given Mark. All Mark knew was that it had been injected with something like an EpiPen. He'd only been able to get in two or three good punches to Rudy's midsection before blackness descended.

Billy had called one of his Agency contacts right after we'd finished taping up our former captors, using way more tape than they'd used on us. (Intelligence: learning from your mistakes. Wisdom: learning from someone else's mistakes.) He'd told the contact to get somebody out to the auditorium immediately, if not sooner. Mark and the venue proprietor had been found tied up and unconscious in a supply closet and brought to this hospital.

Mark had awakened before we got to the hospital, and apparently hadn't been the most genial and cooperative of patients, judging by the looks on the nurses' faces.

Once we'd been assured of some privacy in Mark's room (the nurses were only too glad to leave him to us), Billy and I explained why Rudy had done what he did. Mark's face had remained hard while we were talking, and even now I couldn't pick up a clue as to how he'd be dealing with it. One thing was certain—he was not happy. Whether he would accept Rudy's children being taken as a mitigating factor was still up in the air.

The kidnappers were now in the custody of Agency officials. We'd stayed right where we were until the men in the black SUVs had shown up to take them off our hands. One of the agents had driven us to Dr. Phil's house, where we'd dropped our assumed auras. Dr. Phil and Misha were both "invited" to come to a local Agency facility to answer some questions. Mark was currently frothing at the mouth to talk to them. To Rudy, too, though he'd apparently disappeared into the ether with Simon and Phoebe. Couldn't say that I really blamed him.

"Billy, could you do me a favor and track down my clothes? And my phone. I mean, I'll walk out of here in this hospital gown if I have to, but I'd like it better if I can avoid mooning strangers in the elevator."

"I'll see what I can do. For the sake of the strangers." Billy grinned and left.

Mark waited until he was safely out of earshot to address me, quietly. "Have you started your period yet?"

Whoa. Blunt much? I felt a blush rising to my cheeks. "I . . . I . . . no. But I'm sure I will soon. The tests were all negative."

"You weren't wearing your patch when we were together"—trust him to be so annoyingly observant—"and had received a dose of fertility hormones."

"True, but I'd only had the patch off for a short while. I'm sure I'm fine."

"Look, you and Billy have obviously worked things out. But I want you to know if there are consequences to the other night, and Billy isn't okay with it, my offer still stands."

I swallowed. Twice. "Thank you. It means a lot to me. I'll tell you when . . . um, when you can stop worrying."

"Why didn't you get married when you were at the city clerk's?" Again with the blunt.

"Al or Candy?"

"Both. They work for me. Did you think they wouldn't tell me?"

I shrugged. "I suppose not. Doesn't matter now anyway."

"It does to me." Mark's eyes were intent.

I sighed. "Al brought me flowers, and I realized I couldn't get married without my dad walking me down the aisle. It wouldn't be right."

He nodded. Understanding, I thought, but also a little . . . disappointed? Had he been hoping I hadn't been able to go through with it for another reason?

"Mark, listen—" I stopped myself when I caught sight of Billy in the doorway.

He carried a short stack of clothing sandwiched between a pair of shoes on the bottom and a cell phone on top. "Where did you find this suit, anyway? Big Lots? Seriously, your hospital gown is more flattering."

Mark summoned a grin. "Are you dissing my fade-into-the-background working-stiff clothes? I'll have you know I paid seventy-nine bucks for that suit."

"Worth every penny. As are your—Payless?—loafers." Billy handed him the stack.

"Thanks, bud. I owe you."

"You do. Ten dollars, to be precise. That's how much I had to give an orderly to tell me where they were hidden."

"Why'd they hide your clothes?" I said.

Mark twisted his mouth wryly. "It's what they do when you threaten to leave against an Agency doctor's orders. Okay, anyone who doesn't want to see my pale fuzzy butt better leave. Wait for me downstairs. I may need you when I talk to Dr. Carson and her husband."

I stopped myself before I blurted out his butt wasn't fuzzy at all, but from the amused look Billy was giving me, the thought might have been plain on my face.

Dr. Phil looked as shocked as I'd ever seen her. Misha was looking a bit gob-smacked himself. They were seated in a small parlor in a safe house on the outskirts of Houston, having a cup of coffee with Mark. They ignored the cookies on the coffee table.

Billy and I were watching from behind a small two-way mirror. It was framed on the parlor side, and so looked more like a regular mirror. Still, it wasn't likely to fool anyone with half a brain, and both of Mark's "guests" kept glancing at it nervously.

My eyes kept darting back to the cookies. They appeared to be chocolate chip, and not from the grocery store shelf either. Bakery, or possibly even homemade. How could anybody sitting next to those, sipping coffee, not eat one? Or, you know, half a dozen?

"Is that your stomach growling, cuz?" The amusement in Billy's voice was plain.

Damn, I was starving. "Maybe. But a gentleman wouldn't comment on it."

He hugged me from behind. "A *gentleman* wouldn't do a lot of the things I do." Leaning his head down close to my ear, he whispered the less-than-gentlemanly activities he had planned for later, some of which included feeding me cookies. And ice cream. Naked. Unless, of course, I preferred him to act like a gentleman.

I squirmed. "It's possible gentlemen are overrated."

Billy laughed and turned up the volume on the speaker a tiny amount. "Shh. I think we're supposed to be paying attention to this."

"In that case, stop breathing on my neck. It's distracting."

Dr. Phil put down her coffee cup, folded her hands in her lap, and looked Mark right in the eye. "You're saying it should have been me. From what you're telling me, it *would* have been me, if not for my kidney stone." Her voice sounded tinny coming from the speaker.

"That's what your brother told my colleagues," Mark said. Calm. Cool. Professional.

I chewed the inside of my bottom lip. "Why'd he have to tell her? Can't he see it's upsetting her?" I knew how it would make me feel if one of my brothers had planned to set me up like that.

Billy gave my hand a small squeeze, like he understood what I was thinking. "That's the idea. He wants her upset. It's harder to hide what you know when you're emotionally off balance."

Phil stared for a minute into the middle distance. Finally she nodded, accepting what Mark had told her. "I understand why," she said at last, sounding like she was trying to convince herself. "His kids were in danger. He didn't have a choice." She looked at her husband, the love blooming in her eyes. Was she thinking of her own future child?

"Where is he now? Where did he take the kids?" Mark's demeanor still showed no outward emotion.

"I don't know. And that's the God's honest truth. I imagine he's taken them somewhere they won't be found by the Russians."

Mark gave Misha a hard look. "We'll be talking more about the Russians later. For now, tell me about Alec Loughlin. I suppose you don't know where he is either."

Misha shook his head. "No. He came to me at my office— once—after he failed to capture Ciel on the day of the flight. He kept ranting about government-controlled imposters and how they'd replaced 'his' Phil with some sort of alien. He wanted to know if I was in on it. Held a knife to my throat and demanded to know where the real Phil was, so he could do what he was paid to do."

"Did you tell him about adaptors?" Mark wasn't bothering to keep the steel out of his eyes, or his voice, anymore.

Misha had started to sweat. "I told him to take me instead. I was the one the Russians really wanted. He said no, they had insisted on Philippa because without *her* they would never be able to control me." Misha leaned forward, extending his hands toward Mark in a gesture that begged for understanding. "They were right. There is no way I would let them control my company, and what it does for the United States. But if they had Philippa . . ."

"Did you tell him about adaptors?"

"Yes! I had to. He would have slit my throat and gone after Philippa."

"And Rudy? Did you tell Loughlin you'd learned about adaptors from your wife's brother?"

Misha sagged against the back of the sofa. "Yes. I did."

Mark seemed strangely relieved by his answer.

"Why is he okay with that?" I said softly to Billy. He knew what I meant.

"Because it means Loughlin doesn't have some sort of magical ability to recognize adaptors. Or an adaptor-spotting technology. *That* is what scared the spook the most, and I can't blame him."

"I can see how Loughlin might have guessed I wasn't Phil, if he knew her that well. But he saw through the other astronaut aura I borrowed, too."

"Can you be certain he didn't see Phil's ID tag or name patch?"

I thought back. "No, I can't be absolutely sure. But what about the Japanese aura I was wearing at the skating rink?"

"Rudy could have easily found out who was assigned to your security detail, which would lead right to you no matter whose aura you happened to be wearing. And if Loughlin was threatening to make sure the Russians hurt his kids . . . well, let's just say if Rudy was willing to give up his sister for them, I doubt he'd have any compunction about endangering a few stray adaptors." Billy's voice was wryly understanding, but his underlying anger was apparent. I had a strong feeling he was on the same page as Mark with regard to Rudy.

Mark had refilled all the coffee cups, pulling back from his foray into "bad cop" territory, taking a moment to digest what Misha had told him. "So Loughlin, in his head at least, had reason to go after adaptors."

Misha nodded. "It seemed to give him a new purpose. He was . . . I don't know, *offended* by the idea of adaptors. Said your existence was dangerous to 'real' human beings."

Lovely, I thought. *He could take a page from Billy's birth mother's book.*

I glanced at Billy—his jaw was tightly clenched. He must've had the same thought. I took his hand and leaned my head against his shoulder. He stiffened at first, but then put one arm around me and pulled me to him. That was good. He needed to know I was there for him.

"Is there anything else you can tell me about Loughlin?"

Misha hesitated. Mark jumped on it. "What?"

"My drone. I gave it to him."

Mark just stared at him.

Misha leaned toward Mark, hands upturned, his body language begging for understanding. "I thought if I gave him the technology, he could give it to the Russians instead of giving them us. Don't you see? It was a way to get rid of Loughlin and the Russians, too. He was supposed to leave us alone after he got it."

Mark twisted his mouth briefly. "How'd that work out for you?"

Misha flushed. "Not as well as I'd hoped. As you know."

"Does Rudy know?"

"About the drone? No," Phil said quickly. "We didn't want to involve him in something the government might not approve of. By then we knew he was already going to be in enough trouble without that."

"Is the technology classified?" Mark asked.

Again, Misha hesitated. "No."

"But?" Mark said, voice hard.

"It might be, once the government gets wind of what it involves. But I haven't finished the design. There are still bugs to be worked out."

"Is it dangerous?"

"It depends on who sets its controls, and what they're delivering," Misha said.

"Does Loughlin know how to operate it?"

Misha nodded bleakly. "I showed him. It was part of the deal—he was afraid the Russians wouldn't accept it as payment otherwise."

"Anything you want to add? Did you hand the Russians anything else they might weaponize and use against our country?" Mark couldn't quite keep the disgust out of his voice.

"No! I swear that's it. And the Russians have scientists working on similar technology—it was only a question of who would get there first. That is the drone's only possible value to them, to beat the Americans to the punch. But that in itself is worth a lot to them."

Mark rose to leave.

"What now?" Misha asked. "Are we going to prison?"

"No," Mark said. Though he kind of looked like he wouldn't have minded sending them up the river. "Now you'll be taken back to your home. Your security detail will be tripled until we find Loughlin. Dr. Carson, your mission will go on as planned. No one wants to jeopardize its success."

Relief flooded her features, spilling out of her eyes. "Thank you." She looked like she wanted to say more, but couldn't seem to find the words.

"One thing—if you hear from Rudy, you have to let me know immediately. He may think he can guarantee his children's safety, but he's wrong. It would be a whole lot better for him—and the kids—if we find him before the Russians do. Or before Alec Loughlin does."

Dr. Phil nodded. "What will you do with him?"

"It's not for me to decide." Mark's neutral expression gave nothing away, but I suspected it was a good thing for Rudy that Mark wasn't going to be the one judging his actions.

The cookies were every bit as heavenly as I'd thought. Combined with the rich flavor of the coffee, it was like chocolate and caffeine were doing a happy dance on my tongue. (Yeah, yeah. Sue me. I wasn't going to feel guilty over half a cup of coffee when I was ninety-nine-point-nine percent sure there was no way I was pregnant.)

Mark had brought us into the parlor after Dr. Phil and Misha were taken home. We were discussing our next move. Well, Mark and Billy were discussing. I was mostly listening, because it's rude to talk with your mouth full.

"So, how worried should we be about that drone?" Billy said.

"It's certainly something to add to the list," Mark said. "Misha was an idiot to think the Russians would take it and leave them alone. Why settle for a golden egg when you can control the goose?"

"Naïve," Billy agreed. "Speaking of idiots, do you think Rudy gave Loughlin inside info on adaptors?"

"I do. Loughlin knew the Russians had Rudy's kids. He could have used it to coerce all kinds of useful information out of him, like how there's a relatively large enclave of adaptors in New York, and, later, where Ciel lived in D.C. He's one of the few people who had clearance to access my personal files. God damn it, I *trusted* him. He should have trusted me." He paused to take a breath, reeling back the little emotion he'd allowed to show. "I won't make that mistake again."

Billy nodded, obviously understanding how dangerous trust can be in the world of covert operations. "So, Aunt Helen? Loughlin killed her only because she was, what, the first adaptor he came across once he got to New York?"

"Possibly. If he even killed her himself. He might have employed the same guy who went after Ciel at the skating rink. We're matching his DNA against traces on all the victims."

I shuddered at the memory, almost choking on a cookie. There'd been a hell of a lot more than a trace of his DNA on me. I'd been covered in it.

Billy patted my back. Mark got me a glass of water from the bar in the corner and continued speaking. "I suspect Aunt Helen was first because her routine was so regular. She walked in Central Park every day at the same time, no matter what the weather. She was old, slow, and an easy target. Plus, it was a good bet her funeral would draw most of the adaptors in the area in to one spot where they could be easily photographed. Once he had pictures, he could always take his time and pick them off as he came across them."

Billy nodded. "And right now he's probably waiting until adaptors are easier to get to. He has to know such a high level of security can't be maintained indefinitely."

"That would be my guess," Mark said, and then looked at me thoughtfully. "Except in Ciel's case. He might have something against adaptors in general, but he seems to have fixated on her for some reason. He didn't wait to try for her in D.C., or at the ice rink either."

"What the hell makes me so special?" I muttered.

"Could be he blames you for his failed attempt to snatch Phil. Whatever the reason, I don't want you to go anywhere alone until we get him." He might have been talking to me, but he was looking directly at Billy.

Billy got the message. "I won't let her out of my sight."

I twisted my lips. "Well, damn. That's going to make wrapping your Christmas present problematic."

Chapter 27

"Grumpy climbed to the top of the tree in the living room again!" Mom hollered. "Somebody get him down—my hands are full. Patrick? Thomas? James? Brian? For God's sake, will one of you get him down before he shreds the angel?" She hurried into the dining room with a huge tray of cinnamon rolls and Moravian sugar cake fresh from the oven.

Christmas morning in the Halligan household is a boisterous affair in any given year. Add seven cats (named by Jenny after Snow White's dwarfs—she'd been a huge Disney fan) to the equation, and "boisterous" morphs into "chaotic" quicker than a fledgling adaptor flits through auras.

Coincidentally, we had one of those, too, Santa having delivered Molly's dearest wish. She was officially on the road to full-blown adaptorhood, and delighting in exhibiting her new talent to everyone. It had (naturally) been her idea to bring the three cats the Doyles were fostering—Dopey, Doc, and Sneezy—so they could visit with their friends. Happy, Sleepy, and Bashful were running around in blissful joy at being reunited with their brethren. (Grumpy apparently preferred the tree to his feline friends.)

The whole Doyle clan had shown up on the doorstep at the crack of dawn, all of them wearing red- or green-plaid flannel pajamas beneath their heavy coats, their feet encased in sturdy, fleece-lined slippers. Our families traded off every year, one taking Christmas Eve, the other Christmas morning. Frankly, I was glad it was our turn for Christmas morning, because it was damn cold outside, even for the short walk.

Molly, Sinead, and Siobhan had each carried a cat (one short-haired tuxedo, two long-haired gingers). Auntie Mo and Uncle Liam had hauled giant bags of garishly wrapped gifts, slung over their shoulders. A resigned-looking (and no doubt well-armed) contingent of Mark's agents accompanied them, and had taken up positions outside with our own long-suffering guardians.

Billy was the only Doyle missing from the gang when they arrived, but only because he'd insisted on remaining with me overnight in the basement. Which might have been romantic, except for that whole being-my-parents'-house thing, and besides, Brian had stayed downstairs with us the whole night. I suspect Mom put him up to it once she found out Billy wasn't spending the night in the bosom of his own family. (Thomas and Laura were using my room again, and James and Devon had the room James had once shared with Brian. Ha. Hope they enjoyed those bunk beds.)

Of course, Brian had smuggled some of his special cookies into the house, and had snacked on them liberally as we watched *A Christmas Story* yet again. It hadn't taken long for him to fall deeply asleep, so (according to Billy) we were as good as alone. During the rest of the movie, he had done his level best to convince me, via a whispering campaign and sneaky caresses to my ridiculously

sensitive inner elbows, that fooling around in one's parents' basement was a sacred rite of passage, and since I'd missed it as a
teenager, he would be happy to help me through this essential
developmental milestone.

I might have succumbed to his persuasive techniques if, a) I
hadn't been afraid Bri would wake up with a bad case of the
munchies in the middle of things and, b) if Santa hadn't brought
me my own special gift earlier that week. Or maybe it was Mother
Nature. Whoever. My period had finally started. Sure, it was
almost over, and technically I could adapt around it, but frankly
I didn't want anything—not even a short partial adaption—
messing with my plumbing until I was sure everything was back
to normal. We'd compromised on mutual foot massages, the
one I received being twice as long as the one I gave. Which was
only fair, because his feet were twice as big as mine. (Hey, you
can't argue with math.)

"Ciel, guess what—I got a drum set! A real one. It's *awesome!*"
Molly said, once she was done (for the moment at least) shifting
through auras, and was adequately stuffed with sugary goodness.

"Whoa! Fantastic, Molls. Who's it from?" I asked. Auntie Mo
and Uncle Liam couldn't be that masochistic.

Thomas had a huge smile on his face, one arm around Laura.
(We were all in our flannel pj's, too. Tradition dictated it.) "I
believe Santa left it for her. He probably heard rumors about the
great "Wipe Out" solo at our wedding and figured she needed a
professional set."

"Mmm-hmm. Santa is special that way," Auntie Mo said. The
glint in her narrowed eyes as she looked at Thomas told me there
were going to be many loud toys in his offspring's future.

Mom clapped her hands. "Okay, everyone, you know the drill.

Retire to the living room and start tearing paper!" She reached down and snatched a bow out of Happy's mouth as he whizzed past. "And do *not* let the cats eat the ribbons! I don't want to see any of them running around later with streamers under their tails."

Once upon a time, Mom and Auntie Mo had insisted on an orderly distribution of gifts, with everyone taking turns opening them, and much oohing and aahing over each present in turn. They'd given up on it years ago—there were too darned many of us to keep organized, and it would have taken until dinnertime to get through everything. Frankly, none of us—including Mom and Auntie Mo—had that kind of patience.

Billy pulled me down next to him on the floor close to the tree—an eight-foot-tall blue spruce chaotically decorated with every homemade ornament my brothers and I had made from birth onward, intermingled with the genuine antiques my father was fond of giving Mom every year. (Normally, it was littered with silver tinsel, but Mom had heard it was dangerous for cats, so she had painstakingly removed every last piece of it.) The lights were the multicolored, big-bulb kind. It should have been a tasteless mess, but somehow it was beautiful, even attached to the ceiling with fishing line as it now was.

Billy scanned the crowd. "Guess the spook's not coming this year."

When Mark wasn't in one of the far reaches of the planet for the holidays he usually spent the day with us. Sadly, more often than not, Christmas seemed to invite crazy happenings requiring CIA intervention by someone with Mark's special skill set. He never talked about his own family, if he even had one. I'd asked Thomas about it once, long ago, but he'd ignored me. When I'd pressed him, he'd told me not everybody was as lucky as we were, and to drop it. For some reason—possibly fear of what kind of pain I'd find buried inside Mark—I'd never pursued it.

"Not sure," I said. "Thomas said he might stop in later, if it looks like things are quiet on the Loughlin front."

Billy gave my nose a quick kiss. "Good thing he assigned me to watch you. It's the one job I'm willing to do on Christmas Day." He grabbed a package from under the tree. "Hey, Molls, heads up!" He tossed it across the room to her like it was a football, which, coincidentally, it was. She was thrilled, as were all the others in the crowded room when they dug into their own loot. Most of the gifts were simple, thoughtful expressions of affection, nothing terribly extravagant. Joke gifts abounded, as both families considered laughter to be the best present you could give anyone.

Billy's necktie—the one with lumps of coal and "naughty" written on it in all the different fonts—was well received, by Molly in particular, who'd also gotten him a tie—a green one with spines. "Get it? It's a cacti!" She chortled her delight as the rest of us groaned. "And you can't complain, because you only told me not to get you a *Christmas* tie. Ha! Gotcha."

"Thanks, squirt." He slipped it around his neck and quickly knotted it, careful not to flatten the spines. "Now come here and give me a hug."

Molly beat a hasty retreat. "No way!"

Billy pulled me to him instead (the spines weren't really sharp) and whispered, "I won't put on yours now, but don't worry, I'm sure I'll be able to think of an appropriately 'naughty' use for it. Later."

I shivered. "What a coincidence. I'll be giving you the rest of your gift later."

"What'd Billy get *you*, Ciel?" Siobhan said, parading around in the cowboy hat and boots I'd gotten her. (They added a certain panache to her flannel pj's.)

Billy looked down at me and grinned. "If you'll excuse me for a minute, I have a retrieval to make."

"Where are you going?" I said, puzzled when he put his coat on.

"Well, knowing a certain someone's propensity for snooping, I took precautions. Candy kindly agreed to keep something in her vehicle for me." Candy had drawn the short straw for Christmas Day duty, along with a fresh recruit. (Al and another guy had been on watch until midnight, so he hadn't escaped entirely, but at least he was getting to spend Christmas Day with his family.)

"Oh, wait, Billy . . . as long as you're going out, take some cinnamon rolls and coffee to the gang outside. Let me get a thermos and some cups." Mom bustled off to the kitchen, talking the whole way. "I do wish they could come in and join us. It's so cold out there, and not to be with your family on . . ."

Billy waited by the front door while Mom loaded up a care package. I waited with him. "Need any help carrying my present in? If it's heavy, I'd be happy to give you a hand."

He tugged my hair. "Patience, cuz."

"So, not heavy? Bulky, then. I'm great with bulky."

"I'm not going to tell you how big it is. I'm not giving you any hints at all. Anyway, it's only a few more minutes. Surely you can hold out that long."

I stuck my nose up in the air. "Huh. Of course I can. Don't bother to hurry. My patience is infinite."

Mom came back, still talking. ". . . not to worry, I put it all together so you can carry it. Tell them to call if they need anything else." She handed a huge box to Billy. "Now, if you need help I'll get Thomas. Or James. Or—"

Billy grinned. "Auntie Ro, if you could carry it from the kitchen, I'm sure I can manage it the rest of the way."

Mom beamed at him. "Thank you, sweetie. Here, let me find a scarf for your neck."

"Never mind that. I won't be but a minute." He was out the door before she could start rummaging through the closet.

Mom hooked her arm through mine and started walking me back to the others. "He's always been the nicest boy. Full of mischief, but so sweet. I can't tell you how happy Mo and I are that you two finally realized you loved each other. Do you think he got you a ring?"

Yikes. "Slow down, Mom. Don't you have enough on your plate right now?"

She laughed. "Oh, honey, you'd be surprised at how big my plate is. There's always room on it for another helping of love."

In the living room Thomas and Laura were gushing over the handcrafted cradle Dad had brought in from his garage workshop. Looked like he'd spent every spare minute from the time he'd heard the good news working on it. The lines were simple, in the Amish tradition, and the wood was stained a medium brown, the same color as Thomas's hair.

Mom rushed over to them. "Wait . . . there's more." She pulled one last package out from under the tree. She'd taken the precaution of tagging it with her own name, to make sure it wasn't opened out of turn. "This goes with it."

The happy parents-to-be ripped off the paper to reveal a cradle mattress and six fitted sheets.

"And this," Auntie Mo said. Her addition was the softest baby blanket ever knitted. (I touched it, so I was certain.) Apparently she'd used every color of baby yarn she could get her hands on,

307 ALL FIXED UP

and hadn't followed any particular pattern. It was gloriously hideous, and I could tell by the way Laura rubbed it against her cheek she loved it with all her heart.

I must have looked at it expectantly, because Mo slipped another package to me. As I'd hoped, it was a replacement afghan, even uglier than the one I'd lost in the fire. I wrapped it around me like a shawl and told her she was the best aunt ever.

A big group hug and ten minutes of everyone raving about the cradle and Mo's knitting later, I began to wonder what was taking Billy so long. I went to the front hall and peeked out one of the sidelights, expecting to see him shooting the breeze on the street with Candy or one of the other agents, testing my "infinite patience." I saw two SUVs, but no Billy. Maybe he was inside one of them. It was hard to tell with the tinted windows.

After another five minutes, I stopped being impatient to see my gift and started worrying. It shouldn't be taking this long. Billy liked to tease me, but I didn't think he'd take it this far, not when he knew the strain we'd all been under waiting for Loughlin to be caught.

Maybe I should check . . .

I got my coat from the closet and quietly slipped out the front door—no point in getting anyone else jazzed up over what was probably nothing. Candy and her cohort were in the SUV across the street, gratefully sipping Mom's coffee and chowing down on cinnamon rolls, their firearms within easy reach. When I asked about Billy, they said he'd gone back into the house right after he'd left the box of goodies. They'd watched him every step of the way.

"He checked his phone as he opened the front door. Looked like he might be reading a text."

"Huh. Maybe he's in the bathroom. Or . . . look, he said he was coming out here to get my present. Could it be something that requires, I don't know, setting up or special presentation?" He could have sneaked past me while I was preoccupied with the cradle crowd. Maybe he was in the basement right now, preparing a surprise for me.

"Well, he did seem pretty excited about the present. But if you want me to come check the house again, I will. Joe can hold down the fort out here for a few."

Her cohort smirked. "Oh, sure. I'd be happy to sit out here freezing my ass off while you go warm yours. Of course, there might not be any cinnamon rolls left when you get back."

Candy practically growled at him. "Touch mine and die."

I laughed, pretty sure she was joking. "No need. Stay here and defend your rolls. I'll track down Billy myself." And my present, because damn, I was really curious now.

Chapter 28

Mom was passing through the center hall on the way to the kitchen when I came in. "Ciel! What were you doing outside? Are Joe and Candy okay? Do they need more cocoa? Coffee? Rolls? Never mind, I'll send more out when the quiche is done—I know they'll want to try it. It's a new recipe. Peanut butter and oysters, with a dash of—"

Jesus, spare them. And the rest of us. "Mom, have you seen Billy? I seem to have misplaced him."

A timer went off in the kitchen. "Try upstairs. I heard the floor squeaking up there, and everyone else is in the living room." She scurried off to check her latest avant-garde culinary masterpiece.

Leaving my coat on the banister, I went upstairs and peeked into every room, including the restrooms and closets. (Pro tip: Never look in your parents' closet if finding a French maid's outfit, a Thor costume, and a copy of the *Kama Sutra* might scar you.) Billy was nowhere to be found.

My phone buzzed, giving my left boob an unexpected tingle.

(Why didn't pajama pants come with pockets?) I was ready to give Billy some hell, figuring it must be him. But it wasn't.

"Ciel Halligan?" The accent was way too Australian for comfort. Loughlin.

Crap. What should I do? "Yes . . ." I started swiping the screen, looking for the app Mark had installed for me to record conversations. (Yeah, totally illegal without letting the other party know. I'd let Mark deal with the ramifications.)

"I hope you're having a good time with your family. Pleasant neighborhood you have there. Please give your mother my compliments on the tree. It's the prettiest one on your block. And the fishing line? So clever of your father."

A chill went through me.

"Thank you. I'd invite you over for a closer view, only you might have a hard time getting in." That hadn't sounded too shaky, had it?

"I expect I would. Mr. Fielding has been a royal pain in my backside with all his pet security guards. So I'm afraid you'll have to come to me instead."

"Oh, really. And why would I do that?" I said, keeping my voice pleasant. Just another telephone convo with a murderer.

"Because if you don't a state-of-the-art, highly specialized drone will drop a pound or so of C-4 at the base of your parents' very old brownstone. Doesn't take much to make those collapse, does it? Could get messy for anyone inside."

Crap. He hadn't given it to the Russians? "What?" I said, trying hard not to let on how badly he'd shaken me. "You're being ridiculous. You couldn't possibly . . ." Could he?

"Oh, I can. And I will. Thanks to Mikhail Yurgevich's technology."

Jesus. He did have it.

"I don't believe you. If you could kill us all as easily as that, you wouldn't be warning me about it now."

"Ask me what I want, Ciel. Ask me why I need you."

"Why do you need me?" I echoed automatically, still dazed, trying to stall for time, praying a good idea for dealing with this madman would come to me.

"I need you because *you* are going to get me my money from the goddamn Russians so I can get goddamn Bratva off my goddamn back. You are going to perform your fucking magic one last time so I can sell them Philippa Carson."

"Why don't you just sell them the drone instead? Isn't that what they're after?"

"I tried. They wouldn't take the deal. Somehow they figured out if they control Misha, they'll get the drone *and* any other brilliant technology he might come up with in the future. Imagine that. Russians with brains."

Same thing Mark had pointed out with his golden goose reference. "Right. But if that's the case, why wouldn't you go after the real Dr. Carson? She's the one you need, not me. Not that I'm suggesting it."

"Thanks to your Mr. Fielding, she has a goddamn arsenal around her, and her idiot husband has been put someplace out of my reach. And since her brother and his children have disappeared, too, I don't have sufficient leverage to persuade *her* to come see me without her army of guards."

"The way you do with me."

"Yes. The way I do with you."

I had to keep stalling. "But what good would it do to give them me if Phil is still in the public eye?" I paced the upstairs as I spoke, walking blindly from room to room, keeping my voice low.

"Oh, I imagine Mr. Fielding will find a way to keep her out of the spotlight while you're missing, protective as he is about your kind." The way he said "your kind" made it sound like we were vermin. "You know, at first I thought you should all be wiped off the planet. But now I can see where you might have your uses."

"Yeah, well, you don't get to decide who lives and who dies. You're not God," I snapped.

"Shut up." He gave me an address in a commercial area not far away. "If you leave right now you should be able to get here in seven minutes. If you're not here, the drone will drop—and detonate—its cargo. If anyone other than you leaves the house in the interim, the drone will drop its cargo *immediately*. Trust me, they won't be able to get far enough away to escape the effects of the blast entirely."

Jesus. "But I can't go anywhere alone. The security guards follow me everywhere."

"Have one—and only one—of them drive you. My advice? Pick your least favorite. And don't get any ideas about warning your watchdogs, because if anything happens to me the drone will automatically make the drop."

"I still think"—*prayed*—"you're bluffing."

"You saw what I did to your condo." I could almost see him shrugging. "You think I'm not capable of this? Seven minutes, Ciel. Leave now. Tick-tock." He disconnected.

Fuck! I needed time to think. And time was something I didn't have. I crept down the stairs, grabbed my coat from the banister, and left the house, careful to make sure no one saw or heard me.

Candy had the window down by the time I got to the SUV.

"What? No more cinnamon rolls?" Her smile was infectious; I couldn't help but return it, no matter how sick I felt inside.

"I think Mom has something in the oven for you guys. But, listen, I remembered a present I forgot to pick up. For, um, Billy. I'd feel really bad if his gift to me is better than mine to him, you know? Could I get a ride? It's not far."

"Sure. Hop in. But what's open on Christmas?"

"Um . . . it's not. I called the owner—he made me something for Billy's car—and he's meeting me there. Hoo-boy! I had to promise to pay through the nose, but it will be worth it. Look, can we please go? I need to get back before Billy realizes I'm gone, or he'll know I didn't remember"—geez, I was talking as fast as Mom—"and his feelings will be hurt. Hey, I know! Candy, could you go find Billy and keep him distracted until I get back? Don't tell him I'm gone. Or anyone. Please? I'd be *so* embarrassed." I gave her a beseeching look I'd learned from watching Billy.

"What? Me, go into the nice warm house where more cinnamon rolls are baking?" She grinned at Joe. I didn't correct her misconception about the rolls. Who would go in for peanut-butter oyster quiche? "If I must, I must. And about time, too. My bladder is about to blow."

I swallowed hard and tried not to look at Joe. If Loughlin killed him, I would be responsible for his death.

Stop it, Ciel. It was him or Candy.

Even more, it was one of them or everybody in the house. I'd think of something to save him when I got there. In the meantime, I had precious few minutes to decide my best course of action.

If I went with Loughlin, I'd be sold to the Russians as Dr. Phil. If I didn't cooperate, he'd blow up my family. No choice there. I'd do it, and worry about escaping later.

But even if I could get away from the Russians somehow, and drop Dr. Phil's aura, I might be in Russia. Alone. No ID. No passport. Not knowing the language. *(Note to self: learn more languages.)* As much as I wanted to think of myself as badass material, capable of saving the day single-handedly, I was totally out of my element. There was only one intelligent thing to do.

I brought up the voice recording of my conversation with Loughlin and forwarded it to Mark and Billy. I was going to have to trust them to know the best way to handle the situation without getting my family blown up.

Chapter 29

The address Loughlin had given me turned out to be a small storefront coffee shop. I told Joe it was where I was meeting the guy who had Billy's present, hoping he wouldn't notice I'd failed to mention it earlier. He seemed to take it in his stride. Still, he was alert, gun in hand as we approached the building.

The door was locked, but it only took a second for a man wearing a cap with the store logo on it to open it for us, stepping back after he did. Joe went in ahead of me. His instincts were good, but not quite fast enough—he only had his gun halfway lifted when the wires hit his face, instantly locking his muscles.

Loughlin came at him, knife extended.

"*Stop.* If you kill him, I swear to God I won't cooperate, no matter what."

I must have sounded sincere, because Loughlin pulled up short. He stared at my face for a few seconds, flipped the knife over, and clubbed Joe on the back of his head, hard.

The Taser stopped sending its jolts of electricity. Joe stopped twitching and fell to the ground, unconscious.

"If you want to keep him alive, pull him to the back room." Loughlin sounded like he didn't care one way or the other. "But you better hope there's something to tie him and gag him with back there, or he's dead. Remember, you still have a lot of other lives to consider."

I glared at him. I couldn't believe I had found him attractive the first time I met him. His ugly soul seemed to shine through his eyes now. "Yeah, and you have Bratva and *your* life to consider. Don't push me too far."

"Do it. Now."

I picked up Joe's feet and started dragging. Between his wool coat and the freshly waxed floors, it wasn't as hard as it could have been, even though he was kind of a big guy. Or maybe all my workouts had paid off in stronger muscles.

The shelves didn't have any handy rope, but they did have aprons. I cut the ties off several of them with some blunt-tipped scissors I found, wound them together, and used them to bind Joe's hands and feet. I made sure I did an excellent job of it, because Loughlin was watching me closely and I didn't want to give him any reason to reconsider leaving Joe alive. Finally, I cut a thick strip from one of the aprons and worked it into Joe's mouth, knotting it snugly in the back. He wouldn't be going anywhere when he woke up.

"Enough. We're leaving." He'd exchanged his knife for a small handgun while I was working on Joe. Guess he still didn't trust me.

My phone buzzed in my coat pocket. I tried to hit "ignore" without being noticed, not wanting to tip Loughlin off to its presence, but apparently he had excellent hearing.

"Answer it. Put it on speaker phone. Let's see if you've done anything stupid."

It was Billy. My heart thumping, I swiped the screen. "You're on speaker."

"Hi, cuz. In a bit of pickle, are you? Where are you, the back room?" His voice was purposefully light, but I could hear the underlying tension.

Loughlin lunged for me, realizing at the same time I did that Billy must be close. "You just couldn't keep your mouth shut, you little bitch!"

"Yeah. He has a gun," I yelled over him, fast. Loughlin slapped the phone out of my hand and pulled me in front of him.

"Duck, Ciel. *Now,*" Billy said from behind the door. His voice was followed instantly by the door crashing open. I tried to bend over, but Loughlin had one arm around my neck and his gun to my head. So I stomped on his foot, and elbowed his gut with as much force as I could muster.

The crack of a gunshot was the last thing I heard before everything went black.

A sharp sting on my cheek woke me. Who the hell was slapping me?

"Ciel. *Cuz.* Are you okay?" Billy's face hovered over mine, paler than I'd seen it since the day of the pregnancy test in Houston.

I pushed myself up. "I'm fine." Loughlin lay on the floor beside me, his head bent at an odd angle.

Billy nodded once, and then was beside Joe, checking his pulse, pulling off his gag, cutting the binding at his wrists and ankles. Joe didn't show any signs of coming around. After a second,

Billy came back to me and pulled me to my feet. "Come on. We have to go."

"Wait—are you okay? I heard a shot."

"So did I. Scared the shit out of me. Fortunately, you threw his aim off. I couldn't risk shooting him—thought I might hit you by mistake, the way you were twisting in the breeze—so I had to resort to the old tried-and-true neck twist. Luckily, I'm a fast son of a bitch when I'm scared shitless." He paused briefly to give me a hard kiss. It tasted like relief. "We're going to have to work on that passing out thing of yours, though."

"Hey, his elbow was clamped around my neck! He cut off my air."

"I'm just glad he didn't cut it off permanently. Now, come on." He pulled me toward the door he'd just kicked down.

I tugged him to a stop. "We can't leave Joe here—he could be seriously hurt. Loughlin hit him really hard."

"You can call for an ambulance from the car. Right now we have to go. Mark needs backup."

Shit. "The drone. Can you stop it?"

"If we can bring it down before somebody sends the signal to the blasting cap."

We were there in under three minutes, according to the phone I kept holding after I called 911, but it felt so much longer. On the way over, Billy told me nobody except Mark and his agents knew anything about the drone. There was no point in panicking the family when we couldn't risk evacuating the house for fear it would cause whoever was controlling the drone for Loughlin to set it off before everyone was out.

"You and I are going to walk in like everything is normal. Then you're going to stay downstairs with everyone while I slip up to the roof."

"Mark's on the roof?"

"Yeah. The rest of the team are watching from street level, in case of a low approach. If there is a drone, we'll shoot it out of the sky."

I sucked in a breath. "But won't that set it off?"

"Not if we can disrupt the signal to the blasting cap. C-4 is actually quite stable—it takes a special detonator to make it blow. If there was time to get some jamming equipment here, we could block the signal, and wouldn't have to worry about it at all. What we have to do now is get it to the ground and hope we can remove the blasting cap before the operator gives the cell phone it's probably connected to a call."

"And if you can't do it in time?"

His grip on the steering wheel tightened. "Then there'll be a hell of a bang. And not the fun kind."

Candy was in front of her car, gun in hand, scanning the sky. Seeing me, she must have wondered where Joe was, but saved her questions. The other agents were doing the same, each of them covering a different direction. We didn't pause to talk.

Inside, everyone was still in the living room, laughing while Molly taught Laura the "Jingle Bells, Batman Smells" version of her favorite carol. If tradition held, my brothers would start in next with "We Three Kings of Orient Are . . . trying to smoke a rubber cigar . . ."

This might be the last Christmas we ever spend here together. A lump lodged in my throat at the thought.

I'd never be able go in there and keep my shit together. Since we hadn't been spotted, I followed Billy up the stairs instead. He gave me a look over his shoulder. I set my face and followed. When we were far enough up the stairs not to be heard, I said, "You don't want them to see me and ask questions right now. Trust me on that."

He studied my face, briefly. What he saw must have convinced him, because he didn't argue. "Fine. You can help watch for the drone. The more eyes, the better." He pulled a pistol out of his coat pocket, a nine millimeter, and put it in my hand. "It'll be a big enough target. Shoot the propellers."

I took it, hiding my reluctance. I don't like guns, but I knew my aim was decent. "What about you?" I said.

He winked and showed me his dimples. "Don't worry. I always carry a spare."

My room, now with Thomas and Laura's suitcases in it, was at the back of the house. Billy and I used to sneak up to the roof through my window to spy on James when we were kids. Of course, all James was doing was staring at the stars. It was his astronomy period.

The trellis didn't seem quite as sturdy as it had when we were kids, or else I was more aware of the danger now that I was an adult and no longer immortal in my own eyes. The roof was pitched, but maneuverable. Still, it was prudent to keep your center of gravity low. Mark knelt, hips on heels, my grandfather's shotgun in hand as he scanned the skies. The relief on his face when he saw me was gratifying. I tried to ignore the flash of guilt I felt at seeing it.

"Does that thing work?" I said. As far as I knew, no one had fired it since Granddad had died.

"Billy said it did the last time he and James took it to the range. No reason it shouldn't. So, did you get him?"

Billy nodded, his eyes expressing grim satisfaction. "He's no longer a problem. Any sign of the drone?"

"Nope. No idea which way it's coming. Glad you're here—I'm starting to get a crick in my neck from all the twisting. Take a section of sky and watch it. Tell me if you see it."

Billy pointed me one direction; he took another. Between the three of us, we had the sky covered. While we were waiting, I asked Billy where he'd gone after he got my present from the car.

"Got a text from a number I didn't recognize telling me I'd find something interesting waiting for me out back, but it would only be there if I came alone. I think it must have been Loughlin making sure I wasn't with you when he called you."

After a minute or so more of strained staring, up and down and side to side within my third of the sky, I said, "Maybe he *was* bluffing. Or maybe he called it off when he saw I came—shit! There!"

I pointed the nose of my gun above the trees and houses on the next block over. It was as big as I remembered, but somehow it gave off a more sinister vibe. In Dr. Phil's backyard, operated by a boyishly exuberant Misha, it had seemed like a giant plaything. Now it looked like a freaking flying robot spider. I shuddered, fighting the urge to take a dive off the roof. I *hate* spiders.

"*Down*, Howdy. Now!"

I dropped my hips to my heels, still pointing the pistol. Mark and Billy eased their way closer to me, both with guns trained on the creepy-looking thing. It whined like a giant mosquito, getting louder the closer it got. It would be over us in a matter of seconds if we missed—

Two loud cracks sounded. I joined in as soon as I heard them, straining to keep my hands steady. Shots came so fast I couldn't keep count. Within seconds half of robo-spider's arms, with their whirling helicopter blades, were gone. It fell out of the air, hitting the pond in front of the lovingly constructed grotto in my parents' backyard. The two agents who were back there got the hell out, fast.

"Is that it?" I said, lowering my gun to my side. "Are we safe? Do we need to get the blasting cap out?" I edged closer to the top of the trellis. "I can do it. I can get down there faster than—"

Billy and Mark appeared on either side of me, each taking hold of one of my arms, holding me back. "Geez, guys, it's not like I was going to jump. I'm going to use the trell—"

The explosion shook the house beneath us. A cloud of dust and debris rose high into the air, sending bits and pieces of Dad's grotto—and his poor koi—raining down on us.

Well, crap. But at least the drone hadn't been close enough to collapse the house, thank God.

I sat back on my haunches. "Sushi, anyone?"

Chapter 30

Initial inspections showed the explosion hadn't caused structural damage to any of the homes in the vicinity. It had shattered windows in our house, and in some of the neighbors' houses, knocked knickknacks off shelves and rattled dishes in china cabinets, but no lasting harm done. Well, other than to the grotto, which had pretty much disintegrated, and the pond, which was now a crater. (Dad said he'd been thinking about enlarging the pond anyway.)

Mark had gotten on his phone immediately, making sure there was a net of agents out there to pick up whoever was controlling the drone. If anyone. Because according to Misha—the first person he'd called, to verify the range of the drone so he'd know how wide to cast the net—there wasn't necessarily anyone controlling it. Loughlin could have programmed it on a set course ahead of time. It was perfectly capable of delivering its payload without real-time human control.

Once it was ascertained that everyone was safe, and the initial shock had dissipated, Mom and Auntie Mo organized us into teams to sweep up glass and tape thick sheet plastic over the broken windows. Before Mark left to wade through red tape and tie up loose ends for his bosses, I pulled him aside into the library and music room. All the family pictures had toppled from the piano, and books were scattered on the floor.

"What is it, Howdy? I need to go make sure things are getting wrapped up."

"I know. I won't keep you. I just wanted to tell you . . . I mean, this past week has been so busy, I never got a chance . . . it didn't feel right to text you, and Billy was with me every minute, like you told him to be, so I couldn't call, and well, I, um . . ."

His face went carefully blank, but not before I saw a flash of something—disappointment?—in his eyes. "You started your period."

I nodded, swallowing hard. Not because *I* was disappointed—I honestly wasn't sorry not to have impending motherhood hanging over me like some big procreational Sword of Damocles. "Yup. So you don't need to worry about me anymore."

His mouth quirked. It was almost a smile . . . but not quite. "Old habits die hard. But I'll adjust." He ruffled my hair and kissed the top of my head, just like old times.

I stopped him when he turned to go. "Mark . . ."

He looked back, with a questioning tilt of his head.

"It might have been good for us, right? If things had been different."

"Yeah, Howdy. It might have." This time it was a smile, but it was the kind you see on the face of someone having a pleasant memory of a loved one who'd died. Melancholy. It simultaneously broke and melted my heart.

"I never stopped loving you, you know," I blurted, appalling myself.

Jesus, Ciel, just because something is true doesn't mean you should say it out loud, especially if saying it might hurt the other person.

I rushed on, trying to fix it, to make him understand. "Not even after my relationship with Billy grew so fast. You said it yourself . . . old habits."

God, that sounded worse, like he was in the same category as a nicotine addiction or something. Crap, shut up before you fuck up your friendship beyond all repair.

But my mouth wasn't taking advice from my brain. "See, the problem is, I love you both—and nobody can tell me that's not possible, because I damn well know it is." I sucked in a breath too fast, and nearly choked on it. "Jesus, I'm really making a mess of this, aren't I? Like I do everything. The thing is, Billy doesn't just love me. He *needs* me. And I guess . . . I need to be needed." I screwed up my mouth in an effort not to cry. "It's one of my quirks."

He nodded, not touching me, his eyes as soft as I'd ever seen them. When he spoke, his voice was a tiny bit hoarse. "Howdy . . . I understand. I do. Don't worry. It'll be okay. We can make being friends work. I promise."

And then he was gone.

Shit. Why had I said anything beyond letting him know I wasn't pregnant? That would have been the smart thing, the kind thing, to do. Now he probably thought I was trying to keep him dangling, in case things didn't work out with Billy. And I *wasn't*.

The lady doth protest too much, methinks.

Great. A fine time for my bitch of a subconscious to channel Shakespeare.

But this time I didn't automatically leap into denial. Instead, I worked like a fiend for the next hour, trying to assess my feelings in an adult way. Sweeping, taping, hauling things too damaged to be repaired out to the garbage, anything to keep my hands busy while my mind tried to sort out what I truly felt, and for whom.

Molly found me in the basement. "Ciel, come on—Auntie Ro says we've done everything we can here for now. We're all going to my house. You have to carry a cat."

So we all trooped over to the Doyle homestead, dusty, disheveled, and exceedingly happy no one was injured, cats inclusive. Grumpy had draped himself over my shoulder and was, near as I could tell, actively engaged in unraveling the Grinch sweater I'd changed into. When Uncle Liam started singing "Jingle Bells" along the way, we all joined in. Molly switched to the "Batman smells" version for the second verse. We all—even the parents—joined in on that one, too, laughing it up in our post-trauma giddiness at being alive.

Happily, the Doyle house had escaped damage. Mom and Auntie Mo set to work in the kitchen preparing lunch, deftly maneuvering between cats who were trying to convince them feline starvation was imminent. (Another thing to be thankful for: the peanut butter and oyster quiches had been forgotten in the chaotic aftermath of the blast, and had burned to a crisp.)

Dad and Uncle Liam retired to the study to research building plans for a new, improved grotto and a bigger pond. Thomas, Bri, James, and Devon helped Molly set up her new drum set in the basement while Laura, Sinead, and Siobhan watched and offered suggestions. Looked like there was an after-lunch recital in the offing. Considering Molly only knew the one number, it was probably not such a bad thing all of our ears were still a bit numb from the blast.

Billy cut me away from the herd and took me upstairs to his old room. He closed the door and produced a small package from behind his back.

I must have looked alarmed, because he tugged my hair and said, "Don't worry, it's not a ring."

"Huh. I wasn't worried at all," I said, relieved all the same.

I ripped off the iridescent light green paper and flipped open the velvet case. The piece was almost exactly like my parachute pin, only with two canopies instead of one. I looked up at him, puzzled.

"I got it back from Thomas after he told me how you ran into your burnt-up condo like a big dummy"—I stuck my tongue out at him—"to get it. Even after I was such an idiot in Houston."

"Why the extra canopy? It's beautiful, of course, but you didn't have to do that."

"It's the emergency 'chute for when I'm acting like a fool. Ciel, I *will* always be there to catch you, I swear. But I can't promise I'll never do anything stupid again." He smiled ruefully. "Being me and all. The extra is to remind you not to give up on me. And to remind *me* that you're my parachute, too."

"It's gorgeous. I love it. But, damn, it's going to make my other present to you look so lame by comparison."

"I don't need anything else—I love my necktie. Actually, I was kind of hoping the rest of my gift would be what we *do* with the tie." He grinned wickedly.

"Oh, you can count on that. But I got you something else you might find handy." I rummaged through my shoulder bag and pulled out a package wrapped in blue paper with a flat silver ribbon around it.

"Feels like a book," he said after careful inspection.

I quirked my mouth. "Can't put anything past you savants."

"Ha ha. Now, let's see what you think I'd like to read . . ." He ripped it open and burst out laughing. "Can't fault your reasoning." He tossed *Relationships for Dummies* onto the water bed and jumped on beside it, sending waves rolling through the mattress. "But I think I prefer hands-on learning. Come here."

"Billy! This is your parents' house."

"Wuss."

"We can't—"

"Wimp."

"Someone might hear—"

"Chicken."

"I am *not* chicken. I simply have certain standards of behav—" He started clucking.

And that's all it took. My heart leapt so high I thought it might fly out the top of my head. I knew part of me would always love Mark, but Billy was the one who made my soul sing with laughter. I might tell myself I chose him because he needed me to fix him, but I needed him every bit as much.

"*Argh.* You are impossible," I said. My heart might be singing, but my brain was still worried about getting caught.

"Improbable, maybe, but not impossible. Aren't we all?"

I wasn't sure if he was talking about men in general or adaptors. I was going to ask, but the question somehow evaporated when he shifted his weight, making the mattress ripple enticingly.

I bit the inside of my cheek and tried to stem the rush of heat to my . . . um, yeah. To be honest, I'd wondered more than once what it might be like to make love on his relic from the seventies. The possibility of all that wave action was intriguing.

"Damn it," I said, admitting defeat. I locked the door and returned to his side. "Okay. But we have to hurry. They'll be waiting for us downstairs."

He pulled me down and rolled on top of me, rocking us both on gentle waves. "Finally having the object of my adolescent fantasies in this bed with me? For real this time, instead of my lurid imagination? Trust me, hurrying won't be a problem."

I lifted my mouth to his and kissed him, slowly, ending with a heartfelt sigh. "Pleeease tell me you have a condom." I know. Not exactly romantic, but I wasn't quite ready to trust my future to the patch on my hip yet.

Dimples dented his cheeks. He dug into his pocket and pulled out a handful, in assorted colors and textures, no less. "Lady's choice."

Acknowledgments

First and foremost, I'd like to extend a very special thank-you to Robert Hanley (NASA Flight Operations) for his helpful—and entertaining!—information about all things astronautical. If anything I've written seems off-kilter to the NASA nerds (Renee' Ross, I'm looking at you) who may be reading, let's just blame Robert, shall we? Oh, all right. Let's *not*. My conscience won't allow it. The fact is, I may have taken a few liberties here and there. It's what fiction writers do. But the kidney stone? *That* we can safely blame on Robert.

Second, thank you to my brother Eddie for introducing me to Robert. (See above.)

Third, thank you to my other two brothers, Steve and Rick, so they won't think I'm playing favorites.

Fourth, thank you once again to my mother for the "God punishes right away" thing. I've gotten a lot of mileage out of it over the years. Plus, if I mentioned all my brothers and left her out, no telling what The Big Guy Upstairs might do to me.

Special thanks to Karla "Kuddles" Nellenbach, aka "Grumpy Bear," the sweet . . . er, I mean totally badass cruise director for the Ciel Halligan Advance Reader Copy tours. She's the one who sees to it that an ARC gets mailed through the pipeline from one volunteer early reader to the next. Speaking of which, thank you to all my early readers! You guys are the best.

My eternal gratitude goes (again) to my generous crew of critique partners, beta readers, and cheerleaders: Elise Skidmore, Kris Reekie, Julie Kentner, Sarah Meral, Tiffany Schmidt, Tawna Fenske, Emily Hainsworth, and Sara Walker. You guys have saved me from more typos and continuity blunders than I'll ever admit to publicly. (Oh, wait. I guess I just did. Oops.) Of course, some mistakes always slip through, no matter how many eyes search for them. What can I say? It's like some sort of law in the publishing universe.

Additionally, I'd like to thank my lovely niece, Allie Cappelli, for the family discount on proofreading. There's more pumpkin-spice pound cake where that came from.

My heartfelt gratitude goes once more to the members of Team Ciel: Super-Agent Michelle Wolfson, Editor Extraordinaire Melissa Frain, Editorial Assistant par Excellence Amy Stapp, and the host of other Tor denizens who have made it possible for me to share Ciel's stories with you. You guys rock!

Finally, thank you to Bob, always and forever the keeper of my heart.